THE RETURN OF
THE DWARVES
BOOK 1

THE RETURN OF THE DWARVES

BOOK I

MARKUS HEITZ

Translated by Sheelagh Alabaster

Arcadia

First published in Great Britain in 2024 by

Arcadia
an imprint of
Quercus Editions Ltd
Carmelite House
50 Victoria Embankment
London EC4Y 0DZ

An Hachette UK company

The authorized representative in the EEA is Hachette Ireland,
8 Castlecourt Centre, Dublin 15, D15 XTP3, Ireland (email: info@hbgi.ie)

Cover design: Guter Punkt, München / Anke Koopmann
Cover illustrations: Elm Haßfurth / elmstreet.org
Translation: Sheelagh Alabaster

Die Rückkehr der Zwerge was originally published in German in 2021 by
Verlagsgruppe Droemer Knaur GmbH & Co. KG, Munich, Germany.

A CIP catalogue record for this book is available
from the British Library

PB ISBN 978 1 52942 486 7
EBOOK ISBN 978 1 52942 487 4

10 9 8 7 6 5 4 3

Typeset by Jouve (UK), Milton Keynes

Printed and bound in Great Britain by Clays Ltd, Elcograf S.p.A.

Papers used by Arcadia are from well-managed
forests and other responsible sources.

PROLOGUE

Girdlegard

To the north of the United Great Kingdom of Gauragon
In the foothills of the Grey Mountains
Kingdom of the Fifthling dwarves
1023 P.Q. (7514th solar cycle in old reckoning), spring

The massed waters of the Emerald Falls thundered unceasingly over the precipice edge, plunging thirty paces into the wide natural basin below the cliff. Clouds of spray played round the wide green expanse of the Towan river. Tiny droplets drifted on the wind to land on the leaves and bark of the trees in the heavily wooded landscape. Bright sunlight formed a picturesque, and seemingly perpetual, iridescent rainbow in the air.

Water vapour landed in the dark braided beard of a dwarf, standing, dressed in light armour, on the edge of the Towan at a sensible distance from the shingle bank of the broad riverbed. The droplets shimmered like decorative pearls next to the jewelled clasps in his damp beard hair.

Barbandor Steelgold of the clan of the Royal Water Drinkers was not at all concerned about the drops running down the deep grooves and scars on his weathered face. His strong hands held the elaborately engraved steel head of his battleaxe, the shaft planted firmly in the pebbles of the riverbank. From a distance, this solidly built dwarf could have been a wanderer taking a short break on his journey.

Barbandor's brown gaze was firmly fixed on the surface of the green waters swirling past, ten paces below him. There was a fresh smell of flowers and a tang of wet stone. Nature was awakening to new life in the meadows and woods of these, the southernmost foothills of the Grey Mountains.

Barbandor had volunteered for this tour of duty. He did it gladly whenever the time was right.

This happened frequently.

Whenever there had been cloudbursts over the distant Grey Mountains, or during the deluges that followed the spring snowmelt, or if there was heavy rain over the peaks and slopes of the old abandoned homelands, the River Towan would grow in size and power, bringing with it some unusual freight. Anything the floodwaters carried would eventually be washed up at the side of the river. The Emerald Falls were a likely place to find interesting items.

Sighing deeply, Barbandor turned his head to look to the north, a melancholy expression in his eyes. The Grey Mountains. Or at least what was left of them after the many earthquakes and disturbances that had occurred in the past hundreds of cycles. Where once had stood majestic peaks whose names were widely known, the impressive, ancient mountain slopes an inspiration to those seeking beauty – and many strange rock formations echoing the shapes of monsters and animals – were now broken cliffs, unlovely mounds of stark stone and soaring, ugly ridges. Daily, clouds of smoke belched forth from the recently formed volcanoes. The venerable landscape of the Grey Mountains had been obliterated and new movements in the earth were constantly forcing new peaks upwards on top of the ancient foundations of the Grey Range. The land had not yet come to rest.

The sight upset him, even though he had never had the chance to set foot in the old homelands. Neither he nor many generations of his fellow Fifthlings.

The halls with their age-old carved pillars were consigned to ancient history. As were the treasure chambers, the rich mines, the workshops and the forges which had once rung with the sound of metal being worked, and the beautiful crafts carried out so skilfully by the gifted dwarves of yore. All that was left was the memory of past glory, held fast in song and fable, and celebrated in fragments of documents that had survived from the old times. Drawings, paintings and innumerable songs. Such sad songs.

Nobody knew what the situation was like in the interior of the ancient homeland.

'Vraccas, I beg you, tell us what we did to deserve such harsh punishment?' murmured Barbandor.

The living could not provide the answer.

More than one thousand cycles before this, all the Children of the Smith had been forced to flee overnight, when the earth had begun to tremble and shake and volcanoes had erupted. They fled to avoid their Fifthling tribe being buried alive by the Grey Mountains. In fleeing they had lost both the High King of all the tribes and also his legendary weapon Keenfire, the fire-bladed axe. This enormous loss affected not only all the dwarves, but also the whole protected land of Girdlegard.

The same thing had happened to the Secondling tribe in the Blue Mountains to the south. Only the Firstlings in the west and the Thirdlings in the east had been spared. They waited in their defensive settlements in the red and black rocks of their homelands, even though those lands had been changed for ever.

Worst off were the Fourthlings. The dwarf folk of this kingdom had been adversely affected by more than just the earthquakes and eruptions; the whole of Girdlegard had been struggling with the consequences of this for many hundreds of cycles.

Secondlings, Fourthlings and Fifthlings now lived in fortified settlements near the mountains. They were faced with uncertainty about when, if ever, they could return to rebuild what had been destroyed.

So many things are uncertain. Barbandor closed his eyes, letting the spray from the falls refresh the lids, cooling the hot tears that had been beginning to sting.

His soul, however, could not be calmed. Nothing could really help make up for the pain of losing one's homeland.

'What are you standing around for?' Giselgar Hardblow's snarling voice came from behind him. 'What's up? Have you fallen asleep standing up? Or are you scared of Elria's curse?' There was a dull thump and a rattling sound. 'Come on. Make yourself useful.' There came the metallic screech of a cart's wheel brake. 'There's going to be something special today. Can feel it in my old bones.'

Barbandor was grateful for the diversion. He quickly wiped away the spray and the tears from his face.

'Old bones? What do you mean?' He turned to look at his friend, who was sitting on a cart pulled by a shaggy black and white pony. 'You're only ten cycles older than I am.' The wagon was loaded with metal poles, hooks and several nets.

'But they were ten cycles full of hardship. That's the difference. Harsh cycles count double. No, I'd say threefold, by Vraccas!' Giselgar jumped down from the driving seat, fastening the reins to a vinegar tree whose leaves made a colourful canopy. Like Barbandor, Giselgar was wearing the lightest of leather armour, unusual attire for dwarves. But when working near deep water, a chainmail shirt or heavy metal armour was not a good choice. Unless, of course, you were dead set on drowning. 'And that's why you'll need to be working much harder than me.' Giselgar took out his collapsible spyglass from its case on his belt, extended it and studied the surface of the water carefully, checking in particular both banks and the shingle at the edge. 'Find anything, did you, while you were hanging around doing nothing?'

'I was just about to . . .'

'Ah, here comes an excuse. Why did you leave Platinshine before the rest of us, if you . . .' Giselgar stopped sweeping the spyglass from side to side and quickly adjusted the focus. 'Curses! May lightning strike the greedy scavengers! Why on earth didn't you drive them off?'

Barbandor turned to where Giselgar was looking. Among the larger rocks rearing out of the water to form a stepping-stone path over the Towan river, there was a group of humans jumping around, equipped with hooked poles and nets and sacks. Others were carrying wicker fish traps.

'They weren't there when I looked before,' Barbandor said defensively with a scowl, bridling at the accusation.

'You didn't see those long'uns because you were dreaming, staring at the Grey Range and willing it to come close,' Giselgar commented, putting away the spyglass. 'Quick now, grab some tools and let's get down to the riverbed. Those greedy-fingered wretches mustn't get there first if there's anything that belongs to our tribe.' He reached back on to the cart and grabbed what he could carry. Metal poles clanged noisily. 'Get a move on! If they find a single brooch before we get there, I'll take the pony out of the traces and you'll be pulling the cart back to the settlement yourself . . .' He raced off, sliding agilely down the bank.

After evacuating from the old homeland, the Fifthlings had always tried to collect anything the emerald-green waters might wash out of the old mine workings and tunnels to end up here in Girdlegard. They were keen to preserve the legacy of their heritage, keeping it safe against some future cycle when they might be able to return to the mountains.

Barbandor stared at the pebbles at the edge of the water where his companion was standing. Like every dwarf, he knew of the curse Elria had pronounced. The water goddess had commanded her element to drown all the Children of the Smith wherever occasion arose, even be it in a shallow puddle.

A raging river would be a breeze for a goddess wanting to drown you.

Giselgar did not seem to be affected by any fear of the water. He was two paces away from the river, fixing his poles and starting to fish around in the emerald depths.

Right, let's do this. Barbandor took a deep breath and put his battleaxe in the holder on his back. He grabbed rods, poles and nets and went down to join his friend. *It's not like it's the first time I've done it.*

That feeling in his heart when the sounds of the water intruded on his hearing in spite of the noise of the waterfall itself – the crashing roar and the bubbling of the swirling waves – no, he wouldn't call it actual *fear*. *Discomfort* perhaps would be nearer the mark.

The humans had noticed the two dwarves and were yelling incomprehensibly at them, obviously jeering and making gestures to drive them off. They were not keen on competition on the flotsam and jetsam front.

'These shoe-pissers. It's the same performance every time,' laughed Giselgar, loud enough to carry over the river's noise. 'Hey, you lot! Don't even think of trying to steal any of our treasure,' he shouted. 'You're to show me anything you've found, got that? It's ours. It all belongs to my people!' He put spectacles on his nose. The specially ground lenses made of a semi-precious stone allowed him a better view through the water to what might be lying on the riverbed. He used his nets like an expert as he poked around in the shallows. 'Elria, if you need to drown anyone, take yourself one of the long'uns, all right? Not one of us.'

'I can see why the humans would want to collect whatever they can. They must be hoping to come across something that could be enough to feed their families and bring them a little prosperity.' Barbandor was four paces away now from his friend; he placed the magnet stone carefully in the fixture on one of the poles. There was a hook at the end. He rammed the wrought-iron pole securely into the earth of the riverbank. To calm himself down, he pulled out a wad of tobacco to chew. It was reassuring to taste the mint and cinnamon.

'It's still theft from us, though – they'd be stealing from our tribe,' Giselgar insisted, pulling back the rod. In his net he saw a piece of silver as big as the palm of his hand. There was a ruby set in it. He retrieved it with a satisfied grunt and put it in his leather bag. 'You're not going to take their side, are you?'

'No, but I can understand why they do it, that's all I'm saying.' Barbandor moved his magnet stone carefully around in the water, sweeping the pole from side to side. 'Something like what you've just turned up would keep a whole family through the winter, wouldn't it?'

'Well, maybe. But it's spring now. The long'uns should get to work tilling their fields and planting vegetables if they want to be able to eat next winter.' Giselgar had had a second find: a massive gold ring shone in his fingers in the sunlight. As he stowed it away, he cast a questioning glance at Barbandor. 'If you're starting to have doubts about what we're doing, and you want to let the long'uns have some of our treasure, why do you always volunteer for this duty? You've been doing it for ten cycles.'

'That's because . . .' He raised his eyes once more in to where the view of the Grey Mountains was hidden behind the spray and the rainbow of the waterfall. 'Because I'm hoping to find a message. Not just antique bits of treasure that belonged to the dead.'

'You want a message from some Fifthling that's survived all this time?' Giselgar laughed. 'Never. The Stone Gateway and the High Portal were both completely buried. Along with everything the dwarves knew there. There's no one alive. It's been more than a thousand cycles.' He pointed to the river. 'That's where your legacy is to be found, floating past, straight in front of our noses. Save what you can, Barbandor, before those vultures grab it for themselves. Wretched mudlarks and thieving scavengers! If they find anything at all, they'll sell it for a cow or ten sacks of mouldy grain, without a single thought!' The older of the two dwarves appealed to his friend. 'One single coin, however small, from the old orbits is without price for us. It is what is left of our ancestors, of their culture, their craftsmanship and their knowledge. It all has to be returned to its rightful place. *All of it!*'

Barbandor nodded and moved his magnet stone along. He was not going to give up his private hope that a message, a signal of hope, might come.

'You hang on over here, young whippersnapper. I'm going to try further along.' Giselgar shouldered his equipment and walked across the shingle towards the spot where the humans were fishing from the stepping stones. They were casting nets and using fish traps. 'I'm going to make sure the long'uns know how to behave themselves.'

Barbandor neatly lengthened the pole he was using by attaching an extension rod. He pushed it further out into the surging current. 'Right you are.' He left his companion to deal with the jeers and insults he would probably encounter from the humans.

In times of catastrophe you looked for simple explanations. The humans were wont to blame the dwarves and their god

Vraccas for the perpetual earthquakes and the volcanoes and the rugged bald heights of new peaks that had emerged in the middle of their territory, and so for all the difficulties that Girdlegard was facing, they would let their anger and resentment out on any dwarf they came across.

Barbandor watched the band of treasure seekers.

It was a group of about a dozen men, dressed in simple wool and linen garments. Some of them had inflated leather rings and pieces of cork to help them in the water if they lost their footing and slipped into the raging Towan. Searching for the treasure of the Fifthlings was a dangerous undertaking.

That was why Barbandor preferred to be a little further away from the water, standing on the bank in relative safety. To his surprise, he noticed a wooden chest floating past. It bore dwarf insignia. There did not seem to be any fastenings, and, since it was bobbing along on the surface, it was most likely to be empty. Barbandor let it pass. *Maybe some human further downstream can make use of it.*

Giselgar was meanwhile making his way downriver, showing no fear. A shouting match had broken out between the angry dwarf and the jeering scavengers, who were apparently from the nearby village of Smallwater. The settlement had about fifty huts and houses and the people there had the reputation among the Fifthlings of playing host to looters and unscrupulous thieves. Adventurers from other regions and treasure seekers who were less courageous did not like to work in the vicinity of dwarf villages, so they would gather further downstream. To search the dangerous waters of the river, they employed the labour of their voluntarily enslaved workers of the doulia caste.

Barbandor could not understand everything that was being shouted. And he did not wish to. He hated hearing these endless tirades, the insults, the derogatory chants about his own folk.

Why, Vraccas? Why? With a deep sigh, he moved his pole to cover a different area of the water. *What have we done to ever . . .*

There was a sudden jerk. The magnet had found something made of metal and the grasping hooks had caught the object fast. Almost overcome with excitement, Barbandor felt his fingertips tingling with anticipation. *Is this the special thing Giselgar thought we'd find today?*

He pulled it carefully to the bank and quickly became aware of how heavy it was. *I bet this will be a chest full to the brim of treasure!* His boots sinking securely into the shingle, he hauled with all his strength, grinding his quid of tobacco between his back teeth in the effort of landing his catch.

But his catch refused to come to the surface.

Curses! Elria is holding on fast to this one! Barbandor turned to Giselgar, ready to shout for assistance. Then he noticed the column of black smoke filling the spring sky. Something in the village was on fire.

Before he could call to his friend, a net, spanned by the Smallwater people between the stepping stones, had caught hold and pulled one of the men into the water. Luckily he had a rescue rope coiled round his arm. He was going under, struggling for air, in spite of his leather ring and the cork belt.

Next, a solidly built fellow was yanked off his feet on the riverbank. He had been attempting to fasten down a fish trap. He was dragged screaming through the shingle before the rope gave way. He was covered in cuts and grazes and rubbed an injured hand on his tunic.

That's some dangerous undercurrent. Barbandor's brown gaze was fixed on his pole and he tightened his grip. *I'm not letting Elria win here.*

'Giselgar!' he yelled. 'Over here! I've got . . .'

Suddenly a coarse hand with long curved fingernails shot up out of the foaming emerald waters and grabbed his pole.

A green-skinned arm and the rest of an orc, in full armour, followed. The current swirled splashing and boiling around the orc's body, as it hauled itself up out of the water, holding on to the magnet rod, and spitting out the river water it had swallowed.

The markings on the bone necklace and the engraved symbols on the rusty arm protectors and leg greaves were unfamiliar.

'By Vraccas!' Barbandor exclaimed, dropping the magnet pole in astonishment. 'A pig-face! You're not what I was fishing for!' He tried to get a more secure foothold in the pebbles at the edge of the river and grabbed his steel axe out of its holder behind his back. He spat out his tobacco. 'Dare put one of your filthy feet on land, I'll have you on your way to Tion, your creator!'

Immediately, Barbandor realised that it had not been the undertow that had dragged those two human treasure seekers into the river. And he knew why the settlement was burning. Other monsters must have made their way to Smallwater, and would be wreaking havoc there and slaughtering villagers in order to eat them.

The hefty orc had heaved itself upright, pulling a curved sword out of its belt. The sword was as long as Barbandor was tall. The orc grunted and stumbled knee-deep through the water towards the dwarf, brandishing its weapon threateningly. Its gaping mouth revealed black fangs like the tusks of a wild boar.

'A real live groundling! I knew it. I've always said you're more than a heap of bleached bones, rusty armour and mouldy bits of leather, back in the abandoned mineshafts.' As it moved, water trickled out of the monster's leather tunic and the well-made lamellar armour. 'At last! I'll have your ugly skull for a tankard. And I'll wipe my arse with your nice soft beard!'

Barbandor could not work it out. This beast was not one of the salt sea orcs and certainly didn't belong to the notorious fire eaters who tended to hang out near the lava fields in the north. And definitely not one of the horrors from the orc fortress Kràg Tahuum; those were said to be the worst examples. And the brightest. The way this one was talking sounded awkward and there was no trace of any dialect used normally by orcs.

I know! He must be from the Grey Mountains! The idea shot into Barbandor's brain.

Very occasionally, heavy rain or the spring ice melt would drive monsters out of their caves or sweep them from the Outer Lands and spit them out in Girdlegard. Mostly they'd be dead and not necessarily all in one piece.

But he'd never caught sight of one like this.

'So, you fancy my beard, do you? Go on, then. But try a taste of my steel first. You won't be very thirsty after that!'

Terrified screams and the howls of the dying reached Barbandor's ears from over by the river crossing.

More beasts had emerged from the river. The humans, trying to ward off the attack with poles, nets and knives, were no match for these opponents.

'I've been waiting such an age to find one of you to kill!' With a wild shriek, the orc flung itself forward, boots dragging through the shingle, kicking up handfuls of river pebbles to hurl. 'And I'll take your skin for a drinking flask. That'll go nicely with the skull mug.'

Barbandor held the head of his axe in front of his face for protection against the hail of stones. 'Devious, of course, like the rest of them!' he muttered. Using his axe, he fended off the giant sword on its downward path, bending his knees slightly to absorb the violence of the blow. He was able to force the orc's sword to one side. This gave him a way in, between the orc's raised arms, breaking the monster's cover. He pushed home the blade of his weapon.

The polished metal sank in the orc's neck to the depth of half a finger and the monster staggered back, gurgling, dropping its sword and grabbing the shaft of the dwarf's battleaxe. Greenish-black blood dripped from the neck wound, where the axe blade was now stuck fast.

'You're not keeping my axe.' Barbandor drew his dagger, bent down and rammed it into the towering monster's right boot, fixing it firmly to the ground. 'Or we could swap. What do you think?' Barbandor neatly avoided the kick coming his way and did a backward somersault to get at the giant sword cast aside by the screaming orc. His hands closed round the hilt. 'Here you are. I'll give you back your weapon and you give me back my axe.' He whirled round and slung the heavy sword as if it were a hammer he was throwing.

Whizzing through the air, the sword sliced through the orc's hand and buried itself deep in the monster's chest, penetrating the armour with ease. Metal plates flew off with the force of the blow. The sword stayed put and Barbandor let go.

What with the gaping slash injury and the pinned foot, the orc could not keep its balance. Yelling blue murder and spitting blood, it landed full length on the shingle, frantically trying to lever the sword out from its own ribcage using the hand that was still working.

'Thanks so much.' Barbandor retrieved his axe swiftly from the orc's neck and used the impetus to follow through with a sharp whack on top of the monster's head.

The steel went easily through helmet, skin and skull. The monster collapsed. Quite dead.

Barbandor looked around for Giselgar. His friend had meanwhile killed off two orcs with his club. Four of the humans were lying dead on the stepping stones or on the bank. The Towan must have done for the rest of them.

'They're in Smallwater,' Barbandor shouted, raising his voice over the roar of the river. He rushed over to the cart. 'We've got to get there and help the long'uns!'

Giselgar shouldered his blood-smeared war club and scrambled across the shingle and up the bank. 'Where did these beasts come from? As Vraccas is my witness, I'd swear they must have grown gills!'

'Rubbish!' Undoing the tethers, Barbandor jumped on to the cart and seized the reins. 'They've come from the Grey Mountains!'

'Never!'

'It's true! The orc I was fighting thought I was a legend.'

'What a joke! You're not that famous, you know.'

'Oh, ha, ha! I mean the fact I was an actual dwarf! It'd only ever seen dead ones before. You know – skeletons.' Barbandor pointed over at the Grey Range. 'They came from over there. Out of the abandoned mines. It told me so.'

'But ... but that would mean ...' Giselgar screwed up his eyes and surveyed the road to the settlement. 'Look! Down there! More of the long'uns!'

Some elderly people were staggering along towards them on the wide path, accompanied by women and children. Even from a distance it was obvious they were waving frantically for help.

'I beg of you – get us away from here!' It was a young woman. She was carrying a badly injured young child bleeding from a vicious bite. 'The village is lost. They just barged their way in. Everything's on fire.' The rest of her words were swallowed in sobs.

'Get the wounded up on to the cart,' Barbandor told Giselgar. 'And then let's get out of here!' Even though humans did not usually regard the dwarves as their friends, Barbandor adhered strictly to the commands of his creator, Vraccas, who had decreed it was the sacred task of the dwarves to protect the inhabitants of Girdlegard. 'They'll be safe enough once we've got them inside our walls. Then we'll come back with a troop of fighting dwarves and deal with these beasts.'

The two dwarves promptly jumped down and helped the injured and the infirm up on to the cart, then drove off.

They had hardly taken the turning to Platinshine with their laden cart when they heard the sound of a deep reverberating horn, with other bugles joining in to the cacophony, along with the grunts and growls of the orcs thundering along in hot pursuit.

'Hurry! Or you'll be lost!' Barbandor jumped down.

'What in Vraccas' name are you up to?' Giselgar was trying to bring the vehicle to a stop.

'I'm going to head them off and divert them.' He gestured to his friend to get going. 'You make sure these people are safe, then hurry back here with the best warriors you can find!'

'Of course. We'll be back to rescue you!'

'No, you won't.' Grinning, Barbandor ran his thumb gleefully along the edge of his battleaxe blade. 'You'll come back to see if you can still catch one of the beasts alive. By the time you're back with reinforcements, I shall have had to dispatch all the pig-faces for the sake of my own health.'

'What are we supposed to do with a live one?'

'If we catch one, it can tell us what the orcs are up to in the Grey Mountains. Now, get going!'

'Good thinking! Make sure you leave some to share with us. Don't be selfish.' With a hearty laugh, Giselgar drove his Smallwater charges off and the pony and cart disappeared in the trees. 'May Vraccas be with you!'

He will be! Barbandor took a couple of deep breaths and listened out for the screech of the bugles as the orcs drew closer. He had realised how anxious his friend had been in having to leave him here, though he had tried to hide the worry in his voice by striking a cheerful note.

Barbandor, on the other hand, was feeling quite different.

He was not afraid of having to fight a load of orcs. He could rely on his trusty steel axe and on his own expertise with the weapon. He'd sort this all out, and no mistake. Lead these idiot monsters a dance and keep them busy until Giselgar got back to him with the troops.

But we do certainly need to keep one of them alive. Let's hope at least three or four of them got out of the river downstream.

Selecting a fresh wad of tobacco to chew, he strode round the bend in the road to spy on the approaching company of monsters. And this is when his confidence took a considerable blow. Four dozen armoured grey-green beasts were snaking their way up through the undergrowth in a long double column, already snuffling the air with their short, slit snouts.

And they were moving very fast.

Faster than Barbandor would ever be able to run.

I

Girdlegard

Brown Mountains
Brigantia
(formerly the kingdom of the Fourthling dwarves)
1023 P.Q. (7514th solar cycle in old reckoning), spring

The lantern swung from side to side, turning the walls and roof of the tunnels into a hectic dance of dark and light and illuminating the faults and fissures in the rock. The brightness was magnified with mirrors and directed forward by means of metal flaps on the lantern; the rays of light pierced the surrounding blackness and a rhythmical metallic squeaking noise came from the carrying handle as it moved.

Klaey was the one holding the lantern pole; he was the leader of this troop of ten. They had come a long way from their home in Brigantia. 'Take care, mind you keep quiet to listen out for any sounds the rocks make,' he said, passing the order back over his shoulder. The reflected light flattered his face with its neatly trimmed dark beard. 'I've no desire to end up buried under a collapsed roof.'

There were murmurs of agreement.

Eight orbits previously, they had crossed the Brigantian border, and now they were in the no man's land of the Brown Mountains with its network of corridors, endless tunnels, and chambers with vaulted ceilings at giddy heights. A real labyrinth. But Klaey and his little unit were not without a plan as they made their way through the ancient realm of the groundlings who had fled a thousand cycles before, when the earthquakes had started.

On the contrary.

They often had to climb or squeeze themselves through gaps in the rock or force their way perilously under half-collapsed bridges. Their journey had shown them all the construction skills of the earlier inhabitants, who, deep under the earth, had built impressive halls and chambers decorated with consummate artistry and specialised tools. No other folk in Girdlegard could match these dwarves for engineering skill and handiwork. Most of it had already been lost as the hundreds of cycles had passed: broken, plundered, covered in scratches, paint and slogans. Everything, that is to say, that the earthquakes had not already destroyed. The enemies of the groundlings had taken their revenge and had stolen anything they could haul away.

With *one* exception.

And it was just that exception that Klaey and his selected band of trusty friends were searching for. Again and again he wiped the dust from his face and brushed bits of crumbling rock out of his dark hair, which he wore long and plaited and shaved stylishly close on the right-hand side of his head.

The young banner officer cadet was in no mood for taking a rest or admiring the ruins and the stone remains of the Fourthlings' work. In exactly eleven orbits' time they were due back in Brigantia from the scouting mission they were supposed to be on. Otherwise their absence would be noticed and there would be awkward questions to answer on their return. For example, what was a low-ranking member of the supply corps doing, taking troops out on a manoeuvre on his own initiative? The Omuthan might well be rather displeased.

'Apparently there should be a right turn after this tunnel. And then we ought to find a gate. A locked gate.' To Klaey's immense relief, they had not come across anyone or anything on their way that could have caused them a problem. No monsters. No spectres. Occasionally they found the remains of some orc that had not got the better of a sharp blade, many hundreds of cycles previously.

'And then we've done it?' Ayasta pushed her way to his side. Like the rest of the unit, this fair-haired young warrior was sporting a lightly padded armoured tunic. Nothing too heavy that would be difficult to march in on their long trek. It was bad enough having to carry all their food and the equipment they were going to need. 'It's gone well, hasn't it?' She took the lantern and shone its light around where they had halted. 'So, if we're getting closer to the forgotten hoard now, won't you tell me again how rich I'm going to be?'

'How rich *we* are going to be, you mean. It will be for all of us,' Klaey corrected her, laughing. He rubbed the sweat from his brow with the back of his hand, touching as he did so the decorative brand on the bridge of his nose. It was warm down here underground. And then they were all excited about the prospect of immense fortune awaiting them. 'Hundreds of gemstones. Whole rooms full of rubies, diamonds, emeralds, sapphires and all that other stuff. Everything the dwarves will have left behind in their workshop. It's where they kept all the jewels from the mines in the north-west. The gem chippers always intended to go back and retrieve their treasure once the mountains came to rest.'

His band of soldiers gave whoops of excitement.

'Rubies!' Ayasta squirmed with pleasure. 'I'll have a wonderful necklace made with the rubies! And then I'm going to buy myself a country estate, outside Brigantia, of course, and . . .' The others' laughter broke rudely into her train of thought.

'You idiots! Bleating like a load of sheep! I think my plan is amazing. I want to spend the evening of my life at ease on the bank of a lovely river, in a beautiful posh house. And I'll have masses of trusty doulia slaves to do my bidding . . .'

'They'll steal from you. And then brigands and vagabonds will come and take over and grab everything you've got,' Klaey embroidered, grinning. 'If you've got a smidgeon of sense, you'll not only leave Brigantia but get away from Girdlegard altogether.'

Ayasta shrugged her shoulders. 'Maybe I haven't got a smidgeon of sense. But how about you all come and visit?' She turned round and shone the light in their eyes, shaking her fist. 'Don't you dare try and steal my stuff, though! I'll steal it right back!'

The company, who didn't like the lantern dazzling them, met Ayasta's plans with mocking laughter. A half-hearted handful of thrown gravel came her way.

Klaey went back to examining the scribbled map covered with dwarf runes that he had taken off one of the lower orders in his military supply unit. The simple-minded soldier had been making preparations for his own excursion and had been easily caught out on a lie. The clumsy excuses as to why he would be needing the armour and provisions he was storing had piqued Klaey's interest. One thing had led to another and the soldier had met a sudden tragic end before the map changed hands.

Klaey compared the translated descriptions on the map with their actual location. His light-blue eyes took in every detail. Moving the lantern around revealed the corridor he had been expecting to find. But the way was blocked with a wall made of great lumps of granite; to the right there was a tunnel.

'Almighty Cadengi, give me strength!' he exclaimed. *Curses! The way is blocked.*

One by one the others made their way over and stared at the impassable obstacle. Some of them started to mutter.

'It's going to be harder than we thought, folks. Out with the tools and roll your sleeves up! Let's get stuck in!' Klaey placed the lantern on the floor. 'It's nothing we can't handle.'

'Are you absolutely certain we're in the right place?' Ayasta looked at the map and pointed at the symbols. 'What if the runes haven't been translated right? Did you get the chart checked by one of the scouts before we left?'

'How could I have done that without letting everyone know about all the jewels awaiting us, right *there*' – Klaey gestured with the tip of his pickaxe at the wall. 'Do you really want to share it all with my brother?' He didn't let on that he had been the one who had done the translation. He had always been gifted with languages and as a child he had enjoyed deciphering unfamiliar scripts. It had taken him only a few orbits to work out the patterns in the runes. This facility was something he owed to his mother, he thought, and to the special circumstances of his birth.

The passage walls echoed with heated arguments. Nobody was keen to let others in on their expected prosperity.

'Right, then. Let's get to work.' With this encouraging suggestion, Klaey handed his pickaxe to the blonde soldier. 'It shouldn't take you more than half an orbit. As long as you keep at it.'

Ayasta cast an offended glance his way. 'So you don't intend to get your own hands dirty?'

'Indeed not. I am the leader. And I'm standing guard.' Klaey nodded towards the dark tunnel to their right. 'I shall be protecting you with my life so that all of you can safely dig your way through to the treasure store.'

'Such a noble leader.' Ayasta got to work with the others, picking away at the gaps between the massive stones, ready to lever the granite blocks out one by one. 'But if you're not sharing in the work, I think you should accept a smaller share of the treasure. We'll have been working our arses off. Just to let you know how things will be . . .'

Klaey grinned and watched his unit for a while as they laboured and hammered away. Then he took a few steps into the dark tunnel and sniffed. *Stuffy. Airless.* Obviously no one had been in this part of the Brown Mountains for a long, long time. Any trace of a draught would have indicated that somewhere nearby there might be some kind of opening, or a connection up to the surface through which other creatures could have found their way in.

But that was not the case here, so Klaey remained calm and relaxed.

He took out his prepared tobacco pipe. It was as long as his forearm. He sucked at it without lighting it. He loved the way the luxurious aroma of the kedonit spread over his tongue. He would light his pipe in celebration as soon as he had the first of the gemstones in his hands. *I shall have deserved it.*

Every so often he got his troop to stop their hammering so that he could listen out. But there was nothing – neither any dangerous cracking noises from the roof nor any strange sounds emanating from the tunnel. Apart from themselves, there were no living creatures around and the Brown Mountains were not about to collapse and bury them alive.

Stone dust hung in the air and was visible in the lantern light. There was a distinct smell of sweat. The constant metallic scraping of their tools was hard on his ears.

After a while Ayasta called him over. She was covered in a fine layer of filth. 'We're through!'

'Already?' Klaey made his way past his soldiers as they stood aside for him. Behind the wall was a double portal. 'Well done!'

The fantastic workmanship the groundlings had put into the construction of the two doors of the portal was stunning. Iron bands as thick as a finger bound the heavy kergan wood. There was not a speck of rust on the metal. A huge lock secured the entry, along with many chains fastened with padlocks. Although it had only been a question of deterring visits from robbers, the groundlings had not spared their efforts, displaying all the mastery of their craft. The doors and the fastenings showed ornate carvings and ornamental runes decorated with gemstone slivers.

'We'll be seeing those real jewels soon with our own eyes. This is what we came for.' Ayasta wiped the dirt and sweat on her face, creating a spontaneous kind of warpaint decoration. 'I could really do with a nice cool flask of wine.'

'You'll soon be raking in enough gold coins to buy yourself barrels of the best.' Klaey held up the drawing to show the others. 'You see! This is the very door! Just like it's marked on the plan here.'

Everyone cheered.

'Right. Here we go!' Klaey kissed the lucky charm he wore round his neck and then got to work with the wires and hooks and the fine tools he would need to unlock the complex metal mechanisms. The lantern gave him the light he needed for the task.

'Why go to such trouble?' said Ayasta, taking a long drink from the flask she carried at her belt. 'Let's just bash the door down with a nice big stone.'

'No.' Klaey poked at the iron cover of the hefty lock. 'If we use force there's a chance of triggering some kind of a trap and we'd all be done for. The groundlings have always known how to keep their treasure safe from marauding hands. I'm not going to risk everything when success is so close. Patience is the name of the game.' Klaey turned calmly back to his task, working with great concentration until a succession of clicks indicated that the mechanism was about to give way. 'Here we are, ladies and gentlemen.' He wound the chains out from the fastenings, then stood up and placed his hands on the two handles of the double doors, pushing down. 'Behold! Our treasure!'

But however hard he pushed and pulled at the handles, the doors refused to open.

Dirt trickled down from the edges of the doors and there was a considerable amount of creaking, but the door remained firmly closed. The intruders were not about to be admitted.

'What's happening? You told it to open up, didn't you?' said Ayasta. 'You chose not to exhaust yourself with the hard work like the rest of us, but now you're too weak to open the doors? How about you use your terribly impressive voice and sing them a nice little ditty?'

'To Tion with the wretched groundlings! You know what? It's barred from the other side!' Klaey glared at the doors in anger. *I'm not giving up now!* He kicked the door several times and there was a crash – the double doors gave a little. *I want my treasure.* 'Come on, everyone. One, two, three.'

A human battering ram was established – a double row of soldiers took a run and set their shoulders against the heavy wood. With a splintering noise, the doors finally sprang open.

Klaey and Ayasta were the first to go through, closely followed by the rest, stumbling and falling over each other in their eagerness.

They did not need the lanterns to see where they had ended up. A huge vaulted hall with numerous columns and painted glass lights on the walls and the ceiling. The reddish light thus provided showed beautiful wall paintings and decorations on the pillars. The pictures told the story of a single warrior, showing him sometimes in combat and sometimes on a journey. He might be reading. Or resting.

'This is no groundling workshop!' Klaey took a closer look at the perfectly executed paintings. The brilliance of the colours was extraordinary. The creatures and the warrior portrayed here were so lifelike you could have expected them to step down any moment from the walls and continue their fight under the domed ceiling of this very hall. Strangely, the hero wore no conventional armour but seemed to have metallic plates actually fixed permanently into his flesh. His weapon was depicted as a black tionium spear adorned with shimmering runes.

Klaey's troop spread out, staring at the dimensions of the hall, eighty by a hundred paces. The columns were as high as the mast of a sailing ship. On the long side of the hall, quite close to where they stood, they could see the proper ceremonial entrance. It was an enormous double door of solid metal.

'And in no way is this place anything like abandoned!' Ayasta turned on Klaey, fury in her voice. 'I see no jewels. No treasure at all!' When the dwarves' door had crashed open, much of the masterly wall decoration that had been on the plaster behind the door had been destroyed. The damage to the wall was acutely obvious. 'Where in the name of all the blazing demons of the world have you brought us, you fool?'

Klaey stared at the map in utter confusion. He thought his way back through the recent orbits but could not work out what had gone wrong. *I should have taken out my lucky amulet and kissed it before we broke down that door.*

'Where? I brought you where—'

'Hey!' The voice of one of the soldiers further away echoed back down to them. 'Come and have a look at this!'

He was indicating a long, white stone platform in the centre of the hall. It stood about one and a half paces high and there were lights focused on it from the four corners of the ceiling. They showed those same engraved tionium armour plates, armoured gauntlet and runic spear that featured in the paintings; one of the armour sections was holed, where something the size of a crossbow bolt must have passed through.

If Klaey had at first assumed the plinth with its carvings and elaborate filigree work was marble, he recognised his mistake when approaching for a closer look.

'Is that . . . bone?' he muttered, shuddering. 'By the mother of Cadengis! The whole thing is made out of bones!'

The reliefs and the borders had inlaid gold and vraccassium patterns. Black tionium and polished silver decorated the altar, together with a selection of jewels that shimmered and sparkled in the light.

'Holy shit! We've landed in Dsôn Khamateion!' Ayasta pointed to the huge figure in the nearest wall painting. 'It's an *älf*!'

And here is its armour. Klaey stepped slowly away from the bone plinth. The map had not shown where the corridors really terminated – he would never have knowingly ventured into älfar lands.

'This is the älf's memorial.'

'Almighty Cadengis, be with us!' Ayasta did not move back. 'The black-eyes have taken over your abandoned workshop cavern and turned it into a tomb!' She pointed to the most valuable of the gems on the altar. 'Still, plenty of stuff up for grabs, though!' She pulled out her knife. 'Come on, everyone. Help yourselves.'

With a sudden rumbling sound, the mighty bolts securing the huge entrance were pulled back. A series of clicks followed as further fastenings were opened. The real entryway revealed itself.

'Quick, everyone. Hide!' Klaey ducked behind one of the pillars. There wasn't time enough for all of his scattered troop to escape back the way they had come in. 'Don't attack till I give the order! With any luck, maybe they won't notice us.'

'I'm not leaving without a souvenir.' Quick as a flash, Ayasta had dug a diamond out of its setting on the plinth and then ducked down on the side of the bone platform furthest from the entrance doors. She stowed the stone away and kept the dagger in her hand as three älfar strode ceremoniously over to the altar.

A black-haired female älf in a flowing, floor-length dark blue robe gathered at the waist carried in her hands a bundle of glowing incense sticks. Her companions, both in full armour, followed at a respectful distance. Although their bronze-coloured armour was made of metal, there was a rustle rather than a clanking sound as they moved.

Is she maybe a priestess? Klaey was hardly aware that he was holding his breath. He hoped his people had all found good hiding places. Even if there were only two armed älfar warriors to contend with, there was little hope of winning, given that a single shout would surely bring more guards running into their venerated hero's memorial chamber.

Crouched behind the platform, Ayasta had her eyes tight shut – like a child convinced no one could see her. She kept the dagger ready to attack in her right hand.

The graceful female in the blue robe knelt down at the plinth, holding up the glowing incense sticks and waving them in circles, making shapes so that the smoke trail left mysterious patterns in the air. As she did this, her voice kept up a low chanting. The two warriors bowed their heads.

They haven't seen us! Klaey was jubilant. *We're going to escape with our lives! And with rich pickings to boot!* The soldier he'd taken the map off was, of course, already dead, or Klaey would have been making a mental note to kill him when he got back as punishment for having led them into this danger.

The other half of his mind was on the words spoken by the älf woman; he concentrated on finding speech patterns and repeated sounds. He wanted to understand their language. He had never heard the like. It was darkly poetic.

The grace and elegance and the immense skill in decorating armour, devising fabrics and weapons – all this the älfar shared with their arch-enemies, the elves. In the half-light here, you would not be able to distinguish between them. But if exposed to sunlight, the eyes of an älf would change colour and go black. This would reveal the true nature of the älfar: incredibly cruel and very, very dark.

Klaey was extremely keen not to fall into their hands. These creatures painted pictures with the blood of their victims and he surmised they would make ghastly but stunning works of art with his own skin and bones. But only if they considered his remains to be of the correct quality.

From the hole in the wall the Brigantians had made on bursting through, there came a faint clanking of chains; the volume of the noise was steadily increasing. It sounded as if someone in shackles were shuffling this way.

Klaey looked over to the gap they had made in the wall. *What's this? By Cadengis . . .*

In staggered a dwarf. Coming into the low red light, there he was, hands in irons and a gag in his mouth. His beard was filthy, his leather boots torn and in the same miserable condition as his leather tunic. His build was on the scrawny side, suggesting he was probably a Fourthling.

No, no, no! Stay there! Don't come in! Before Klaey could intervene, the dwarf had staggered past, into the hall, groaning, falling to his knees, chains rattling and clanking.

The female älf rose to her feet and stared at the manacled dwarf. Then she swept the room with her eyes. At an order from her, the two warriors moved to the right and to the left, brandishing their spears, going off to search the vaulted hall. For her own part, she separated the bundle of incense sticks, keeping them in her hands. She waited calmly.

Where did that groundling come from? Klaey placed his hand on the hilt of his rapier and squinted over to the exit that might save them. *Has he come from some prison or other? One of our prisons, maybe?*

A shout, a weapon clanging and the sound of a body thumping to the floor indicated the start of the fighting Klaey had been afraid of. One of his soldiers had been discovered and killed. *So now they know we're here. The game's up.*

Ayasta jumped up from behind the altar and was about to hurl herself at the älf priestess. 'Finish off the black-eyes!' As she spoke, she stabbed at the heart of her opponent with her dagger. 'Or we are lost!'

The elegant dark-haired älf woman moved neatly aside, jamming the burning incense sticks into the girl's face again and again, before delivering a kick to her chest, knocking the screaming blonde Brigantian off the altar. There came the sound of Ayasta's neck breaking against the edge of the plinth. Ayasta slipped dead to the floor, her face disfigured by black and red burn marks.

'Withdraw, everyone!' shouted Klaey and raced for the gap in the wall. 'Retreat! Get out of here, or else . . .'

A slim black sword blade stabbed down out of the dark of the passageway, piercing Klaey's thinly padded armour.

'Stay where you are,' someone whispered in a strong accent. 'I'm going to need you.'

A tall figure in a hooded robe pushed the groaning Klaey, fixed on the double-edged blade as if on a spit, before him back into the hall. 'You are going to be a great help. Just like that groundling.'

The sword was yanked out of his body. Klaey collapsed next to one of the pillars. *Whatever is happening?* Klaey tried to close the wound with his right hand but the blood came pouring through between his fingers.

The figure moved over to the grand entrance and bolted and barred the doors to prevent anyone escaping. Then it swept into the midst of the fight – on the side of the soldiers from Brigantia, attacking the älfar warriors from behind – only to subsequently turn on the hopelessly outmatched men and women of his unit and slaughter them.

Klaey watched, bleeding heavily, as the hooded figure exchanged a few words with the priestess, who had been on the point of attacking him, before he felled her with a blow on the left shoulder. Then he lifted one of the Brigantian swords and poked the blade around in the wounds inflicted on the fallen älfar.

He must be trying to put the blame on us. Klaey struggled to understand and then collapsed in a heap from the pain.

The hooded figure took the pieces of armour from the plinth along with the gauntlet, placing it all in a carrying sack. He took the rune spear in his left hand.

It was hard for Klaey to follow because his vision was blurring over. He heard the dwarf give a last gasp and then slip down.

After a while, the slight rasping sound of the tionium armour plates shifting in the sack came closer.

'My thanks, human scum. You have served me well by taking all the blame.' The blade was placed at Klaey's neck. 'Or you will have done, of course, once you all are dead.'

'But what . . .?'

'Your death' – white-hot pain shot through Klaey's throat – 'bears the name of Mòndarcai.'

Girdlegard

To the north of the United Great Kingdom of Gauragon
In the foothills of the Grey Mountains
Kingdom of the Fifthling dwarves
1023 P.Q. (7514th solar cycle in old reckoning), spring

'Wake Gundelgund! Get her and her sister up and ready!' Barbandor shouted, catching his breath after racing across the open stretch of land between the woods and the outer curtain wall of the dwarf settlement. 'At once!'

Barbandor had long since abandoned his fishing tackle; all he was carrying was the bloodied battleaxe in his right hand. The cart with Giselgar and the human casualties was a long way in front, already through the gate. He had nearly caught up with them, but there were still a good five hundred paces till he was in safety.

Using trickery and the shortcuts he knew in the stony terrain by the riverbank, Barbandor had managed to confuse the four dozen orcs and lead them quite a dance. But finally the beasts had worked out what he was doing and they had driven him into a corner. He had sent three of them to their god, Tion, with mighty blows from his axe. After that the only hope was to race for the safety of Platinshine's protective walls. Ignorant humans liked to think of this settlement as being a fortress.

From there Gundelgund and Gindelgund could come to his aid. Just as long as, that is, they were quick enough off the mark. Sometimes those sisters took a long time to get ready for a fight.

An arrow whizzed past and buried itself in the soft earth in front of Barbandor. *That was too close for comfort!* Three further shots followed, which he avoided by running in a zigzag. The beasts were worryingly adept with their short bows and could use them accurately while careering along at full tilt. He heard their yelps of delight when they discovered the rampart wall.

'Do you really think you can win?' Barbandor gasped, staggering, as a further arrow landed between his feet. It was not enough now to rely on swerving out of danger. He fell flat, rolling over and over, his hand firmly on the handle of his axe.

Let's get out of here! He tried to push himself up but an arrow hit him in the lower leg, pinning him to the ground.

He hurled himself about, shouting – and saw the next shot heading his way. This arrow had a string attached to it. *They want to harpoon me like a fish!* In the nick of time he drew in his uninjured leg and managed to avoid the vicious barb. *I'm supposed to provide your supper, am I? A nice little snack?*

The orcs charging towards him were less than fifty paces away. Five of them stopped and readied their bows. The others were armed with various bladed weapons.

'You miserable beasts!' With great difficulty, Barbandor got to his feet, supporting himself on his upturned battleaxe. 'Let's be having you!' He skilfully manoeuvred his weight on to the sound leg and lifted his heavy weapon with both hands. Greenish-black blood and bits of orc skin and hair were sticking to the head of the axe. 'By Vraccas! Listen good, you orcs! I swear I'll send ten of you on your way to your creator before you get the chance to use my skull for a drinking vessel. And I'll eat my own beard so you don't use it to wipe your arses!'

Barbandor thought he could feel the ground shaking under the impact of the orcs charging towards him. He saw their gaping muzzles and ink-stained teeth. A delighted roar escaped them as they anticipated killing their prey. He saw the mountains of muscle and flesh towering over him where the armour did not cover them, and the jagged blades they were brandishing. And those dreadful tusks.

I'm heading for the Eternal Smithy, and no mistake!

Determinedly, Barbandor lowered his dark head and selected a victim from among the orcs. He would kill this one before he was forced to yield to their violence. *One at the very least. And after that, as many as I can manage.*

The five orcs waiting at the back fired off their arrows. The missiles rose as black streaks, but suddenly they broke up in mid-air as if they had been shattered by an invisible power. Clumps of earth sprayed around and the eight orcs at the front fell to the ground without uttering a single cry. They lay motionless, bleeding from countless wounds.

'By Vraccas! Serves you right!' yelled Barbandor, relief obvious in his voice. *My thanks, sisters! Well done, Gindelgund and Gundelgund!*

Ten orcs lumbered forward over the bodies of their fallen companions, but again they were struck down as if by a phantom hand. Dust and grass whirled around in the air.

The rest of the band of orcs came to a halt in confusion, not ten paces away from where Barbandor was. Although the dwarf was almost near enough to grab, the monsters did not dare approach. They growled, sniffing at the air, trying to work out what it was that had done for the others. Two of them bent over the corpses, grunting, and tried to examine the bodies, running their fingers round the circular wounds, from which the blackish-green blood oozed.

Neither their helmets nor their armour had been able to protect them.

'Don't like that, do you?' Barbandor remained on high alert, his axe in his hands, ready to defend himself. 'What are you waiting for? Come and get me if you're tough enough!'

In the meantime, the five orc archers in the rear had placed barbed arrows on their bowstrings and were taking aim at the dwarf.

The noise of the snuffling orcs was now mixed with a sudden deadly whizzing sound, followed by several crashes.

Helmets, armour and bodies alike were peppered with holes and the archers' bows dropped to the ground, shattered into pieces. The archer orcs collapsed soundlessly.

This was the prompt for a yelled order from one of the remaining orcs, and the two dozen monsters still standing whirled around, abandoning their dead and also leaving the dwarf victim they had been so sure of.

'Didn't I tell you so?' Barbandor gave a malicious laugh. 'Feel like a wager, maybe? Gindelgund and Gundelgund will be firing again any time soon.'

Even before they had taken ten strides, the whirring in the air was heard once more and the retreating orcs were hit from behind. Their thick plating and the padded leather armour were shot through, releasing gushing fountains of green blood. The last of the monsters had been downed.

Thanks be to Vraccas! On looking around, Barbandor noticed the dwarf runes on the ground. The symbol was less than half a pace away from the final orc to succumb. *That was a near thing!* His eyes were stinging with sweat, but the tension eased, making way for the intense pain in the leg still transfixed by an orc arrow.

He heard hooves fast approaching.

It was his friend Giselgar, bringing him a brown pony to ride. 'What did you do that for? Why didn't you kill the pig-faces in the wood? These iron bullets are expensive, you know!' Giselgar joked.

'I thought I'd bring the orcs to meet the sisters. The two girls don't often get the chance to come out to play.' Barbandor snapped off the feathered shaft of the arrow, but without dislodging the barbed tip. He would leave that difficult task to the healers. He gritted his teeth against the pain and got himself up on to the saddle, taking the pony slowly over to the settlement. 'Did they enjoy their outing?'

'Oh, by Vraccas! Indeed they did.' Giselgar kept pace with his friend. 'But we've more or less run out of the ammunition discs. We'd have had to go and get more bullets.'

Barbandor glanced back over his shoulder at the bodies of the slaughtered orcs, already being visited by crows and vultures. With their sharp beaks, the birds picked and pecked at the softest parts, tearing off bits of warm flesh.

'Vraccas was on my side,' he murmured.

'He certainly was. On mine, too. You remember what we found in the river?' Giselgar was grinning from ear to ear. 'We got top-class finds out of the Towan. Pieces from the treasure hoard of the High King himself. The hallmarks prove it.'

'Congratulations. All I got out of the water, though, was an ugly beast keen to have me for its dinner.' Suddenly Barbandor felt dizzy. 'Pity we didn't keep one of them alive. I . . .' It wouldn't be the first time that orcs had used poison on their arrows. Usually it would be to immobilise the prey until they had had a chance to collect it. 'I must get myself to a healer.' He found it difficult to get the words out. As he spoke he tipped forward on his pony, face on its neck. 'The arrow . . .' *I must not fall asleep.* But his eyelids were heavy and he could not keep them open. *Just for a heartbeat, not for long. Then I'll soon feel better.*

When Barbandor finally managed to force his eyelids open, he found he was lying in a soft bed. It wasn't his own. He had been dressed in a linen nightshirt and there was a dim light coming from a petroleum lamp at his bedside.

The windows showed it was dark outside. Night had come to the settlement.

I must be in healer Glamdulin's care. He sat up slowly and removed the sheet from his injured leg.

They had taken the orc arrow out and the wound had been cleaned and bandaged. The black thread-like marks on his calf showed how close his leg had been to succumbing to the poison. He was lucky to have escaped an amputation.

Thanks be to Vraccas! Barbandor had a raging thirst. Over by the door of his chamber he could see a water jug and a beaker.

Cautiously he got up and limped over to the sideboard to pour himself a drink. He gulped some of the water down and then wiped his face to wash the dirt out of his dark beard. *That's better. But a good tankard of black beer would really hit the spot.*

The door was open a little and his eye fell on the view through to the next room, where Master Glamdulin, and his friends Giselgar and the town councillor Gesalyn were sitting at a table. There was a human female of middle age with them. *Who would that be?* He pushed the door open a bit more, to hear and see better.

'... the chance to visit this settlement.' The fair-haired woman was dressed in startlingly white clothing: cuff boots and a leather skirt, bodice, blouse, gloves and a hat with a conspicuously broad circular brim. The only things that were not white were the feathers on her hat: two bright orange feathers, one on each side. They seemed to glow, almost. 'I apologise for keeping you waiting, lady councillor.'

Silver-haired Gesalyn, a chainmail-shirted dwarf in the best of years, looked unimpressed. 'We were not expecting you.'

'And we certainly weren't waiting for you,' muttered Giselgar, half under his breath. Giselgar was still wearing the padded leather tunic from the river expedition.

'Girdlegard people seldom do expect me, I find. But it is the law, of course.' The stranger remained polite. It seemed she was more than familiar with frosty receptions.

'It is not the law that applies here in the United Great Kingdom of Gauragon, however. We follow their laws and are grateful for the land we have been granted.' Gesalyn filled the tankards with beer and passed one to the visitor. 'That is not to say we are inhospitable. If you are hungry, please say and I shall prepare some food for you.'

The stranger reached for the mug of beer and tasted some. 'So it's true what they say about the flavour of your black beer. You dwarves know a thing or two about brewing.' She wiped the creamy foam from her top lip. 'And about making good jewellery, of course.'

'Did you want to buy some?' Giselgar sounded annoyed.

'Indeed I should like to take something back for my mistress. As is my right, of course, under the law,' she replied. 'Most of the other dwarf settlements have already paid their dues.'

'But we've heard about some who refused to do so.' The grey-haired healer Glamdulin drained his tankard abruptly. He was wearing a dark nightshirt and a dressing gown, indicating that the visit had come as a surprise. 'Don't you dare threaten us.'

'Why? Because of the bullet-hurlers you've given women's names to?' the stranger returned. 'Yes, you've made yourselves a fine weapon. It's a tightly wound metal spring, I understand, that can shoot iron balls out with great accuracy over several hundred paces.'

'I think you'll find the penetrative power is a match for the scales of any dragon's skin,' Gesalyn added. 'I wonder if you'd heard that, too?'

Barbandor suddenly realised who this must be. Quite a celebrity sitting here with the councillor and the other dwarves. *It's Stémna, of course.* The woman in white travelled through the various lands as the messenger and representative of the largest of all the dragons in Girdlegard, collecting tribute for her scale-clad mistress. Ûra the dragon saw herself as the supreme ruler of Girdlegard, given the superiority of her powers. She demanded her subjects pay tribute to her. Valuable tribute. Paid regularly.

Like dragons everywhere, Ûra had a weakness for precious jewellery and metalwork and was always keen to increase her hoard of treasure. However, she did not stoop to flying down from the sky, the slopes of the volcanoes or from her mountain-top lair to collect the tribute herself. Instead, she sent Stémna. The woman was one of many human Voices the dragon employed and she had been carrying out this office longer than anyone else.

I wonder how old she is? Forty cycles or less? Barbandor thought she was physically unremarkable; she was impressive only in the choice of costume. He assumed, however, that long'uns would probably find her attractive. He had heard rumours purporting that she was immortal, or at least invincible because she drank Ûra's dragon blood. And she bathed in it. It was also said that any settlement, town or village that objected to producing tribute, and refused to do so, tended to go up in flames soon after. *May Vraccas help us!*

'Not at all. There is no need for either of us to issue threats,' Stémna said soothingly. 'As you will know, everyone in Girdlegard pays tribute. Humans. Monsters. Elves. Älfar. Meldriths. And the dwarves.'

'Why have you never been here before? Or one of your predecessors? This is the first time you've visited our fine town of Platinshine.' Glamdulin drank again from his refilled tankard, then put on eyeglasses to study the visitor closely through the lenses. 'Why specifically this very orbit? Why come now?'

Stémna gave a wise smile. 'Let's say it's fate.' She pointed to Giselgar. 'The Smallwater people told me you had saved something you found in the Towan. So good of you. A ring and a silver amulet straight out of the treasure hoard belonging to the High King of the Fifthling realm. The river has been generous indeed.'

'No way! You're not having that!' Giselgar leaned back in his chair, crossing his arms firmly over his chest. 'Find your own treasure in the river. I can lend you my equipment.'

'Be quiet, Giselgar,' Gesalyn told him, gathering her silver hair back to tie at the nape of her neck. Barbandor thought how relaxed the councillor looked.

'So it is true.' Stémna raised her drink to Giselgar. 'Have you any idea what I normally demand as tribute for my mistress?' Her voice became quieter and its tone colder. 'If you hand over these items, you will have come off well. I am only giving them such a high value because they are from the royal treasure hoard.'

'Now, please, Stémna,' said Glamdulin, trying to stay calm. 'You must understand that this is part of the history of our race. Our ancestors made these things. For Ûra, it might be a piece of jewellery, but for us, it represents incalculable worth.'

'And this is why we would appeal to you, and to your mistress, to consider us supplying a different item in tribute,' Gesalyn added.

Stémna looked at them over the rim of her drinking vessel as she took another sip of the beer. 'What did you think the orcs were looking for in Smallwater and in the Towan? Did you think they were there by chance?'

'They'd . . . been looking for the ring and the amulet?' Giselgar took the items out and showed them round. 'What have I missed? What makes these things so special?'

'Hand them over, Master Dwarf. My mistress will know the answer.' Stémna's smile was cool. 'I'll tell you the answer next time I come.' She held out her hand for the objects.

Giselgar suddenly drew a short battleaxe from his belt. 'No! Like I said: choose something else for your mistress.' Angrily he drove the blade of his axe into the wood close to the stranger's fingers. The table shook and the tankards jumped. 'Souvenirs of our own ancestors are holy relics for us.'

Barbandor was struck by how calm Stémna remained. It was as if she was sitting in the sunshine having a refreshing drink with friends. 'You have made your decision,' she announced, getting to her feet. 'I thank you for the excellent beer, Councillor Gesalyn.' Slowly and carefully, to avoid any suspicion that her gesture might be construed as a threat, she took out one of the two orange feathers decorating her white hat. 'A memento. A souvenir of my visit. Let it be a reminder to you to think again about your words.' She poked the end of the quill upright into a gap in the wood and headed for the door. 'I'll be back tomorrow—'

'No need, dragon slave. Save yourself the trouble.' Giselgar pushed past her, opening the door to the courtyard, where several of the Smallwater people had been waiting with bated breath to discover the outcome of the meeting. As they were now in Platinshine, the fate of the township was one they would share. 'You heard the councillor's offer. It's up to you to think again, not us.' His right hand was on his axe hilt. 'Otherwise we'll be more forceful in our arguments next time we meet. Consider the possibility of greetings from Gindelgund and Gundelgund.'

Barbandor's blood was chilled by the way Stémna smiled. 'You'd be surprised how many times I've been threatened, Master Dwarf. But as you see' – she spread her arms wide – 'I am still alive.' Then she stepped out. 'Innocent people of Smallwater! I advise you to leave here immediately. The walls of this fortified township may seem to offer protection, but the representatives of the dwarves have decided to refuse my mistress, Ûra, the tribute that is due.' She sketched a bow towards the trio of dwarves and then again towards the humans, before she crossed the courtyard and disappeared.

That will probably have been a mistake. Barbandor's eye fell on the orange feather stuck upright in the wood. There was an unusual glow dancing around it, like a candle flame. *I wonder if it's true, what she said about why the orcs had turned up.* What was the mystery surrounding the ring and the amulet?

He became aware once more of the pain in his leg. He took himself back to the couch, mug in hand, and lay down, groaning quietly.

His thoughts were whirling.

Unlikely that orcs would plunge into the icy waters of the Towan and let the raging river wash them out from the Grey Mountains without very good reason. Perhaps Stémna was right and they had wanted the precious items of jewellery. Or maybe they were scouts, spying out the land before planning an invasion of Girdlegard, in spite of Ûra and the other dragons. *Just let them try. We'll stop them.* This was exactly why the fortress of Platinshine had been built.

Since the realm of the Fifthlings no longer existed, and there was no one left in the tunnels and ravines of the Grey Mountains who could hold back rampaging beasts from the gates, the dwarves had constructed their defensive forts. Platinshine, Mountainshine, Smithyfort, Goldenwall and all the rest. These fortified villages and townships had, with the Gauragon Great King's permission, been put up at regular distances from each other in the foothills of the range of mountains in the country's north. Those mountains had still not come to rest; they were unpredictable, often shifting dangerously. The fortified towns were equipped with sufficient weaponry and, above all, with enough iron determination to repel occasional attacks on the part of marauding monsters. They would deal with incursions of that sort long before the ruler's official forces marched in from the nearest garrison. Most Children of the Smith still very much saw themselves as bound by their oaths of allegiance to their creator, Vraccas, pledging to protect all the inhabitants of Girdlegard.

Exhausted by his efforts, Barbandor took a drink of the water and put the mug on the small cupboard next to the bed. In the morning he would ask to be shown the ring and the amulet.

He closed his eyes with a sigh.

He was not too concerned about Platinshine. They had a double curtain wall with watchtowers to help keep the two thousand dwarves who lived there safe. Plenty of guards and archers to ward off trouble from robbers or the odd random orc or other beasts from the Grey Mountains.

He was just dropping off when he heard a loud hissing sound from the next room. It was followed by a hot wind that blew his door open. A dazzling flash of light shone through Barbandor's closed eyes and a wave of terrible heat surged towards him.

Without pausing to think, Barbandor instinctively rolled out of bed to find protection from the tongues of flame. Alarm bells could be heard through the broken window. Alarm bells and screams.

There are creatures of light – the elves.

Then there are creatures of darkness – the älfar.

And in between there are the meldriths.

Hundreds of cycles ago, when the älfar first infiltrated the elf people in order to spy on them and encroach on the lands of Girdlegard, and there were matings between elves and älfar, meldriths were the result. Nobody had thought it was possible. I presume some kind of alchemy was used by the älfar in order to disguise themselves as elves.

I made a study of meldriths. Dead ones and living ones. My research showed that the dominant genetic feature in their makeup was the darkness. Meldrith children turned into älfar, but with varying dark powers, and they acquired manifold other aptitudes that I was not able to investigate fully. Their eyes did not turn black in the light.

The good thing is this: because of their history, they see themselves as being servants of goodness and they keep up fragile relations with the elf realm. The pure-blooded älfar do not acknowledge them, but regard them as shameful freaks of nature resulting from a malicious whim of Sitalia.

Dar Whjenn, academic expert in the fields of flora, fauna and the laws of nature

Meldriths?

I never had anything to do with them. And have no wish to. When their eyes go white in the sunlight and they smile nicely – because, on the whole, they are not ill-intentioned – well, that's when I see myself lying dead with my throat cut.

Rekarda, female marine merchant from Palusien

They are a masterpiece produced by various deities – but I couldn't say what they are like. The elves trade with them, though, so I can only hope they are nearer in their worship to Sitalia rather than Inàste.

Ucerius, priest of Palandiell

II

Girdlegard

Free town of Malleniagard
1023 P.Q. (7514th solar cycle in old reckoning), spring

Bright afternoon sunlight came streaming in through the sloping windows of the crowded attic workspace belonging to Sparklestone's High-Class Ornamental Jewellery and Gemstone Studio. The workshop building was in the yard behind the prestigious luxury store on one of Malleniagard's best streets, where the wealthiest and most cultured of local families would come to spend their coins.

That daylight, magnified in intensity through cut crystals, was directed in by polished metal sheets down on to the benches where two skilled dwarves were at work. The studio smelled of stone dust, sun-warmed wood, and the herbal tea steaming in their mugs on the counter.

While Gandelin, the stockier of the two, was using a pedal-driven mini-drill to mark his design on a white marble cameo inlaid with amethyst, Goïmron, tall enough to be taken for an undersized or juvenile human, was putting the finishing touches to his jasper gemstone. He was lost in deep concentration on his task. At present the two of them were on their own in the workshop, the other four gem polishers and goldsmiths having headed off home to their families.

'Right. Enough.' With a sigh, Goïmron put down his cutting tool and had another look at the intricate item he had been working on for two full orbits so far. At first the jasper had not wanted to yield, but now his etched outline of the splendid North Gate had been imposed. The image was the size of a normal silver coin. He had worked from sunrise to sunset, completing sketches, doing the preliminary carving, finessing the details, and perfecting the design with the help of his magnifying lenses to rule out any tiny faults. 'So? What do you think?'

'What do I think?' Gandelin put the cameo brooch down and got up from his chair to come and stand next to his friend. He looked at the piece, picking it up and turning it over, studying it carefully, before handing it back to Goïmron.

'I'd say you have the least artistic talent ever exhibited by a Fourthling, to be frank.' He patted his friend on the shoulder in sympathy. 'Not even an orc would want that piece. Not even as a gift. But he might use it as a sling-stone, of course.'

Goïmron had been secretly afraid the verdict from his friend would be something of that nature. 'Don't be so hard on me!' A sigh escaped him. He tended to do a lot of sighing in this workshop. 'I've really tried my best.'

'So has the stone.' Gandelin sat back down and pointed to his own jasper creation. His respectable dark brown beard and the ornamental clips in his prolific beard showed him to be a proud dwarf, even though, as a Fourthling, he was smaller and slighter in stature than those of the other four tribes. 'See those tiny little cracks at the edge? The stone chose to start splitting rather than be further ruined by you.'

'You are too kind.' Goïmron's blue eyes narrowed. 'I think you're going a bit far.'

'We both know the score: you are not destined to be a gemstone carver. But you could be a trader. You'd be better suited to that. Or you could be a quality surveyor in the mines.' Gandelin smiled. 'I don't know anyone else in Malleniagard who can judge a stone's provenance and quality at first glance like you can. You're better than your father ever was. And he's a legend in this community.'

Grumbling, Goïmron chucked his gemstone failure on to the display cloth. A human might have judged it pretty enough, but for the merciless eye of a Fourthling dwarf it did not pass muster.

'That's not how my family sees it. I mean, about myself.' He took off his leather apron and slung it on to the hook near the door. Under the apron he was wearing a simple pair of breeches like the townspeople favoured. He could sometimes even pass as one of them. He kept his black curly hair short and affected sideburns to create the right impression. No matter where he went in Malleniagard, his appearance helped him to avoid trouble. 'And anyway, there are other things I plan to do in my life. I'm not cut out for gem carving.'

'Really? By Vraccas! Who'd have guessed it?' Gandelin countered, taking off his own apron. He preferred the traditional garb of the Fourthlings: a tunic belted at the waist. 'Let's go to the Trusty Tankard. Black beer's on me this evening. With a drop or two of honey mead. What do you say?'

'I don't feel like going to the tavern.' Goïmron noted the failing sunlight. 'I've got to go see Solto. He's told me he's got new stuff in.'

'So you want to waste your time and money looking through his overpriced junk?' Gandelin rolled his eyes and rubbed his well-groomed beard. 'You are, indeed, a hopeless case.'

'Someone has to honour our heritage. Whatever we can find that comes to us from our ancestors is important.' Goïmron was adamant. He had taken this role upon himself. He would be in charge of preserving every dwarf item of historic value. 'Jewellery. Writings . . .'

'Last thing I knew, you'd spent a fortune on a granite tooth-pick with a tiny sliver of diamond on the tip. It was supposed to have come from the Brown Mountains.' Gandelin shook his head crossly. 'Cheap rubbish produced in a doulia sweatshop somewhere in Brigantia.'

'Why not come with me? You can advise me. With your undoubted expertise, you can help me keep an eye out for Solto's trickery and stop me making expensive mistakes.' Goïmron got to his feet and put on his natty conical blue hat with its grey embroidery.

'That is a terrible look. No sane dwarf would be seen dead in a hat like that. You look like one of the long'uns. Well, a smaller version of one.' Gandelin could not disguise his disapproval. 'Long'uns are all very well, don't get me wrong. They pay us for our work. But that doesn't mean I've got to grovel . . .'

'I'm not trying to ingratiate myself. I'm just trying to keep out of trouble.' His slight build often made him the target for insults. But there was open aggression, too. Whereas the Secondlings and Fifthlings in the north and south had built fortifications at the foot of the mountains surrounding Girdle-gard, the original Fourthling lands had, for hundreds of cycles, been taken over by robbers, murderers and vicious beasts who had made their incursions virtually unchal-lenged. Brigantia was a painful, toxic thorn in the flesh of the humans and they often blamed the Fourthlings. Only the Fourthlings. Not the other dwarf tribes. Five large fortified border posts had not proved sufficient to keep out the war-mongering Brigantians. 'Come on, you know I'm not much of a fighter.'

'You mean you don't *want* to be a fighter,' argued Gandelin. 'No, that's wrong. I've seen you fight once.' He glanced at the item on the workbench. 'It was as pathetic as this poor attempt at stone cutting.'

'How good that you never try to flatter me, friend. But occasionally it would be nice if you did.' Goïmron sighed and made for the door. 'See you in the Trusty Tankard later on, maybe.'

'No. After the tavern, I'm off to see Doria Rodana de Psalí. It's the final performance, starting soon after sunset. Full house . . .'

Goïmron burst out laughing. 'So *you* are going to watch a puppet show? Be careful – the way you're dressed, you'll stick out like a sore thumb among all those children. Hey, and don't forget to take your axe.'

'On the contrary, the whole town will be there,' Gandelin said. 'It's absolutely not just for kids. She's a brilliant performer, that Doria Rodana. She puts on a virtuoso show. She does shadow theatre, you know – silhouettes, and the rod puppets, too. And all the different voices. The stories are amazing. She's taken her show to all the courts in Girdlegard. She even performed in front of the dragon herself. Or so they say.' Gandelin added more onyx clips to his dark brown facial hair.

'Kids' stuff.' Goïmron chuckled. He put the red gemstone in his pocket. He could claim the jasper had split and was worthless. That way he wouldn't have to show it to Master Sparklestone. The loss would be deducted from his wages, but he'd prefer that to having to put up with any more sarcasm. 'Grown dwarf and still going to puppet shows? Who'd have thought it? And look at him, will you? Scrubs up nicely . . .'

'You just have no idea about the power of storytelling.' Gandelin opened the door out to the courtyard, letting his friend go first. Then he fixed on his weapons belt and locked the door behind them both. 'But I shan't hold it against you. I'll go to Solto's with you to make sure he doesn't cheat you.'

The two dwarves strolled along to the Broad Avenue in a roundabout way. The wide thoroughfare led from the fifth to the third of Malleniagard's eight hills. This was where Solto kept his curiosity shop.

The pavement and streets were busy; carts, coaches and other vehicles rattled along on the cobbles, and many people were out riding. You had to mind where you walked. The display windows of the tall, brightly coloured half-timbered buildings were attracting the shopping crowds.

The fifth hill was known for its good bakers and butchers and also for the dwarves' goldsmiths shops and breweries. This was where most of the dwarves lived. Goïmron and Gandelin were based in this quarter. They had been friends since childhood but they could not have been more different. Even though Malleniagard was not where they were originally from, they felt at home here in the largest of the five free towns in Girdlegard. These towns were independent, of course.

Malleniagard had about two hundred thousand inhabitants; mostly humans, and some from the doulia caste. There were a fair number of dwarves here, as well. Occasionally one could catch sight of more exotic creatures such as elves and meldriths, or even a srgàlàh or a parsoi khi. And visitors from the Outer Lands, naturally, who would travel in from overseas and undertake study trips for educational purposes. They were all made welcome, provided they behaved properly and respected the free town's laws. Such hospitality and open-mindedness towards foreigners and strangers was not necessarily the rule in other parts of Girdlegard.

But Malleniagard, founded more than seven hundred cycles ago by Mallenia of Idoslane, and furnished with impressive fortifications, was regarded in the United Great Kingdom of Gauragon as an undesirable exception. The most quarrelsome of the Ido dynasty had not wanted to agree to the various realms being amalgamated, as this had meant the end of Idoslane itself. This town, built out of a spirit of proud defiance, was seen as a warning and a monument celebrating the achievements of the female ruler. Many a war had passed Malleniagard by, but little success had accrued to Gauragon. Idoslane's heavy cavalry was still notorious, along with the battle wagons that had wreaked such havoc in the plains.

'Who would have thought the town would attract so many new residents? The founders would have been very surprised.' As they walked, Goïmron glanced at the other hills, with their strong walls, defence towers, and ramparts equipped with sling devices and catapult emplacements.

'I was told the senate is putting a stop to any more immigration. There's not enough suitable accommodation.' Gandelin purchased a crunchy butter hail-stick at a stall and shared it with his friend. 'Malleniagard is as popular as ever.'

Despite the enormous size of the town, things were usually calm, and there was little in the way of criminal activity. Flags and banners fluttered in the gentle breeze and the rays of the setting sun were reflected on the slate roofs and wooden shingles. The two dwarves could smell the malt from the nearby brewery.

At last they reached Solto's curiosity shop. As soon as he stepped over the threshold, Goïmron felt the usual tingle of excitement. The bell on the shop door awakened his hunting instinct.

'Ah. Our dear Master Chiselcut is back again. How nice to see you.' The chunkily built antique dealer came out in his multicoloured decorative robe with its batwing sleeves. He popped out from between his glass display cases, which held extraordinary collections of likely and unlikely items from all over Girdlegard and beyond.

Everything was available. At a price. People would pay astronomical sums. 'I've put a few items aside for you.' He affected an annoying lisp, which was part of the theatrical effect he was aiming for, and which had given his shop its extensive reputation. He turned to Gandelin. 'Are you also interested in our selection, sir?'

Gandelin chewed and looked the shopkeeper up and down. 'My interest is limited to stopping my friend here being ripped off.' His right hand went casually to the axe at his side. 'Don't want him buying any more rubbish, junk dealer. Cheap doulia-made toothpicks, for example. Things made of dodgy marble.'

Solto's eyebrows shot up but he made no reply. 'Do come with me, Master Chiselcut.' With his hand on Goïmron's shoulder, he guided him confidently through the curtain to the alcove. 'I've got new items from the mountains to show you. Some will undoubtedly have come from the land of your forebears.'

Goïmron felt his excitement increasing tenfold. Of course he was aware of the potentially dubious provenance of what Solto was going to be showing him, accompanied as they would be by extravagant claims implying the dealer had personally ripped the items from the maw of a monster with his bare hands. Most of the stuff Solto sold would have washed up somewhere from the floodwaters, but occasionally there would be a selection of valuable items collected by plunderers wandering through abandoned mountain regions. In spite of such looting being strictly against the law, adventurers would still organise themselves into gangs and sneak past the dwarf settlements. Or they would use previously untrodden paths to get round to the Blue and Grey Ranges. Sometimes these thieves would spend many moon phases in the crumbling underground corridors, dilapidated mine shafts and half-collapsed halls. They could amass a fortune for themselves. However, some would pay with their lives before they could ever realise their riches.

Sometimes the jewellery and gemstones or the scraps of ancient documents – on paper or carved into stone – would have been supplied by Gauragon or Khalteran soldiers who had been repelling an invasion of monsters and would have pursued their quarry deep into the tunnels to finish them off. If the soldiers came across things the dwarves had left, they would take them and sell them when they got home. Dangerous military missions like those were rarely successful for humans. It was generally left to the dwarves to keep the beasts out.

And then again, much of what was on offer here would be fake. As indeed Gandelin did not tire of stressing.

With a theatrical gesture, Solto lifted the curtain aside. 'Behold! Behold and wonder, Master Chiselcut!' Goïmron was confronted with bales of rotting fabric, piles of rusty pieces of armour, shattered weaponry and broken shields. He was relieved to also find some small stone tablets, parchment rolls and map fragments. *Perhaps I'll find something here.*

'Take your time, Master Dwarf. Have a good look through,' murmured Solto, as if he was showing off the most magnificent hoard of dragon treasure ever found in Girdlegard. 'I'll make you a good price.' He disappeared swiftly into the shop where a wealthily dressed family had just entered, accompanied by a number of doulia slaves.

'I'll get straight to work.' Goïmron was in a fever of excitement. 'Come and give me a hand, Gandelin.'

His friend did not move, continuing to lean against the wall with a disdainful expression, arms crossed. 'No one else would give a copper coin for that junk. If it weren't for you, Solto would have chucked all that rubbish away.'

'You never know what might turn up.' Goïmron began carefully sorting through. Some of the items fell apart in his hands. 'I'll take my collection to Enaiko one day and they'll welcome me with open arms.'

'Oh yes, the city of knowledge.' Gandelin grinned. 'So you fancy yourself as one of the scholars?'

'I am a preserver. The scholars are all in Enaiko already. I'll just bring them things for their research.' Goïmron sat down on the carpet. Ever since he had been very young, he had dreamt of visiting the town at the foot of the Blue Mountains where dwarves studied ancient wisdom and examined objects that had come from the bygone realms of the Secondlings and Fifthlings. In the course of the centuries, Enaiko had become a celebrated centre of science, alchemy, art, music and healing. The brightest of minds were attracted to the place. 'I have a really good collection.'

'You'd better not mention the granite toothpick, then.' Gandelin surveyed the great heap of objects. 'Boring. I'm off to the Trusty Tankard.'

Goïmron shot a reproachful glance at his friend. 'Aren't you at all interested in what your ancestors wrote about the old times?' He held up two battered tablets with dwarf runes scratched into the stone surface. 'If it weren't for me, things like this would be lost for ever.'

'You can't even read them, though.'

'I'm . . . learning . . .' The ancient symbols were still a closed book to Goïmron and most of his fellow dwarves. The writing presented quite a challenge. The generations that would have been able to decipher the script were long gone. 'Look at all these mysteries! All this knowledge!'

'It could be a recipe for herb beer, of course. Might even be tasty.'

'Yes, or it could be describing . . . something really important. Something that might affect our future, for when all the tribes are united again under our High King. Like they were a thousand cycles ago.' Goïmron's face darkened. 'You don't think that could happen, right?'

'No, I don't. Nobody's thinking of choosing a High King. Not unless the Fourthlings take back the Brown Mountains. And *that's* hardly likely. Not going to happen in our lifetime, is it, Goïmron? Be realistic.' Gandelin went out, muttering, 'I'll be in the tavern. If I'm not there, wait for me and I'll see you after the performance.'

'You'd rather be off playing with puppets? Is that really more interesting than helping me solve the riddles of our history?

And who's going to protect me from buying fakes?' He watched his friend leave. 'As you wish,' he mumbled, turning back to sorting through the enormous pile. In his head he mulled over what Gandelin had said.

It was a seemingly unsolvable problem for his tribe – getting the Brigantians out of the Brown Mountains. And then it was said the älfar had established themselves a realm in a far distant valley to the north. Hundreds of them, disguised as elves, had moved into Girdlegard, multiplied and were looking to get back up to their original numbers. They were planning to take over.

We'll never do it on our own. Goïmron continued sifting through the pile. *We need a High King to unite the Children of the Smith and drive all the horrors out of Girdlegard.* He got up and stretched with a grunt. *To unite us and save us from the otherwise inevitable disaster.*

Only when Solto brought him a lamp did he notice how time had flown. Vraccas had created dwarves to live underground, so he was able to see well even in dim light.

'Have you found anything, Master Chiselcut? Because I want to shut the shop.' Solto's voice had lost its affected lisp. The business day was coming to an end. He looked at the sorted items. 'I see. So *that* is what you've selected?'

'Yes.' Goïmron got up from the carpet and stretched his limbs. 'Three dozen stone tablets, eleven pieces of parchment and the broken dagger, please. I've taken a fancy to the engraving on the hilt.'

'Fine, fine. Let me just quickly work it out . . .'

Goïmron pulled out his rather sorry-looking piece of jasper. 'Would that do? You could keep the change and put it against future purchases.'

Solto pursed his lips and examined the piece of jewellery. As he held it up against the lamp, his colourful, wide sleeves swept the bench.

'This is rather nice,' he said. 'Of course, it's not quite up to the usual Sparklestone standard of workmanship, but, do you know what, Master Chiselcut? I rather like it.' He quickly pocketed it. 'And because I like it, I'm prepared to throw *this* in as well. You can carry your acquisitions home in it.' Like a stage magician, Solto removed a linen cloth that had been covering a wooden chest. 'I can't get it open, but it feels empty and it's got no value. Rather than me putting it on the fire next time the weather turns cold, why don't you take it?' He hooked the lamp back up. 'Get a move on, though. My other half is waiting for me. I'm supposed to be cooking dinner. It's our anniversary. And thanks to you, of course, I've now got a nice little gift for her.' Solto turned round and strode back through the shop, ushering his last customers out.

Well. Goïmron regarded the unexpected extra item. *Not bad at all.*

There were dwarf runes burnt into the wood and engraved into the metal bands – warnings against unauthorised opening. No owner's name and no clues as to where the chest had come from. The wood was in a bad state with some bits splintering off. The lock, however, appeared to be as good as new.

Goïmron grinned. He recognised the type of security fastening. There was a keyhole, but in fact the lock was controlled by a quite different mechanism. To open the chest you would have to press some of the rivets in a certain order.

It did not take long for him to work it out.

Rust – and the harsh treatment the elements had subjected the chest to – actually made things easier. Goïmron could hear which of the rivets were reacting to his touch. The lock clicked open.

He lifted the curved lid.

Inside was a book. A single volume. It was securely stowed in a side drawer and thoroughly packed in waxed paper to keep damp from damaging its pages.

Oh. This is really something! Worried that Solto might charge him extra, he concealed the book under his jerkin and proceeded to load his purchases into the chest. After a friendly leave-taking, he left the curiosity shop and dragged his new property back through the streets of Malleniagard.

It was thirsty work, especially going uphill. It was a good thing that he and Gandelin had arranged to meet up at the Trusty Tankard. He was pleased to find a table free and some good beer ready. He got them to add a shot of extra-strength honey mead to his. This orbit had been one that needed celebrating.

I wonder what I've been given here? There was plenty of candle-light in the taproom, where people were laughing and joking and swaying along to the music provided by a couple of rather tipsy bards, so he took the book out and carefully removed the wax paper covering.

What he found was a notebook bound in decorated leather. The loose-leaf pages were numbered. It appeared from the numeral runes that the various entries originated from different cycles.

A recipe book? A reference book? A collection of the best-ever orc jokes known to dwarfkind? Or maybe some sad old dwarf cataloguing his stomach troubles. Goïmron prepared himself for disappointment and turned to the title page.

In elaborate script was written the following:

> *The Adventures*
> *of*
> *Tungdil Goldhand*
> *His own experiences from*
> *his time in the Black Abyss,*
> *written by himself.*
> *First Draft*

Goïmron peered at the handwriting in disbelief. *It can't be!* 'By Vraccas!' he exclaimed.

The assembled company of dwarves joined in enthusiastically to the toast he appeared to be giving while the humans shushed them. They wanted to listen to the singers.

Goïmron went red and raised his tankard, trying hard to make sure that he didn't let a single drop of beer touch the precious book. *It can't really be by Goldhand!*

His hand trembled as he turned the page.

> To allow better oversight
> as to the content of this book
> and the chronology of my adventures

> Chapter I: how I came to be in the subterranean realm

Goïmron's eyes raced from side to side of the text as he drank in the import of the chapter descriptions, all inscribed in impeccable handwriting. There were occasional corrections, done very neatly. In every case, the exact solar cycle date was given for the various events.

And it was this aspect that gave him the greatest surprise of all.

'It must be a fake,' Goïmron stammered, as he downed the rest of his beer in two draughts, while leafing swiftly forward in the notebook, his fingers flying. He used two small stone tablets from his wooden chest to keep the pages weighed down. It was vital none of the loose pages got lost.

> Chapter XXIII: how I made my way back
> and how I was found

'By ...' *In the name of Vraccas!* He gestured with his empty tankard for a refill. *But this is all less than a quarter-cycle ago. This last winter. That's going by the old reckoning, of course.*

The dwarf who ran the inn brought him over the beer he had asked her for. She looked at the notebook. 'I see you've joined the storytellers?'

'Indeed. I'm just getting some ideas.'

Goïmron shielded the handwritten runes protectively with his arm. To distract her he tapped the wooden chest and showed her the stone tablets he had bought. 'This is some of the junk I've just bought at Solto's.' He gave a nervous laugh. 'All completely made up, of course.'

'I'm glad you are turning to stories, little lad. You'd never have made much of a gemsmith, would you?' she said, making her way back to the bar.

'Good to know that everyone in the whole of Malleniagard thinks so highly of me,' he called over to the landlady. He turned his attention back to the date given for the final chapter. *Unbelievable! Spring 7514.*

No mistake.

Written by Goldhand himself. The words swirled round in Goïmron's head. *That would make him . . . more than one thousand cycles old.*

But no dwarf had ever reached that kind of age. On the other hand, there had never been a dwarf like Tungdil Goldhand.

Goïmron was on fire, giving off sparks of excitement like a piece of amber that's been rubbed hard. Or like the life-forge of the Divine Smith when the bellows were used. He talked himself down and tried to be reasonable.

Solto had not told him where the chest had come from. Anyone could have made up a story and pretended it was by Tungdil. They could have used their imagination to invent things that might have happened to him in the Black Abyss.

I've got to read the whole thing. Check all the details. And examine the way the adventures are narrated. He took a draught from his fresh beer and settled down to read. It got more and more exciting as the story unfolded.

It was a completely different world he was being shown. Cruel and sinister but still fascinating. Everything was described so clearly and the events related were accompanied by deep insights from the author. It was easy to grasp the depths of helpless despair the dwarf had experienced. The flaming-hot fury in his soul, expressed in the most convincing of words. It kept Goïmron riveted. He turned the loose pages more and more quickly as he raced through the narrative. After many more beers, he finally arrived at Chapter XXIII, the end of the story – the end so far, that is.

Time had flown by. The bell went for *last orders, please*. The two musicians had stopped playing and sat slumped on a bench.

Goïmron had not a single doubt in his mind. *This is definitely Tungdil. The real Tungdil. He's still alive. And he's in the Grey Mountains and he's guarding the remains of the Stone Gateway.* He sat back against the wall, aware of the momentous nature of his discovery. He had in his possession the undoubtedly genuine memoirs of the greatest hero Girdlegard had ever known. And that same dwarf was waiting to be found. *Only Tungdil Goldhand could ever bring unity to the five dwarf tribes.*

It was irrefutably clear to Goïmron that he must go to the Grey Mountains and make his way through the mines, tunnels and halls, facing monsters, boiling lava and all the other challenges and discomforts that awaited. *It is up to me to find him. That is why Vraccas has sent me the book. Because we Fourthlings have got to atone for what we did.* He clapped his hands, suppressing actual laughter. *He chose me. Me, the keeper and protector of our heritage.*

In spite of the amount he had drunk, Goïmron was conscious of the fact that he was certainly not the hero type himself. The only weapons in whose use he was adept were darts. He was an ace at the dartboard. But fighting orcs and rampaging monsters? He was not cut out for that.

Gandelin! He must come, too. He emptied the tankard and ordered a final refill. *Well, maybe not just Gandelin. Wouldn't be enough, would it?*

Another alcohol-fuelled idea came along. *Him and me – we'll set off for the Thirdling kingdom tomorrow.* They could get the armour and equipment they would need and recruit other dwarves to go with them. The king would endorse the mission once he'd been told about the memoir. *Goldhand was a Thirdling, after all. Originally, that is.*

Goïmron grinned, well satisfied with how the evening had gone. His hitherto dull and disappointing life had suddenly taken a different turn. Things were looking up.

I want to see the expression on Gandelin's face when I tell him. He looked towards the door. *Where has he got to? Wasn't he supposed to come straight after the performance? It must be long finished by now.* His grin was broader now. *Of course. The devil will have found himself a nice little dwarf. Or she will have found him.* Goïmron grasped the handle of the tankard. *But I've got something more important than bed and fleeting pleasure . . .*

Not totally gracefully, given the amount of black beer inside him by now, he raised the tankard. 'In the name of Vraccas!' he enthused, not caring about the droplets splashing on his beard-less face.

'To Vraccas!' chorused all the dwarves still in the hostelry.

The noise roused the snoozing musicians, who grabbed their instruments again and started to play.

Girdlegard

Brown Mountains
Dsôn Khamateion
1023 P.Q. (7514th solar cycle in old reckoning), spring

Klaey opened his eyes wide. Instead of a shout only a husky sound emerged. His throat was excruciatingly painful and his chest burned like fire.

'Good. That's the hardest part.' The heavily accented voice was pleasant enough. Klaey saw the finely chiselled features of an älf countenance floating in front of his eyes. The bright red pupils held a contemptuous expression and the smooth complexion was chalk-white. 'Samusin was watching over you.'

Klaey took a cautious look at his surroundings. He had a heavy bloodstained blanket over him as he lay on a simple wooden bench in a cell made of blocks of black stone. Sunlight streamed in through tiny arrow slits in the walls. He could only remember as far back as events in the sepulchre. *That cut!* His left hand went up to his throat and encountered a bandage. The lucky amulet had gone. *And the chest wound?* There were bandages round his upper body, too.

'It will be some time before you'll be able to speak properly. A blade damaged your vocal cords.' The pale-skinned älf stood upright, hands clasped behind him. His slim physique was clothed in an elaborately embroidered dark red robe with a high, close-fitting collar; he wore a sword and a dagger at his belt. The quality of the fabric, and the weapon sheaths, knife hilt, belt, neck adornments and the silver ring holding back his long sloe-white hair all indicated an älf of high standing. 'You'll be known as Crow or Croaker, I expect.'

Klaey wondered why this strange älf had rescued him. *Probably not out of the goodness of his soul.* Why would a thief be treated kindly, particularly when found red-handed inside a hero's monument? Judging by the pallid skin, the red pupils and the very white hair, some alchemy had been used in the past by this älf's ancestors. Such effects could last for many generations, it seemed. *It'll be the result of all that deception, smuggling themselves into Girdlegard, disguised as elves.* The älfar, arch-enemies of every creature in Girdlegard, were regrouping. No outsider had ever set foot in Dsôn Khamateion, not for many hundreds of cycles. *No one, that is, except, apparently, for me.*

The älf put his head on one side. 'I can read you like a book. My name is Vascalôr. It's due to my intervention that you are still alive, human. Don't thank me. I expect you to recompense me for my trouble.'

Klaey sat up carefully. 'What do you want me to do?' he asked, his voice a rough whisper. The pain in his upper body and throat could not compete with the utter terror he was feeling. The white in the älf's eyes turned black as a random ray of sunlight touched his face.

'Some may deduce that you turned up in the sepulchre with your captive dwarf, then were surprised by the priestess and killed one and all. Except for yourself.' Vascalôr looked at him disdainfully, observing his reaction. 'But I don't think that's the whole story. While yes, you Brigantians would not have stood a chance against a single one of our warriors, two of our soldiers were killed. Stabbed with immense precision.'

A quiet voice at the back of his mind advised Klaey to keep his counsel. So he made an effort and listened calmly to what the älf was saying. *Don't let him see that you are terrified.*

'Something tells me that it was all planned to look that way. But what really happened was different.' Vascalôr gave an icy smile, displaying perfect teeth. 'Am I right?'

Klaey nodded slowly.

'Don't be under any misapprehension, human. I can tell if you are lying. If you try to trick me, you will die in the blink of an eye.' The älf remained cool and calm. 'Did someone else show up? Who ran off with the armour and the spear, leaving you, the treasure and the other holy relics behind? Did you see them before you were killed?' He brought his left arm forward, raising a forefinger. His fingernail was transparent as glass.

'A single gemstone from the plinth would keep one of you miserable creatures in comfort for the rest of your life. We found the missing gem with one of the Brigantian women.' He lowered his arm. 'But you mortals can do nothing with the armour or the spear.'

'It was the map,' stammered Klaey painfully. 'We thought . . . We thought . . . we were in a dwarf . . . workshop. The Fourthlings . . . Looking for their treasure.'

'What map?'

'I had a sketch. We used it . . . That dwarf . . . he wasn't with us . . . He came out of the opening we'd made in the wall.'

'And this map is where? It must have been taken by someone who escaped.' Vascalôr nodded. 'I *knew* it. When I saw the injuries inflicted on our warriors I knew I was right.' He broke off in full flight and gestured to Klaey to continue.

This was a life or death moment for Klaey. 'I will . . . tell you everything. Exactly as it . . . happened.'

Vascalôr drew a deep breath. 'I'd advise you not to start bargaining . . .'

'I want. Back. To go back. To Brigantia.'

'Tell me what I need to know. Then you'll be free.' But the veiled smile on the pale visage told Klaey the real story.

'No. I want you . . . to take me there . . . When I'm safe . . . I'll describe . . . everything I saw.' Klaey placed his hand on his sore neck. His once charismatic voice was lost. He could taste blood when he tried to speak. The thought of never again being able to sing horrified him. 'Not until . . . I'm safe . . .'

The älf reacted with an incredulous laugh. 'You think you're a cunning little thief, don't you?'

'I owe you my life. I shan't forget that. But as you . . . seem to be the only one in Dsôn Khamateion who wants me alive . . . I need to take precautions.' It hurt to speak. 'What's the good of my heart still beating . . . if I get an arrow . . . in it the moment I leave this cell?'

Vascalôr acknowledged the truth of this with a supercilious smile on his white face. 'Someone who understands logic, I see. What's your name?'

'Dagwin,' he lied.

'That is not your name.' The spectral älf challenged him immediately. 'That makes me even more curious as to who it is I have here.' His hand shot out and he pressed the wound on Klaey's chest violently with his outstretched fingers, making Klaey yelp with pain. 'If I have to ask again, I'll pull out a few of your arteries and make you eat them.' The pressure on Klaey's wound was increased. 'Or shall I reach in and grab hold of your heart?'

'Klaey!' he gasped, trying to wrench himself away from the vicious fingers. 'I am . . . Klaey . . . Berengart.'

'Well, what do you know? A Berengart.' The älf took his hand away. 'The Omuthan's youngest brother. That's good news. I'd seen the clumsy family brand on your forehead, but it's good to have it confirmed.' He put his hand behind his back again. 'That means you are twice as valuable. So, did he send you?'

'No. He doesn't . . . know . . . that I'm here.'

'Makes no difference. He'll hear soon enough.' Vascalôr took a few moments to think. 'Right. Agreed. I'll make sure you get away safely and I'll take you back to Brigantia. In exchange, you tell me everything on the way. The mighty Ganyeios of Dsôn Khamateion owes me a favour.' He nodded to Klaey. 'Just like you owe me your life. Never forget that, if one day you take your brother's place. Be assured, I shall remind you.' The älf turned to the cell door. 'I'll have you brought some fresh clothing. We'll give you a couple of days' respite for your wounds to start heal-ing before we set off. We won't want your siblings to get too worried about you. Orweyn Berengart will be glad to embrace you again.'

'How long . . . have I been here?'

'Six orbits.' Vascalôr opened the door and stepped out of the sunlight, so his eyes resumed their normal colouring. 'Congratulations, Klaey. You are indeed unique. You have survived älfar captivity. You have been in Dsôn Khamateion and an älf is going to see you home.' Vascalôr laughed as he left the prison. '*That's* certainly never happened before.' He let the door slam shut behind him.

When Klaey tried to get up to see out of one of the narrow windows, the injuries to his throat and chest prevented him and he sank back on to the mattress.

But he already knew: his brother would be anything but delighted to see him once more.

Never annoy a srgālàh. He will find your tracks just like his teeth will find your throat.

Proverb from the Sinter realm

Once, when we were half-dead of exhaustion and hunger, we came to a srgālàh settlement and we learned about these creatures' sense of hospitality.

You will find they are generous, friendly and help-ful, once you have grown used to their ways. And they certainly are not like large talking dogs. The grace of their movements gives them a majestic air.

Entry in a Gauragon patrol record book

When the srgālàh had drunk too much of the corn milk and had run out of jokes, he looked round to all the others, tapped his muzzle and said: 'These earthquakes, you know, they're not sent by Vraccas. There's something alive right down there under the earth. I can smell it. And it's digging its way up. You'll see.' I love these horror stories. They're my absolute favourite!

Entry in a Gauragon patrol record book

III

Girdlegard

Red Mountains
Kingdom of the Firstling dwarves
Seahold, eastern harbour
1023 P.Q. (7514th solar cycle in old reckoning), spring

'A smidgeon more to port.' Xanomir set the second sail of the small boat as it danced up and down on the waves. 'We've got to get away from the cliffs or the breakers will smash us.' Laughing, he jutted his grey beard into the spray at the bow, enjoying the weather. 'Nice wind today, eh?'

At the stern, his friend Buvendil adjusted the tiller, keeping a keen eye on the red crags shimmering in the light. 'Yes, good sailing weather.' Both dwarves were of middle age and stockily built, and all the time they had spent at sea had turned the skin of their faces, necks and arms the colour of leather. They had selected light clothes for the trip. It would dry quickly and if you fell in, it would not drag you down. 'The sunlight's going right through the water. Perfect for diving today.'

'I wonder what we'll find.' Xanomir looked back behind their vessel, *Elria's Defeat*. The harbour entrance to the dwarf fortress of Seahold was growing smaller and smaller. His folk controlled the entry to the sea tunnel that the earthquakes and the sea itself had gouged out on both sides of the Red Mountains. Over hundreds of cycles, gigantic fortified harbour townships had grown up on the east and west sides of the range. 'Let's keep our eyes peeled. This must be the spot.'

Xanomir and Buvendil were among the Children of the Smith for whom neither water nor Elria's curse held any terror.

On the contrary.

For the past two generations, Firstling dwarves had been exploring sea, lakes and rivers, building boats and actually swimming happily in any kind of water. They were in the minority, of course, but this third generation was exhibiting growing confidence around the watery element.

Xanomir went even further.

He set about combining old traditions and new ways. As an engineer and a smith engaged in research, he felt this was his duty. This was often awkward for him because sometimes his inventions failed to work. Or rather, failed to work as planned. Such setbacks never stopped him or even lessened his urge to experiment. Buvendil was a kindred spirit in this regard. They shared the excitement of new inventions. And they shared their life.

'There you go!' Buvendil, his blond beard plaits waving in the breeze, pointed to a break in the cliff shaped like a gateway. 'There it is.'

Xanomir's excitement grew and he dropped anchor. Obediently, the boat came to a halt and rocked up and down with the waves. 'Let's make a start.'

Buvendil secured the tiller and went over to the capstan, to which something, hitherto hidden under a waxed cloth, was chained. 'Have you come up with a name yet?'

'Still thinking. A name to annoy Elria, but also compliment her.'

'Like *Elria's Defeat*?'

'I see what you mean – that was issuing a bit of a challenge, wasn't it?' Xanomir tapped the side of the boat. 'But then again, we've never sunk, have we?'

'Yes, we have,' Buvendil contradicted.

'No, that wasn't us sinking. We just ran aground.'

'But we sprang a leak. And then we sank,' his friend went on stubbornly. 'In the harbour. With everyone watching. They laughed themselves silly.'

'But we didn't drown.' Xanomir removed the tarpaulin to reveal a steel construction the shape of a three-quarters sphere, two paces high. There were portholes set into its sides and it had weights attached to sink it to the seabed. A long tube of hollow creeper tendrils was joined in an ingenious and not altogether confidence-inspiring fashion to a set of bellows. Air bags had pressure valves attached. The whole construction had spikes all round to deter attacks from predators, so it looked like an oversized puffer fish with a large bite taken out of it. It also had a spring-loaded mechanism that could fire iron-tipped darts. 'How about the *Elria Bonnet*?'

'What's wrong with *Diving Bell*? That's what it is, after all.'

'That's too mundane. We must include the name of the goddess.' Xanomir operated the pulley, heaving the *Bonnet* up into the air to swing out over the calm surface. 'I'll hop down and then you let it down over me, right?' He quickly stripped off down to his loincloth and then went over the side. 'I can check the pitch seams and the resin hemp fibre seals.'

The ice-cold water really brought him alive. Dwarves were tough, and this had proved a great advantage with the diving.

Buvendil unwound the capstan chain slowly, lowering the *Elria Bonnet*. 'I'm sure the seals will hold. Don't forget to give a sign. I shan't be able to hear your voice once you're inside.'

Xanomir swam down under the *Bonnet*. 'Slowly!' he shouted at the heavy porthole glass while he closed the air valves. Laughing, he made the appropriate gestures, knowing his friend would not be able to understand what he was saying. *I should calm down.*

Buvendil lowered the weighted diving bell and down it went.

To communicate, if necessary, Xanomir had five small inflated pig bladders he could write on with waterproof ink. They could be released up to the surface for Buvendil to catch. They had rehearsed this as a method to use while the engineer was still ironing out the flaws on his new speaking tube system made of rubber and resin.

The inland sea was only fifteen paces deep at this spot and the current was not strong. Conditions here made it an ideal place for experimenting, avoiding curious eyes and mocking comments.

Xanomir inspected the seals, seams, rivets and screw fittings carefully. *They are all intact.* He tested the porthole surrounds with his finger. *All good!*

In the course of the last cycle he had tried out many different ideas: moulded diving bells, or tin capsules, with each new prototype sporting progressively more glass. In order to maximise the length of time he could stay underwater, Xanomir had experimented with barrels of fresh air tethered near the *Bonnet*. As soon as these containers were under the bell, he could release the air into the diving capsule by adjusting the tubes made of rubber or hollow plant tendrils. That way he could renew the breathable air and increase the size of the air bubble within until there was enough room for him to sit down on a seat in the dry. He had managed to stay submerged for one and a half or even two full sandglasses. The next feature had been the development of the release tap to get rid of the stale air and to take in fresh.

Xanomir's newest wheeze was the *permbellow*. This was a pressurised permanent bellows construction that allowed for the constant pumped exchange of air. He had not yet given it a more elegant name. The permbellow allowed him to keep the interior of the diving bell completely dry. Well, it had worked on the model.

In front of the inspection window, a slate appeared with the words *here we go* written on it.

Xanomir deftly opened the valve above his head, and he felt the strong blast of air entering the *Bonnet*. At first, the water level went up, until the pressure equalised, pushing the water down and forcing it out of the undersea vessel.

'Well done, Vraccas! Praise be!' the dwarf cheered. He wrote a message with his indelible pen and sent it up for Buvendil. All he needed now was to sort out a better solution for operating the permanent bellows. He had to come up with a machine. *I know what: a wind-up steel-spring mechanism.*

Xanomir wished his father could have been around to see his achievements. An engineer himself through and through, he had never given a jot for others' doubts or mockery. He had paid for his courage in the end with his life. Elria had taken him. *I'm doing this for you, Father, too.*

Xanomir had a thousand ideas going through his head for a type of diving vessel that could be made to move along underwater, and which could be heated. He sat on the special bench seat and dried himself on a towel. He cast a glance out through the porthole glass that had been specially designed to withstand the extra pressure when drifting along on the seabed.

The sunlight slanting down from the surface created a strange ambience unlike anything on land. Fish swam up, curious to investigate the diving bell. Sea grass was abundant here and there were cold-water coral structures and any amount of tekuli shells clinging to the rocks.

It was at moments like these that Xanomir pitied anyone who was too frightened even to enter the water, let alone to dive underneath the surface. His plan for an undersea boat could change that for everyone. These ideas had been his father's, but the king himself had forbidden the research to go ahead – the monarch had been afraid of the goddess Elria exacting revenge.

Under the earth. Underwater. Xanomir grinned. *In my view, that's as truly dwarf as anything can get.*

His simple *Elria Bonnet* construction would allow a maintenance crew to examine the foundations of harbour defences so that faults could be repaired before the sea found a way in.

Water will always find a way. Xanomir eyed the waterproof seams and seals. *But not here, it won't!*

A shadow swept past the window and then there was a clang as something hit the side of the diving bell.

The dwarf looked out in horror. The fisherfolk from Strandil and Flunders had warned him of a beast that had been destroying their nets. *Is this the same creature?*

The bell was attacked again.

This time Xanomir saw the fish. It was at least four paces in length. *A saw-finned seawolf!* These armoured creatures were hated because they destroyed nets and emptied traps and used their sharp fins to damage fishing equipment.

The fish, with its huge head and long teeth, was circling the spiked *Elria Bonnet*, unsure what to make of it. After a while it approached, opening its jaws to take a trial bite at the porthole window.

Watching in horror, Xanomir noticed a decorative chain stuck between the creature's teeth. *For Vraccas' sake! Does that mean it's eaten someone?*

When the armoured fish closed its mouth, the glass of the porthole cracked. Its sharp teeth had found a weak point.

This is for you, greedy guts! Xanomir pressed a button to release the spring-loaded darts at the predator. The tiny bolts shot through the water like harpoons, piercing the fish in many places. The creature sank and bobbed on the current, streaming blood. *You won't be ruining the fisherfolk's livelihoods anymore.*

Xanomir quickly dived down and swam out of the diving bell and fastened a new line to the sharp tail fin, tethering the creature to the back of the vessel before he returned to the *Elria Bonnet*, closing the air valve and bringing the device up to the surface.

'I'm back,' he called, climbing on to the boat and going to the capstan to wind up the chain, ready to help his friend lift the undersea vehicle. 'And I've brought us some lunch.' His catch was a significant size. A few too many pounds for Buvendil to manage on his own.

'All perfect,' Xanomir announced, cranking the winch to lift the *Elria Bonnet*. 'I hope you like fish?'

'Why?'

'I've caught the armoured saw-finned seawolf that's been bothering the fisherfolk.' He pushed the wet grey hair back from his face.

'I wondered why the diving bell was so much heavier this time.' Buvendil was soaked with sweat. Winding up the chain had taken it out of him. 'We need a machine for that, Xanomir. Or next time it'll finish me off.'

'I'll think of something.'

Soon the diving bell was on board and safely stowed away once more under its tarpaulin.

The four-pace-long seawolf fish in the bow of the boat looked even bigger dead than it had done alive, in the water. The iron-tipped darts had gone right through its head and made holes in its body. Blood and a yellowy brown liquid dripped out on to the deck.

'You didn't aim very well. That yellow stuff's from the gall bladder,' said Buvendil. 'It'll ruin the taste. Chuck it back. We can't eat that. Let Elria have it.'

'Just a moment.' Xanomir wrapped himself in a blanket and carefully opened the creature's jaws to extract the chain he had noticed. Attached was a rusty amulet with a design of two crossed hammers. 'That's dwarf handiwork.' On the obverse he read out the name Hegomil Coalglow.

'What? It can't be!' Buvendil was incredulous, but on inspection it proved true. 'How on earth does Coalglow's medallion come to be in the mouth of this fish?'

'Who is that?' Xanomir dried himself quickly, changed his wet loincloth for a dry one and slipped his tunic on.

'You mean: who *was* that?' His friend thought back. 'He disappeared, it's said, maybe three hundred cycles ago from one orbit to the next. I know because my father is mates with Coalglow's grandson.' Buvendil rubbed the rusty metal. 'He was one of the best climbers we had, says my father. He knew more about the Red Mountains than anyone else.'

'So what age can those armoured fish get to?' Fastening his belt, Xanomir stared at the dead creature in disbelief. 'Do you think the seawolf can have eaten him? Surely not. Dwarves can live a long time. But to live for three hundred cycles?'

Buvendil drew his knife. 'Let's have a look.'

Girdlegard

Free town of Malleniagard
1023 P.Q. (7514th solar cycle in old reckoning), spring

The performance on the market square on Malleniagard's second hill had long since finished and the audience had mostly wandered off.

Gandelin was still sitting on the steps of the fountain, his eyes glued to the travel wagon, where a handful of excited children were hanging about. The puppeteer's young apprentice was entertaining them with some simple conjuring tricks. It must have really looked like magic to the boys and girls. *THE MAGIC OF THE PLAY*, it said in large letters on the side of the caravan, and underneath the words there were drawings of some of the different theatre puppets.

In a warm glow, Gandelin went over to join them. Doria Rodana de Psalí's wonderful performance had entranced him; he had never seen anything so moving. Silhouettes, puppets, lighting – it had all combined to create a magnificent spectacle. And then there were all the different voices and the sound effects. *And that amazing music!*

When the curtain had come down at the end, all the people had applauded enthusiastically, throwing silver and gold coins on to the little stage, even though they had already paid an entrance fee. That stage had seen wonderfully poetic stories recreated by the puppet mistress and her assistant.

The soft metallic tones of the barrel organ issued from inside the wooden caravan. The melody seemed to want to go on for ever.

The song had featured in the play at the moment when the white dragon was killed. Doria Rodana must be a really courageous woman to dare to perform this work, a story about the death of the self-appointed supreme ruler of Girdlegard. *I can't imagine Ûra would approve.* Doria Rodana de Psalí was giving people hope, encouraging them to think that one day all the bitterness and evil would pass and the good times could return.

But where was she? She had left it to her young trainee, who could not be more than sixteen, to collect up the money and thank the spectators. The children were not about to give up and go home. The puppeteer herself was keeping in the background.

Because he had waited so patiently, Gandelin caught sight of her starting to dismantle the stage and put away the scenery. He judged Doria Rodana to be about twenty. She was small and slim, which made him think she would be perfect for Goïmron. Her face was pleasing, with high cheekbones, and her blonde hair was in a short pageboy cut. Her skin was lightly tanned and her lips inky black, as were her fingertips. Gandelin could only guess whether this was a dye, a tattoo or perhaps an unusual natural colouring. Her clothes were simple. She obviously was trying not to be ostentatious.

The most attractive thing, Gandelin thought, was the hypnotic effect of her voice. Everyone had been drawn to it. *I can understand why she is so sought after to perform in all the grand houses of Girdlegard.*

He wondered how best to tell Doria Rodana how much he admired her work. Obviously she would be sent any amount of messages and praise after each performance. His unsophisticated words would not be able to compete. *But I could offer to help her with stowing the scenery perhaps?* He got up and went over. *That way at least I could be useful.*

'Right, that's it for this evening. It's getting late,' the apprentice announced, finishing her magic show by handing one of the children the paper rose she had just conjured up out of her sleeve. 'Hurry home, sweeties. Before Ûra comes to eat you up.' She gave a roar and pretended to grab some of the little ones, her hands forming claws as they shrieked with delight, escaping her and scuttling off through the darkening streets.

Gandelin bowed, greeting her politely. 'May Vraccas be with you.'

'Thank you.' The young apprentice pushed back her long hair. It was dyed half brown and half black and reached past her waist. Her eyes were a mixture of blue and hazel and her expression friendly as she looked the dwarf up and down.

'What can I do for you, Son of the Smith?' She pulled her light-brown mantle closer to protect her from the chilly evening wind.

Gandelin gave a friendly smile. 'I wanted to offer my services. Could I help dismantling the stage? To say thank you for the wonderful performance? I saw your mistress was having to do it all by herself. It looks like hard work.'

'That is kind of you, Master Dwarf. But it's not necessary. I'll be giving her a hand.' She sketched a bow.

Gandelin laughed. 'But look. I could carry five times what you can. Go on, let me help.' He walked round to the other side of the caravan. 'Let's ask your mistress. What is your name?'

'I didn't catch yours, either.' She stood in his way. 'No one gets to disturb her. I'd have to ask her first if she agrees.'

'Then please tell her it's Gandelin Goldenfinger from the clan of the Stone Turners from the tribe of the Fourthlings. I am a master carver of gemstones and cameos and I work for the well-respected Master Sparklestone.' He remained where he was, so as not to seem threatening or pushy in any way. 'What about you?'

'Chòldunja. Just Chòldunja. Aprendisa. It's my first year with my mistress, learning the art of puppetry. And she *is* the very best.' She did an exaggerated courtly bow. 'It is an honour to make your acquaintance.' As she bent low, a pendant fell forward out of her neckline. 'If I'm ever as rich and famous as my mistress, I will come to you and ask you to make me a cameo brooch. I promise.'

The simple wood and bone talisman she was wearing caught Gandelin's expert eye. His friendly feelings towards the young woman disappeared at once when he noticed the pale pink stone, a small one about the size of a fingernail.

'Where did you say you were from?' he asked, his voice sharp.

'In the last few orbits we've been . . .'

'No. I mean you. Where are *you* from, Chòldunja? You're not from Gauragon, are you? I can tell from your accent.'

The young woman stood up straight, surprise and suspicion on her face. She tossed her hair back. 'Why is that important?'

Gandelin pointed to her necklace. 'Because that is a moor diamond. They are the rarest stones in the whole of Girdlegard.' Anyone but a stonecutter might have thought it was costume jewellery, some cheap piece cut off another stone. 'And it's pink. It's been coloured.'

Chòldunja hastily tucked the pendant inside her dress. 'You're quite wrong. It's only glass. Coloured glass.'

'In the name of Vraccas!' Gandelin could not hold back scornful laughter. 'You want to tell that to me, a Fourthling dwarf? We are the best jewellers and gemstone specialists far and wide. You can't fool me with a story like that.' He frowned at her. 'I know as well as you do where moor diamonds come from. There is only one place they get to be worn.' He stared at her eyes. Her multicoloured eyes. 'It's virtually impossible for any outsider to get one. Thus it follows—'

'You are wrong. It is glass,' Chòldunja insisted stubbornly. 'As I said: glass. Coloured glass.'

Gandelin was not to be convinced. 'Does Doria Rodana de Psalí know your secret?'

The apprentice ground her teeth with rage.

'So, she doesn't. I see.' He placed his hand on the shaft of his axe. 'I am letting you know, to make myself quite clear, that I shall be going to report you to the Senate if *certain things should happen* while your mistress is here in Malleniagard. And the Senate will inform the king of Gauragon. That will go badly for you and maybe also for your mistress.'

'I haven't—'

'Do we understand each other?' snarled Gandelin. 'You can thank your lucky stars I'm not going straight to the guards.'

'Yes.' Chòldunja gave in, though he could see she was seething. 'But there is no need to be angry. I've got nothing at all to do with whatever you think I'm involved in. I swear. As Vraccas is my witness.'

Gandelin's fury dissipated. 'I won't say anything. Now introduce me to your—'

Strident male voices could be heard coming from behind the caravan. And the high voice of a woman protesting her innocence.

'My mistress is in danger!' Chòldunja turned and ran off. 'Those idiots have come back like they threatened they would. The moor should swallow them up.'

Gandelin followed her, concerned, holding his weapon. 'Let's call the guards.'

'But they *are* the city guards.' Chòldunja hurried behind the wagon.

When the dwarf rounded the back of the vehicle, he was confronted with an ugly scene.

The slight figure of the puppeteer was being grabbed by the throat by one of the three armed guards, who was shaking her, his face red with anger. 'Don't think for a moment I've forgotten,' he yelled at her. 'For . . .'

To Gandelin it did not look as if the trio were investigating a crime. It seemed to be a personal matter. 'What is happening here, officer?'

The three members of the city watch looked at Chòldunja, then at the dwarf.

'Ah. A dwarf to the rescue,' said the obgardist, releasing his hold on the woman's throat and taking her by the scruff of the neck instead. 'Save your breath. She's a Brigantian and she's going to cool her heels in our cells until we've finished investigating.'

'You? An obgardist? Isn't that more a matter for your captain?' Gandelin hooked his thumb over his belt buckle. 'What is this about?'

'None of your business.'

'Maybe Senator Molka might be interested? Or the lady Senator Sandberg? They are both good customers at the shop where I work. At Master Sparklestone's. You will have heard of him?' Gandelin spoke with quiet authority. 'I'm sure they would want to take this on. It must be a matter of grave security import to the township, the way you are choosing to deal with this vulnerable young lady here.' He noted the red marks on her throat. 'Doria Rodana de Psalí is a celebrated artiste who has performed at the greatest courts in the land. She will be acquainted with more aristocrats than you have hairs on your head. If you are making an official charge here, perhaps you might like to think again.'

The obgardist cast a furious glance at her. 'Get out of Malleniagard. Out! By the end of today. You are a fraud. Don't ever come back here.' He hurled her against the side of the van and kicked her. 'Or I'll do what the dwarf advised.' As the apprentice ran over to her mistress with a cry of distress, he reached out and felled Chòldunja with a blow to the face. 'And you—'

'That's enough!' Undaunted, Gandelin drew himself to his full height, though each of the three humans were much taller. 'Otherwise it'll be the two of us fighting. You wouldn't want that, I'm warning you. Nobody enjoys fighting a dwarf.' He scowled, baring his teeth threateningly.

'Fighting a *Fourthling*. You're no proper dwarf. Couldn't be scared of you if I tried.' The obgardist turned round and his two colleagues followed suit. 'Get out of here, you sham,' he repeated, shouting at the puppeteer over his shoulder.

Gandelin turned to the young women. The puppeteer helped her apprentice up. Chòldunja's nose was streaming blood. 'Will you be all right, or shall we get to a healer, Doria Rodana de Psalí?' he asked.

'Please just call me Rodana, respected Sir Dwarf.' She flashed him a grateful smile. Her right cheek was marked with a graze. 'You were a great help. I thought I was going to end up in a prison cell and being badly beaten.'

There's no way she's any kind of a fraud. Gandelin's gaze swept round the market square. Nobody seemed to be looking out of their windows, so the ugly scene had not been publicly witnessed. 'What was the idiot talking about?'

'I can read people's thoughts from their eyes or their gestures and reactions. I used to do that before I took up working with marionettes. I used to travel around as a kind of fortune teller.' As she answered, the timbre of Rodana's voice was fascinating. 'In those days, that obgardist was a simple city guard and he used to boast that I could never succeed in reading his mind.'

'But he was wrong?' Gandelin grinned. 'And he has never forgiven you.'

'I admit I went a bit far, and I forced a few unpleasant confessions out of him in front of his friends. And the audience. That was difficult for him and ruined his career. He'd have made it to captain by now, otherwise.' Chòldunja was sitting quite still while Rodana wiped the blood away from the brave apprentice's face. The young girl did not even whimper. 'I assume he had accused me of something and brought his friends along as witnesses. What a good thing you turned up, Master Dwarf.'

'My name is Gandelin.' He bowed. 'I was happy to help.' He indicated the wooden stage that still needed dismantling. 'I really came over to tell you how much I admired your performance and to ask if I could assist with the heavy work.'

'That's most kind.' Rodana was holding her lower back where she had been so violently kicked. 'I think he's done me an injury here.'

'I'll have it all stowed away neatly in no time.' Gandelin got to work taking down the temporary construction, following Rodana's detailed instructions. He was delighted to have been able to help her. As he worked, he asked her about her puppetry career, how she made the marionettes and built the scenery. She told him how she had started out in this field. While they talked, Rodana helped Chòldunja roll up the swathes of fabric and pack away the scenery flats. As they finished their work the little barrel organ went silent, as if it knew it was no longer needed.

'My thanks, Gandelin.' Rodana stretched out her hand. Her tiny fingers seemed as fragile as glass in his grip. 'I would like to invite you to eat with us, but I should feel safer if I left Malleniagard straightaway. Fate sent me this brave dwarf in my hour of need. That won't always be the case, I'm afraid.'

'No need to thank me. Reward enough to be able to talk with you.' Gandelin bowed once more. 'You are a fantastic artiste. Girdlegard needs a storyteller like yourself. You give everyone, whether simple folk or powerful citizens, the hope they long for.' Then he winked at her. 'But let me give you some advice: if the dragon invites you to perform for her, you might consider choosing a different play.'

Rodana gave a merry laugh. Gandelin was very close to falling in love with her. The mere sound of her voice had a strange effect on him. 'May Vraccas' blessings be with you, Gandelin Goldenfinger from the clan of the Stone Turners. You are a credit to your folk.' She disappeared into the wagon.

Gandelin went over to where Chòldunja was busy getting the two carthorses ready. 'May your journey go well and good luck with the trip.'

'Thank you for what you did. I would never have been able to stand up to those guards.'

'And because you already have trouble enough, I shall keep quiet.' Gandelin had not forgotten the rose-pink moor diamond she wore around her neck. 'If we meet again another orbit and I see the stone change colour and turn dark red, I shan't hesitate . . .'

'That will not happen.'

'Chòldunja! Can we set off now?' It was Rodana, perched up on the driver's seat. 'I'm keen to get as far away as possible before it's dark.'

'Yes, mistress.' The apprentice hurried over and climbed up. The reins snapped and the powerful horses started off.

'I shan't forget. I shan't forget you and your kind. Look after your mistress.' Gandelin waved after them and started off for home, his mind full of the memories of an unforgettable evening. *Yes, Goïmron would have fallen head over heels for Rodana*, he thought. *They would have made a lovely couple.*

Rodana's relief on taking the road out of Malleniagard was indescribable. The wagon rumbled through the cobbled streets, going up and down the hills, heading for the West Gate. The meeting with the obgardist had shaken her. Vraccas had sent her one of his own, saving her from the worst outcome, whereas Palandiell, the humans' own patron goddess, had done nothing to help. She was still feeling tense. She would feel better once outside of the busy township built on its eight hills.

'Shame we had to go.' Chòldunja looked at the houses and waved back in response at the people who greeted them. Some applauded or cheered. 'The takings were great, mistress.'

'But we nearly lost everything.' Rodana directed the horses along the road leading west. 'You know? I'd completely forgotten about that incident long ago. What horrid revenge he wanted . . .'

'But it turned out all right.' Chòldunja rubbed her swollen cheek where the guard had hit her.

'You call that "all right"? My back is really painful. I feel like one of the horses have kicked me. And that guy could have broken your jaw. Or your neck.' Rodana arranged herself an extra cushion to be more comfortable. 'Why don't you get some sleep? We can swap over when I've got us a few miles out of town.'

'Yes, mistress. Thanks. I will.' The apprentice got up.

'Tell me, had you met Gandelin before?'

'Why do you ask?'

'You were talking quite seriously while you were harnessing the horses. I thought you must know each other.'

'Oh, no . . . that's . . . not . . .'

'What were you talking about? It looked pretty serious.'

'Gandelin was suggesting going to the Senate to complain about the obgardist.' She opened the hatch into the caravan. 'I told him not to bother, because it might mean more trouble for him. The town watch might make things difficult for him. And maybe hurt him.' Chòldunja disappeared through the little doorway into the sleeping area.

'Good thought.' Rodana brought the horses to a halt and looked around. She did not know these roads at all. 'I think I've gone the wrong way. All right, horses, sorry about this. Let's find the gate.' She had to keep going back on her tracks. Sometimes the streets proved too narrow for her vehicle. The horses were obedient and patient as they made their way through the darkened lanes.

When they got to the West Gate, there were two big freight wagons waiting to leave the city. The city guards were checking their loads and examining the paperwork. Rodana halted. Suddenly she heard a noise from back in the wagon.

'Chòldunja? Everything all right?'

The little door opened and the sleepy apprentice stuck her head out. 'Did you call, mistress?'

'What was that noise?'

'That was me . . . I fell out of bed.'

Rodana laughed and told the horses to move on. They moved up in the queue. 'Go back to bed. I can cope for a bit.'

'Thank you, mistress.' Chòldunja popped back into the sleeping quarters, yawning profusely. Soon Rodana was taking her mobile puppet theatre out of Malleniagard, to the applause and cheers of the guards on the West Gate.

Time to stop worrying.

Girdlegard

Black Mountains
Kingdom of the Thirdling dwarves
1023 P.Q. (7514th solar cycle in old reckoning), spring

Goïmron was secretly glad that nobody else in the crowded wagon took him for a dwarf. None of the other passengers had reacted in any way when he got on. His clothing and appearance generally made him look like a rather undersized human, with his beard shaved off completely apart from the sideburns.

The people were jam-packed, standing or sitting on their luggage. Some had ducks or hens in poultry cages while others had goats and sheep with them. His heavily laden pony did not attract attention.

His disguise was a precautionary measure. Goïmron did not know how the world outside Malleniagard might deal with the likes of him. He really was not cut out for fighting. Or for dwarf heroics. Heroes used heavy weapons and lots of armour, but all he had was his dagger and his favourite set of darts, the latter useful if there were an opportunity for making a few coins in a wager or winning some free food or beer in a hostelry on the way. Many was the time he had won himself a free meal in the Trusty Tankard.

The wagon rumbled to a halt and the doors opened. 'Whitefields' was announced by an official on the ramp wearing the light-green uniform of the Gauragon cavalry. 'Welcome, passengers. If you are intending to continue your journey with the rail coach, please note we will be staying here for around one full sandglass.'

Grasping the bridle of his pack pony, Goïmron took his leave of his fellow passengers and walked down the ramp.

The rail coach had not been invented by the human inhabitants of Gauragon but had been developed from a system which bygone dwarf wisdom had produced. Over the course of recent hundreds of cycles, some of the rails originally used by the dwarves in their express tunnels underground had come to the surface during the successive waves of quakes and earth shifts. Humans had adapted the transport principle and had laid more rails and built larger trucks to accommodate freight and passengers alike.

Sometimes the rail coaches were pulled by horses or by tamed monsters. And sometimes they ran on a system of wheels operating by gravity on the sloping terrain. Humans did not share the dwarves' natural talent in technical matters and it was for this reason that only certain stretches of the Great Kingdom territory were held suitable for rail-coach travel.

Fortunately, there was a connection that ran from Malleniagard to a spot about ten miles distant from the Black Mountains. This saved Goïmron a significant amount of walking. He no longer had enough money to hire a second pony for him to ride. Master Sparklestone had declared he must be mad when Goïmron had explained his plan, but he did give him permission to go, telling him that having time to himself would help him come to terms with the terrible news. He told him he would be welcome to come back to work any time.

Not just Goïmron but the whole Fourthling community in Malleniagard had been deeply shocked when Gandelin's dead body had been found in a side street. He had been robbed of everything, even his belt buckle and the clasps in his beard. He had been murdered with his own axe. It must have happened on his way home after the puppet show.

I should have gone along with him to the show. Then he would still be alive. Goïmron led his pack animal down to the street and headed west, where the territory of the Thirdlings rose in a forbidding mass of high peaks and dark cliffs behind the gentle green foothills. *Then you would have accompanied me here on my mission, Gandelin. I know you would.*

People were milling around the rail coach, with its ten truckloads of passengers. There was freight to be unloaded. Some wagons had luxurious cabins where the wealthy were served food and drink. Most of the passengers travelled seated on wooden benches, or on layers of straw on the carriage floors.

The four exhausted giant trolls who had been harnessed to pull the train were being exchanged by a group of officials for a fresh team.

Children and adults watched as the huge beasts, eight paces tall, were led out like tame dogs. They were stupid creatures. And obedient. No comparison with their wild siblings of a thousand cycles previously, who had come rampaging through into Girdlegard via the fallen dwarf kingdoms.

Although the monsters were tame, humans insisted on extra security measures. The trolls wore iron bands around their skulls. These had a device controlled by a chain. In case of mutiny, a mechanism would fire bolts into the rebel creature's head. The overseer could operate these at the first sign of trouble. Metal springs would send spikes through the brains of any troll threatening danger. Death would be instantaneous.

If they were not so dangerous I would feel sorry for them. Goïmron led his pony out of the loading bay. Outside were refreshment stalls offering snacks and delicacies. Other booths sold lemonade, beer and wine. Warehouses the size of temples were being filled with the goods which had just arrived by rail.

The huge trolls were kept outside some way off, chained up and concealed behind a small wood. Occasionally you might catch sight of a troll arm or a head through the bushes.

Two Gauragon guards in light green were checking the paperwork provided by newly arrived passengers. They stopped him.

'So, my lad.' The older of the two men held out his gloved hand. 'Where are you from and where are you heading?'

'I am from Malleniagard and I'm going to the Black Mountains,' Goïmron answered. 'But is that any of your business, sirs?'

'You are in Gauragon,' the younger man explained. 'We can't just let anybody come marching through our lovely kingdom whenever they feel like it. Subjects of the state need to have papers.'

'But I am not a subject. I am from the free town.'

'Exactly.' The older man took over. 'That means you need a visitor's pass.' He pointed to the left where there was a long low building next to the warehouses. The building sported the flag of the United Great Kingdom. 'You can apply over there. It will cost you one gold coin for each day of your visit. If you outstay your visa, there's trouble in store. It gets pricey.'

Goïmron did some quick sums in his head. He did not even have twenty silver pieces left. 'What if I can't pay?'

'We send you back to Malleniagard.'

'If you get caught here without a pass, my lad, you'll be in prison before you know it. Hard labour until you've paid off what you owe the state.' The older of the two guards waved him off. 'Either pay up or move aside. There's others want to come through. You're holding us up.'

Goïmron was horribly disappointed. His destination lay tantalisingly close. Only ten miles away. All that separated him from it was one gold coin. *Where can I get one?*

He couldn't sell his pony or his equipment. Or his clothes. Or his provisions. *It'll have to be my set of darts. And the tobacco and the bergschaum pipe.* He started unpacking his luggage. *It might just be enough.* 'Would this . . .?'

The men smiled knowingly.

'No exceptions. No bribes. No goods in lieu. Move aside, boy. Quickly now before I turn nasty.'

Goïmron had never felt so completely helpless. He had no money to get him back to Malleniagard and without this wretched visitor's permit he would not even be allowed to walk back to the border. *I am absolutely sunk. All for the want of one gold coin.*

'Just let him through,' came a woman's imperious voice. 'He is my guest.'

The two guards turned round in astonishment.

Goïmron squinted past the men to see who had spoken up for him, and with such authority.

'Consider his gold coin paid.'

He saw a dwarf woman with copper-coloured hair sitting in full armour on a black horse. Her armour was partly composed of black plates and partly of silver chainmail. From the hips downwards she had a long skirt that would allow the maximum of free movement in combat. In her right hand she carried a war club that ended in a vicious narrow blade. The handle lay casually on the saddle in front of her. Her face was round with a pointed chin and decorated with dark blue tattoos.

'By Vraccas!' If Goïmron had considered his friend Gandelin a dwarf of impressive stature, he was adjusting his opinions now.

Behind this Thirdling he saw two muscular, mounted warriors in similar armour. One, with a black beard, had a long-handled axe carried in a supporting holster at his saddle, while the bald one had an interestingly dyed beard in blue tones. His preferred weapon seemed to be a war flail, and he carried a silver casket under his arm. Goïmron guessed neither of these two would have any trouble splitting an orc in half with one hand. *Even with that flail thing.*

'We can't . . .' The younger of the two guards attempted to protest but his older comrade dug him in the ribs with his elbow.

'We can't prevent that and we have no wish to,' he said, continuing his companion's sentence. 'Take him with you. But if he wants to leave Gauragon to go to the Black Mountains . . .'

'Then I will ensure he has the appropriate papers.' The copper-haired dwarf woman motioned to Goïmron to step over to join herself and her impressive-looking escort. The tattooed device on her left shoulder was one he thought he recognised. 'Come, friend. Let's go. It will be raining soon. We need to be sitting in the warm chatting over a good mug of spiced beer.'

'Gladly.' Leading his pony, Goïmron walked past the guards who were now dealing with other passengers. Next to the magnificent horses of his rescuers, the animal looked pathetic. *Just like me, I suppose.*

The two mounted dwarves appeared to be enjoying the incident. They also bore tattooed devices on their skin, just nowhere near as elaborate as the patterns belonging to their leader.

'We should have brought a barrel of black beer along for the way back. The going will be slow, Hargorina,' said the one with the blue beard and the flail. 'Because he's on foot. Maybe should start on a calming pipe. A nice smoke might stop me getting too impatient.'

Hargorina! Goïmron immediately realised who it was he was dealing with here. He looked again at the heraldic device. *Of course. This was Hargorina Deathbringer, the great-granddaughter of that one-time king!* She had already impressed him by her appearance, but learning her identity filled him with awe. She had the reputation of being the best warrior the Thirdlings had. The tattoos bore witness to her many triumphs in battle.

'I'll be as quick as anything,' he stammered. 'I'm good at running.'

The Thirdling with the huge battleaxe at his saddle made some complicated gestures.

'He says: "I bet you are!"' Hargorina was interpreting the signs.

'What else is a little quarter-dwarf going to do when faced with an orc?' said the blue-bearded one. The two warrior dwarves burst out laughing.

'Let him be.' Hargorina shared the joke, he could see. The dark lines on her face showed that she was smiling. 'Don't take it amiss. Belîngor and Brûgar have never met a Fourthling before.' She indicated the one with the black beard. 'Don't be surprised at Belîngor. He has taken a vow of silence. He only speaks in emergencies. If he breaks his vow he has to do penance.'

'Thank you for helping me like that.' Goïmron felt his voice sounded unnaturally high. A scrawny little dwarf with a scrawny little voice.

'Can't leave you to starve in Gauragon if you're heading for the Black Mountains, can we? You are a Child of the Smith and we stick together. Well, that's the way I see it. Old rivalries are best forgotten.' The red-haired dwarf turned her horse, slowing it to a walk and letting the reins hang loosely over the pommel in front of her saddle. 'Would you like to ride with one of us?'

Goïmron felt affronted by the warrior dwarves' gurgles of laughter. He imagined himself seated in front of one or other of these huge contraptions of steel and iron, like some blushing maiden being carried off as a bride. 'No,' he said. 'I shall run.'

'That'd be cos you're good at running away?' teased Brûgar, to his companion's delight. 'Like all the Fourthlings.'

Hargorina indicated to her dwarves that they should exercise some restraint. 'As you wish. But if we get caught in the rain because of your being slow, we shall blame you. You will owe us one. On top of the gold coin I've already paid out for you.' She took out her flask and drank. 'What are you called?'

'Goïmron.'

'The rest of your name?'

'Goïmron Chiselcut, clan of the Silver Beards, tribe of the Fourthlings,' he replied. He was beginning to feel calmer. Walking next to Hargorina and leading his pack pony, he found his voice sounded stronger now, as it should.

'And in Malleniagard, what is it you do?'

'I am a skilled gemstone carver in Master Sparklestone's workshop.'

'By Lorimbur, quite something,' he heard Brûgar whisper. Belîngor snorted. 'A gemstone scratcher.'

Hargorina ignored them. 'But you are dressed like one of the long'uns: your hairstyle, your lack of beard ... Why is that, Master Chiselcut?'

'It's my choice.' Admittedly he had always chosen the way of least resistance, but this would make him appear to these Thirdlings like a complete idiot, a dwarf weakling.

'Right.' Hargorina's tone remained amicable. 'I had assumed you dressed like that so as not to attract attention, living among the humans.' She was directing her mount by thigh pressure alone. 'I thought maybe because you were ashamed of your origins.'

'Never.' He felt sick to the stomach to be lying. None of them would understand. *And indeed, how could they, being so impressive in stature themselves?*

'It would be a mistake if so. It's true the long'uns do not hold us dwarves in high esteem, and especially your own folk, that is. But for thousands and thousands of cycles we have been protecting them. Lorimbur's tribe still does that. Take pride in the achievements of your ancestors, Goïmron.' Hargorina smiled. 'Eventually you will regain possession of your Brown Mountains. It will happen.'

He sighed and thanked her with a nod and a rueful expression. *That would be too wonderful for words.* 'I wonder if I might be the key to that future,' he said.

'You?' Hargorina's bright red eyebrows shot up. 'Oh, *now* you're making me wonder what kind of a Fourthling we've found here.' She was about to say more, but their talk was suddenly interrupted by shouts and screams of horror coming from back where the rail coach was drawn up.

Goïmron turned round. And froze.

Two of the trolls had attacked their supervisors, trampling them under their massive feet. It had come too quickly for the men to be able to trigger the chains controlling the punishment bolts. The humans' battered corpses were stomped into the dust. The trolls, all eight paces high of them, were roaring, kicking out and blindly hurling barrels, boxes, animals or even humans around – anything that came to hand. The monsters had ripped out roof timbers and were smashing them into the hated rail-coach vehicles they had always been forced to pull.

Passengers were screaming and trying to get away, while the Gauragon guards fought to control the situation, hurriedly summoning archer support and spear catapults.

Incited by the leaders of the mob, those beasts still tethered were howling along with the others. Their noise was echoed by the monsters in the distant wood.

They won't dare to attempt to escape. Not yet. Goïmron gripped the bridle of his pack pony firmly to prevent it bolting. *But what happens if they do?*

The two giant trolls rampaging free obviously grasped the potential danger facing them from the catapults. They rushed over to the machines and flattened them, together with their crews, with brutal blows of their makeshift clubs. Randomly torn off limbs and bloodied blocks of wood flew through the air.

'I've always told the long'uns this would happen,' Hargorina commented calmly as she watched the mayhem. 'You can't train the beast nature out of the trolls. Never. Tion does not allow it.' She looked over at Goïmron, who was feeling overwhelmed. 'Stay where you are. We'll be right back.' Then she brought her horse round and held out her long-bladed war club. Her battle cry resounded as she galloped to the fray. 'For Lorimbur!'

Belîngor grinned at Goïmron, wiggled his black eyebrows and charged after his leader.

'Let's show the long'uns how to do this. Watch and learn, little quarter-dwarf. But don't try this kind of thing yourself.' The bald-headed Brûgar tossed him the silver casket he had been carrying. 'Here. Look after this. You should be able to manage that.' With a wild shout he dashed after the other two, whirling his war flail.

Catching hold of the heavy box, Goïmron had to take a couple of steps backwards. Under Brûgar's arm it had appeared to be light as a feather.

Meanwhile Hargorina was attacking the first of the giant trolls from behind. Even on horseback she only reached up to the knee of the hair-covered monster.

Mesmerised, Goïmron watched the Thirdling dwarves' manoeuvres.

Hargorina leaned back and sliced through the creature's ankle tendons with her sharp blade while Belîngor attacked in the same way from the other side.

Howling with pain and fury, the beast whirled its arms but could not keep upright. It plunged to the ground in agony, its arms supporting it.

Hargorina and Belîngor were back in position and cut at the creature's forearms. Once more, they slashed through ligaments, and the troll collapsed.

Brûgar rushed up and, with a swipe of his flail, activated the bolt mechanism on the troll's skull. There was a loud snapping sound as the steel spikes drove into the beast's head, piercing its brain.

Goïmron witnessed the exact moment of death in the troll's eyes.

'Brûgar! Get to the bullet catapult!' Hargorina commanded, as she turned her attention to the remaining troll, which she was now circling. 'Get it working.'

'Understood.' The bald dwarf turned his horse back and raced to the unmanned catapult that could hurl out plum-sized shot – as long as the spring mechanism was tightly wound and the magazine fully loaded.

But the beast did not fall for Hargorina's diversionary tactic. It bounded up on to the roof of one of the warehouses. The roof collapsed under its weight. Dust and flour rose up in clouds, colouring its hairy pelt white. It quickly grabbed itself two humans who had sought shelter inside the building, and swallowed them nearly whole. Blood dripped down from the corners of its mouth as it uttered a shout of triumph.

'Brûgar! Hurry up!' Hargorina cried, halting her mount.

'We can't get at the troll through all that rubble. Drive it out over to us.'

Belîngor whirled his axe in anticipation.

'Yes! Let's be having it! I haven't even had a chance to get my combat pipe lit.' Brûgar had meanwhile wound up the clockwork mechanism. Goïmron watched, impressed and enthralled, as the Thirdling swung the catapult around to aim at the troll. 'Here we go!' he called. And the shot was fired.

The spring-loaded device for the sling hurled out its metal balls in quick succession as they were fed in from an overhead contraption. The hits the beast took in its unprotected flesh were devastating even for a troll that measured eight paces in height. The creature screamed in pain as holes were punched into its skin and black blood gushed out of the injuries it sustained. In panic it attempted to take cover within the remains of the building.

That is so loud! Goïmron covered his ear – only able to protect one since he could not let go of the box.

Brûgar knew what he was doing with the catapult and, in spite of all the rubble and the wooden beams in the way, every third shot hit its target. 'Let's have you out of there,' he shouted with a laugh. 'Give us a chance to kill you properly.'

The monster launched itself upwards again.

Goïmron saw how it towered up against the grey sky, swinging its club and heading straight for the Thirdling who was working the catapult. *By Vraccas! He must get away now!*

Brûgar stood firm at the sling machine, adjusting the firing muzzle upwards and targeting the charging troll and sending out missile after missile. But then the metal spring exhausted its power.

No! Goïmron was convinced this meant the end of the Thirdling.

The troll landed with a mighty crash, falling to its knees. Its raised club went right through the catapult, destroying the machine. Brûgar disappeared in a cloud of dust.

'For Lorimbur!' yelled Hargorina, galloping up and slashing the cowering beast along the width of its lower back. The wound was so extensive that the flesh gaped open, revealing the white bone of the spine, soon hidden again under a gushing fountain of blood.

Goïmron felt ill, and an acid taste rose to the back of his mouth.

Before the roaring troll could get to its feet, Hargorina followed through, and in a death-defying move, rode straight underneath it, with her bladed club raised high so that it cut the unprotected throat. Another black fountain of blood shot out.

While this was happening, Belîngor passed the monster's right flank and grabbed at the end of the security chain. Goïmron heard the clanking and the crunch of the bolts as they were released. The troll collapsed, giving a death rattle, crushing several distraught humans and a sales booth under its body. Beer barrels burst open and the alcohol mixed in with the beast's black blood.

'Brûgar!' called Hargorina, standing up in the stirrups for a better view as she searched for him. 'Tell me you are alive?'

'Yes, I am,' came a shout from the cloud of dust by the first dead troll, and then there he was, having climbed up on to the creature's back, his war flail held casually against his shoulder. He rubbed the blue tattoos on his face as if fresh from the barber's shop. 'And I intend to stay alive for a considerable time to come.'

The surviving humans cheered the three dwarves and thanked them for the rescue. Goïmron noticed the Gauragon supervisor operating the lethal chains on the remainder of the unruly trolls, killing them as a precaution. One monster after another fell. The men, women and children expressed their satisfaction at seeing this done. From the little wood in the distance, where the other trolls were kept, came howls of distress.

Goïmron had no pity in his heart for the creatures. But he still did not find it right to execute them in that way. *Nothing to do with me.* He gazed at the Black Mountains. *That is where my destiny awaits.*

Hargorina came riding over to him. 'Task completed, Goïmron. Let's get back underway again.' Her bloodstained war club was held down by her side, black drops running off the blade. 'That made a nice change. But it was not a good fight.'

'Oh, but it was,' said Goïmron, although inside he had died a thousand deaths. He tapped the heavy casket. 'I kept it safe.'

Brûgar came over, hearing that last exchange of words. 'Let me welcome you to the inner circle of the bravest of the brave, quarter-dwarf,' he said, mockery clear in his tone. 'You and your pony both. The true heroes of the day. Without the two of you to protect it, the casket would surely have been lost.'

The first raindrops started to fall from the light-grey sky. They clinked and clanked on the leader's armour. Proudly she raised her face, streaked as it was with blood, to the shower of rain, putting out her tongue to catch the moisture, some of which made pearls in her red hair.

Goïmron understood the significance for him of the rainfall. *This means the drinks will be on me. I see.*

Why is the sea the whore of all the rivers? She always lies beneath them and they all empty themselves into her.

Joke among the seafarers of Litusien

IV

Girdlegard

Brown Mountains
Brigantia
1023 P.Q. (7514th solar cycle in old reckoning), spring

'After the last bend we will reach the top of a steep slope. Then we go three paces down on one of the main paths.' Klaey was being carried on a litter by two human slaves who were also carrying the provisions on their backs.

He was bright enough to know not to tell the spectral älf in the dark red robe the whole story until he was safely back in Brigantia. Occasionally he would hint he had more secrets to disclose. This way he could ensure his älfar escort would protect him from danger. In his present weak state of health, he would have been hard put to fight off a one-armed gnome child.

'The entrance can't be seen from below,' he croaked. 'That's why it was never noticed.'

'Excellent.' Vascalôr gestured his instructions to the slaves, so as not to have to address them with words. He was playing along with the secrecy agreement and realised he would have to wait until the end of the journey for the big reveal. In the meantime, he was assiduously noting down every word Klaey divulged about events in the memorial hall. He did not, however, disclose the significance of the pieces of tionium armour, the runes on the spear or the identity of the warrior depicted in the many frescoes and other paintings decorating the walls of the sacred monument.

So we both have our secrets to keep. Klaey tried to find a more comfortable position on the stretcher chair. The injury he had sustained to his abdomen smarted in warning. But his speech was improving and he was managing to talk without fighting for breath. Still croaking, though. 'I expect they will have reported me missing.'

They had three female and three male soldiers as escort, providing both protection and a front for their excursion. The älfar troops looked like shadow spirits in their dark hardened-leather tunics over black clothing. The only sounds came from the slaves' footsteps or the creaking of the wooden stretcher poles. Or from Klaey himself. The älfar always moved silently.

'You'll have a good excuse for your absence,' said Vascalôr. 'I'll see to that.'

For the journey to Brigantia the little band had chosen the same route taken by Klaey and his troop through the mountains. The älf was looking for possible clues concerning the robbery and those involved. Whether or not he had found anything, he kept strictly to himself.

At the top of the cliff Vascalôr halted and studied the path, which was illuminated by lanterns and led down into a tunnel whose roof was ten paces high. 'There's nobody there.'

There were some roof supports roughly constructed out of wood and bricks, but practically nothing left of the original vaulted architecture designed by the Fourthlings, cleverly engineered to take the pressure of the rocks above. Earthquakes and distortion had destroyed much of the evidence of the dwarves' skill. Only small sections of their decorative carvings remained to be seen through layers of dirt.

'We take a left now. That will bring us directly to my brother's conference chamber. Someone there can tell us where to find him.' Klaey's torso wound was hardly causing him any pain but he was too weak to attempt any climbing. 'You should lower me down first. Otherwise there'll be trouble as soon as they notice you.'

'Because they'll think that seven älfar are enough to conquer the whole of Brigantia?'

As Vascalôr turned back with a scornful expression, his long, sloe-white hair swept round. 'They can't be very confident about their own defences.' He turned to his soldiers. 'Shall we think about invasion? Shall we see how far we can get into the realm of these thieves and cut-throats?'

The soldiers laughed quietly. One of them responded to his leader's words by indicating their captive.

Klaey did not let on that he was now able to understand much of the älfar language. He also had a good idea of the content of the notes Vascalôr was making in his little book. He had managed to decode in his head the script the älfar used. Had he not been captured by them, he would never have had the opportunity to work this out. *I'll certainly be the only one in Brigantia with this knowledge.*

Vascalôr motioned to the human slaves to put the litter down. At his orders they placed the carrying harness directly round Klaey's body over the woollen garment he wore. The harness was then connected to a rope so that he could be lowered to the broad passageway; this was a technique they had used before at steep sections of the march.

'You won't have forgotten our agreement, o smallest of the Berengarts?' Vascalôr was watching the slaves at their task. 'Don't assume you are safe and then refuse to tell me the whole story just because you are back in Brigantia. I can kill you quicker than you can blink.'

They could hear the rumble of an approaching cart.

'I know. That's why I shall be keeping my word.' Klaey had reached the right level and was now standing in the tunnel, leaning his weight against the stone wall.

A number of Brigantians came along with a trolley cart full of rattling barrels in tow. When they noticed him, they slowed their pace, glancing upwards to see where the rope was coming from.

'Greetings,' said Klaey with a smile. 'You know who I am.'

The men and women stood still.

'Of course we do. Your face is on posters everywhere. They're looking for you,' a brunette observed in a surprised tone of voice.

'What's that you're wearing?' asked one of the men. 'What kind of clothing is that? Are you a woman now?'

'I've been lent it.' Klaey did his best to stand up straight and create a dignified impression. 'So, I have been reported missing, have I? Good.'

'No. Not missing. *Wanted*,' the brunette replied drily and the group all laughed. 'Your elder brother has put up a reward of ten gold coins for anyone who can drag you along to him. That's what it said on the posters.' The woman stepped forward. 'Must be my lucky orbit. Easy money. And it's not far to where the Omuthan is.'

Before Klaey could answer, Vascalôr landed silently next to him, drawn sword in his hand. The shining tip touched the woman's throat. 'I'm not sure it's *really* your lucky orbit, human,' he said darkly. 'You see, *I* found him first. The ten gold coins are mine.'

The other älfar arrived without a sound and stood round the group, again all pointing their drawn swords. None of the Brigantians dared even draw breath.

Wanted. That's an unpleasant development. In spite of this, Klaey tried to relax. He had seven excellent guards protecting him.

He could talk to his brother about what it said on the posters. 'May I introduce Vascalôr? He is the . . .'

'The ambassador from Dsôn Khamateion. And I saved his life.' The pale älf took over, his eyes alert, the pupils burning. 'I present no threat as long as none of you does anything silly.'

'No . . . No, nobody . . . will,' stammered the brown-haired woman, squinting sideways along the double-edged blade at her neck. She glanced over to the cliff path where the slaves were making their way down, bumping the empty stretcher along with them. 'Shall I take you to the Omuthan?'

'That would be extremely helpful.' Vascalôr sheathed his sword neatly. 'Perhaps I will hand on one of the coins for your assistance.' The other six älfar also put away their weapons. 'What is he wanted for?'

Klaey was also keen to learn this but he already had a nasty suspicion. 'It must be some sort of misunderstanding.'

'The notices say desertion of duty, ignoring orders and disrespecting the Omuthan's authority,' the brunette said as she turned to lead the way off. 'This way. I saw him enter the conference chamber with the zabitays a little while back.'

'No. None of that is true. I told you, it's just a misunderstanding.' Klaey had thought as much. His prolonged absence had had consequences. But as Vascalôr had said, *I have a good excuse.*

The mixed column moved on.

Klaey was put back on the stretcher chair. He welcomed this because it would emphasise his vulnerability and weakness. With luck, his brother would therefore treat him more mildly. The three charges against him would otherwise carry drastic punishments. Brigantia was not built on loving kindness among its citizens, but based on strict rules. The Omuthan would act swiftly to condemn even the slightest of misdemeanours, coming down with the full weight of the law. The sudden appearance of the älfar in Brigantia would, he hoped, distract his brother's attention from the real reason for his disappearance. *I really need a new lucky talisman.*

The brunette Brigantian let her people go off with the trolley of barrels while she took the new arrivals to the conference hall. She went to stand firmly by the door. She was apparently really going to wait for Vascalôr to give her some of his reward money once the interview with the Omuthan was over.

The group were escorted to Orweyn Berengart by the ruler's bodyguards, who, obviously impressed at the sight of the visitors, remained close to the älfar. For greater security the zabitays quickly summoned reinforcements armed with spears, pikes and crossbows.

Klaey doubted this would prove sufficient if Vascalôr were to decide to attack. *An älf can beat anyone.*

He knew that he had brought sevenfold death incarnate right into the heart of Brigantia.

The conference hall door opened. Inside they saw a huge table and many chairs. This was the great chamber where the Omuthan would hold counsel with his most important advisors, to discuss the situation at the borders of the land, to plan attacks on Girdlegard, to arrange limits on immigration from the Outer Lands, or to investigate untoward events in Brigantia itself.

Orweyn was seated on a three-pace-high platform from which, in the distant past, the Fourthlings had looked down at the decorative mosaic pattern on the floor, showing a map of their realm. There were many gaps in the work of art, where, in the course of hundreds of cycles, the precious stones had been stolen.

Orweyn's scant white hair was well groomed and plaited, tied with a black silk bow at the back of his neck. His dress was sober, consisting of knee breeches, doublet and a perfumed scarf. Even with the decorative Berengart brand on his brow, the overall impression was of someone harmless.

But if anyone were to underestimate the fifty-year-old, they would be making a mistake. Klaey knew he was an excellent strategist, a fine mind, and completely unforgiving. Once in his armour, Orweyn was transformed into a fighting beast.

'My smallest brother.' To his right and to his left he was protected by shield-bearers and archers with short bows ready to fire. 'I never for a moment thought you would be brought to me by älfar.'

Klaey struggled to sit up, his face a picture of pain. 'Dear elder brother,' he croaked, his new voice suited so well to his pretended distress. 'I am well enough. Please don't worry any longer.'

'I was not aware that the pay in Dsôn is so low that seven älfar have come along, eager to share the ten-coin reward for bringing me my good-for-nothing brother. And you were carried all the way here?' Orweyn placed his hands on the balustrade. 'Start talking. Where have you been hiding? And what's wrong with your voice?'

The spectral älf stood confidently, as if the Berengart conference chamber were his own. 'I, Vascalôr, envoy from Dsôn Khamateion, have come to bring you the only survivor from a cowardly and perfidious attack on the most sacred of our memorials.' He glanced at Klaey. 'In order to thank him for his assistance, we saved his life and promised him a safe escort to his home.'

'How do you black-eyes come to be in Brigantia without being noticed?' Orweyn asked.

'That was my doing,' said Klaey, retaining his troubled and pained expression. His brother did not appear to be overly pleased to see him. 'While on patrol I discovered a secret way through to Dsôn Khamateion and was about to explore with my troop when we found ourselves in the middle of a fight.'

'So that is why you disappeared. A hidden pathway. You wanted to outdo your siblings. To have something to boast about.' Orweyn was grinning. 'Maybe that was it. But I have my doubts about the truth here.' He gestured politely to the älf, saying reassuringly, 'Please understand I am not accusing you of lying. But you both seem to have agreed on the story.'

'No, eldest brother! That's really exactly how it was.' *Well, nearly.* Klaey got up slowly from the carrying chair and stood slightly bent over because the wound was troubling him. 'I was trying desperately to get home.'

'And you wanted to talk about a treaty, didn't you?' added Vascalôr. 'That is why I am here to see you, Omuthan.'

'Oh, what could that be about? How would it be of any interest to us in Brigantia?'

'We owe your brother respect for his courage in discovering and exploring the pathway. He paid a heavy price for his brave actions. He lost his voice. But for the future we should agree that there should be no further incursions into Dsôn Khamateion from Brigantia,' Vascalôr began in a diplomatic tone. Diplomatic but threatening at the same time. '*For the present* I stand here before you in peace. And I am, as you see, accompanied by only six of my warriors.'

Orweyn gave a quiet laugh. 'Understood. You're saying you could have brought a whole army to kill us all and take over Brigantia.'

'That would indeed have been a possibility, Omuthan.' Vascalôr's smile was smooth. He raised a hand to receive a leather roll from one of his soldiers. 'We have prepared a non-aggression pact.'

Orweyn let his gaze wander over the walls and floor of the chamber. 'Ah yes, these mountains. Insane, isn't it? Still so many secrets after all this time. Some good ones, and occasionally a very unpleasant surprise. However, what you are asking puts me in a difficult position.'

'Namely?'

'Brigantia's population is growing in size and we always need more land. Places we can live. We have given shelter to all kinds of different creatures and they all have different needs as to their environment. Some like it dry and cool, others like cold caverns. It is important that we are able to offer everybody their ideal conditions.'

Vascalôr's fake smile disappeared. 'Let me be quite clear. We are not here to conduct negotiations on this matter, Omuthan.'

'I shall want compensation for lost opportunities. Because if I sign your treaty, I would be restricted in my expansion westward.' Orweyn put his hands in the pockets of his breeches. 'What do you suggest, Envoy?'

Vascalôr went quiet. His stony face was starting to show thin black anger lines, emphasising his pallor.

Meanwhile, Orweyn had turned to Klaey. 'Let's come to your case, banner officer cadet. I have no idea what your true intentions were, but at the time you disappeared, one of the supply team was murdered. I had known him for a very long time. Patvos. May Cadengis watch over him. He had told me about an old Fourthling chart that could take him to a treasure chamber of the dwarves. I was intending to send out a scouting party.'

'Is that so? What a coincidence,' Klaey replied innocently, clutching his wounded chest. The fact that he was perspiring heavily could be accounted for by the effort involved in standing.

'No. It was *not* a coincidence. You were seen coming out of Patvos' rooms.' Orweyn drew his hands out of his pockets. 'Well?'

'Oh, *that*! That's easily explained. The good fellow owed me money.' Klaey did his best to appear honest. 'He was in debt to me and many others, you know. He used to drink. And gamble.' Others in the room murmured assent to this. 'Patvos was telling me he'd soon be rich enough to pay everyone back. With interest.' He stared at his brother. 'He will have told lots of people that story when he had had a bit too much to drink. Someone must have wanted to make sure of his fortune. But it wasn't me, brother.'

'Is that so?' The Omuthan rubbed his head. He was obviously deep in thought. 'Right. For the time being, I shall send you to the healers where you can be kept an eye on. As soon as you have recovered your strength, you will receive your punishment, like any other banner officer cadet, for having absented yourself from duties without leave. And I shall be interrogating you about the murder.'

Klaey pretended to be grateful, but he remained deeply concerned. Things were not going smoothly at all.

Orweyn turned back to the älf. 'Have you had time to reconsider your position?'

'I have,' said Vascalôr with a condescending smile. 'I am going to eschew the ten gold coins offered as a reward.' Behind their visors Klaey could see the älfar all grinning. 'I shall have to take advice about everything else.' Slowly he placed the treaty document roll on the conference table. 'I shall consider the matter as having been discussed and having been accepted by Brigantia. With only the details still to be decided.'

'Details are always important, Vascalôr. I shall sign nothing until the amount of compensation due to us is clarified.' Orweyn, surrounded by military shield-bearers and crossbowmen as he was, felt secure enough to stand firm on this.

'Understood.' The älf drew himself up, his red-eyed expression murderous. 'So you are choosing to live in a state of constant insecurity, Omuthan, until that pact is signed. Your choice.'

Klaey suddenly had a brainwave. He realised how he could profit from the situation.

'Elder brother, you are sure you want to gamble with the lives of all the humans and creatures in Brigantia in this way?' In a croaking voice, he addressed himself also to the many Brigantian guards standing in the hall. 'Provoking the wrath of Dsôn Khamateion is a dangerous undertaking. They might feel pressurised into demonstrating their power. It would seem that we would be the ones to benefit from the treaty.'

Orweyn's head shot round. 'Don't you dare, banner officer cadet, to speak like that. Who here is the Omuthan?'

'Of course. But as a Berengart, I do belong to the council. I shall do so as long as I live and as long as our family is in authority in the land.' Klaey swivelled round to look at the other men and women as he spoke. 'For the good of our realm and to ensure the spoken agreement is honoured, I shall place myself in the hands of the älfar as a hostage. For you' – and he pointed to each of them in turn – 'I am prepared to make this sacrifice, and I shall travel back to Dsôn with them. Let it be known! Announce it throughout Brigantia that a member of the Berengart family is ready to place his own life in jeopardy for the nation's sake.'

Thunderous applause met his words. They cheered him, calling out his name and drumming on their shields.

Vascalôr bent to speak to Klaey, murmuring in his ear, 'What are you up to? You are to stay here in Brigantia. I have no use for you.'

'But what if there's more I can tell you about the robbery than I originally implied?' Klaey's response was made without noticeably moving his lips. As he muttered to Vascalôr, he raised his hand to acknowledge the guards' admiration.

'I already know a great deal,' Vascalôr said, challenging him. 'What could you still have to offer that would make it worth my while to protect your shabby little life and save you from your murderous brother?'

Klaey played his trump card. 'I know the name of the person who undertook the robbery.' He climbed back into the invalid chair, while the Brigantian guards cheered him for his selfless conduct.

The älf's white eyebrows shot up and a black fury line crossed his face at lightning speed. 'You little bastard!'

'My brother would agree with you there. He is frowning just like you.' Overwrought now, Klaey could feel the blood rushing in his ears. *Samusin, I beg of you. Let this miracle happen.*

Girdlegard

Black Mountains
Kingdom of the Thirdling dwarves
1023 P.Q. (7514th solar cycle in old reckoning), spring

Goïmron managed the remaining few steps to the double portal of the assembly hall, where four dwarves in dark ceremonial armour with golden embellishments were standing guard, implacable expressions on their faces. His pulse was racing.

He was holding Tungdil Goldhand's precious notebook clutched under his arm; this was the best, indeed only, piece of evidence he had and he was gambling everything on its being accepted.

Although he had in the meantime seen something of the Thirdling kingdom, he was dumbfounded at what he saw here. To the right and to the left of the corridor, whose ceiling was twenty paces high, were statues denoting the tribal founder Lorimbur. Most portrayed him in warlike pose or standing in triumph over a vanquished foe. The enemies were, for the most part, monsters, but there were also a couple of dwarves shown with shattered skulls and punctured torsos, under the boots of the hero. These were reminders of the far-off times when the Thirdlings' relationship with their brother and sister dwarves in the mountains had been characterised solely by hatred.

In the express tunnels, as well, on the way here, it had been obvious that the builders and engineers had not held back with their urges to add decoration to certain stretches, with paintings on walls and ceilings. As one rushed by in the transport trucks, the pictures seemed to come to life. In other places, the images showed a continuous narrative in which the figures appeared to move due to the speed of travel.

'How fantastic it must all be in the other kingdoms?' Goïmron wondered. He spoke instinctively in a low voice as he examined the statues. As a dwarf with an expert eye for detail, he became aware that the actual quality of stonemason, blacksmith or goldsmith work was not of the very highest order. No real evidence of skills the Thirdlings could have been celebrated for. *I saw their real abilities back there in Whitefields.*

'You have never left Malleniagard before, have you?' Hargorina was at his side. It was thanks to her, of course, that he was going to be able to approach the king without waiting the normally obligatory ten cycles to get to the top of the list for an audience. She was dressed in her martial armour with its long-skirted leg protection and her custom-made club. She carried it as if it were light as a feather. She wore her copper-coloured hair in a plait gathered and perched on the top of her head like a scorpion's tail. 'Haven't you seen the Firstlings and their marine fortifications, either?'

'No. Never. What for? They would have chased me off, anyway.' It occurred to Goïmron now that it was a pity he had not, in the past, at least attempted to visit other places.

He was, of course, well acquainted with the traditions and songs of his kind, and he had acquired much knowledge about the history and skills each dwarf folk possessed. He could sing the songs and he could play their stone-strike game, and he had joined in with the various community choral performances of an evening at the Trusty Tankard or at the annual festivals. His parents had been keen on all of that. But Malleniagard was still a human settlement when all was said and done. Dwarves were very much in the minority.

Past history prevented any Fourthling from paying a friendly visit over the border to the present-day dwarf realms. There would have to be a very important reason for entering another kingdom. Not everyone would be prepared to recognise an ancient diary of the legendary Tungdil Goldhand as being a suitably important reason for a visit.

Here again, Hargorina had proved to be a true blessing. She had sorted the matter with the guards at the West Gate. From there they had taken the newly repaired express tunnel service all the way to the heart of the realm where King Regnor Mortalblow of the clan of the Orc Slayers resided with his family. His ancestor had once held the post of Thirdling chancellor in the time before the Mortalblows had taken over as rulers following the demise of Hargorin Deathbringer. How exactly this change of power had occurred was not to be gathered from his copper-haired escort. For this reason Goïmron suspected that particular handover had not been entirely voluntary. Whatever the background, it was clear that the Mortalblow clan's hold on power was well established. The Thirdlings had followed him and his descendants rather than obeying the Deathbringers.

Goïmron stole a glance at Hargorina. 'Thank you for everything you are doing for me. And for not ignoring me back at the border where, like an idiot, I'd otherwise have had to go crawling back to Malleniagard, having achieved absolutely nothing.' Dressed as he was in quasi-human costume, he felt smaller than ever in these surroundings. He had abandoned his recent attempt to grow a beard. It had looked odd and had not felt right.

'I was glad to help.' Hargorina signed to her four guards in their ceremonial black and gold armour for them to open the double doors to the royal audience hall. 'Even though you and your mission remain total mysteries to me.' She cast a curious eye on the book he was carrying. 'I hope that was worth risking my reputation for.'

'It is.' Goïmron ran his fingers caressingly over the leather binding. 'This is unique. The only copy in the whole of Girdlegard – no, in the whole known world. That is why I must tell Regnor about it.'

The entrance stood wide. With a clash of metal on metal, the four guards presented arms with military precision, their pikes being three times as long as their bearers were tall.

An older dwarf was waiting to receive them. His armour was more restrained, consisting merely of silver chainmail under a black velvet cloak. His past campaigning prowess was recorded in blue and black tattoos on his face. This was a warrior dwarf of great repute. He wore a broad white leather belt at which a huge steel axe hung. His long hair was the white of sloes and worn loose on his shoulders. His beard covered cheeks and mouth.

'Hargorina Deathbringer. What are you presenting our king with here?' The two of them clasped hands, and then Goïmron felt his own hand seized in a vice-like grip. 'Would this be a Fourthling?' The older dwarf ran his eyes over him. 'Yes, I see it is. At first I thought it might be a stunted long'un.' He grinned. 'You are on the small side, aren't you? The most delicate of all the delicately built ones. What is your name, my boy?'

Goïmron put a brave face on things and answered politely. He was going to have to get used to being treated like this. Teasing was to be expected. Teasing. At the very least. *I'll have to be prepared to hear the same from the king.* 'Goïmron Chiselcut.'

'Go on.'

'Of the clan of the Silver Beards.' Inconspicuously he rubbed the hand that had been painfully squeezed. 'I am grateful to have the chance of an audience.'

Hargorina did the introductions. 'This is Romogar Bloodstab of the clan of the Leaf Bells, royal master of ceremonies and in charge of all official events and arranger of audiences. Pay heed. He will advise you on what to do and what not to do when you are in the royal presence.'

'You are the last ones on the list. That is why the Hall of Impatience is empty. That's the name I give to the foyer where petitioners wait, simmering with eagerness,' Romogar explained. 'Right. It is quite simple: the better the king's mood, the more likely you are to have your petition granted.'

'Of course.' Goïmron was ready to pay careful attention to the master of ceremonies' quick speech.

'He has an aversion to jokes. He strongly dislikes being interrupted. He detests it when someone goes on and on. And what he hates most of all: Fourthlings.' Romogar was revelling in the horrified expression on Goïmron's face. Hargorina burst out laughing. 'Forgive me. I could not resist the joke.' Romogar clapped him on the back. It felt as if he had been hit by a catapult stone between the shoulder blades. 'Never say "by Vraccas". And make sure you praise either his beard or his hairstyle. At least once. Except?'

'Except?' Goïmron could not think what Romogar was referring to.

'Except if your compliment is going to constitute an interruption.' The master of ceremonies rolled his eyes. 'Stand up straight and pull yourself together, boy. Fourthlings have a hard enough time. And you are a particularly scrawny example.'

Hargorina cleared her throat. 'Stop terrifying him. He's anxious enough as it is.'

'He will be going into battle. Metaphorically speaking. He has to be prepared for it,' Romogar countered. 'Right. What is your petition to the king?'

'I should have . . . to His Excellency . . .'

Romogar lifted his right hand to cut him off. 'Never use that title. Don't say "Your Excellency" or, worse, "Your Highborn Noble Majesty". He hates the way the humans bow and scrape. Call him "my king". Or just "king".'

'Understood.'

'And what are you asking for?'

Goïmron's head was swimming by now. 'I shall tell him when I see him.'

Romogar cast a reproving glance at Hargorina. 'What is this? What's all the secrecy for?'

She shrugged her broad shoulders, and as she did so, her plated armour clanked slightly. 'I couldn't get him to tell me.' She rested her long-bladed war club casually against her shoulder.

'It is a matter of considerable import for all the tribes and for the whole of Girdlegard,' Goïmron stressed, choosing his words carefully, although sweat was streaming down his body under his clothes. 'I swear it to you both. By Vrrrr . . . By all the gods.'

'Right. Now I am really curious.' Romogar took the lead. 'Through the next door and we'll find ourselves in front of the king and his council. Are you ready?'

'His council?' Goïmron's anxiety level shot up. 'But I thought . . .'

'The king never hears petitioners on his own. In his decisions he always considers the advice and opinions of others.'

Romogar had got as far as the next set of doors. Here again there were armed guards in ceremonial uniform. 'Keep my instructions in mind.' Romogar's broad hands were already on the doors. 'The best of luck, my boy, with whatever it is you are hoping to achieve.' Then he opened the doors to the actual audience chamber. 'Vraccas may be with you, but . . .?'

'But don't mention his name,' murmured Goïmron under his breath.

The twin doors swung back noisily, revealing the throne on its dais. The stone plinth was studded with pieces of polished precious metals.

On the throne sat the bushy-bearded King of the Thirdlings, wearing a white wolfskin draped over smoke-coloured steel armour; his gauntleted left hand gripped a spiked sceptre. His complexion was dyed dark blue.

Four other dwarves, male and female, were seated with him at a long conference table constructed from basalt. His councillors were in elaborate robes and armour and they loomed over the table ready to adjudicate on the next petition.

'My king,' Romogar's voice rang through the hall. 'I present the last of this orbit's petitioners. Behold. This is Goïmron Chisel-cut of the clan of the Silver Beards of the Fourthling folk.' He ushered him forward. 'He comes with a mysterious secret matter to put before you, and claims it is of the utmost importance for all the Children of the Smith and also for the whole of Girdlegard.'

'Good luck,' whispered Hargorina, moving over to stand by a pillar at one side.

Goïmron stepped forward.

The ceiling of the chamber was supported by huge statues of kneeling dwarves, and the ornaments on the walls resembled the weapons the Thirdlings employed in combat. There were paintings showing battle scenes from the distant but glorious past. The chamber's illumination came from enormous chandelier lanterns which hung suspended on long chains and had glass sides covered in a wafer-thin layer of gold, so that their light cast a warm glow. In the hall the smell of steel and stone was dominant, just like in a forge.

There were a good ten paces he needed to cover. It seemed endless. *Does one stay silent until one reaches the royal throne? Or do I address him now?* Goïmron's head was buzzing. *How far away should I stand?* His anxiety increased with each step. All those eyes on him – the king, the councillors, all the armed guards – he felt faint. *Vraccas, don't abandon me!*

Regnor broke through his thoughts. The right-hand side of the king's face was decorated with dwarf rune tattoos.

'Welcome to the Black Mountains, Goïmron Chiselcut.' The voice was deep and thunderously loud. 'You are the first of your Fourthling tribe in over one thousand cycles to dare to enter our territory. This must mean that you are the strongest of your kind. On the inside, at least.'

The assembled council allowed itself some quiet laughter.

'King Regnor, I thank you for permitting me an audience.' He halted four paces away from the throne and bowed. His mind was in utter turmoil but he managed to put the most important part of his mission into words. 'Tungdil Goldhand is alive.'

A murmur went round the chamber.

Regnor leaned forward, allowing his bushy blue beard to fall like an avalanche over his armoured chest. 'Have I been mistaken in you? Did the Fourthlings send, not the strongest, but the most stupid of their number?' he thundered. 'How can you . . .?'

Lifting Tungdil's book like a shield, Goïmron said, 'My king. I bring you his memoirs.'

Speaking as quickly and clearly as he could, he told how he had come into the possession of the leather-bound journal. 'It is written in one hand. The record is full of detail that could never have been made up, but that must have been actually witnessed.' He concluded his speech: 'The final paragraph is dated . . . last winter.'

Regnor looked him up and down. 'I have yet to understand why you have come, Goïmron Chiselcut. You wish to present the book to me?'

'No, my king. I have come here to ask for a troop of soldiers to accompany me to the Grey Range. To look for him.' Goïmron was struggling to control himself. He forced himself to stop shaking. 'Tungdil Goldhand is alive. The mightiest hero of the Thirdling tribe, having often saved Girdlegard from destruction in the past, is now waiting to be found. Once he returns, we can unite all the tribes and ensure the return of harmony. We can eradicate all the dragons and the monsters from Girdlegard and peace and prosperity will reign once more.' He advanced slowly and proffered the book. 'Look at it, my king. Read his lines. It is no deception. I am utterly convinced it is authentic.'

Regnor took the pages and leafed through. 'If that were the case, then Goldhand would be over one thousand cycles old. No dwarf ever attains that age.'

'Goldhand is no ordinary dwarf. All the things he went through. Maybe that's what has let him survive so long. For this very purpose.' Goïmron stepped back to his original place. 'I . . .'

'So you're saying some ancient dwarf should lead us against dragons, monsters and murdering armies?' one of the female councillors asked. She was seated, dressed in chainmail reinforced at the shoulder with spikes. She had long-skirted armour-plated protection for her legs. This was the traditional military garb for the Thirdlings.

'No, I'm not saying that he . . .' Goïmron began.

'And if he were to assert a claim to the Thirdling throne?' objected a one-eyed dwarf in furs at Regnor's side. 'Are we supposed to depose Regnor in exchange for him? Like chucking out a rotten apple?'

Goïmron turned to face him. 'Why should that—'

'Or what if Goldhand demands to be made overall High King of all the tribes?' This from another concerned female dwarf in a moss-green padded velvet tunic over her chainmail.

'Would that be such—' Goïmron struggled to get his voice heard.

'Are you really trying to get us to help you conquer the Brown Range because the Fourthlings can't manage on their own?' interjected an older armoured dwarf angrily as he rose to his feet. 'You come here to an audience with Regnor thinking you can win him round with some trumped-up story about Tungdil Goldhand? Telling us he is the sole survivor of the Fifthlings, sitting in the ruins of the ancient halls, locked in by lava, just waiting to be found and liberated?' Furiously he slammed his fist on to the table. 'If he were truly alive, he would have got himself out of there hundreds of cycles ago.' He stabbed a finger towards the book. 'This is outright forgery, Goïmron Chiselcut, whether you or someone else is the perpetrator of the deceit. The effrontery! The bare-faced cheek of it!'

Along with the rest of the council, he continued to inveigh against Goïmron, mercilessly heaping allegations on insults.

No! Nothing like that! Only with the utmost difficulty did Goïmron manage to retain his composure. Had he taken a single step back, it would have given his accusers the opportunity to gloat. *Why are they so incensed?*

Regnor raised his hand and his advisors fell silent. 'This is the liveliest session in a long time,' was his amused comment. He ran his fingers over his beard. 'Right, Goïmron. I believe you.'

From one heartbeat to the next, delighted surprise permeated his being. 'My king, that—'

'I believe you,' Regnor repeated. 'I believe that you are convinced of the truth of what you are telling us. But these pages are a complete and utter fantasy – someone's idea of fun. Who knows who wrote it? Or indeed, when?'

'But the date proves . . .'

'That date can have been added a hundred cycles ago. Or even a thousand. Possibly Goldhand himself may even be the author. But it is of no import to us to learn of his experiences in the Black Abyss. It has no effect on our present-day lives.' Regnor chucked the book back at him and some of the loose pages fluttered out. 'He and his son perished in the Grey Mountains with many of the Fifthlings when the earthquakes and the volcanic eruptions began. They were lost, as were all their halls and their treasures. The survivors in their settlements await an opportunity to return when it is safe to do so. The same is the case for the Secondlings at the foot of the Blue Mountains. Likewise your own tribe, Goïmron Chiselcut.'

Goïmron was clumsily attempting to gather in the scattered pages. He replaced them in the leather cover. 'You are mistaken, King Regnor.'

'It is you who are mistaken. You are absolutely obsessed with believing a mighty rescuer will return.'

'He has done it before.' Goïmron held up the book. 'He came back from the Black Abyss. From a place of unmitigated horror.'

'But that return did not involve an absence of a thousand cycles, did it?' Regnor was taking deep breaths, and resting his tattooed chin on his hand. 'It was very brave of you to approach me with this petition of yours. But I shall not be sending any troops to search for a ghost in the Grey Mountains. It is dangerous there. There are constant rockfalls and the mountains are still on the move. The place is full of monsters crawling about in the ruins of the Stone Gateway. Why would I do it? For *what* exactly?'

'For the sake of the greatest hero the Thirdlings ever knew,' was Goïmron's bold response. 'King Regnor, he is there. We—'

'I thank you for your visit, Goïmron Chiselcut. It was entertaining and refreshing to meet a Fourthling who has not lost his courage. Use your courage wisely as you go through life. May your future be long and fruitful.' Regnor got to his feet. 'You should be an example to your tribe. Gather an army. Take back – in a hundred cycles or two – what is rightfully yours. My best wishes accompany you. The audience is at an end.' He nodded and looked past Goïmron. 'Let him be given food and drink. And give him suitable clothing for the return journey to Malleniagard. And see he is accommodated comfortably overnight.'

The master of ceremonies took Goïmron gently by the arm.

'My king, if you should change your mind, please let me know,' he called in utter despair.

'Enough now. We leave,' muttered Romogar.

I have failed. Dejected, he watched the king and his council leave the chamber. Some of them glanced back at him, a few with sympathy on their faces, the others with outrage. *I have not succeeded.* As if in a trance, he allowed Romogar to lead him out. He was unaware of what was being said to him. He held the book tightly against his chest. *Should I set off on my own to find Goldhand?* He would never manage a hundred paces alive in the Grey Mountains.

'Well, *that* went really well, didn't it?' Hargorina joined them at the door. 'You presented a totally nonsensical request and they are still letting you leave the kingdom with your head and all your limbs still attached. Well done.' She winked. 'Only joking, Goïmron. Just like the joke about the gold coin you owe me.'

'I am not in the mood for jokes.' He gave a heavy sigh.

'Here comes something that's *not* a joke. I think you are a courageous dreamer. I share my king's opinion on the matter, but you have proved that a strongly held conviction gives one inner strength. In spite of everything.' Hargorina clapped him encouragingly on the shoulder. 'Hang on to that attitude, Goïmron, and you will go far.'

'So far it's brought me to complete failure in the Black Mountains and it'll let me go as far as back to Malleniagard, I suppose.' His tone was bitter. Touching the leather cover of the book, he said, 'I was so sure I would find a ready ear.' *What a fool I was.* The words spoken in the council chamber resounded in his head. They ate away at any confidence he had arrived with. *A dwarf surviving more than one thousand cycles? But he never turns up?* He cleared his throat. 'Well, I must admit it was an entertaining outing. I don't know of anyone from Malleniagard who can claim they travelled to the Thirdling kingdom.'

'And were welcomed to stay one night in the land, of course.' Romogar had escorted him back to the corridor leading to the waiting room. He summoned a guard and gave her the king's instructions. 'I hope you will like your stay here, even though your petition was not granted. I found it quite thrilling, your story. Get the book printed up. The long'uns will buy the story. You could make a small fortune.' He bade him farewell with a hearty handshake. 'May your journey be easy on the morrow. You will be given everything you need.'

'No, I shan't,' whispered Goïmron. *I have been given nothing of what I need. And neither has Girdlegard.*

'I must get off now and deliver the box we picked up in Whitefields. But I'll come round later this evening and we can talk. We can go out for a mug of good spiced beer,' Hargorina suggested. 'I'm keen to hear everything about life in

Malleniagard and about the Fourthlings who live there. It must be fascinating.'

Goïmron realised that she was just being kind. The warrior girl did not want him to be left alone to wallow in his thoughts. 'I think I'd rather stay in my chamber,' he said. That was the last thing he thought he could take – being surrounded by towering Thirdlings who'd mock him with names like quarter-dwarf. *They'd be throwing me round the room for fun.* 'It has been a long day. I'm tired.'

Hargorina nodded, understanding how he felt. 'Then I'll come to bid you farewell in the morning.'

'You don't have to. I'll be leaving very early.' Goïmron was grateful to her for saving his life and standing up for him. At the same time, he felt ashamed. 'Please come and visit me if you ever come to Malleniagard. I can show you the sights.' He held out his hand. 'It has been a great honour to meet you, Hargorina Deathbringer.'

'The honour has been mine, Goïmron Chiselcut. Whatever some Thirdlings may have said or what they may say in the future, you are an honourable dwarf and a very brave Fourthling.' She released her grip on his hand and turned to the corridor. 'Never forget that.'

His smile was rather forced. *An honourable dwarf and a brave Fourthling – and an unmitigated fool.*

'Take me to my accommodation, if you please,' he asked the guard, who set off at once to escort him.

After marching through various opulently furnished corridors, Goïmron found himself sitting in a comfortable room whose floor-length window gave on to a cavern one hundred paces high, where a waterfall cascaded down to feed a lake and a river. There was a row of forges and smithies on the bank of the river and he caught the faint sounds of metal being worked by water-driven hammers. He could clearly see the glow of the furnaces.

There was an inviting meal on the table: several different dishes with appetising smells – fish baked in stone sand, root dumplings, various types of bread, truffle butter, rock-chickens and other meat delicacies that were new to Goïmron. The dwarf tribes each had their own traditions when it came to cuisine.

Next to the food he saw a small barrel labelled *finest strong black* and an attractively fashioned copper tankard with a note stating it to be *A gift from King Regnor to the bravest Fourthling of his acquaintance.*

Lost in thought, Goïmron clutched the leather book. *This nonsense is the reason Gandelin died. Because I absolutely insisted on reading it all the way through instead of meeting up with him. I could have saved him.* He suddenly felt impelled to hurl the book out of the window. *No good came of it.* Furious with himself, he threw the book into the corner and drew himself a beer.

He felt the effects of the strong brew on an empty stomach immediately. He was not strongly built compared to these war-like Thirdlings; they would likely be able to put away a full barrel of this size without feeling the worse for wear. However, in his present mood, the idea of drowning his sorrows and his dark thoughts seemed appealing.

After the third tankard the room was spinning. He hungrily grabbed the mountain goat ham and the mushroom sausage before opening the window to go and sit on the balcony to admire the view.

A gentle breeze wafted on to his face, moving the sideburns and his curly hair. The sounds from the forges were mixed now with music, laughter and the singing emanating from the neighbouring houses.

Someone was giving a virtuoso performance on the hurdy-gurdy. The tune being played was the old lay of 'The Lonely

Dwarf' they had often sung in the choir back in Malleniagard. *Gandelin and me . . .*

Goïmron was overcome with melancholy thoughts. He drew a deep breath and joined in the singing. He sang of his sadness and grief from the fullness of his heart. He sang of his disappointment and his feelings of failure. He was so lost in the melody that at first he did not notice that more voices had joined his own.

More and more figures had appeared at windows and on balconies, singing the song of 'The Lonely Dwarf'. It seemed that even the forge hammers were keeping time over there on the banks of the river.

A sense of grief overcame Goïmron. He stopped singing just as the Thirdlings were launching into the next verse. *Oh, Gandelin. I am so very, very sorry.* He took a drink and lifted the bundled pages that were untidily gathered in the leather folder. *By Vraccas! We grew up together in the streets of Malleniagard and I have let you down.* He hefted the book in his hand. *Fantasy! Make-believe!* Unsteady on his feet under the influence of the drink, he reached back his arm. *To Tion with it!*

He had thrown the book with enough force to send it right into the cavern opposite. As it turned in the air, it came open and a tail of loose pages followed its flight in an arc.

The wind caught the numerous closely written pages and scattered them in a black and white cloud whirling round in the cavern. The paper danced like a swarm of butterflies.

By Vraccas! That's what I should have done straightaway. He drained his tankard and, with tears streaming, he intoned the last line of the song.

The last of the melody died away, echoing inside the cavern.

From right and left he heard applause. It was directed only at his own singing. He quickly wiped away the moisture from his cheeks, realising that he was being observed. He did not want it to seem that his emotions had got the better of him because of the song.

'As Lorimbur is my witness,' said Hargorina, appearing behind him, 'that was so moving. It got me from the ends of my red hair right down to my graceful toes.' She approached him, clapping her approval. 'Now we know you are the best singer in the Black Mountains. They'll all be striving to compete with you. They won't want to lose out to a Fourthling.'

'I was not intending anything like that.' Goïmron tried not to reveal how drunk he was. 'Were you going to sing along?'

'No – I can't sing at all.' She was wearing a long, simple, earth-coloured dress with black embroidery under a metal breastplate, with a sword at her side. *A striking appearance*, thought Goïmron. She almost looked as if she were in disguise. Her long copper-red hair was hanging loose in waves around her head. 'I came to say that I'm going to come with you tomorrow.'

'I'll manage to get to the rail station alive.'

'I don't mean to the rail station. I mean all the way to the Grey Mountains.'

'What?'

'King Regnor has changed his mind.' Hargorina grinned. 'You are going to get your troops.'

'By Vr–!' Coming in from the balcony, he just managed to restrain himself from giving a triumphant shout, as he did not want to attract the anger of Lorimbur's descendants. He grabbed the muscular warrior dwarf round the waist in an enthusiastic embrace. 'That is amazing!'

She laughed and patted him on the back. 'Great, isn't it? You did it. You convinced them.' She freed herself from his arms. 'Ah, I see they gave you a barrel of the finest strong black. I'll join you.'

'Of course! We've got to celebrate!'

Hargorina went over to the table and, not seeing another tankard, filled an empty dish with the delicious beer. 'I'm curious about the book.' She raised her drink in a toast. 'May I borrow it until the morning? I'd like to get an idea of why it so fascinates you.'

The book! Goïmron felt a shiver down his spine.

He slowly turned his head to look over into the cavern, where the pages were slowly drifting round in circles.

They say no magic rune is more wonderful than a book.

And I would add: a miracle has nothing to do with the real magic of enchanted runes and books.

Excerpt from
The Collected Wisdom and Sayings of a Magus
by Master Perticus

V

Girdlegard

Red Mountains
Kingdom of the Firstling dwarves
Wavechallenge, western harbour
1023 P.Q. (7514th solar cycle in old reckoning), spring

Xanomir Waveheart took a deep breath of the fresh, salty air. 'This sea is really different from the one in the interior of Girdlegard,' he commented to Buvendil, who was standing by his side on the foremost wall of Wavechallenge's circular harbour. 'Wouldn't it be wonderful to sail out and away to explore new oceans?'

'And how exciting it'd be – being attacked, or kidnapped, or even eaten alive,' replied his friend with exaggerated enthusiasm. 'Amazing, eh?' He laughed as he finished combing out his sun-bleached beard.

'That's rotten of you. Stomping on my dreams like that.'

'I'm merely pointing out the possible dangers involved in seafaring.' Buvendil pointed to the horizon. All that was visible now between the headlands was an empty stretch of water. 'Of course, all the ships come from somewhere. From far distant realms. But that doesn't mean it's peaceful out there. Why should it be any safer than life on land?'

'You're right. And anyway, Vraccas has already given us a task.' He glanced at the diving bell about to be lowered. 'And our task does not consist of exploring the distant seas.'

'Instead it is to protect Girdlegard.' Buvendil put his comb away and went over to the diving contraption to check the chains securing it to the winch. 'And that's what we're doing.'

Xanomir nodded and turned to where the tunnel went straight through the Red Mountains and the Firstling kingdom to connect the two bodies of water. The sea water had found itself new paths after the widespread destruction caused by the earthquakes, floods and landslides.

Some referred to this as a 'wonderful opportunity' while others called it an 'incalculable danger' for Girdlegard. In Xanomir's opinion, the truth of the situation lay somewhere between those extremes.

To minimise the dangers, the Firstlings had established the fortified town of Wavechallenge out here in the west, on its little spit of land, in order to check out vessels wanting to enter Girdlegard. Ships arriving from the Outer Lands docked at the circular quay area with its ring of warehouse buildings. Here they could be boarded and searched. Crew and freight were checked for infections or for contraband. If everything was deemed in order, the vessel would be permitted to proceed through to the main lock where paperwork was to be verified, and pilot fees, customs duties and harbour dues had to be paid.

If a ship's master could not pay the tolls, the vessel would be sent to a side arm of the port, impounded there, and after a period of one moon cycle, the freight, together with the boat's fitments and equipment, would be confiscated, should the sum due in the intervening time not have been forthcoming. If, on the other hand, a shipmaster were able to find the money owed, or if he paid in part with goods from his cargo, he would be allowed to continue his onward voyage.

Tugboats manned by rowers would then move the ships into the tunnel through the Red Mountains, a distance of some miles. It was strictly forbidden for crew members to leave their vessel at any stage. There were severe punishments for any contravention: imprisonment, hefty fines, or even execution in the case of a repeat offence. The Firstlings were adamant: they wanted no foreigners disembarking in their kingdom.

Xanomir was not fully au fait with the defensive devices installed in the tunnel. In fact, apart from the king, the only people with access to such information were a few elite tunnel guards and a limited number of the maintenance crew for the hidden machines, which included catapults and ramming equipment. It was widely known, however, that any enemy ship or vessel breaking quarantine regulations could be destroyed within moments of its entering the tunnel without permission. At the other end of the tunnel, officials at Wavechallenge's sister fortress of Seahold would conduct a further inspection before letting a vessel pass.

On looking down, Xanomir realised what he had forgotten. He muttered a curse under his breath. 'I'll have to go back to the harbour master's.'

'Why?'

'I left my other toolkit there.' Xanomir headed off. 'We'll get this finished today.'

'Well, hurry! Look at those clouds. If the sun goes in, we won't see a thing down by the foundations.' Buvendil rattled the chains and hooks to test them and then tapped them with a small hammer. Any damage not visible to the naked eye could be discovered if the sound changed subtly. 'What about your underwater lamp? How's that going?'

'Nearly done,' Xanomir called back over his shoulder. 'Back soon.'

He and his friend had been summoned here because the most recent earthquake had resulted in cracks to the fortifications.

The *Elria Bonnet* would be deployed to inspect the foundations and determine how far down the fissures went, before the next storm could loosen any sections that might have become unstable.

On going through the tunnel, Xanomir had also noticed other cracks. Gaps and chinks had appeared on the roof and walls. *The masons will have their hands full to repair it all.*

Xanomir had by now reached Bendabil Pincergrip's office. The tool bag was next to the desk where the harbour master sat, eyeing him reprovingly.

'Vraccas be praised!' Xanomir exclaimed. 'You've kept them for me.'

'Yes, but you nearly lost them.' Bendabil twiddled the ends of his moustache. His face was a weathered dark brownish black from its constant exposure to the elements. The skin was furrowed like old leather, which made the beard hair look silvery in contrast. The harbour master was sometimes given the nickname of Leatherface.

'Rubbish! Who's going to steal a set of tools?' Xanomir wanted to know.

'Foreigners, that's who.' Bendabil pointed through the window to a freighter which had recently arrived in port. 'The *Shushkumush*. Come in from Tritania. Two of her crew were seen grabbing the tool bag but my watchmen got it back off them.' He pushed it over to Xanomir with his foot. 'They pretended it had been a mistake.'

'That would have been a nuisance. It's got all the tools and special parts I need for making bolts and screws.' He turned his dark-eyed gaze to rest on the ship. '*Shushkumush*. Weird name.'

'And it's got strange dimensions. The vessel's lying low in the water as if fully laden. But it's empty according to the ship's manifest. And there's nothing extra under the hull. I had a good look with the underwater mirror,' said Bendabil. 'I wasn't born yesterday and wasn't about to rely on her lading docket. Must be made of the heaviest kind of wood there is. Whatever they want to load, it won't be much. Maybe a hold full of cotton wool.'

Xanomir was already fascinated by the puzzle. 'I must go and take a look.'

Bag shouldered, he was already half out of the office and on his way to the main lock where the *Shushkumush* was moored, when the gates opened and a tug started to pull the vessel through. Seen from above, the ship had the form of a river barge. *Sides a bit too flat. The centre of gravity would be too high,* thought Xanomir. *They'd never get far on open sea. Not even ten miles.* The smallest wave catching the vessel would swamp the deck and the hold would be flooded. *They must have hugged the coast to get here. But all the way from Tritania?*

Usually it was doulia slaves that came from there – humans who volunteered for menial work in order to honour their god Doul with their penitent and austere way of life. It was the strangest religion Xanomir had ever come across. There were many new divinities from overseas arriving with the trade ships, but they found no new converts in Girdlegard.

Xanomir walked slowly back along the ridge of the walls watching the three crew members at work at bow and stern. The ropes that had tethered the ship to the quayside bollards had been released and the *Shushkumush* was drifting towards the tunnel entrance. *But they're not doulia. The clothing's wrong. And their hair.*

As Bendabil had said, the whole thing was odd. Just as odd as the amulet belonging to Hegomil Coalglow that he and Buvendil had found in the seawolf's maw. As expected, they had not found any dwarf bones in the creature's stomach. It remained a riddle as to how the pendant had come to get stuck in the seawolf's teeth.

Suddenly the large boat came to a jerking halt, and there was a grinding sound as if the keel were scraping along the canal bed. But the ugly figurehead was still ten paces away from the actual tunnel entrance.

Xanomir was struck with a horrible suspicion. *Surely not?* He stepped on a piece of stone by accident and the pebble shot out into the lock, landing not with a splash but with a bang three paces in front of the *Shushkumush*, at the height of the vessel's deck. Then it rolled off and splashed into the water.

The three sailors on board exchanged glances with each other and then looked up at the dwarf.

Oh curses! Watersnakeshit! Xanomir waved to them as if nothing were wrong and as if he had not noticed what had happened to the stone. *I must report to the harbour master.*

One of the sailors waved back and another was seen reaching under a tarpaulin, while the third disappeared swiftly down a hatch.

The one at the tarpaulin pulled out a spring-loaded slingshot device that had an ammunition magazine attached – and he raised it, aiming at Xanomir as he fired. 'Wretched groundling!'

'Sound the alarm!' shouted the dwarf, dropping to the ground. 'Attack! We are under attack!'

Two shots whizzed by over his head. He would have been hit had he not had the gumption to protect himself with his toolkit bag. The leather was peppered with small holes but there was enough metal in the contents to keep him from harm. Hastily he crawled backwards to the shelter of a bollard.

Peeking out, he could see the *Shushkumush* now brightly illuminated. The spell that had camouflaged it had lifted and instead of the barge it had appeared to be, its true dimensions were clear.

A battleship.

What had seemed to be crates for transport goods revealed themselves as weapon emplacements. The innocent-looking shape of the barge was now threatening in aspect, and rows of oars appeared along the sides. At a whistled signal, the ship, with its metal bowsprit spar, was propelled towards the gate.

And at first impact, the bolts holding the entrance gave way. The lock had not been constructed with the need for defence against invasion in mind.

The foreign ship sped towards the tunnel, cutting through two lines of barges waiting at the end of the lock. The metal bowsprit, in the shape of an axe head, sliced through the wooden planks, and crunched the smaller vessels as though in a nutcracker.

May Elria punish them! Xanomir came out from where he was sheltering and watched the attackers in horror. The iron bollard showed indentations from the shots fired at it.

On deck, the firing machines were shooting bolts at the guards on the quayside who were rushing to activate the spear catapults. Alarm horns sounded in the port and in the fortress.

Without a magnifying spyglass, Xanomir was not able to make out what manner of beings these were. *Are they real humans or are they in disguise?* There was no sign of any heraldic device or flag denoting their origin.

The battleship had increased its speed and was racing forward to the tunnel entrance, creating a huge bow wave. At that very moment, four enormous stone boulders, each a ton in weight and suspended on chains, were released from the roof of the tunnel. They crashed on to the wooden planking, holing the deck of the galley that had been moving at speed.

Xanomir heard screams from the rowers, and the oarsmen lost their rhythm. Some of the oars stood at strange angles, while others were abandoned and slipped out into the water. The ship came to a halt.

The four boulders were wound back up, causing more damage as they were hauled up on their chains. The defence crews on land wanted to make absolutely sure of their effect. Long iron barbs were sent shooting up from the water like the spikes in a mantrap. The ship broke up.

Bodies were seen tumbling from the decks as the vessel fell apart, and they were met with bolts, metal balls and arrows fired from slits in the tunnel walls. Occasionally there were sparks when the shots hit the manacles on the unfortunate galley slaves.

A further two boulders crashed down from the roof, putting a final end to the vessel.

Fire suddenly broke out on what remained of the ship, to Xanomir's surprise. Then he noticed the apertures in the tunnel walls pumping out an unquenchable mix of petroleum, pitch and oil. Clouds of black smoke emerged from the tunnel. Any crew still on board would be burning to death with their ship.

'Quite a display!' said Bendabil, appearing at Xanomir's side. 'How long did it take to sink her? Five, six breaths, maybe?'

'I was too busy to count.' Xanomir brushed the dirt from his clothes. He had not sustained any injury. *Thanks be to the jolly bollard and to my toolkit.* 'I realised they had a camouflage spell but they saw I had worked it out.'

'Looks like you've saved Girdlegard from an invasion. That's all that matters.' Nervously twiddling the ends of his beard, Bendabil nodded at him and said, 'I shall be making specific mention of that in my harbour master report. You might get an award from the king.'

Xanomir watched the charred timbers finally disappearing under the surface. 'I wonder who they were.'

'It was a shark-class galley. Nothing like that's been seen here for at least a hundred cycles.'

'And who ran them?'

'Wrotland. But that realm no longer exists. I would assume what we had here was a band of audacious pirates wanting to get their hands on some loot in Girdlegard. Nobody would have suspected anything, with the spell disguising them as a kind of slow river barge. They would have been able to sail about wreaking havoc on the inland sea for ages. Then they'd have slipped away with their fortunes made.' Bendabil scratched his ear. 'The customs inspectors will be in trouble. They should have seen through the trick. And how come I noticed nothing when I did the mirror examination of the hull?' He clapped Xanomir on the shoulder. 'You have done well. Come over to my office later. I'll stand you a drink.' He needed to get back to alert the salvage operators. 'Excuse me, I'll be off. The wreck must be removed or the trade ships can't get through.'

'Thank you!' Xanomir called out.

Pirates with the ability to use magic like that? Unlikely. And certainly unlikely that pirates would have a couple of hundred galley slaves at their disposal or want to have to feed them for the length of a raid in unknown territory.

Xanomir resolved to make his inspection of the foundation walls of the fortress as meticulous as possible. No fault, however slight, must escape notice. There was something sinister behind this attack, he was sure. *Something bigger yet is planned.*

He turned round to go, picking up his tools, but the damaged leather bag ripped and the contents crashed down on to the quayside.

Girdlegard

United Great Kingdom of Gauragon
Province of Grasslands
To the west of the Grey Mountains

Kingdom of the Thirdling dwarves
1023 P.Q. (7514th solar cycle in old reckoning), spring

As he rode along, Goïmron battled with trying to put the pages of Tungdil Goldhand's book back in the right order. His horse was trotting slowly behind the rest of the troops and he did not need to take charge. *Have I really got all of them?* He checked the numbering and the dates one more time. It wasn't easy with a headache.

Around them there was a pleasant aroma of flowers and fresh grass. The bees were buzzing and flocks of songbirds swooped and rose again in the spring air. Goïmron, however, was in no mood to appreciate the beauties of nature. He had a hangover from the unaccustomed indulgence in strong beer over the last two evenings. And his back hurt from having had to constantly bend over to gather up the scattered pages of his precious book as he ran through the cavern. They had been forced to lose a whole orbit before setting off for the Grey Mountains, because of his drunken idiocy in throwing the book from the balcony. He had taken on the task himself of collecting the papers from where they had landed on the rocks and pebbles, in the branches of trees or among clumps of cavern thistles. Some had had to be plucked out of the water. He did it all himself, as penance, realising the enormity of what he had done in a self-indulgent fit of melancholy and despair.

Some of the records had been damaged and some pages were illegible now. *I'm sure I'm still missing the final page.* He had been pretty sure that he had managed to find it originally. *Curses. No!* That would be the page with the hero's actual locality when he inscribed the last section of his diary. Goïmron's pounding head was not helping as he racked his brain to remember the details. *More water. Rinse that beer out of my system. That's the thing. Then I might remember.*

Hargorina dropped back to ride next to him. She wore the normal Thirdling protective garb and had her war club in its holster on her saddle. She had fastened her copper-red hair back in a twist at the nape of her neck. 'You've done it, I see.'

'Yes.' He kept quiet about the missing final page.

'Excellent! Now you must have a look at this view. We're approaching the best bit of Grasslands here. From tomorrow the landscape will be uglier.' She smiled. 'We're making good progress even with no rail transport this time. And the weather is on our side.'

'Glad to hear it.' Goïmron's backside was already quite sore. His parents had taught him to ride as a child back in Malleniagard, but he'd not been on a horse much recently. 'When do they reckon to repair the station at Whitefields?'

'It's usually quite quickly done. That incident with the trolls – it's not the first time. The long'uns are skilled with their timber and nails.' Hargorina called out an order to Belîngor, riding at the front, to increase their pace. 'Are you pleased with your troop here?'

'Of course. King Regnor has been . . . generous. He has given me his best people.' Goïmron did not wish to appear ungrateful. After the initial news from Hargorina about the royal change of mind, he had imagined a force of fifty or a hundred would be leaving with him for the Grey Range. Instead, the band consisted of the silent Belîngor, his bald-headed companion Brûgar, Hargorina herself, and five armed soldiers. Then they had two pack animals to carry their supplies and tents in case they had to sleep in the open. Goïmron was not feeling totally confident about the problems he might be confronted with in the kingdom of the Fifthlings.

Hargorina took a deep breath of the fresh spring air. 'It's good to get out now and then, isn't it? A bit further than a trip to Whitefields. We've lots of nice valleys and lakes and rivers in the Black Mountains, but a good ride through open country is lovely. A change. But you've not even been looking, have you?'

Goïmron wished he had a bit of shade for his face. He had omitted to bring his sunglasses, which were fashioned from thin slivers of nephrite stone held in a frame. 'So what did I miss?'

'Two pretty villages and lots of fields of yellow high-raps flowers in full bloom, draped over the gently rolling hills like a golden ribbon.' Hargorina took out her distance eyepiece to sweep the horizon. 'There's a small town. We could ... No, maybe not. They've got the black flag up. It's a good thing we're far enough away from them. I've no wish to share their plight.'

Goïmron was well aware of the black flag's significance. It meant they had a case of suihhi and the population was warning visitors to keep away.

The United Great Kingdom owed its existence to the emergence of this deadly plague, against which only a few humans would be immune. They called it divine providence. Many thousands had fallen victim to suihhi four hundred cycles previously, in the north-western part of Girdlegard. Those in Girdlegard with resistance to the disease had taken advantage of their situation. Quick as a flash they had invaded and conquered the surrounding area, incorporating those realms into Gauragon. Since then they had defended themselves against any attempt from outside for people to win the lands back they had lost. Nowadays the Gauragarians, although in the minority, numerically speaking, were still in control. If ever there was a whiff of a revolt, the suihhi virus, which had been carefully conserved, would be released in whatever village or township that was rife for insurgency. Everybody without disease resistance would succumb to the plague. Rebellion over. And without a fight.

'Do you think it was a punishment action?' There were many people in Malleniagard who had immunity, just as the dwarves did, and the älfar and the elves and most monsters. The virus seemed also to be ineffective against the population of Brigantia. Elsewhere in Girdlegard the fear still reigned that an occurrence of suihhi could cross the border and spread. 'Or maybe a spontaneous outbreak?'

'We haven't heard any rumours of an uprising against King Gajek.' Hargorina gave an order and Belîngor changed direction towards the north. 'We would know if there were anything happening because we've got one of his officials stationed at our Eastern Gate. And people in Whitefields would have been full of the gossip.'

Goïmron was aware of the pact the Thirdlings had with Gauragon: the dwarves controlled the stream of migrants from the east wanting to enter the Great Kingdom. A delegation from the ruler was posted at the eastern entry point under the supervision of a border customs officer. Together they decided who should be given entry permits. The Thirdlings made a packet out of this, earning fees from Gajek. Goïmron looked up at the daystar in surprise. 'Why are you altering our route? Is it because of the suihhi flag?'

'I don't want to end up in Rhuta by mistake.' The red-haired warrior dwarf shrugged her shoulders. 'Some may see it differently, but I am of the opinion that magic and the Children of the Smith should have nothing to do with each other.'

Oh, but they are connected. At the mention of the magic realm, Goïmron had a great idea. 'We ought to pay Vanéra a visit, I think. We could borrow a famulus from her. As support.'

'You've got the sharpest weapons and the best fighting force in Girdlegard. Why would you want some rotten magic stuff?' Hargorina argued. 'And anyway, she's not a proper maga. She . . . she just polishes her . . . She only rubs away at her hundreds of weird artefacts until she gets them to do things she can't really control. She's like someone at a fairground. That's all.' Hargorina's round face darkened like a thundercloud. The dark blue tattoos emphasised her displeasure. 'Going to Rhuta would be a really bad idea.'

'We can't know what dangers await us in the Grey Mountains.'

'There certainly won't be any silly wizards and wand-wavers.' Hargorina adjusted how her hair was tied back.

'But there might be beasts that can't be handled with conventional means. Your weapons might be useless,' Goïmron insisted doggedly. 'We will divert for Rhuta, Hargorina.'

'Since when do you order me about?' she said, challenging him with a grin.

'Ever since the king gave me the soldiers.' Goïmron's stomach was rumbling. All that joggling about on horseback was causing havoc with his insides. 'Please. Let us go and visit the maga.'

'If you insist. But if she gives us one of her little wizardlings, he'll have to bring his own cart for all his magical bits and pieces.' Hargorina galloped off to the head of the troop. 'But your use of the word "please" – now that is a magic thing.'

The band of soldiers changed direction once more and they reached the official border of the magic realm by evening.

At Rhuta's border they found colourful banners fluttering in the breeze and a large sign bidding visitors welcome. The notice made clear that newcomers had to register with the required form. And to pay a not inconsiderable sum for permission to enter. On a golden shelf under the sign there was a tall mirror, its frame generously decorated with gems. Next to the mirror there was a square metal chest at least one pace in height, length and depth.

Hargorina ordered the troops to halt and then she called Goïmron forward. 'Your idea. So you do the doings,' she said, remaining in the saddle.

There was not a soul in Girdlegard who did not know that entry to Rhuta was only gained with the express permission of the maga. And that there were only certain routes that could be chosen. Anyone not conforming to the rules was never seen again.

'Of course.' Goïmron slid to the ground, noting the discomfort in his thighs and seat. He moved stiffly over to the mirror.

As a jewellery expert he could not help giving the gems in the frame a critical once-over. He pulled a magnifying glass out of his pocket and on closer inspection observed how the stones had been polished in the old fashion, using techniques none of the present-day long'uns had ever acquired. This was evidence that the jewels had been set more than two hundred cycles previously. He noted mountain crystal, noble garnets and opals. They sparkled in a unique way that Goïmron assumed must be to do with the light. The gems were not of the highest quality. He noticed tiny enclosures in the mineral, slight colourations or even magic runes engraved in their surface.

'Excellent handiwork,' Goïmron noted with satisfaction.

'The sun's going down, Master Jeweller. Hurry up,' Brûgar called impatiently, as he prepared a journey-break pipe. The others liked to call him the Chimney on account of his pipe-smoking habit. There would always be an excuse. He had a great selection of different types of tobacco in his pouch, more than one might find in a specialist shop. He was prepared to sell his wares if asked.

'Get the registration sorted or we'll ride on to Wolfsgart and find somewhere to stay there,' said Hargorina.

Admonished, Goïmron put his magnifying glass away and pressed the various stones in the required sequence. He was impressed to see them light up, as if they contained tiny suns.

Instead of his own reflection in the mirror, he saw the image of a young woman in a bright yellow famula robe. She was seated at a table polishing an engraved staff made of light-coloured wood. 'Who are you and what is your request?'

'What did I tell you?' Hargorina complained in the background. Her comment was louder than strictly necessary. 'A wand-waver.'

Goïmron gave an amiable nod and made a bow. 'Goïmron Chiselcut and I'm here with a delegation from King Regnor. We are on a special mission and are in need of assistance from the Maga Vanéra.'

The young blonde-haired famula broke off from her polishing task. 'What is the mission?'

'We are travelling to the Grey Mountains to look for Tungdil Goldhand.'

'Who's that?'

Goïmron almost choked. 'The greatest hero in the whole of Girdlegard!'

'Never heard of him.' She shrugged. 'And you've lost him?'

'He is missing.'

'Been missing long?'

'About one thousand cycles.'

Her eyebrows shot up. 'You are taking the – Gomson Flitziron.'

He decided to overlook her disrespectful mispronunciation of his name. He was worried she might cut off the interview if annoyed. 'No. But I can explain everything to the esteemed Maga Vanéra, when we –'

'The Esteemed Maga is not to be disturbed. She is engaged in creating a new artefact. Using another artefact.' The famula picked up her polishing cloth and breathed on the coin-sized zircon on the stick's handle. 'That will take ten or twenty orbits. You'll have to wait to tell her your joke.'

Goïmron sighed. He had known it would not be straightforward but now it was looking impossible. 'Don't you think she might take a break sometime?'

Her shrill laughter was like a slap in the face. 'Of course not, Gordon Shamiron! It is a very complicated procedure. It is highly demanding work and cannot be interrupted.' The famula dabbed a drop of oil on to the wood. 'Come back in twenty orbits' time. I will inform the Esteemed Maga of your visit and enquire as to her opinion about your request.' She cast a doubtful look at him via the mirror. 'A dwarf aged one thousand cycles. Needs to be rescued from the Grey Range, even though the mountains there are covered in lava and newly formed cliffs? Have I got it right? And you're called, what was it? Gollom . . .?'

'Thank you for your help,' he broke in, irritated. When he touched the stones again the famula's picture disappeared and he saw his own reflection. *Complete and utter failure.*

He was not going to suggest to the group that they attempt, in spite of this mishap, to cross the border, travel through to the capital and try to see the maga. *Too dangerous.* He took up Hargorina's original idea and returned to his horse. 'Off to Wolfsgart, then. I'm hungry.'

'Aren't you thirsty? Don't want a beer?' she teased.

'Or a brandy?' Brûgar wiggled his bushy eyebrows and finished filling the bowl of his pipe. 'Supposed to be very good.'

Goïmron climbed back into the saddle as the others laughed at him quietly.

Of course. Always ready to mock . . .

They were just setting off when a female rider in conspicuously bright white clothing came out of Rhuta at speed and raced past them on the road to the north. She was wearing a wide-brimmed hat on her pale hair. The hat sported two long orange feathers, one on each side of the crown. The rider did not look at the dwarf company.

Belîngor watched her progress with a puzzled expression on his face as she raced past in a cloud of dust. He waved his hands excitedly in the air using his sign language.

Hargorina interpreted: 'By the beard of Lorimbur! Do you know who *that* was?'

For Goïmron the question was unnecessary. *Everyone* in Girdlegard knew who she was.

At that moment they heard a piercing shriek overhead. Their horses shied in terror.

A gust of wind whirled dust up round them.

They were able to make out the form of the massive white-scaled body reflecting the setting sun's last rays as it flapped mighty wings to rise into the dark blue of the evening sky. The size of the creature leaving Rhuta and the elegance of its movements as it flew brought home to them just how powerful Ûra was.

Watching the creature glide away through the skies, Goïmron wondered whether the young famula had been telling the truth. If some conflict had occurred between the maga and the dragon's emissary, then it was inevitable that the ruler would now be dead. Nobody could survive an attack by Ûra. *Not even Vanéra.*

Girdlegard

United Great Kingdom of Gauragon
Province of Grasslands
1023 P.Q. (7514th solar cycle in old reckoning), spring

Rodana returned at dusk to the place where the accident had occurred. She cursed the bad luck that had sent her the misfortune of a broken wheel, just as she was too far from the township of Richcrumb to organise a swift replacement. She had left her apprentice in charge of the caravan, with all the puppets and the scenery flats packed away inside. She had taken the broken wheel and ridden off on one of the horses to get it mended.

From some distance away, she saw the glow of the fire and smelled the goulash being prepared in an iron pot. Chòldunja was sorting out their meal. The young woman had proved skilled with setting traps in the countryside as they travelled, so there was always enough meat for dinner if they had to stop overnight far from a village or town.

As Rodana approached, she realised that the stage was set up. *What is she up to? Does she want to rehearse?*

Chòldunja was ambitious, she knew. She wanted to learn everything there was to know about working with marionettes and the silhouette puppets. In any free time she found, she would get out the puppets and practise manipulating them, making sure she could move their limbs smoothly. She would try out the marionettes suspended on their horsehair strings, trying to create the impression of life. She was obsessed with learning the wonderful art of puppetry. But why put the stage out? It took time, and was a lot of work, to erect it and then put it all away again carefully without causing any damage.

'Chòldunja!' Rodana rode up and dismounted, untied the fastenings holding the newly repaired wheel and, grunting with the effort, laid it down on the ground. 'I'm back!'

'Very good, mistress,' came the response from the far side of the cart where the fire was and where the stage had been set.

'We'll move on in the morning. Your goulash smells wonderful. I caught a whiff of it from quite a long way off. Even against the wind.' Rodana took the saddle off the white horse and led the animal over to graze on the nearby verge. 'Why did you put the stage up?' The second horse was also grazing and greeted its partner with a friendly whinny. 'You know it's so easy to damage the material.' She walked round the caravan – and stopped in surprise.

'We . . . we have a visitor, mistress.' Chòldunja sounded somewhat intimidated. There was a woman of maybe forty sitting at her side and Chòldunja was serving her some hot tea. 'Forgive me for not giving you any warning. She told me I mustn't.'

'You know you always appreciate my dramatic appearances, Doria Rodana de Psalí. At least I hope you do.' Everyone in Girdlegard knew Stémna, with her white hat and the two orange feathers. She was seated on a stool under a cloud oak tree, sipping at her tea. 'Fresh mint! Delicious.'

Rodana came slowly nearer and sat down opposite. *A truly dramatic entrance indeed.* 'The Voice of the dragon. What an honour.'

'Not everybody says that when I turn up. Either they beg or they pay what my mistress demands.' Stémna peered through the steam from her tea. Her eyes glowed the same orange colour as the decorations on her hat. The rest was white: the leather skirt, boots, blouse, bodice and the light mantle, shining bright in the gathering dusk. 'Can you guess why I got your apprentice to erect the stage?'

'I presume you want to see the play.' Rodana concealed her rising fear. It had to happen one orbit, but she had not expected it today. *Not so soon. And not under these circumstances.*

'*That* play is what I want to see performed.' Stémna waved her white-gloved hand. 'I have heard such good reports from so many spectators, so I thought I really must see it myself. On my own. Without an audience. So that I can concentrate on every sentence.' Her eyes narrowed. 'On every. Single. Word.'

'I'll be interested to hear your opinion.' Rodana turned down the peppermint tea Chòldunja was offering.

'You will certainly hear what I think of it.' Stémna leaned back against the tree and took off her hat, placing it in her lap. 'Don't hold back. No improvising. Play it with your apprentice. Exactly like you always perform it.' She gestured towards the small town in the distance. 'Exactly the way you did it in Rich-crumb these last three orbits to such rousing applause.'

This will be the death of me. Rodana tried an excuse. 'I'm really very . . .'

'Tired. Of course. You've had a long journey and I expect you haven't eaten yet. Just a normal performance. Nothing special,' said the messenger considerately. 'Just do the play, Mistress Doria Rodana de Psalí.' She wrapped the sides of her mantle over her legs to keep warm. 'I shan't eat up all the goulash. It's not really . . . my thing . . . There'll be plenty left for you after the show.'

'I've put everything ready,' Chòldunja murmured, her voice shaking slightly. She placed the kettle down next to the fire.

Rodana gave her an encouraging smile. 'Well done.' She got to her feet and placed an arm round her apprentice's shoulder. In the dim light the black fingertips made it look as if the tops of her fingers had been cut off. 'Let's get started.'

Together and in silence they went behind the stage and set up the lighting apparatus: lanterns with coloured foil inserts. After last-minute adjustments to the scenery, Rodana took up the rod puppets and erected the parchment screen on which the shadows would be thrown to create their lifelike illusion.

'If she kills me when the performance is over,' she whispered to her protégée, 'you must make a run for it. Just inside the woods you'll find a river. Swim downstream as fast as you can.'

'Mistress, I—'

'Just do what you're told,' Rodana said sharply. 'It's quite enough for just the one of us to die. One day you'll have your own travelling show.'

'Are you starting soon?' came Stémna's voice. 'Your audience is getting impatient.'

'Can't we change the dangerous bit?' Chòldunja asked as she wound up the mechanical organ and started the overture music.

'I am sure Stémna already knows the entire text.' Rodana grasped the puppet rods for the dragon shape and held it in front of the lamp. 'She wants to know if it's true what people have reported.' *Like a judge reviewing the evidence before condemning the prisoner.*

The performance began.

Rodana and Chòldunja put on the same show as on so many previous evenings. The young girl's voice went a bit high occasionally because of her nervousness. Even Rodana found her hands shook from time to time manoeuvring the puppets. She was not entirely pleased with how things were going. Both women found they were perspiring a great deal, what with the heat of the lighting and their intense anxiety, but time passed surprisingly quickly.

'When mighty Ûra fell dead at the feet of the elves, humans, meldriths and dwarves, the heroes and heroines fell into each other's arms.' The final words of the play were coming up and Rodana wanted to speak them clearly and with emphasis. If they were to be her own last words, they should be effective ones. 'The worst of all the beasts lay spent and vanquished on the ground. And eternal peace was born among the peoples of Girdlegard.'

The music's last two bars faded away.

Rodana and Chòldunja looked at each other apprehensively, holding their breath, as they laid the puppets aside.

Sudden applause was heard. Applause from a single source.

'Fantastic!' Stémna called. 'Come out, both of you. I must congratulate you.'

'Remember what I said,' Rodana whispered, stroking a strand of the girl's hair back into place. 'Through the woods to the stream and then swim for your life.' She placed a kiss on her brow and stepped out, followed by the young trainee, who was fighting back tears.

Standing together, they received the poisoned applause offered by the dragon's envoy, who was on her feet, and had placed her hat back on her head.

'Absolutely fabulous performance,' was Stémna's enthusiastic verdict. 'The voices, the scenery, and the writing, of course. Music, too, and lighting effects. Anyone would think you had a big crew of assistants behind the scenes.'

She approached, pointing with outstretched hands. 'But see – it's just the two of you. Amazing.'

'Thank you. I'm glad you liked it.' Rodana could see the envoy was genuinely impressed. She bore no weapon in her hand and neither was she holding a noose ready for the gallows. And they were not turned to ashes by a sudden rush of fire from the dragon up high. 'I–'

All of a sudden Stémna's expression became serious and her delight vanished. 'My approval is based on the performance. Not the content. But I totally understand why the humans are so taken with the show, no matter in which region in Girdlegard. And even the orcs and the älfar and all the other creatures of Tion would welcome it, were my mistress to be vanquished.' Stémna sat down and helped herself from the tea kettle hanging over the fire. Although she was wearing gloves, she must have felt the heat of the metal handle. She seemed unaffected by the sensation. 'Now listen to me, both of you.'

Rodana sat down slowly, with Chòldunja by her side.

'Travel around, Mistress Doria Rodana de Psalí. Do your show about Ûra being defeated. Perform it all over Girdlegard. Give the humans that feeling of hope and joy and let them rejoice in the impression that the dragon is dead. That the dragon could be killed.' Stémna gave the ghost of a smile. 'At least in their imaginations. Reinforce this idea in their collective minds. They will adore you for it. And they will talk to you in their enthusiasm. They will tell you things. Tell you everything. In the towns. In the villages. Out in the countryside.' She blew over her drink. 'You two must write down everything they tell you. All their plans. What they may be cooking up. The slightest hints of any thought of rebellion against my mistress.'

'You want me to spy for you.' Rodana breathed out in relief. Anything was better than immediate incineration. You could find a way out of almost anything. But not out of the prospect of imminent death.

'You will both be the eyes and ears of Ûra. You will report on the common people and the nobility alike. They will have no inhibitions about talking to you because you are known to be a brave rebel. As soon as you catch a whiff of insurrection against Ûra, all you need to do is call me.' She took one of the orange feathers out of the hatband and tossed it into the air. As if guided by a magic hand, it drifted over and landed on Rodana's lap. 'Breathe on the feather and say my name, and I'll be with you within a quarter-orbit ready to hear your report.' She put her mug down on the floor. 'And, of course, you may summon me in an emergency. But it shouldn't be too dangerous.'

Rodana did not touch the glowing feather lying on her lap. 'And . . . if I should refuse?'

'Plucky of you to even consider that option. And similarly daring if you were to have the idea of not reporting back when you'd heard rumours of insurgency.' Stémna pointed at Chòldunja. 'Go on, admit it. That had occurred to you both, hadn't it? I can read it on your faces. It's written there. As is your wish to kill me.'

Rodana felt she had been caught out. Her apprentice looked quickly down at the ground. She attempted a lie: 'We would never dare to do that.'

'In order to be absolutely sure about that and to give you an incentive, may I suggest you take a look past the caravan. Look over at the horizon.'

They lifted their gazes.

At first they only saw the stars in the firmament, but then they could not help but see the sparks shooting up to join them. And the glow of fire in the distant darkness.

But that's where Richcrumb is. Rodana stared at the dragon's envoy. 'What have you done?'

'Just supplying your motivation.' Stémna smoothed down her white skirts as if she were ironing her innocence. She went over to her horse. 'Every place that you visit will go up in flames if you neglect your obligations. And your own homeland as well. You will bear the responsibility for the deaths of many innocent folk. Soon Mistress Doria Rodana de Psalí and her apprentice will be reviled as arsonists and your reputation as puppeteers will be trodden in the mud. As indeed you will be, yourselves.' She got up into the saddle and looked down at the two women. 'The same thing will happen if you let on to anyone about your mission.' She grasped something from her belt and tossed it to Rodana over the fire. 'Here you go. A bag of gold coins. As your reward. There will be more to come.'

'You are as much of a monster as the dragon herself!' Chòldunja shouted, incensed.

'You? You call me a monster?' Stémna hooted with laughter. 'Just mind your tongue, girl. Or you'll be landing in the cooking pot like those animals you trap for dinner. Or you'll end up in my mistress's stomach. She is partial to delicacies.'

'May your soul go to Tion!' Rodana said, horrified.

Stémna nodded sagely. '*Now* you sound like all the others. What a shame. So you're not special, after all.' She clicked her tongue at her horse. 'Have a good journey.' She rode swiftly away from the firelight.

Rodana did not watch her leave but turned her gaze towards the burning township of Richcrumb. She told herself that the

suihhi disease had broken out suddenly and many of the inhabitants would have died soon anyway.

It did not help.

Girdlegard

United Great Kingdom of Gauragon
Province of Mountainhigh
1023 P.Q. (7514th solar cycle in old reckoning), spring

Goïmron was surprised at the speed they were making considering they were not using the rail transport. The gentle hills
and lush valleys with their excellent roads allowed them to
make good progress without the horses getting tired and then
having to take rest breaks. As the Gauragon monarch, King
Gajek, routinely toured his kingdom from palace to castle in
turn, much attention had been given to establishing good communication by road between the various regions. Apart from
anything else, it was essential to have the capacity for swift
troop movements in times of war.

This was all playing out to Goïmron's advantage for his
mission.

'Look! There's the high ridge.' Hargorina was pointing to the
volcanic mountain range as if anyone might have missed it. It
reared up, after all, a good eleven thousand paces to the sky. On
the right-hand side the cone was visible, while on the left of the
mountain there were heaps of rubble and precipitous cliffs. A
thousand cycles previously, this mountain had emerged following earthquakes and fountains of lava, while everywhere else
in Girdlegard the ground level had sunk. Sometimes it was only
a question of a few paces; sometimes the difference in levels
could be a mile or more. 'I think the last eruption was only ten

cycles ago.' Goïmron took his spyglass out of its case to study the ridge in detail.

The colour of the stone changed where the ground was broken up. It was as if giants had painted the volcano in a variety of tints, rendering the lower slopes all the shades between ash grey and soft pink. Around the edge of the crater, some of which was hidden in cloud, there were thick lines of petrified black basalt running down.

'Isn't that where Ardin hangs out?' Goïmron searched the heights but could not find any sign of the dark blue dragon who had taken up residence in Girdlegard after the first volcanic eruptions. The resultant heat and fumes were what attracted the scaled beasts. Ardin was the second-largest dragon invader. Sensibly he had chosen not to challenge Ûra for supremacy in the area.

'That's what they say, yes.' Hargorina turned to Belîngor and Brûgar, who were talking using a mixture of signs and actual words. The blue-bearded dwarf had a travel pipe hanging in the corner of his mouth. It held more tobacco than the normal version, and it burned more slowly. The smoke smelled of cherries. 'What are you two cooking up over there?'

'It'll be some trick to play on me.' In the interim Goïmron had picked up how to read the sign language Belîngor liked to employ because of his vow of silence. Why, however, he had taken this vow remained a mystery for any outsider. He would have to earn Belîngor's trust to find that out. Through the lens of his spyglass, he could pick out tiny specks gliding along a far slope. 'Flame flyers!'

These airborne snake-like creatures lived on and around the dragons. They freed the dragons' skin and scales from parasites and fed mainly on leftovers from the carcasses of mountain goats found in crevices on the cliffs. Hot-blooded like the dragons themselves, they chose to bring up their young in the warmth of the lava fields. Their blood was the temperature of boiling oil.

'Flame flyers don't present a danger. They won't come down to the plains. It's too cold for them.' Hargorina rode up to speak to the warriors at the head of the convoy, then reported back. 'The others want to make a detour.' Her tone suggested she agreed with the plan.

'Is that so?' Goïmron lowered his scope. 'Do we need to get supplies?'

Hargorina gestured towards the heights. 'Over that way, on the slope, less than ten miles from the road, there's an old dwarf settlement that is said to have one of the greatest wonders of the last four hundred cycles.'

'So they want to visit the Lava Voice,' he said with a sigh. 'Did you tell them that's where the flame flyers hang out?'

'They nest higher up. On the edge of the crater. They like the heat. The settlement is at about eight hundred paces up. It'll be easy enough with the horses.' She looked expectant, with her chin jutting forward in anticipation. 'It should interest you as well. Maybe you'll discover something to take to the city of knowledge? When you take them the rest of your collection, I mean.'

He could not object now. *I should never have told them about that.* 'Right. As you like.'

'Great! We can be there by nightfall and set up camp. I'll let them know.' As she rode off again, she called back to him, 'Put your leather protective gear on.'

Strange, Goïmron thought. *How come she doesn't mention the fact that the settlement is a heap of ruins? Does she think maybe I don't know the legend?*

Way back, the dwarves that had been driven out of the mountains had taken over this ridge and founded a city. It had been wonderful and strongly fortified. The name was Crownsteel.

In worship of Vraccas, the dwarves had created the Lava Voice. They had set up a series of valves and chiselled pipes in the rockface where natural wind channels already existed, fed by the heated blasts from the lava deposits. With these valves, the multifarious sounds could be adjusted, just as an instrument can be tuned. Depending on the mood of the ridge and on gusts of wind from the depths of the mountain, a variety of tunes could be played, resounding far and wide over Gauragon and reaching all the way to the Grey Mountains. An additional effect was that of flammable gas, ignited by sparks, showing through holes in the rock to form a splendid visual display.

It was said there had been a similar spectacle in the Grey Mountains in the time preceding the earthquakes. Goïmron had read about this phenomenon in old documents he had found in the curiosity shop. It had been in a place where elves and dwarves had lived in harmony together. Unlikely kind of set-up, in his view.

But Ardin the dragon disliked the music being played near his eyrie. His ears were offended by the clanging noises the Children of the Smith used to produce using the lava steam. So he flew down over Crownsteel, destroyed the town with fire and slaughtered the inhabitants with tooth and claw. It took one night and one dawn to kill eight thousand souls. No one escaped and no stone remained in place. *Only the Lava Voice itself had survived. As if to mock those who had created it and to whom it had brought annihilation.*

Goïmron could not help feeling curious. *I wonder how many dwarves have actually ever visited Crownsteel.*

Using his sign language, Belîngor communicated his meaning: *'I don't know anyone from the Black Mountains who's ever been. By Lorimbur! I am as excited as the first time I went into battle.'*

'So, just a little bit, then,' said Brûgar, twiddling the tip of his blue beard into a point. 'And don't worry about the flame flyers, Goïmron. If one comes at you, we'll be sure to protect you.' As usual, his face was half hidden in a cloud of tobacco smoke.

'I am made of stronger stuff than you may think,' Goïmron retorted, not wanting to be more specific in his claims to physical prowess.

He was actually looking forward to the detour. It would not cost them more than one orbit. Admittedly, after the disaster of Rhuta, he would have preferred to continue straight on with their planned route. *But when else would I have the chance of seeing a dwarf masterpiece like the Lava Voice?*

They travelled up the colourful mountainside on what remained of the original tracks. Goïmron put on his padded leather armour as they went. Occasionally they came across weathered runes chiselled into the stone, praise of or prayers to the god Vraccas. And here and there were old monuments to Ardin's victims. Some of these had the image of particular dwarf countenances carved into the surface.

At dusk they took the final hairpin bend and in silence they rode up to what remained of the fortified walls of Crownsteel. The elements had weathered the stone and the mortar had crumbled away, but you could still see the burn marks and the gouges where the dragon's claws had slashed in fury.

Their horses' hooves made the only sound now as they rode through the ruins that spread out on each side.

'The city must have been splendid,' said Hargorina, with emotion in her voice. 'Just look at the artistry in the carving. You know, even the broken reliefs are better than anything we've got . . .' She bit her tongue.

It struck Goïmron that there was no sign of any item made of metal or bone or leather or wood. There was nothing except rock. Vandals, animals, rain and wind had stripped the place of anything belonging to the original inhabitants.

'The Lava Voice is over there!' Brûgar used the mouthpiece of his pipe to point over to the west, where, about three hundred paces further on, the horns and pipes could be made out on the cliff face.

'*By the axe of Lorimbur! It's taller than four cloud oak trees on top of each other!*' Belîngor was grinning from ear to ear. '*The valves and flaps are still intact!*'

'No, we are not going to try to find out whether the Lava Voice can still sing,' Goïmron stated decisively. He could read the signings and knew just what the other dwarf had in mind. 'You said you wanted to *see* it. You didn't say you needed to *hear* it.' Of their own accord his brown eyes turned up to the crater where a dull glow was visible. 'Ardin lives up there somewhere. I do not wish to make his acquaintance.'

'Nor do we.' Hargorina issued an order to the troops and they headed over to where the musical dwarf masterpiece was. 'But keep your eyes peeled, everyone. You never know what may be nearby.'

Goïmron kept his anxiety in check. He had the best Thirdling warriors at his side and he was wearing armour. You could not ask to feel safer than that. *Except if maybe we had a maga with us . . .* Out of the corner of his eye, he saw a pale glow showing through the piles of stones from a collapsed tower. The smell and the noise indicated there was still an active stream of lava. At night a pool of molten stone would probably show up as an enchanted spectral phenomenon.

Hargorina suddenly called for quiet.

Goïmron strained his ears. He could not hear anyone coming. Only the incessant slight whistling of the wind swirling around the crevices of the rock. All of a sudden, the sound of the wind altered. It got louder and deeper in tone. *That's never the wind.* He took out his spyglass and focused it on the Lava Voice. There had been a change in the valves – some had closed. Others had opened. The vegetation was moving in the draught coming from the openings or from the flammable gas. *Curses!*

'Someone has activated the instrument,' he told Hargorina.

'Are you sure?'

'It must have been done by hand . . .' A tall slim figure in a green, hooded mantle crossed his field of vision, holding ropes that came from the operating chains for the flaps and valves.

'I can see an elf!'

'What's that you say?' Brûgar grabbed his own telescope. 'What are the pointy-ears doing in Crownsteel? That's blasphemy.' He knocked his pipe out and stowed it away. 'They are insulting our dead.'

Goïmron could clearly see the elf making his preparations. 'He's setting the Voice up to sing.'

'Let's stop him before he brings the dragon down on us.' Hargorina pressed her heels into the flanks of her horse to make it lunge forward. 'Don't anyone kill that elf! I want to find out what the blazes it thinks it's doing.'

Goïmron followed the others as they dashed over to where the elf was. He still had his spyglass out. *What's behind this?* He had not seen any other elves. *This one's here on his own. So it can't be intended as a trap to get Ardin.*

The tall slender elf folk had been forced to leave the north of Girdlegard over eight hundred cycles ago after the dragons had destroyed all of their largest townships and eradicated any remaining resistance. The new elf realm of Tî Silândur was away to the south, far from the dragons' lairs.

Through his glass Goïmron saw a red glow that hid the rest of the picture. *What on . . .?* He quickly lowered his scope and saw a flame flyer not five paces in front of him. His horse was rooted to the spot in terror.

The creature had the form of a winged snake with a long, sharp beak. It was armoured with a skin of tiny scales where a bird would have feathers. On its back it had four wings, which were fluttering to keep the creature hovering in the air. Its glowing eyes were fixed on Goïmron.

That lava pool in the ruins! That's where it has its nest. Finding himself absolutely alone with this threatening creature, he felt for the slingshot device that was behind him in the saddlebag.

With a shrill squeak, the flame flyer dashed forward, its long beak like a harpoon.

Goïmron caught hold of the handle of the crossbow-like weapon, pulled it up, undid the safety catch, and aimed and fired repeatedly.

The heavy steel bullets swished through between the horse's ears, hitting the flying creature in the body and wings. But it kept on coming.

With great presence of mind, Goïmron slipped down out of the saddle and landed on the rock-hard ground.

The injured flame flyer missed him by a beard hair's breadth. As its hot blood dripped on to the horse's neck, the animal shied and bolted with fear and pain.

Goïmron got up on to one knee and reloaded the sling. He searched the area but could not see where the winged creature had gone.

Then he heard a fluttering behind him. Turning aside, he dropped flat to the floor and aimed again straight ahead. He fired.

Under tension, the metal spring catapulted the balls of steel at the flame flyer as it dived to attack the dwarf. One pellet took it between the eyes and the glow in the pupils vanished. Another hit the tip of its beak and burst into tiny pieces as if it were made of porous pumice stone.

At this the creature plunged lifeless to the ground. The veined wings snapped and hot blood shot in fountains out of the wounds in its body. Steam rose from it in the cool night air. The creature finished just in front of Goïmron's shoes.

Thanks be to Vraccas! He jumped to his feet and activated the winding mechanism to reload the spring. If there was one flame flyer here, there were probably more. *I must warn the others!*

Goïmron was startled to hear the deep tones of a horn. A blue tongue of flame as tall as a house shot out into the evening sky, throwing light on the surrounding ruins. *The elf has actually done it!*

This was followed by other shrill sounds, and four more powerful flames were sent up into the twilit darkness. The sounds were constant – horns and pipes. The valves were old and no longer functioning properly, it seemed. The mechanism was not obeying its activator.

The resultant cacophony resounded over Crownsteel's ruins and reached far into Gauragon, all the way up to the crater of the volcano. The noise was causing the dwarf some painful discomfort. He started to feel giddy.

We must get out of here! Right now! He grabbed his axe and severed the flame flyer's beak. Some of the skull was attached when he sliced it off. He ran off to his horse which had been standing in the rubble. He did not attempt to shout to Hargorina and the others because it would have no point, given all the background noise coming from the Lava Voice installation. *They'll know anyway by now that we have to get away.*

Goïmron got up into the saddle and patted the injured animal's neck to reassure it.

He hurried to stow away the axe and his mechanical sling. He tried to locate the Thirdlings using his spyglass and checked the dark sky for any signs of Ardin.

'Come on, gem cutter, get yourself away. Ride as quick as you can!' Hargorina appeared suddenly from the ruins. She rode past him at a furious pace. 'Get down to the plain! And don't use any lights.' Goïmron saw she had the blond elf lying unconscious across the front of her saddle, its head and limbs bouncing up and down with the movements of the galloping horse. 'The dragon will be here any moment.'

Fine bodyguards you lot are. Goïmron pulled his mount's head round and raced off.

Belîngor and Brûgar flew past, one at each side of him, and the rest of the soldiers came galloping after them. Then there was a mighty gust of wind, throwing up a whirling cloud of dust, obliterating their view of the path.

Ardin! Goïmron cowered down in the saddle. *The dragon's right here!*

A hard object hit him on the back of the head and lightning shot up and down his spine. Pain swept from his head down through to his fingers and his toes. It even affected his breathing.

His vision was failing and his limbs lost their strength.

He collapsed, heavy as a wet sack of grain, falling to the stony ground for the second time on the same evening.

Unfortunate circumstances have brought me to this place.

After vanquishing the Unslayable Ones, we were forced to leave Girdlegard in order to prevent a catastrophe at the Black Abyss.

We fought an enormous number of beasts who had come swarming out, and we managed to beat them back. A protective dome was erected over the abyss and I was thus unable to get out again in time.

So here I remain, cut off from my friends.

But not for ever.

Excerpt from
The Adventures of Tungdil Goldhand,
as experienced in the Black Abyss
and written by himself.
First draft.

VI

Girdlegard

Brown Mountains
Dsôn Khamateion
1023 P.Q. (7514th solar cycle in old reckoning), late spring

Given that he was a brother to the Omuthan of Brigantia, Klaey never thought his life as a valuable hostage would be like this. He had imagined it would be a pleasanter experience. The last comfort he had experienced had been the journey back to the realm of the älfar because he had been carried in the invalid chair.

That had been the last touch of luxury he was afforded.

Vascalôr had sent him straight to this cell, where he could either sit on the narrow bunk, try out a few physical exercises in the cramped conditions, or peer out of the arrow-slit window and see the rockface opposite, but nothing at all of the alleged beauty of Dsôn Khamateion's landscape with its rolling hills and gentle valleys.

His injuries, however, were healing satisfactorily. That is to say, apart from the damage to his vocal cords. Vascalôr had been prescient with his choice of nicknames for his prisoner: he had called him Croaker or Raven. Klaey was not sure what name he should best select for himself. Certainly nothing commonplace. He already knew of so many people who for some mysterious reason bore the name of Raven.

How about Whisperer? Getting to his feet, he looked over at the door, which was opened twice a day. Once for food and once so he could empty the slop bucket. He had to carry the pail along a corridor to tip the contents down a shaft. Then he was allowed to wash himself and his clothes if necessary in a small courtyard. He had to put the wet clothes back on. The only garments he had were a loincloth and a woollen tunic. What his jailers did not know, however, was that he had managed to smuggle in a piece of metal and some wire he had found out in the yard.

Klaey listened out. *Sounds like they've changed the guard.*

All was quiet in the corridor, so he started to work away at the lock on his door. It was not that he wanted to escape; he merely intended to get out and have a good scout around. He had already acquainted himself with the älfar language, spoken and in script, so he expected he would be able to gather some important information. He might later find an opportunity to make use of his knowledge. However, all he had managed on his previous three excursions from his cell was to explore the immediate vicinity inside the prison tract. Today he thought he would try something more adventurous.

The lock cylinders clicked as he wiggled the piece of wire and used the scrap of metal as a lever.

Vascalôr had interrogated him several times, demanding to be told the identity of the one who had broken into the memorial chamber, killing Brigantians and älfar alike. Klaey said nothing until threatened with torture. Then he divulged the required name: Mòndarcai.

Vascalôr's reaction on hearing this was to utter a scream of fury. Anger lines zigzagged across his spectral features and his eyes burned like dark red holes. Apparently the robber was a hated individual in Dsôn Khamateion. After storming out of the cell on that occasion, Vascalôr did not appear again. He had not been back for several orbits.

Klaey heard the click that meant the lock had succumbed to his manipulations. He opened the door cautiously. If only he still had his lucky amulet with him. *I'll have to get myself a new one once I'm out of here.*

As he had hoped, the brightly lit corridor was empty.

My thanks to you, Samusin and Cadengis. With a grin he set about making a dummy for his bed out of blankets so that his absence would not be noticed if the guards took a swift glance through the hatch. *Dsôn Khamateion – here's an end to hiding away. I hope the famed beauty of the älfar land proves as great as the notorious deadly menace of its inhabitants.* He pulled the door closed after himself and locked it, for all eventualities.

Thanks to the conversations he had overheard in the course of previous orbits, and thanks also to his being able to study plans which he had found in the guardroom, he had a decent idea of his surroundings, and he knew which direction to head in to find his way out of the prison.

But on this night he chose to climb the stairs to a small watchtower. Once upon a time this would have formed part of the general defences. But now it was where the guards spent their leisure breaks. It afforded a good view of the area. He soon located the narrow spiral staircase and once upstairs he felt fresh air on his face. He was getting closer to the entrance. He slipped carefully out on to the platform and poked his head over the battlement crenellations. The breeze blew through his long black hair.

Stretched out before him was a night-time vista of the whole of Dsôn Khamateion, cloaked in a light garment of mist, as if the land were trying to hide from prying human eyes. All he could make out were the silhouettes of buildings and some lamplit windows.

Judging from what he could see of the constellations, he reckoned his prison must be at the western end of the town that extended over the entire valley. The built-up area seemed to stretch for at least two miles before giving way to fields and forest in a second valley which Klaey could just make out vaguely in the moonlight through the mist.

'. . . is the last thing I want,' came Vascalôr's voice close by.

Damnation! Never heard him coming! Klaey ducked down under the line of the battlements, using his hearing to work out where the älf was. *Those wretched black-eyes should all be made to wear bells.* He peered round with the utmost caution.

He saw a walkway two paces beneath his little tower. Vascalôr, in his usual high-collared red robe, was standing below him, talking to a female älf. They both held cups of steaming liquid. She was dressed elegantly, but Klaey could not see the exact shade of her robe clearly. Moonlight tended to falsify colours. On her dark hair she had a transparent veil, embroidered in silver. He could see the glint of her jewellery.

'Are you absolutely certain, Vascalôr?' She brought her drink gracefully to her lips. Klaey was affected by the sensuality of her movements.

The ghostly pale älf nodded. The starlight made his white hair look like glass. 'Our spies have confirmed that a handful of groundlings left the Black Mountains in search of their greatest legendary hero, hoping to bring him back.'

'And *who* might that be?'

'Tungdil Goldhand. I unearthed some old documents from the vandalised Fourthling archives. Records from the 6243rd cycle in the old solar timescale the humans use. If what I read there is correct, the groundling would pose a danger for our plans.'

'But would he not already be more than one thousand two hundred and fifty cycles in age? Is that even possible?' She sounded rather bored. 'A myth, surely. Does it really matter if that group of groundlings goes to the Grey Mountains and their deaths?'

'But what if he *does* exist, Ascatoîa?'

'Then we kill this Goldhand.' One of her eyes was completely white, as if blind, while the other was black as an abyss. What Klaey had initially thought was a shadow effect proved actually to be a particoloured face: one half was white. This was undoubtedly the long-term effect of the deceptive modifications once adopted by their ancestors. 'I'm wondering what we could paint with his blood. The life-juice of a dwarf of that incredible age would make a fantastic picture . . . no matter how old and wrinkly the body might be . . . Do you think he still has any teeth?'

Vascalôr drank from his tankard. 'I repeat: the last thing we need would be the groundling tribes uniting. And all inspired by the return of their legendary leader. They could form an army to march on Brigantia, demanding the return of the Fourthlings' territory. I am worried about what that might mean for Dsôn Khamateion.'

Klaey was thrilled with himself for having had the bright idea of coming to this spot on this very night. His brother would be delighted with him for bringing him this snippet of information.

Ascatoîa's laughter echoed from the nearby hillside. 'The groundlings can't defeat us. What an idea!'

'They don't have to. We're surrounded by rock, stone, and mountain peaks. Look. It's their land. If they want, they can make the hills collapse on top of us.' Vascalôr seemed to be uncharacteristically upset at the thought. 'This cannot be allowed to happen.'

'Ah. You're thinking of the wider consequences, I see.'

'I'll get the council and the Ganyeios to send out a force to stop the groundlings before they set foot in the Grey

Mountains. Any spark of hope they have will be dashed out and eradicated.'

'Oh, by Inàste! Send me! Go on, do!' Her variegated eyes glowed with enthusiasm. 'All I've got to paint with at the moment is that pallid blood from Fourthling captives. It's no good at all. Thirdling red will have iron in it. It will be very intense. I'll be celebrated for my art if I can get hold of some of that!' she wheedled. 'And I haven't been able to use my zhussa powers for ages. They are starting to dwindle. Have pity on me.'

The älf laughed. 'Agreed. As your cousin, I shall let you have your fun. But take care not to underestimate the Thirdlings. They are tough.'

'I never underestimate an opponent. Even when there's really no contest,' she retorted, clinking her cup against his. 'The groundlings' deaths will bear my name.' Satisfaction on her face, she drank deep. 'Have you heard the other news?'

'I only want to hear it if it's good.'

'I assure you it is.'

'Right. Tell me everything.'

Exactly! Tell him. And you'll be telling me at the same time. Klaey wanted to rub his hands in anticipation, but he did not dare move a muscle.

'Our ships are underway.' Ascatoîa smiled at her cousin. 'Loaded with the weapons we were promised.'

Vascalôr's hand with the cup froze in mid-air. 'You mean *those* weapons?'

Come on, be specific, for goodness' sake. Klaey stared down at the älf. *Start talking!*

'Exactly. Yes, those very ones. The relief fleet will probably pass the Firstlings' western water gate in the Red Mountains in late autumn. The groundlings won't know what's hit them.' Ascatoîa's necklace began to glow, as if sharing in her eagerness.

'If we're clever, dearest cousin, Girdlegard will be ours before winter sets in.'

In the names of Samusin and the mother of Cadengis! What plot are these black-eyed demons hatching here? Whereas up to now he had been relishing his privileged role in overhearing secrets, his excitement turned to dismay. Whatever it was the mysterious fleet was bringing through the sea tunnel, it must have something to do with combatting the might of the dragons. Otherwise the älfar would not have an earthly hope of overall victory.

'Now *that's* a really nice bit of news.' Vascalôr drained his cup. 'Right. We kill this bunch of groundlings and we find Mòndarcai.'

She had been about to take another sip of her drink but stopped and spat contemptuously. 'Him? Where did you get that name from?'

'The Brigantian named him as the butcher who slaughtered our people and the other dregs. Apparently he introduced himself and thanked him for taking the blame.'

Your death bears the name of Mòndarcai. The terrible memory of those words ran round Klaey's mind. He shuddered and clutched at his throat. His skin crawled with horror.

'Mòndarcai is only a myth.'

'Well, what do you know. Another myth,' replied Vascalôr cuttingly. 'But a myth alive and able to launch itself into our sacred spaces, killing the priestess and the guards, in order to steal Aiphatòn's relics and then disappear into thin air. If this Tungdil Goldhand turns out to be the same sort of myth, what do you think the groundlings will say?'

'Stop making fun of me.' The glow of her necklace faded. 'It could have been any traitor from Dsôn claiming to be him.'

'Why announce that identity to the Brigantian when about to kill him?'

'Perhaps he was an admirer of Mòndarcai? Some stupid ritual,' Ascatoîa argued. 'Mòndarcai does not exist.'

'I disagree. I'd rather not take the risk. I need to find him. I made some notes while I was in Brigantia. There are some clues I can follow up.' He stared at the bottom of the empty cup. 'No matter what that thief wants the relics for, it bodes ill for us. It's essential we get those things back: the armour plates, the gauntlet and the tionium spear.'

'The Originals and Mòndarcai are all made up. Just like the Unslayable Ones.' Ascatoîa tried to reassure him. 'We never found any basis for believing all those tales people used to tell round the campfire. And where could they be hiding in Girdlegard? We've got spies everywhere.'

Vascalôr placed his empty cup on the balustrade. 'I'll be able to give you an answer soon enough, cousin. And don't forget that Tungdil Goldhand used to figure in those old stories, too, that we found in the Fourthling papers.' He turned to go.

'You're leaving me here on my own?' Her tone was sulky. 'First you get me up here with the prospect of a wonderful view and now you're running off? Why don't we wait till the mist lifts?'

'Forgive me.' The spectral älf gave her a kiss on the cheek. 'Our talk has reminded me of something.'

'And that would be what?'

'The Brigantian prisoner. I'll interrogate him one last time, to be quite sure about Mòndarcai. And then that will be it for him. We've no need to keep a hostage. If anyone from Brigantia dares to cross into our territory, I shall have them torn limb from limb.'

'What will you tell the Omuthan when he enquires about his little brother?'

'The big idiot will be glad to see the back of the smallest one.' Vascalôr turned to the top of the staircase.

'Are you sure about that?'

'Absolutely. You should have seen Orweyn's face when the fool forced himself on me as a hostage, merely to escape the prospect of the court martial. I'll put his cowardly blood aside for you. You can use it to prime your canvas.' He disappeared down the stairwell.

Klaey felt ice-cold fear surge through every fibre of his being. *I am of no use at all to the black-eyes. Except to provide ink for one of their cruel paintings.*

If he returned to his cell, he would be killed.

If he tried to escape from the town, he would be killed.

But Klaey had already gained so much in the way of secret knowledge about the älfar and there was more he was keen to find out. Their plans. That fleet of ships. The Originals. He must not die in Dsôn Khamateion.

That's it! Klaey turned his head to survey the fog-covered townscape. *I shall hide here in their midst. I'll find out about their defences, gather all the black-eyes' secret intelligence details. And then I'll disappear, in order to . . .*

Yes. To do exactly what?

Ascatoîa gave a final glance at the outlines of the city buildings and then left. The way was clear. Not a guard in sight.

I'll decide later what to do with my knowledge. Klaey vaulted over the battlements and worked his way down the walls to start his venture into the lanes and streets of Dsôn Khamateion.

Girdlegard

United Great Kingdom of Gauragon
Province of Mountainhigh
1023 P.Q. (7514th solar cycle in old reckoning), late spring

Goïmron landed with a thump on the hard ground of the ruined city, his own horse's hooves narrowly missing him.

The dragon roared and raged in its cloud of dust. The wind caused by its flapping wings brought up yet more dirt, coating the stunned dwarf. *It's imperative it doesn't catch sight of me.* Unable to see clearly, Goïmron worked his way forward until his fingers met a heap of stones that might afford shelter. *Vraccas! Help me!*

The strident noises of the Lava Voice were shrilling and growling in appalling discord, outdoing Ardin's angry howls. Then a scattered beam of flame shone through the dusty air. A ball of heat rolled over where Goïmron was cowering for safety. This was followed by the ground shaking as the dragon flailed around, beating wings and tail against the ruined walls.

Suddenly he felt a hand on his shoulder and caught a whiff of plum tobacco. 'Gem carver? Still alive?'

'Yes, I think so. It's my back.' His response was more groan than speech.

'Let me have a look.' Brûgar felt along his spine and across his shoulders. 'I can't find any open wound, and the bones aren't broken. Can you feel your arms and legs?'

'Yes.'

'Then let's not give up hope. I reckon the monster's tail gave you a whack. I can feel the graze here. It's even left the shape of his scales on your padded armour.' Brûgar splashed Goïmron's face with water and rinsed the dust out of his eyes. 'Stay down. Best wait till Ardin has finished rampaging.' In the corner of his mouth, he had a short-stemmed pipe filled with plum-flavoured tobacco.

As time went by, the Lava Voice grew quieter, until only the deepest horn sound was still competing with the dragon's furious roar. After another crash and some ground tremors affecting the ruins of Crownsteel, the noise died away completely. Ardin gave a howl of triumph. The wind picked up strength and the sound of the creature's flapping wings retreated. A few heart-beats later, the dust had settled and between coughing bouts, the two dwarves stared at each other.

High above their heads, the dragon, now a harmless outline against the sky, was flying off to perch on the glowing red walls of the volcano crater. Seated on a mound of blackened scree, it gave off a long squawk of anger.

At this distance it looks quite harmless. Goïmron would have wanted to have had a better look at the dragon when it was close up. The creature's skin was said to be a sparkling dark blue, with diamonds on its scales. But with his eyes full of dust, he had been half blinded at the time. *Don't suppose I'll ever be that close to it again.*

Crownsteel's ruins had suffered from the dragon's attack. No buildings at all were now still standing. The city was a thing of the past. As was the famed phenomenon of the Lava Voice.

Goïmron could see the pipes and horns of the ancient instru-ment were broken now. And there were claw marks gouged out of the stone. *What a waste. It was something quite unique and now it's lost for ever.* He got to his feet with difficulty. 'Where are the others?'

Brûgar hauled himself up in spite of the heavy armour he was wearing. 'Hiding up on that path.' He gave his Fourthling companion a thorough inspection. 'Only bruises. I can't see any blood anywhere. Not many folk could claim to have got off so lightly after a scrap with an angry dragon.' He slapped him on the shoulder with a laugh and shook the dust out of his blue-stained beard. 'Let's get out of here before Ardin decides he's hungry.'

'What happened to the elf?'

'The idiot pointy-ears that caused the whole fiasco is still asleep. Hargorina sent him off to the land of dreams with a gentle tap on the head.' Brûgar put his pipe away and strode off to collect the horses, which had bolted in terror. They were standing over by the rockface. 'When he comes round, he'll be wishing we'd left him here in the ruins.'

With his back causing him considerable discomfort, Goïmron limped after Brûgar. Glancing up, he saw the dragon high above them slip back inside the crater. *I nearly died.* He was furious with the elf who had endangered them with his silly trick of setting off the Lava Voice. Their whole mission could have been wrecked by his action.

'Did he say anything before she hit him?'

'Yes.'

'What?'

' "No, please don't" and "No, not my nose." ' Brûgar chortled. 'And something about having mercy and "I had to do it. Forgive me." '

'Not very helpful.' Goïmron suspected the Thirdling was making fun of him again. 'So we'll have to wait till he comes round. I'm keen to know his story.'

'We all are. And then we'll give him a thorough beating before sending him home to Tî Silândur.' Brûgar clenched his fist, the metal gauntlet crunching as he did so. 'Oh for the chance to give a pointy-ears a good dressing-down. How long since a dwarf has been able to say that? Two hundred cycles? Longer? Four hundred? I'll permit myself a celebratory pipe. With the most expensive tobacco.'

Goïmron did not contradict him but made a mental note to put a stop to things if they got out of hand. He did not hold with using violence on anyone who was unarmed. Even on an elf. And even one they were rightly furious with.

They were soon back with the rest of the troops. Hargorina prevented any more talk and insisted on their leaving at once to get away from the mountain where their presence might provoke another attack by the dragon. Only once they were safely making camp in the shelter of the white beech wood did the company of dwarves relax. Their horses, too, calmed down at last.

They had dumped the elf by the fire in a clump of nettles as punishment, and he was still unconscious. Even for one of his kind, he did appear to be very young. He had no beard and his hair was worn in long golden braids. Under his torn green mantle he wore leather armour reinforced with iron rings. He would have lost his sword while fleeing but he still had a dagger on his belt.

'Belîngor, try and wake him up.' Hargorina was toasting some cheese on a stick. 'I want to hear what he has to say for himself.'

Belîngor nodded and turned the sleeping form over with his boot, ensuring the elf's face scraped over the noxious weeds.

Only half-conscious, the figure jerked to one side – straight into the next clump of stinging nettles. There followed a set of weird contortions which kept the dwarves amused as the elf tried to squirm away from the discomfort. Coming fully awake, the elf stopped wriggling and sprang to his feet with a string of curses. He stared at the laughing bystanders in disbelief. Then he began to recollect what had happened. His reddened, blistered face turned towards the mountain.

'We saved your life, you know,' Hargorina told him. 'Your stupid actions provoked Ardin's attack. The dragon was so enraged that he destroyed the Lava Voice utterly.' She nibbled at the toasted cheese. 'Have you got an explanation?'

'Tell us, or we'll take you back for the dragon to feast on,' growled Brûgar under his breath. He had four different bags of his favourite tobacco blends in front of him. Belîngor was helping with the selection.

The elf executed a graceful bow. 'My name is Telînâs. I come from Birchbrook. It's a village. The nearest town is Sunroof.' His voice was high and clear.

'That's a long way away. A very long way.' Brûgar had made his selection. He took a burning spill from the fire to light the tobacco. As he drew on his pipe, smoke came out of his nostrils, much like a dragon's fiery breath, only with the more agreeable scent of pine needles. 'Elves have no business being in the mountains.'

'"And they certainly should not be in an abandoned dwarf settlement."' Hargorina translated Belîngor's sign language for the benefit of the elf. '"Where they are up to absolutely no good at all and have managed to bring about the total destruction of the most brilliant instrument our folk have ever devised."'

Goïmron listened in to the interrogation. It was all quite amicable. He would have expected a deal more shouting and violence, considering it was the Thirdlings at work here.

'Was it a test?' He broke in with a question.

Telînâs nodded, rubbing his blistered face ruefully. 'I want to get into the fîndaii, the bodyguards of the Kisâri. The more intrepid the initiation rituals you complete, the likelier you are to be accepted.'

'So you thought you'd have a go at bringing the Lava Voice back to life?' Hargorina munched on the crispy cheese snack she had toasted. She prepared herself a second one. 'And thereby risk a little dance with a dragon.'

'It's said that the horn can be heard all the way to Tî Silândur. I told the fîndaii captain to be sure to listen out.' The young elf looked downcast. He sighed. 'I have failed.'

'Why do you say that?' Goïmron was getting hungry and took some spiced bread out of his lunch bag to toast over the fire. The smell was delicious. 'The Voice did speak.'

'But I had intended to make it play an elf melody. To make it quite clear it wasn't a random event.'

'And for that, my little pointy-ears' – Brûgar raised his war flail menacingly – 'I would in my wildest times have beaten you to a pulp. It would have been extremely blasphemous of you.'

'So? What's to be done with you?' Goïmron bit into his delicacy, releasing the flavours of the herbs in the bread. There was a back note of ham, he noted with satisfaction. *I would give anything for a mug of dark beer in the Trusty Tankard to go with this.*

'I have failed the test. There is no point in my going back to Tî Silândur,' replied Telìnâs. 'My dream of serving with the guards is in ruins.'

Belîngor took out a mushroom sausage and held it over the fire in his bare fingers.

'Serves you right. You've destroyed the Lava Voice. That's ruined, too. But at least it wasn't violated first by being made to play elf tunes.' Brûgar rubbed his blue beard, puffing furiously on his pipe.

Hargorina watched the young elf. 'Even though I don't appreciate what you have done, I must admit you have shown courage.'

'Overly confident, I think. Too courageous for your own good. Never a wise move.' Brûgar added his opinion.

'I am indebted to you noble dwarves of Lorimbur's line.' He looked at Goïmron. 'But you – correct me if I am wrong – are a Fourthling, I think.'

Belîngor's hands gave the message: *'A blindfolded orc could see that with its head in a bucket.'* The company all laughed quietly.

'How is it that you are travelling with them?' Telìnâs asked, scratching at his itching face. 'Oh, I think I know. You are the guards and you're all here to protect him. Are you on a special dwarf quest?'

'Sort of,' Hargorina answered evasively. 'It's not really any of your business.'

'Perhaps it is, though.' Goïmron had had an idea. 'We are going to the Grey Mountains. We are looking for Tungdil Goldhand.'

Telinâs did his best to appear vaguely impressed. 'Presumably a very renowned dwarf ... but the name ... I don't recall ...'

'What? For Vraccas' sake! The greatest hero in the history of Girdlegard? He saved the land so often from destruction.' Goïmron was horrified at this ignorance. He would have expected better from an elf.

'So when was that?'

'One thousand cycles ago.' This was the bit Goïmron did not like. 'And yes, he is still alive.'

'Interesting. I'd heard that the Children of the Smith were long-lived. But *that* long? Really?' Telinâs stretched his red nettle-rashed hands to the warmth of the fire. 'You're sure of that?'

'Yes, I am.' Goïmron handed him a piece of the bread that the elf had been eyeing hungrily. 'How would it be if you came with us? As a way of compensating us for the damage you've caused?' The Thirdlings swivelled round to glare at him in surprise. 'And as soon as we've located Goldhand, we'll be uniting the five dwarf tribes and then we'll liberate the Brown Mountains from Brigantia. After that we'll deal with the dragons, one by one. Girdlegard has waited one thousand cycles. It is time it had its freedom back!'

Belîngor blinked. And sat motionless. The sausage caught fire and he dropped it.

'*You absolutely sure you are a Fourthling?*' he said with his hands.

'There's no doubt about that,' commented Brûgar drily. 'You should have seen him when there was fighting to be done.'

'An elf helping to find the legendary dwarf hero. That would be a signal.' Goïmron was growing ever more enthusiastic. 'Two races that have always disliked each other, seen working hand-in-hand for the common good. For the good of our homeland.'

'Not a bad idea. And it would make up for my having failed my test,' Telìnâs was thinking out loud. 'Right. I'll do it.' He bit into his piece of bread. 'I'd be paying off my debt. I'll stand with you.'

'Elves don't belong in the mountains,' Brûgar repeated stubbornly.

'This one does.' Goïmron was insistent.

'There's a first time for everything, friend dwarf.' Mid-chew the elf's expression altered. 'Don't say there's moon weed in the bread?'

'Yes. Don't you like it?' Hargorina attacked her next piece of toasted cheese with gusto.

'It doesn't like me.' Telìnâs stared at the food sadly. 'It's going to be a hungry night for me, then.'

'If it gives you the runs, best take some of those nettles to wipe your arse,' suggested Brûgar, pulling a face. 'The pain will distract you from your hunger.' While all the dwarves were laughing, Goïmron handed the elf his own water flask. 'Welcome to the company. We'll drink to it later when there's some beer.'

Telìnâs nodded gratefully.

Girdlegard

United Great Kingdom of Gauragon
Province of Fire
1023 P.Q. (7514th solar cycle in old reckoning), late spring

'That's odd,' said Hargorina, studying the surface of the road as they emerged from the dense forest of iron fir, stone spruce and black fern that grew as tall as a man. On the other side there was a raging torrent and a roaring waterfall. Spray coated the leaves and the travellers' clothing. 'I can only see one track. Wheels of a cart. No sign of anyone on foot.'

Goïmron blinked up through the treetops to the sunlight. The sun's power was getting stronger every day. He had been enjoying the tranquillity on the journey and he was looking forward to reaching the Grey Range after one more orbit. His light-hearted mood was now being given a knock. 'So, is that a good thing? Or not?'

Their progress from the foothills to the north had been largely uneventful, even though they had caused quite a stir in the local population. Goïmron never tired of relating their story to anyone who asked: they were off to find the greatest of dwarf heroes. He found it sobering to realise that only two or three of the humans they met had ever heard the name before. Goldhand had been almost totally forgotten. All the more reason, Goïmron thought, to carry on with their mission.

'Well, it's certainly unusual.' Hargorina sent Brûgar ahead to scout out the lie of the land. 'We'll be arriving in Platinshine soon. I'd have expected to find a few travellers about. It doesn't look like anyone is heading for the dwarf settlement at all.'

'Is this the only road that leads there?' Telìnâs enquired. They had acquired a horse for him in one of the villages they had passed through. Apart from a very few small personal items and his dagger, he had no possessions to speak of. His armour had gone up in flames when Ardin attacked. To keep himself occupied as they travelled, he liked to create little figures folded out of leaves to leave at the side of their path. 'Maybe this road will turn out to be impassable, so those in the know prefer a different route.'

'That would be nice if it were true.' Hargorina studied the luxuriant stand of black fern. 'Keep quiet, everyone. And ears peeled. We don't want to end up in an ambush.'

By this time Brûgar had returned from his reconnaissance trip. In the corner of his mouth he held the short stem of his special scouting-expedition pipe. There was a fine sieve fitted over the bowl of the pipe to break up the plume of smoke. This would make it less obvious to anyone watching.

'The walls are still intact,' he reported, as he brought his stallion to a halt beside Hargorina. 'But there are cracks everywhere. The mortar has crumbled away and the basalt and the granite blocks in the towers have disintegrated.'

'What does that mean?' Telìnâs made a puzzled face.

'Fire has raged in Platinshine. Incredibly hot fire.' Hargorina got her horse to speed up. 'Forward! Let's find out what happened to the fortress.'

Goïmron kept his position in the middle of the column of soldiers as they left the forest. On the way, he had cleaned up the flame flyer's severed beak, intending to preserve it as a trophy. He was keen to investigate why it had been the iron pellet that had shattered on impact with the beak, and not the other way around.

The great entrance gate to the fortified township of Platinshine was half off its hinges and the edges displayed obvious signs of burning. Through the gap Goïmron could clearly see the town's tall buildings, most of which seemed to be intact. Only where the fire had completely destroyed wooden beams did you see great holes in the roofs and walls of the timber-framed houses. He noted the acrid smell of cold ashes and burning. *By Vraccas! What happened here?*

They had hardly got through the gate when, riding along the main street, they saw heaps of bones, together with leather and iron items. Some of the armour still had the remnants of the charcoal-black skeletons of those who had worn it. Some parts had melted. Really all that was recognisable was the chainmail and the lamellar armour. Broken roof slates and shards of glass from smashed windows lay scattered on the road.

Goïmron was relieved that the horses did not react nervously, apparently sensing no imminent danger. So it was unlikely there was any threat waiting in the ruins. Occasionally, small rodents scuttled across their path. A black cat on the rooftops followed their progress for a while, then disappeared.

'There's nobody still alive.' Hargorina was distraught. They had reached the town square and saw nothing but smoke stains, broken façades and charred woodwork. 'The Fifthlings have either been burned to death here or they have fled.'

'What kind of fire melts glass and iron?' Telìnâs dismounted and picked up a skull fused into a melted helmet.

From up in the ruins they heard a deep voice. 'I am Barbandor Steelgold of the Fifthling folk's clan of Royal Water Drinkers.' The troops all looked up and saw a dwarf with a braided black beard. He was in full armour and carried a spear in his left hand with the arms of Platinshine on a pennant. The embroidered fabric of the flag fluttered in the breeze. In a harness on his back, the dwarf had a heavy battleaxe.

'I am the last of the watch guarding the settlement and the entrance to the Grey Mountains.' He looked down at the new arrivals. 'What are Thirdlings after, here in Platinshine? You come too late to provide support against the winged white monster.'

'I am Goïmron Chiselcut. Come down and we'll tell you what has brought us to this place.'

Barbandor inclined his helmeted head and shielded his eyes for a better look. 'But you must be a Fourthling. And for added oddity value, I see you have an elf with you.' He took hold of a rope and worked his way down to them using a pulley construction. 'I'll wager your story will be interesting.' He turned round and strode off. 'Follow me. Come and meet the other guests. Time to bring a bit of life back in the place.'

'So it was Ûra.' Goïmron rode up to where Barbandor was walking.

'How come you didn't pay up like everyone else?' Telìnâs asked. 'The dragon exacts tribute from everyone.'

'Because her special envoy was demanding something we were not prepared to supply. She wanted something that belongs to our folk and not in the greedy claws of this beast.' Barbandor tapped his chest. A pendant chain could be glimpsed above his armour. Addressing Goïmron, he swore solemnly, 'As long as I live, Ûra shall have none of it. I would rather toss it back into the river from which . . .' His glance fell by chance on one of the pack animals and he stopped abruptly. 'Well, I'll be . . . ! And by an orc, at that! Where did you get that box?'

Goïmron swivelled round in the saddle to check they would be referring to the same wooden item. 'I bought it. In Mallenia-gard. Why?'

Barbandor slapped his hand over his mouth then slowly lowered it, touching the decorative slides in his beard. 'By Vraccas! I know that chest.' He took a step nearer to inspect the outside of the box. 'Yes. That's the one all right.'

'Is it yours?'

'No. I saw it floating down the river when we found the ring and the silver amulet the dragon's envoy was demanding we surrender. I should never have thought I'd lay eyes on it again.' Barbandor went on walking. 'I let it go because it was empty. So now you're using it as a cabin trunk. Who'd have thought it?'

Goïmron smiled. 'But it wasn't empty.'

'No?'

'I found Tungdil Goldhand's journal inside.' He pulled the book out from inside his mantle and handed it to the last surviving member of the town's watch. 'This book is the reason we've come to Platinshine. We want to get to the Grey Mountains. To look for him.'

'By all the sacred halls of dwarfdom!' Barbandor turned the pages with awe. He stood rooted to the spot outside the remains of the guardhouse as he read. There was a caravan on the square with a placard promising THE MAGIC OF THE PLAY and announcing The fabulous Doria Rodana de Psalí and her true-life stories.

Seeing the name of the puppeteer woman brought back unpleasant memories for Goïmron. For ever and an orbit, that name would be linked in his mind with the death of his best friend. The friend he had failed to accompany on that fateful evening. So many things are coming together. It's all connected.

Barbandor handed the leather-bound volume back. 'It seems to have suffered a bit from being stuck in the box.'

'It was not the fault of the box. I had an unfortunate accident with it.'

It was embarrassing for him to be reminded of what he had done in his drunken rage.

'Orcs came out of the river and attacked us; perhaps they hadn't been after the ring and the amulet, after all. They must have wanted Tungdil Goldhand's writings.' Barbandor went over to the stone steps that led into the fortified guardhouse. The heavy steel shutters had kept out the terrible flames. 'If so, that would make it more likely that he really is still alive.'

'By Vraccas! That's it! They were looking for him. They were searching in the river for a clue as to his whereabouts,' Goïmron said excitedly to the Thirdlings and the elf. 'Did you hear that?' He lifted the handwritten work. 'The orcs were searching for this!'

Belîngor snorted and gesticulated: 'Since when do the pig-faces know how to read?'

'If they're still looking for it, we'll have our hands full.' Brûgar waved his war flail. 'The white dragon's next in line. She can join the queue.'

All the dwarfs laughed, dismounting and tethering their horses in front of the building. Belîngor stayed outside to keep watch.

Barbandor led the company into the dining room where two women were sitting at a table eating, one of them noticeably younger than the other. 'This is Doria Rodana de Psalí and her apprentice, Chòldunja. They came here to perform their puppet show about Ûra. Well, Ûra got here first.' He introduced everyone in turn. 'Now help yourselves to food and drink. Please enjoy the hospitality I can offer you in my capacity as the last of Platinshine's dwarf inhabitants.' He encouraged Rodana to speak to Goïmron. 'He's got a great plot line for you. It'd go with the Ûra story. Or rather with the story of Ûra's death.'

The company spread out on the benches, the wooden furniture groaning somewhat under the weight of Thirdlings in full armour. Barbandor saw to providing what was needed and then placed flasks of cool beer next to the water jugs on the table.

Minted ham. Malted bread. And even the celebrated four-herb roast! Goïmron realised how hungry he was and took a hearty helping. The elf chose food items prepared as simply as possible, such as bread with butter. He did not get on with dwarf cuisine.

Unobtrusively, Goïmron watched Rodana. That was how she asked to be addressed. The blonde woman was short and not of the typical human stature, he found. Her build was delicate and her face finely featured. Almost like an elf. He liked her at first sight. Her skin was darkish and her lips and fingertips black. All in all, someone quite special.

'How long will Platinshine be left without guards?' Hargorina asked Barbandor. 'After all, it's the way into the Grey Mountains.'

'I've sent out rock doves with messages to all the settlements in the area. There should be about two hundred Children of the Smith arriving in less than one orbit to ensure security again for Girdlegard. Before any beasts from the mountains can invade. Or get swept over here in the Towan river.' While the new arrivals tucked in to their meal, Barbandor related what had happened with the orcs and then explained how the dragon's messenger had arrived.

Goïmron saw that Rodana was busily writing in a little notebook. Chòldunja, on the other hand, was eating slowly, eyes downcast, as if she were having to force herself to take food. The most striking thing about her was her waist-length hair, one side brown, the other dyed black.

'What are you noting down?' Goïmron asked Rodana.

'Oh, it's the story. I collect stories. Then I can use parts of them in my puppet show. Audiences love a familiar tale but they also crave something original. That's what the present times call for.' Rodana reached for a tankard and filled it with the tasty beer. 'So, what's your story, Goïmron?' She pushed a strand of light-coloured hair back behind her ear, emphasising her high cheekbones. 'Barbandor tells me you've got a good one.'

'You were in Malleniagard,' he blurted out, although he had been planning to say something quite different.

'Yes, we were.' Rodana looked at him in surprise. 'Is this part of the story?'

'Well . . . yes. I suppose it is.' Goïmron heaved a sigh. 'That's where I live. Same as Gandelin used to. My best friend.'

'Not Gandelin Goldenfinger of the Stone Turners clan? But I know him!' She smiled at the memory. 'A very friendly dwarf. He helped me when I was being bothered by a couple of bullies from the Malleniagard city watch. He even helped dismantle the stage for us.' She glanced over to her apprentice. 'Do you remember Gandelin, Chòldunja? You two had been talking, hadn't you, just before we left?'

The young girl, no older than sixteen, nodded shyly. 'He . . . was very kind.'

'Do remember us to him.' Rodana sipped her beer.

'He is dead. Robbed and killed. That same night. Coming away from your performance and on his way home.' Goïmron found it hard to stay calm. 'He had asked me to come and see the show with him, but . . .' His voice failed as his emotions overwhelmed him.

'No, that's terrible!' Rodana placed her hand on his in sympathy at the news. 'That he is dead – that's awful. He was so friendly . . .'

Chòldunja nodded without looking up. Her long hair slipped forward over her face like a veil, concealing her features.

Goïmron was touched to see how affected Rodana was. He spontaneously placed his other hand on top of hers. 'Thank you, Rodana.' Their eyes met and the dwarf felt light-headed. Her way of speaking. Her sitting so close . . . It was a good feeling.

She pulled her hand gently out from in between both of his. 'Is this going to be your story now that I'm hearing?'

'No. It's only part of the story,' Goïmron stammered. He pulled himself together and put Tungdil Goldhand's book on the table in front of him, opening it up. 'This is how the story goes on.' And he talked and talked. The story was so riveting and he was telling it so fast that Rodana had trouble keeping up as she attempted to get it all down on paper. Sometimes she stopped writing and just listened, chin resting on her hand.

Goïmron finished the tale and quenched his thirst. 'So now you know everything.'

'*That* is the most exciting adventure I've ever heard.' Rodana sat up straight. 'We'll come with you. I want to see it all with my own eyes. It'll be amazing. We can see history in the making!'

'Why not? You'd be most welcome.' Goïmron's heart missed a couple of beats.

'What's that? By Lorimbur, no way!' Hargorina contradicted furiously. 'I've got my hands full minding a quarter-dwarf Fourthling and an idiotic elf. I am absolutely not going to take on protecting two puppeteers that can't stand on their own two feet if there's trouble.'

'Who says we don't know how to defend ourselves?' Chòl- dunja muttered, peering out crossly from under her veil of hair. She stabbed a piece of smoked meat on her plate.

'You can't really stop us following you.' Rodana's tone remained polite. 'We won't cause you any bother, I promise.'

'If I break her legs, Hargorina, she won't get to follow us, will she?' This was Brûgar's amused comment. He was busily filling his dessert pipe. The tobacco this time smelled like buttered caramel. 'Only joking. Don't fret. My bark's worse than my bite.'

'But it would help if you bit her, maybe,' one of the female dwarves from the company butted in. Her name was Gata. She lifted her tankard to toast him. She appeared at first to be about as serious as Hargorina but there was a glint of laughter in her eyes. On her collar she wore a distinctive silver brooch that was intricately engraved with an elaborate device: official seals were superimposed, one on top of the other. Goïmron did not recognise the pattern. 'Let's look at the practical side of things, Rodana. If we meet a load of angry beasts, you can distract them by doing a puppet show. And then we can sneak up from behind and send them off to Tion and Samusin.'

'We'll leave all the puppets here in the caravan. We'll travel light. And we're used to hiking.' Rodana did not let herself be put off by the jokey responses to her idea. 'And anyway, I can make you all immortal by putting you in the next play I write.'

'Oh! Well, in that case . . . Make sure you don't portray me as being smaller than him.' Everyone laughed to see Brûgar was pointing at Goïmron while he said this. 'And don't you forget to give my character a pointy blue beard.'

'I'm coming as well,' said Barbandor, to their surprise. 'We managed to save a few old maps in Platinshine. They might help. You know, I grew up at the foot of Hammerhead, Chimney and Saddlepeak. Those mountains know me through and through. And I know how to read their moods. Let me come along and do my bit to help find Tungdil Goldhand. To make up for having let his wooden box and journal pass me by.' He looked over at Goïmron. 'Don't forget. I saw them first.'

'No objection at all. We can always use a good guide who knows the area,' Hargorina said quickly. 'My thanks.'

'The sooner we find Goldhand, the sooner we can see an end to Ûra's reign of terror.' Barbandor spat into the fireplace. 'I'd happily give my life for that.'

With a loud crash the door flew open.

Belîngor fell into the room. He was bleeding from a number of severe injuries and his armour was hanging off him. He no longer had the strength to use sign language.

'Hargorina,' he croaked. 'Outside . . . there are . . .' He could not finish his sentence.

He was being supported by a srgālàh, a creature two paces tall with a head like a dog and the stature of a human. His armour was also damaged. At his side he wore a curved sword and in his free hand he carried a broad-bladed spear.

'The salt sea orcs have got spies in the town. We managed to beat them off and prevent them getting to the guardhouse. But they're still here,' said the srgālàh in a throaty voice. Belîngor collapsed on the floor of the hall, and the srgālàh supported his head. 'Two of them got away from us.'

The Thirdlings laid hands on their weapons. Brûgar, Gata and two of the others rushed outside to look for the orcs. The fragrantly spiced dessert pipe lay abandoned on the table.

Hargorina and Goïmron turned their attention to the injured dwarf.

'Where's the srgālàh from?' they asked, as he had stepped out of the door to check for danger.

'That . . . is . . . Sònuk.' There was blood trickling out of the corner of Belîngor's mouth, dripping down through his black beard. 'He had been chasing them . . . and he came to my aid. Otherwise . . .'

Goïmron was struck by how weak the dwarf fighter's voice was. The sight of the deep wounds was hard to stomach. Bones had been laid bare and one slash had gone through to reveal the guts. *May Vraccas keep his life-forge burning!*

'Get him up on to the table! We have to staunch the bleeding!' Hargorina was about to lift him up with the help of the others, but the srgālàh stepped in and carried the warrior carefully to the table.

Rodana and Chòldunja quickly moved to make room and Barbandor brought bandages. Hargorina rinsed her hands with brandy to cleanse them and started to handle the wounds. Very soon her hands were covered in blood. The wounded dwarf was screaming with pain.

Sònuk kept in the background, sniffing the air from time to time to check for traces of orc scent. The srgālàh with its elegant dog head resembled a mixture of a pinscher and a greyhound; its pointed ears were pricked upright to catch every sound. The creature had blue eyes with slit pupils and noticed every detail in its surroundings. The dark brown coat showed Sònuk's hackles slightly risen. Its forehead, the upper tip of the ears and its leathery nose shimmered with a gold colouration. The appearance was that of a noble statue.

Goïmron had heard tell of these beings, which refused to be called beasts of Tion's dark chasms. They stood on the side of Palandiell and were creatures of the light. Other races found this hard to credit if they saw a srgàlàh baring its teeth in a smile, displaying sharp canines.

They had arrived in Girdlegard from overseas over four hundred cycles previously in search of somewhere to live in peace and harmony with humans, meldriths, dwarves and elves alike. Few had achieved their aim in this respect, although they had all won a reputation for their determined hunting down of monsters. Even orcs, the smaller ogres and the trolls were wary of these creatures.

Brûgar came back into the hall with the other Thirdlings. 'They've gone,' he reported. 'I shot one of them out of the saddle. It had been riding a bastard-horse. I wounded the other one. Hope it dies a lingering, stinking death. I sent it flying with a spiked ball in its flesh.'

Hargorina cursed under her breath as she worked on Belîngor's wounds. The injured dwarf was biting down on a piece of leather Rodana had placed between his teeth. 'I'm having trouble getting hold of the artery. I'll need to clamp it . . .'

Chòldunja came over to assist. She plunged her delicate young hand into the wound with all the skill of a trained healer or a surgeon with years of experience behind her. 'There. You hold it. I'll stitch it.' Gata handed her a needle and thread.

When the young apprentice turned to one side, Goïmron caught a quick glimpse of the pendant she was wearing. It was made of wood and bone and there was a small coloured gemstone with an unfamiliar aura. He could feel the energy it emitted. This made him uncomfortable. But before he could take a closer look, the talisman had slipped back inside her neckline. *So what was that?*

The whole company stood around in silence looking on and waiting to know the outcome as Chòldunja finished up. Belîngor had passed out. She bit the thread and then dripped more brandy on to the stitches. Everyone sighed with relief. 'He should make it. But he mustn't be moved till the wound is healed,' she announced, and then went to wash her hands in a basin of quickly reddening water that had stood ready. 'That would be at least seven to ten orbits.'

'That means we're one short when we set off for the Grey Mountains. But . . .' Hargorina turned to address the srgālàh. 'I understand you are called Sònuk?'

Sònuk's triangular ears perked up even straighter. 'Nebtad Sònuk. But Sònuk will do.'

'How many pig-faces have you killed?'

Sònuk laughed, showing his teeth. Goïmron found the sight unsettling. 'Do you mean just now or altogether?'

'There are twenty dead ones outside,' Brûgar chipped in, scratching the stale tobacco out of the bowl of his pipe. 'Judging from their appearance, I'd say it was safe to assume he killed most of them.'

Hargorina looked satisfied. 'It seems my good Belîngor trusted you with his life. He would never have survived without your actions.'

'It was you who just saved his life, not me.' Sònuk gave a courtly bow.

'No, it was the girl who did that, really. But without your help he would have died outside.' Hargorina nodded to him. 'I know the good things that are said about your race. We have a diffi- cult task ahead of us. We already have a pointy-ears coming with us, two long'uns and a gemstone cutter, and none of them will be any good at all in a fight.' The assembled dwarves laughed. 'Will you join us?'

Goïmron felt rather put out. After all, it was his mission they were on. Hargorina was going over his head here. But he kept quiet. They could certainly do with another fighter.

Sònuk lowered his head with its long, pointed muzzle. 'Tell me more.'

The SAPPHIRE.

It can be royal blue, cornflower blue, occasionally white, yellowish blue or pale pink. To recognise its qualities, an expert eye is essential. Its defining characteristic is that it is nearly as hard as a diamond.

A sapphire is often applied in the case of eye complaints and is also useful as a treatment in melancholy, or in several physical diseases – for example, when the heart is not functioning optimally. The stone is linked with the element of air, unless the gem in question is a sea sapphire, but these are very rare. Magically gifted persons refer to the sapphire as a stone of truth, friendship, and constancy and it is said to give calmness to the soul. When used together with the appropriate formulae, magic can be very successful.

There is one aspect to be aware of: the sapphire possesses the potential strength of a bolt of lightning, can give warning of hidden danger, and intensifies the power of the imagination. Renowned stage virtuosos used to employ this stone in order to entertain spectators with elaborate magic performances.

Excerpt from
The Forgotten Power of Precious and Semi-precious Stones
by Sparklestone & Sons & Daughters

VII

Girdlegard

Red Mountains
Kingdom of the Firstling dwarves
Wavechallenge, western harbour
1023 P.Q. (7514th solar cycle in old reckoning), late spring

'So we've got at least two thirds of the northern wall checked out.' In the harbour master's office, Xanomir studied the wall chart showing which underwater sections had already been examined. His long grey hair hung free on the shoulders of his blue and white robe. He had braided his short grey beard. 'We should have it all done in three or four orbits' time.'

'It's taking longer than we planned.' Pouring tea for two of them, Bendabil let the hot drink foam like surf into their mugs. His weathered face exhibited the curiosity of an expert. He wore the tips of his beard waxed and twisted up and slightly outwards, somewhat like an insect's feelers.

'What is making the task more difficult?'

'Current and tides are against us. We have come across unexpectedly strong undertow at a depth of twenty paces. This means we've needed to put extra weights on the diving bell.' Xanomir was satisfied that his invention was working, even though the sea had thrown the *Elria Bonnet* sharply against rocks and the wall foundations on several occasions. The thick glass of the viewing porthole had withstood the impacts unscathed. 'Has anything new come up in the course of the salvage works?'

'No.' As Bendabil pushed the mug of tea over to his guest, the scent of mint and lemon wafted through the air. 'We've brought up the corpses of the poor benighted oarsmen. They weren't doulia. No trace of the galley's original three crew members.'

Xanomir sipped his drink and then added some honey from a jar on the table. He liked the extra sweetness but relished how the fresh taste of the tea wakened his senses. 'So the rowers were all in chains?'

'In chains, yes. We noted some unusual decorative scars. And their skin was a kind of bronze colour.' The harbour master slurped his tea as he made his report. 'The ones that didn't burn to death or get shot were dragged to the bottom by the weight of their chains.'

'How many does it take to run a shark-class galley?'

'Only a handful really. The galley slaves do the work. There's no sail so they're independent of the wind direction. And the vessel is easy to manoeuvre. That was the advantage of these Wrotland ships. That's as long as you don't think about the fates of the rowers if the boat goes down.' Bendabil put his hand into the top drawer of his desk to retrieve a small biscuit barrel which he placed on the table.

'Do you think the three foreigners that are missing can have made their way through to the Red Mountains?' Xanomir tried one of the biscuits. A delicious taste of mead and malt. *But how would they have managed to climb those steep slippery cliffs?*

'I don't think so. No one could have survived that catapult bombardment. I expect their remains have been swept away by the current and they'll be somewhere in the inland sea.' Bendabil dipped his biscuit into his tea and bit a piece off. 'We have told the folk at Seahold to report any dead bodies that turn up in their barrier nets.'

Remembering the three figures he had seen on the deck of the bogus ship *Shushkumush*, Xanomir thought about how the men had watched him. Had they been humans or something else entirely? 'They won't find much of them. The current will pound their carcasses on to the rocks and the sphyrae will have cleaned their bones of every bit of flesh.'

'Those arrow fish? What makes you think of them?'

'I caught sight of a shoal while I was checking the wall foundations. They had swum through to the lock.'

Bendabil wrinkled his tanned forehead, creating furrows and folds like hills and valleys on his weathered brow. 'Unusual. First we have the Wrotland galley and then we find sphyrae.'

'What is your thinking?'

'These predator fish don't turn up in our coastal waters normally. Not anymore.' As Bendabil shook his head, the waxed beard tips did not move. He reached for his pipe, ready filled and waiting for him to light it. 'What is it they say? Everything comes round again eventually. Even the shoals of sphyrae.'

'Well, I've no wish to see the return of a Wrotland galley here in Wavechallenge, that's for sure.' Xanomir drank some more tea. The whole matter of the enemy ship and the disguised attackers remained a mystery. How had a powerful magic spell kept them invisible? They had sent to Vanéra to enquire but had so far not heard back. Xanomir assumed the maga did not know the answer and had not wanted to admit her ignorance. Bendabil took another biscuit. 'These are really delicious.'

The harbour master's office door was flung open suddenly and in stormed a white-faced Buvendil wearing a long white and brown linen robe.

'It's gone!' The two other dwarves stared at him in surprise. 'The mobile diving bell. It's disappeared!' His words came tumbling out in a rush and he wiped the sweat from his brow. The little shells woven into the strands of his long blond beard trembled as if in a high wind.

'Now take a deep breath and calm down.' Xanomir pressed his friend down on to a chair. 'It can't have gone.' His newest wheeze to improve its performance was still in the experimental stage. He had been working on how to get the diving bell to move along flat ground by means of wheels, muscle power and the addition of balancing weights. There was still a hitch with the cogwheels and the transmission. 'You must be mistaken, surely. I've just . . .'

'I know, it's in dry dock. I mean, it *was* there. To sort out the movement-lever thingy.' Buvendil's gaze fell on the tempting mead and malt confectionery. 'But when I was about to go and fit the new cogwheel, there was only the tarpaulin lying on the ground.'

Bendabil slid the tin over to him without a word.

'It must have rolled down the ramp. Let's go and have a look. It can't have gone far.' Xanomir took the last but one biscuit, Buvendil the last. 'Let's be going!' There had been so much work invested in the diving bell. No way could it be allowed to turn into a heap of scrap metal alongside the ramming spur from the *Shushkumush*.

Xanomir hurried outside, enjoying once again the view of the town, the port and the proud ships coming and going in the harbour. The houses were built into the cliffs of the Red Mountain for the most part, so that only the wharves and the harbour master's office had needed to be constructed with large slabs of stone. The workers of Wavechallenge tended to live up in the caves where they could admire the sea and watch the weather as it changed. Xanomir quite envied the dwarves and the handful of humans living there. He would not have been so keen on all those steps to climb every orbit. And then you needed ladders everywhere and pulleys to get goods moved up and down. The residents were affectionately known as 'cliff swallows'.

'I . . .' Xanomir stopped short, noticing something unusual. A surprising number of bubbles were rising at the stern of a splendid Ceuwonian caravel just going through the lock into Girdlegard. Neither the vessel's speed nor the current could be responsible. *There's only one explanation!* Xanomir ran off along the harbour wall parallel to the ship. 'Bendabil! Call the watch! Tell them to block the tunnel entrance and raise the barrier spikes. We've found one of the galley crew survivors. And they've got evil intentions.'

'Straightaway!' The harbour master rang the big alarm bell that hung on the outside office wall.

As he ran, stripping off his clothing apart from the loincloth, Xanomir got ready to dive into the cold water from the quayside. Once under the surface, he looked around.

He was good at swimming underwater. He could hold his breath for more than six hundred heartbeats and he could dive down more than a hundred paces without weights; he needed this skill when conducting experiments with the diving bell.

My Elria Bonnet. *There it is!* He could see it being pulled along on the smooth canal bed behind the caravel. One of the air barrels attached to its sides had tipped up and was leaking its contents. That was what had caused the bubbles he had seen. He swam after the diving vessel. Drawing his knife from his boot and gripping it between his teeth, he spied through the inspection window.

Inside the diving bell he saw a large figure vigorously manipulating the motion lever. All the frantic activity was creating condensation on the glass.

There was only a small gap between the canal floor and the lower edge of the diving bell. There was no way he could dive underneath and slip inside. Suddenly the caravel's stern anchor was dropped. The captain had received the signal to halt.

If the thief turns round, he will see me. Xanomir knew the submersible's defence spikes could at any moment be used against him. *I'll have to be quick.*

The vague outline of the figure inside was looking through the window at the anchor falling past.

Xanomir stayed down at floor level and jammed the blade of his knife into the damaged air container. More bubbles escaped. *Let's see how long the thief can last without air.* Under cover of the curtain of rising bubbles, Xanomir swam up, stuck the tip of the knife into the window seal and levered the metal rim out of place. *Let's see if you've worked out how to surface.* He swiftly removed the thick pane of glass and then ducked down out of sight.

Water streamed in.

Obviously panicking, the thief accidentally operated the defence mechanism. Spikes shot out, hitting the wooden air barrel Xanomir was hiding behind. In fear of imminent drowning, the strange figure escaped through the open porthole.

This was what Xanomir had been waiting for.

Pushing himself off from the canal floor, he pursued the thief, grabbing his boot, pulling him back down and striking him on the head with the handle of his knife.

The body of his opponent fell slack.

There was blood on the forehead. Xanomir saw it was an elf wearing light leather armour decorated with runes he did not recognise. *Let's get you up to the surface. Then you'll tell me what you are up to.* Grabbing the elf under the arms, he swam swiftly upwards, aware he was running short of air himself.

Xanomir was suddenly kneed in the groin; this forced him to loosen his grip. He then received a heavy blow to the chest, robbing his lungs of the last of the stored oxygen. For the length of a single heartbeat, he was confronted with the deep black eyes of the furious elf face, glimpsed through a screen of rising bubbles. *Curses! Not an elf at all – it's one of the älfar!* His reflex reaction was to kick out. A knife thrust missed his chin by the breadth of a beard hair but then he felt a stabbing pain in his leg. Xanomir swam back away and up as fast as he could.

He broke surface, gasping for air, and with his dagger raised, he looked around for his attacker.

'Look out! Älfar!' he shouted to the guards standing with Buvendil and the harbour master. 'One of them was inside my diving bell! Get him!'

'Where is he?'

'He swam out. That way.' He pointed forward, then swam over to the quayside ladder. The calf of his right leg had been stabbed through but the blood loss was not too bad. 'He must have headed for the canal.'

The Ceuwonian caravel was waiting to make for the tunnel towards Girdlegard but in front of it in the line there were already four ships being guided through by tugs. Xanomir reckoned his attacker might be on board one of those.

'You're quite sure it was one of the black-eyes?' asked Bendabil, his expression doubtful. 'Why would they want to steal the submersible?'

'Who knows what they might be cooking up.' Buvendil checked out the cut on Xanomir's leg and applied the ointment and bandages one of the guards ran over with.

'That black-eyes had strange engravings on his armour: runes quite unlike the ones our local älfar employ.' Xanomir shuddered at the recollection of those dark pools of blackness that had stared into his face. 'I'm convinced he was not from Girdlegard at all.' He understood the implication. 'Those long'uns I saw on board the galley must have been älfar in disguise.'

The group on the quayside fell silent at this.

'By the sparks of Vraccas' forge! We've got spies in our Red Mountains!' The harbour master was outraged at the thought. He turned to the captain of the guard. 'Run to the fortress and tell them! We must leave no stone unturned till we find them!'

'Wherever they're from,' said Xanomir, scanning the open sea in acute concern, 'there'll be more of them coming, I have no doubt.'

Girdlegard

Grey Mountains
Kingdom of the Fifthling dwarves
1023 P.Q. (7514th solar cycle in old reckoning), late spring

Goïmron had lost track of time. He did not know whether it was day or night outside. They had certainly been down here for several orbits, making their way laboriously, sometimes having to crawl, through the passages and underground chambers and the ancient Fifthling halls, by the light of lantern and torch. It was warm here underground and the troops were all sweating with the effort.

'I think we're on the right path. This passage should take us directly to the Stone Gateway.' He indicated a turning to the right into a now dilapidated five-sided corridor.

'You're sure we've got to go all the way through the mountain?' Hargorina did not sound happy.

In addition to wearing heavy armour, they were having to carry all their food supplies and equipment. They had left their horses at the entrance as it would have been impossible to bring the animals along.

The fact that the entrance was unguarded meant that in the course of previous decades many daredevil adventurers had been attracted by the challenge. The tramping feet of beings who had no business in the Grey Mountains had spoiled the dignified aura of these underground spaces, robbing them of their magic and their beauty. The walls had been defaced by scrawled writing. They had seen the remains of others' campfires, with empty wine flasks and discarded bones from their food. There were indications that people had celebrated feasts down here or carried out dares. The original stonemasons' decorations had been randomly broken off and carvings unthinkingly destroyed.

'Yes. I'm sure. That's what it said on the last page of the journal,' Goïmron replied.

The further they went in, the less destruction they found. But they came across the skeletons of some orcs that had human-made arrows between their ribs. In order to combat these beasts, it was clear Gauragon soldiers had dared to go deeper into the Fifthlings' mountain than the adventurers who had used the halls for their partying. However, the main changes and destruction had been wrought by earth movements. The charts Barbandor had brought along did not always correspond to the new reality of the land. Sometimes they found themselves standing on the edge of a precipice or they saw their way blocked by rockfall. And paths had appeared that had never been recorded on the old maps.

'Friend dwarf, tell me again. Exactly *when* was that? Didn't Tungdil write the book in the winter?' Telìnâs complained quietly to himself about the weight of the load he was carrying. He took out a piece of paper and cleverly folded it into the shape of a swallow, then placed it in a wall niche as they passed. 'He could be anywhere by now.'

Goïmron chose not to respond directly, fearing he might be caught out in a lie. The final page of the book was missing and he was having to rely on his memory of what it had contained. He thought he was correct about having read a reference to the shortcut to the Gateway. But he could not swear to it.

'No. He is sure to be there.'

'Any idea how much further we've got to walk?' Brûgar was chewing on some dried biscuit as he walked. The flavour was cave violet. He had put his hiking pipe away while he ate. 'Surely more than one hundred orbits till we get there. That's if we find an easy way.'

It was clear the Thirdlings were not content with the progress of the mission their king had sent them on.

'Then that's how long it takes,' Goïmron replied stoically.

The srgālàh went up to Barbandor at the head of the column, nose in the air, sniffing out for danger. Rodana and Chòldunja were in the middle, helping to carry the equipment.

Sònuk said, 'Is it possible that you are not the only dwarves down here?'

Goïmron looked at him. 'How do you mean?' He had got quite used to the appearance of this dog-human. He was impressed by what he could do and liked his sense of humour.

'I've been noticing dwarf smell for some time.' Sònuk's golden nose twitched as he tested the air again. 'It's quite strong. I can smell it despite the sweat and tobacco stink our people are producing, which is a better advertisement of our presence than any campfire.'

'Yes, we all pong. But were you just saying you think we've found Goldhand?' Hargorina had been listening. 'That would be great news.'

'I've no way of knowing what type of dwarf it could be. In order to identify Goldhand, I'd need something of his to compare. The book is not enough. It carries too many other smells.' Sònuk was adamant. 'And I don't stink. I'm the only one who doesn't.'

'Charming,' commented Rodana.

'I heard something earlier,' Chòldunja chipped in. 'I have really good hearing, you know, and I . . .'

'Utter rubbish! There aren't any dwarves in the Red Mountains anymore,' said Barbandor, waving his lantern slowly around. He was constantly chewing and took to spitting out the occasional brown stream of tobacco and saliva. Goïmron had politely declined when offered the herb mixture. It made his mouth sore. 'Our tribe has been waiting for so many cycles now for it to be safe to return. We'd be the first to know if there were dwarves here.' He focused the light on a hole in the passage roof. 'What's this, then?'

The column came to a halt. The deep hole showed signs at the edges of a drill having been used. *That'll have been the long'uns prospecting for gold*, thought Goïmron.

'There's another one over here.' Using his lantern, Telìnâs had found a long narrow vertical burrowing, the thickness of a tree trunk. 'They've been using pickaxes.'

'Those greedy humans,' muttered Barbandor, laying his hand on the rock in the immediate vicinity of the hole. There were cracks and fissures to be seen, going in all directions. In some places big chips had come away. 'Can you see what they've done?' Then he suddenly placed his fingers to his lips and even stopped chewing.

In the resulting silence, they could hear a faint crackling sound.

Goïmron saw one of the fissures was getting larger, producing a zigzag pattern as it progressed through the grey rock. *A fresh wound opening.*

'The Grey Mountains have suffered a great deal with the quakes and the earth movements. All these probes in the rock will only be accentuating the damage.' Barbandor's face was serious. 'The old homeland is in a worse state than I had thought.'

'*That* wasn't the noise I heard before,' whispered Chòldunja to Rodana. 'I swear it, mistress!'

'Let's just hope we can get out of here alive . . .' Brûgar muttered. 'Maybe I should start a pipe of hopefulness. What do you say?'

'Better not,' said Sònuk. 'The smell gives us away. And anyway, that stuff is not good for your lungs. It turns them black.'

'Don't you try to tell me that,' the blue-bearded Brûgar said sharply. 'On the contrary. It's exactly what my lungs need!'

'Let us hope that Vraccas will stay with us.' The blond elf looked at the dwarves with an optimistic smile.

'It's Vraccas that's done all of this in the first place,' Hargorina objected. 'What other god had the power to move mountains and shake the whole of Girdlegard? Again and again?'

'Perhaps he does it with the intention of forming new mountains? You know, the same way that a farmer ploughs his fields to get ready for new crops.' This was Barbandor's half-hearted suggestion. He spat out the herb he was chewing and put a fresh leaf in his mouth. 'It is a testing time for us all. We have angered the god.'

'It wasn't us, though. It was always our task to protect the land. Only the dwarves were assigned that task. As you can see by the fact we've come along with the Fourthling.' Brûgar pointed impatiently down the passage. There were drops of sweat on his shining bald pate.

'Firstlings, too.' Goïmron wanted to make the point.

'The Firstlings let anybody through the water gate ready to give them a couple of gold coins,' Brûgar retorted. He unhooked his helmet from his belt and put it on his head, squinting dubiously up at the roof.

Barbandor gave a bitter laugh. 'And you lot allow anyone through if the king of Gauragon wants them in his realm. So stop pretending you're the great defenders with the purest of consciences.'

'King Regnor refuses entry to lots of people. And other beings. But with the Firstlings it's almost as bad as in Brigantia.' Hargorina surveyed the group morosely, shifting her pack and moving her red plait back over her shoulder. 'That's enough arguing. It gets us nowhere. It's a very long way to the Stone Gateway. I think I'm going to have to resole my boots before we get there.'

Barbandor consulted the chart Goïmron handed him, and took the lead. He was grinding his teeth but kept his anger to himself.

'I'm sticking by what I said,' said Sònuk. 'I could smell dwarves. Live ones. And they weren't smoking, either.' He tapped his long nose. 'I can rely on this. Always.'

Chòldunja refrained from doing more than nodding in agreement.

Goïmron noted what was said. He was keen to satisfy his curiosity. 'What else do you get up to, Sònuk, when you're not hunting orcs?'

'I lead a simple life in my village, together with others of my kind,' he answered. 'We srgàlàh are farmers. We keep animals and sell furs.' He grinned. 'Our sense of smell makes us the best hunters in the whole of Girdlegard. We are quiet when we move and we never lose a track. Nobody ever sees me coming.' He looked back over his shoulder to the young elf. 'Telìnâs there could only dream of being as silent on his feet. But I don't mind giving tuition.'

'I'm not sure he'd want to take you up on that offer, generous though it is,' said Goïmron with a laugh. 'But I don't think he will take offence.'

'How could anyone be offended when someone is showing them a better way of doing things?' Sònuk's ears twitched. 'Where I'm from, this would be seen as an honour.'

The company continued their march through the wrecked and ruined Fifthling halls and tunnels, whose original purpose was no longer obvious due to the damage they had sustained. They did not offer anywhere safe to rest, so however exhausted they were, all of them had to keep going: dwarves, elf, humans and the srgàlàh. They found shafts dug by jewel hunters and came across more of the drilled test holes that had been made by gold seekers. Guide marks were sometimes seen on the walls and there were piles of human remains in corners. None of the corpses had been there less than two or three cycles. It looked as if the monsters had been using the tunnels in the northern tract of the mountains as a staging post before moving deeper into the deserted Fifthling realm.

When Goïmron was exhausted enough to want to sit down and sleep in the middle of the tunnel, they opened a huge iron-clad wooden portal and emerged into a simple hall that had stone pillars supporting the roof. Looking up, they saw a large crack in the ceiling. Apart from that, the chamber was untouched by time. No sign of vandals or beasts having ever got this far.

There were empty shelves round all the walls. When forced to abandon their halls, the Fifthlings had taken with them everything they could carry. The only decorations on the walls were stone borders showing simple runes, stylised representations of cereal crops and different types of fruit, together with symbols of Vraccas and his blessings.

Barbandor referred to the chart. 'Here it is. It's one of the storage chambers they kept for brewing their beer.'

'I could do with some fresh beer. Or cold water that doesn't taste of sulphur for once.' Hargorina used her lantern to look for somewhere to settle. They saw old flagons discarded on the ground. 'The wooden shelves will do for a campfire. It'll be nice to cook our food for a change. I can't take cold cheese and ham anymore.'

'What was it they used to put in their beer?' Goïmron sat down on an empty crate next to some pottery shards. The Thirdlings busied themselves gathering timber to burn and Rodana and Chòldunja sorted it into piles, while the elf and the srgàlàh kept watch at the entrance. 'Malleniagard definitely has the best breweries. My cousin is a maltster.'

Barbandor held the map closer to the lamp to study the writing. 'Spices, pepper, orange peel, coriander and different types of sugar,' he said, indicating the abbreviated notes. 'And syrups. Black cherry, grass raspberry, blood peach, blackcurrant and nut-strawberry flavours.' He sat down. 'I remember how they'd tell us about the famous beers fashioned for keeping in small barrels or for jugs. Really interesting creations. Must have been delicious.'

Judging by the shapes of the pottery vessels, Goïmron deduced that the Fifthlings probably let the beer mature with the additional ingredients in the jugs, with corks kept firmly held by wire. 'What about the barrels?'

'Different types of wood, depending on what taste they wanted to achieve. I'd give anything for a cinnamon beer!' Barbandor smacked his lips and lifted up his flask. 'And all we've got is stale water. And having to drink that *here* of all places! If we ever find one of their breweries, I will start to cry, I know.' He got up and went over to help the Fifthling who was breaking up shelves for the fire.

Goïmron sighed and studied the way the hall had been constructed. The firelight was gradually making the chamber easier to see. *I can't think we'll get this kind of dwarf life back in the Grey Range any time soon.* With the light to read by now, he took Goldhand's book in his hands once more. He felt he knew its contents pretty much by heart, and considered the celebrated hero a close friend, but now there was something else. It occurred to him that the task was impossible. How were they ever going to find Goldhand in these mountains, with their thousands of miles of tunnels, chambers, mine shafts and ruined halls? The chances of meeting up with the hero at the Stone Gateway were, in his view now, vanishingly small, even if they ever managed to get there. *I really need some kind of a clue as to his whereabouts.* Goïmron leafed through the pages to see what entries Goldhand had made where. He sat and searched the text for repeated descriptions while the others made themselves as comfortable as they could round the fire.

Rodana and Chòldunja were entertaining the company with shadow puppets made from their own finger shapes, and making up stories about the adventures they would all be having here underground. Glorious tales of victory and prowess, of course. When they told the joke about the orc asking a dwarf the way, everybody's hearty laughter echoed through the chamber.

Curses. Goïmron's eyes were sore and he could not suppress a yawn. Before he could allow himself to go to sleep he must find the answer. *In order to have a proper sense of where we should be heading.* While skimming through the journal, he was also consulting the maps, looking up any location mentioned more than three times in Tungdil's book.

He had soon found a few entries that appeared to have been written in the same location. A place Goldhand referred to as 'Hammerhome'. He compared text and charts once more. It seemed the spot might be less than fifty miles away.

'I think I've got it!' he cried out, waving the map in the air. 'Goldhand will be in Hammerhome.'

Hargorina did not bother to look up from the cheese she was toasting over the fire. The smell was delicious. She sprinkled a little sugar on the cheese to form a layer of golden caramel. 'But didn't you say we had to go to the Stone Gateway?'

'I've had another think. I've been skimming the journal through again. We go to Hammerhome first of all.' He stood up to show them the spot on the map. 'It's the workshop where they forged the hammers and tongs and other tools they needed for working gold. He seems to have been there more often than anywhere else.'

'Makes sense.' Brûgar nodded approvingly, surrounded, as so often, by a selection of tobaccos. 'Let's make our way to Hammerhome. I'll fill this hopeful pipe to mark the occasion.'

Telìnâs had been creating one of his mini works of art: a unicorn fashioned from bits of string. Smiling with satisfaction, he placed it next to him as if it were a living creature.

'Right. I've been thinking, too.' Hargorina was still not looking at Goïmron directly, preferring to give her attention to the cheese she was toasting. 'We'll take this one extra excursion on, my little quarter-Fourthling. If we draw a blank in the forge and there's no Goldhand, then we give up and turn back.'

Rodana and Chòldunja looked at her in surprise.

'But . . .' Goïmron was about to object.

'I'm not spending the rest of my life crawling around underground in these dangerous tunnels. I've the others to think about, too,' the copper-haired dwarf warrior explained abruptly. '*One attempt*. Then we go back home. I've fulfilled my mission.'

Goïmron could not really hold this decision against her, but it brought him close to despair. 'Vraccas will assist us.'

'And so he should. Thank you for not making a fuss. You are more sensible than I gave you credit for.' She offered him a piece of the cheese as a reward. 'Here. Have this. It's done.'

Rodana's expression showed she was not happy with the new announcement, whereas Chòldunja appeared relieved.

Goïmron gratefully accepted the delicacy. His stomach had been rumbling almost louder than the roar of a river bear. He crunched the salty caramel crust and the melted cheese oozed into his mouth. It was the best thing he'd ever eaten.

All of a sudden, Sònuk raised his head, nostrils aflare.

'What is it?' Brûgar rolled his mouthful of cheese around. 'Can you still smell the dwarves?'

'Wait.' The srgālàh sniffed loudly. 'I can't be sure. You all stink so much.'

'Elves never stink,' contradicted Telìnâs.

'Oh, yes, you do. But I was mistaken. It's not dwarves.' Sònuk lowered his head and returned to chewing the dried meat he had brought with him. 'It's älfar.'

Goïmron felt himself grow icy cold and he almost dropped his cheese stick. All their chat stopped abruptly. 'You . . . are joking?'

'No. But I'm probably mistaken again. Nothing to worry about, in all likelihood.'

Barbandor and the Thirdlings laughed and even the elf and Rodana managed a smile. Neither Goïmron or Chòldunja were relaxed enough to join in.

Girdlegard

Black Mountains
Kingdom of the Thirdling dwarves
1023 P.Q. (7514th solar cycle in old reckoning), late spring

'Gunibar: move the barrel four degrees to the right. Ganibar: aim two degrees lower.' Larembar Goodshot gave the directions in a calm voice as he studied the situation through his long spyglass with its complex tubes that allowed a view over the battlements on the Eastern Gate of the fortress. The so-called wall-looker was useful for seeing round obstacles while the operator could stay safe under cover. The solidly built bearded commander of the eastern fortress was in this way able to give detailed instructions to the soldiers working the mechanical slingshot devices at the arrow slits. Even under heavy enemy fire it functioned well.

Four double-axle coaches raced along three hundred paces from the bulwark, whose entrance had been hewn out of the rock in the stylised form of an enormous dwarf's head. If the upper gates came down and the lower ones went up to meet them, the dwarf head showed a mouth grimly baring a fine set of teeth made of polished black steel. The portcullis-like gate also had arrow slits and openings in the stone face through which hot coals, burning oil or slaked lime could rain down on intruders.

Coming close behind these four huge carriages, orcs were galloping along on hairy bastard-horses, brandishing weapons, already sure of capturing the goods being transported. As well as the humans, who would be eaten for their meal.

But the orcs had not reckoned with Gunibar and Ganibar. *Or maybe they just underestimated their accuracy*, thought Larembar. 'Four shots each. Counting down: two . . . one . . . Fire!'

The giant catapults were activated by means of a system of tightly wound steel springs, and fired out heavy iron skull-sized balls. A short salvo was released from each engine. Larembar, in full armour, used his observation glass to follow the success of the shots, noting how accurately they hit home in the middle of the rampaging orc band targeting the merchant caravan whose supplies were so eagerly awaited in Gauragon. The power of the shots was such that they ploughed a path through the pursuers, destroying the armoured bodies. Arms, hands and great lumps of flesh were tossed in the air.

But the beasts had not yet given up. Whipping their mounts to greater speed, half a dozen orcs were hanging on to the wheels of the merchant convoy. High-pitched bugles sounded, urging the monsters on.

Let's stop your mouths with our heavy fodder. Larembar grinned as he watched the scene through his wall-looker. 'Adjust range: Gunibar! Two degrees to the left! Ganibar! Aim one degree higher!' Should the two giant catapults prove insufficient, he had five further devices at his disposal. *We're not going to need those smaller ones.* 'Two more shots each. Counting down: two . . . one . . . Fire!'

The magnifying lenses of the wall-looker gave the dwarf a good view of the catapults' effect on the marauding orcs. The six monsters exploded in a cloud of black blood and burst flesh.

Whoops of delight came from the operators of Gunibar and Ganibar, the two huge catapults, which had a range of over two miles.

'Have you wiped the scum off the face of the earth?' Larembar heard the familiar voice behind him. 'Or did you leave some for me?'

Turning round, he bowed. 'King Regnor. An honour to have you with us in the eastern fortress.'

'I felt like a change. There's always some action where you are. A nice little bit of combat. I fancy a skirmish with the beasts of Tion. Otherwise I'll start to rust.' Regnor dropped his wolfskin mantle from his shoulders, revealing bronze armour, fashioned with skilled mastery and providing hidden blades that could be readily employed in hand-to-hand fighting. Poisoned needle darts could be activated from the breastplate, blinding an opponent. The Thirdling knowledge behind this equipment stemmed from the ancient times of pacts with the älfar. Now their skills served in the fight to destroy evil. Regnor wore a steel gauntlet on his left hand while in his right he carried a long-handled spiked morning star. 'How many are still on their feet?'

Larembar shrugged apologetically. 'My king, you are too late. Gunibar and Ganibar have turned them all to mush.'

The heavy fortress gate opened with a rumbling sound to admit the merchant convoy to the first yard. The way through to the inner courtyard, behind which there was a shiny vertical wall of volcanic rock, remained securely shut. Larembar noticed how relieved the coach drivers looked. The carriages had been shot at with a number of arrows and one of the men had an injured shoulder.

With the entrance opened to admit the merchants, two Thirdling scouts had ridden out to check over the orc cadavers for clues as to where they were from.

Bushy-bearded Regnor snorted his displeasure. 'By Lorimbur's fist! I was so looking forward to a fight!' He gave an experimental swipe in the air with his spiked mace. 'How long do you reckon till the next brutes turn up?'

'It had been quiet for a long time. I think they were attracted out of their lairs by the smell of the goods on board.' Larembar waved at the dwarves below him in the courtyard who were helping the crew with the carriages. 'King Gajek's zolonarius was quite secretive about their consignment. Do you know what their cargo is?'

'Their papers mention dye powder from Uhfey.' Regnor turned to the new arrivals surrounding the royal envoy from Gauragon, who had just stepped out into the courtyard to greet them.

'Powdered colours for the dyers? Unlikely. That's never going to entice pig-faces away from their campfires.' The treaty with Gauragon specified that entry to Girdlegard was restricted to those with permitted access as decided by the Thirdlings. 'Far be it for me to accuse the zolonarius of lying, but I rather doubt our Gauragon friends are sticking to the rules.'

With solemn expressions, commander and king observed what was happening down in the courtyard. The longer they watched, the stranger the conduct of the new arrivals appeared, as they milled round the zolonarius down in the first courtyard.

'We seem to be making them nervous,' Regnor commented, running his fingers through his bushy blue beard.

'It's not a good sign,' Larembar said. 'I'm starting to think we've been deceived about their cargo, my king.'

'Have them arrested. They are not to be permitted to leave the first yard. None of them. Not until my daughter and I have investigated. She is the deputy commander and it falls to her to decide.' Regnor picked up his white wolfskin mantle and slung it over the bronze armour covering his shoulders.

'May Lorimbur have pity on them, should our suspicions prove correct.'

'So, we are to expect Regnorgata to arrive within the orbit, my king?'

Regnor stared at the commander in surprise. Strangely, the tattoos on his face let the right side seem more astonished than the left. 'Did she not get back to the fortress? It was two moons ago I sent her out.'

'No, my king. She left the Black Mountains. And on your orders, it appeared, from the message she sent me.'

'On . . . on my orders?'

'Yes.' Larembar began to feel uncomfortable. It seemed Regnorgata had acted on her own initiative without informing her father. He was not surprised. Everyone knew the relationship between father and daughter had been fractious for many sun cycles now. 'With Hargorina.'

Regnor frowned, his brows scrunched down in fury, almost concealing his eyes. 'Go on.'

'I don't have the communication anymore, but it said she was setting off with a few bodyguards. Heading for the Grey Range, together with a Fourthling dwarf, on a secret mission in your name. I was to speak to no one about it.' He held up his hands beseechingly. 'Don't be angry with me, my king. I am not even the messenger. I'm only the one who met the messenger.'

Regnor turned abruptly and surveyed the scene in the courtyard. 'You!' he thundered, addressing the humans, who jolted to attention and stared up at him, undoubtedly impressed at seeing his abundant blue beard flowing down over the coping stones on the walkway. 'You! The drivers! What have you got in your cargo? The truth now! Or I'll have you thrown out and the catapults will use you for target practice!'

The zolonarius took his jester-like cap off his head and held it in front of himself, as if to catch the threatening words. 'Highness, I . . .'

'Don't you call me *Highness*,' Regnor seethed at him, brandishing his war-gauntleted fist. 'Or I'll give you a bloody nose till you get the title right!'

Larembar was relieved to find someone else was the target of the king's rage. He gestured to one of the scouts who had just returned, indicating he should wait before trying to give his report.

'King Regnor, I wanted to tell you there has been a mistake,' the zolonarius called up. 'What we have on board are crates of moonberries, not dye powder as initially described in the paperwork.'

'That would explain it,' said Larembar. 'The orcs use moonberries to brew intoxicating drugs. They're never going to let a consignment pass without trying to capture it.'

Regnor laid his bare hand on the battlement wall. 'And when I get them to open the barrels, what will I really find, zolonarius?'

'Highness . . .'

Regnor grabbed a spear out of its holder and hurled it at the man without first taking careful aim. It crashed on to the granite floor close to his feet, making sparks fly from the impact, and then slithered to a halt. 'What did I just say, for Lorimbur's sake?'

'*King!* King Regnor, I . . . I am inconsolable. There is a slight possibility that a further mistake may have occurred. I must go and check. A misunderstanding . . .' The zolonarius stammered his way into the next catastrophe. 'But do let me say how much I admire your beard . . .'

'Save your schmoozing flattery! Arrest them all!' Regnor was incandescent with fury. 'Seize their goods and throw the whole lot out of the gates for the pig-faces to come for. And then I can slaughter them all.' The guards moved to surround the drivers and the zolonarius. 'The treaty with Gauragon is hereby revoked,' the king announced. 'From today I will be the only one to decide on who and what comes in through my Eastern Gate.'

'But . . . King Regnor! Listen . . . I . . .' The royal official tried his best to avert the worst, but the armed dwarves corralled the humans and pushed them towards the dungeons, where they disappeared, howling their protests.

'So,' Regnor snorted, turning to Larembar and the scout who was waiting to report. 'By Lorimbur, I enjoyed that! Those long' uns – you can't trust them. Let them fester in the cells for the length of a moon and then we'll see.' He asked the scout to give his report.

'They were blood groll orcs. They very seldom come this far. The cargo must have been extremely tempting for them.'

'So I should hope. I am keener than ever on having a proper skirmish,' said the king. 'We can use the shipment to lure more orcs. Take the carts and park them far enough away from the fortress so they'll come and take the bait and then we can ambush them.'

'As you command, my king.' The dwarf bowed and hurried off.

'Larembar, send your swiftest riders out from the western gate with a message. I need one hundred tharks to follow my daughter to the Grey Mountains.'

'Understood, King Regnor.'

'How can the heiress to the throne put herself in such danger?' he asked angrily. 'The tharks must bring her to me. Bring her here against her will if necessary. They are to ignore any orders she gives.' He slammed his gauntleted hand on to the top of the low wall with such force that bits of stone fell off on to his boots. 'And they can wall that wretched Goïmron Chiselcut up in the tunnels and leave him there with his stupid ideas about Tungdil Goldhand and reuniting the dwarf tribes.' Regnor moved over to use the wall-looker device and observed the removal of the four heavy vehicles. 'Lorimbur, I beg you,' he muttered, adjusting his blue beard. 'Send me some orcs. Hundreds of orcs!'

'Keep watch, my king. I shall be right back.' Larembar went off to compose the message and to select a rider to send it with. It occurred to him how glad he was not to be in the shoes of that Fourthling.

Girdlegard

Grey Mountains
Kingdom of the Fifthling dwarves
1023 P.Q. (7514th solar cycle in old reckoning), late spring

Goïmron raised the lantern higher and went up the broad staircase to the toolmakers' smithy, which bore the legend HAMMERHOME in elaborately carved runes overhead.

Catching his breath, he called down to the Thirdlings following him with the equipment, 'We are here!' He had Barbandor and Sònuk with him while the young elf and the two women brought up the rear. 'We've nearly done it!'

'No, we haven't,' stated Barbandor, shining his lamp on the barricaded stone door, around which the masons had skilfully carved stylised representations of tools. Cobwebs and a thick layer of dust clung to the heavy chains and the padlocks. He spat out a stream of tobacco juice. 'Sorry to have to point it out, but Goldhand is not here.'

Goïmron was not about to accept that his mission had failed. 'There ... there must be another entrance. Perhaps ...' He raced up the remaining steps to the threshold and hammered on the door with the flat side of his axe. 'Hey there! Tungdil Goldhand!' he yelled. 'We know you are still alive! Come forward! Girdlegard is in dire need of you!'

His voice and the hammering echoed through the tunnels.

'But nobody does know, though,' said Hargorina, leaning on the long-bladed war club. 'Please don't shout. I don't think we want to risk rousing anything else that might be in here.'

'There's nothing here,' Barbandor stated. 'Only ghosts.'

Sònuk raised a hand to object. 'And älfar. And dwarves.'

I must see with my own eyes. In his desperation, Goïmron kept hitting the chains and the locks till sparks flew. Dust and spiders' webs stuck to the blade of his axe.

But the barrier held firm.

'What do you think you are doing?' Belîngor pushed past the Fourthling. 'If it was that easy to get through the iron, they wouldn't have bothered to use the chains, would they?' He lit himself the hopeful pipe and came over to study the locks. Smoke covered both face and pointed blue beard. 'It won't work without the right key. Or without a very clever thief who can pick locks. We don't have either of those.'

'But we do have a puppeteer who understands fine mechanisms and uses delicate wires.' Rodana approached and crouched down to inspect the locks. 'Shine your lantern over here.' She unrolled her tool set to reveal a range of tiny hooks and files. 'Let's see if I can do anything.' While Brûgar and Barbandor held their lanterns to help her, the slight figure of the woman bent to the task of examining the lock cylinders. Her dark fingertips looked as if they were covered with the grease and metal filings from the tools.

'I would have thought that goldsmiths and gem cutters would be quite good at this. They have to deal with tiny fastenings and suchlike all day,' said Brûgar teasingly, blowing smoke at Goïmron.

'That's quite different. I've no idea about locks.' He cleared his throat. He would have loved to watch over Rodana's shoulder as she worked. He liked her. He liked her a great deal. And found her attractive. He did not want the others to know this. He had so often been laughed at. So he took out some maps on which he had noted other locations where the ancient hero might be. If Rodana couldn't get the locks open, or if they did not find any clues inside the workshop, he would have to try to persuade his troops to try somewhere else. Even though Hargorina had definitely ruled this out.

'And? Is it working?' Sònuk was observing Rodana's progress closely, as he leaned on his spear.

'I can feel the cylinders offering resistance, but with a steady hand and a bit of time, I should be able to open the lock.' She concentrated on the minute movements she was making with the hook inside the padlock.

'We can wait. Take your time.' Goïmron turned to Hargorina. 'Say we don't find anything in Hammerhome . . .'

She raised her hand to stop him. 'Save your breath, Goïmron. I know what you want to say. I said you had *one* chance. I promised you that. I keep my word. In everything.' Hargorina put down the kitbag she was carrying and her soldiers did the same with theirs. 'We will not be risking lives chasing after some fantasy of yours. All because of some lines in a book that could have been written by anybody.'

'Apart from by orcs, of course,' Sònuk chipped in, making the Thirdlings laugh.

'Barbandor said the Grey Mountains have become unstable. I trust the Fifthling and his opinion, especially since coming down here,' Hargorina went on to explain. 'Each and every moment we spend down here, under the tons and tons of rock and the total weight of the peaks, is highly dangerous. One orbit in the future I shall want a grave of stone. But not here.'

Deeply disappointed, Goïmron put his chart away. 'Understood. And thank you for keeping your word.' He had made his decision. 'I shall keep searching – if need be, alone. You can't stop me doing that.'

'Indeed. We shan't seek to prevent you. It is your own free choice. But we will have fulfilled our task.' Hargorina sat down on the ground, leaning her back against the tunnel wall. She shut her eyes and rubbed a cobweb off her pointy chin. 'Don't take it amiss. This is your vocation. Your mission in life. Not ours. King Regnor was generous to let us accompany you.'

'Whatever his reason was for doing it,' muttered Brûgar, drawing a last puff before putting out his pipe. 'I'm going to select a nice going-home tobacco now.'

Everyone gave a jolt at the sudden sound of the padlock falling open. This was the first of the locks, and the chains were released.

'Still another three to go,' Rodana announced.

Goïmron whooped with delight. 'Excellent! Thank you! How long will you need?' He wanted to give her a hug. *From sheer relief, of course. Only from relief.*

'I'm afraid they're getting more difficult.'

'We can wait,' he said with confidence in his voice.

Hardly had he spoken those words when a shaking and a roaring was felt through the mountain and the ground rocked under their feet. Goïmron had trouble keeping his balance. Bits of debris fell from the roof and cracks appeared in the walls, causing some of the carved runes on the splendid friezes round the door to break off. Soon there was a thick layer of dust everywhere.

This was all followed by clanging and banging noises.

Rodana gave a shriek, then there was an ear-splitting rumble. The rocks were still shaking and shifting, grinding against each other, screeching as if in pain.

'Rodana! What's happening?' Goïmron blundered through the fallen debris over to the entrance stairs. *She mustn't have been harmed!*

The Hammerhome doors lay shattered on the ground. One of the Thirdlings had been felled by them. There was blood coming from mouth and nose, his helmet and his skull were badly impacted and the eyes of the unfortunate dwarf were wide open and unseeing.

The puppeteer had managed to avoid the danger.

'Balendil!' Hargorina came swiftly to the side of the fallen warrior. 'Dead! Curses! The doors have crushed him.' She stared at Goïmron in fury. 'Happy now, quarterling? I've lost one of my best people and it's all your fault. He's been killed by a stupid door. We needed his strength to fight off orcs!' She grabbed Goïmron by the collar and shoved him into the Hammerhome chamber. 'Get in there and look for your wretched ghost! Then do whatever you want. We're going home.'

Goïmron stumbled into the dark of the workshop without replying. The Grey Mountains were gradually becoming calm. The noise died away, but little pieces of stone were still falling. *It wasn't my fault. I couldn't have stopped that happening.* Using his lantern, he tried to see through the dust. *Vraccas! I beseech you! Don't let Balendil have died in vain.*

With time the dust clouds settled and Hammerhome became visible.

The workbenches had been cleared. The dwarves having abandoned the place, spiders and all kinds of small creatures had taken over. There was not the slightest hint of Tungdil Goldhand's ever having been there.

I have made a calamitous mistake. Goïmron was close to tears. All his hopes for finding better prospects for Girdlegard, for leading the Children of the Smith to a glorious future, and for liberating his homeland from the murderous occupying forces had turned to dust. *The same dust that covers everything here in Hammerhome.*

He was overwhelmed with doubts about his mission. He heard Hargorina's words of criticism and he saw in his mind's eye the immense size of the Fifthlings' one-time realm, realising he could never in a thousand cycles traverse it all. And he saw the body of the unfortunate warrior crushed to death by the collapse of the stone door.

How could I have fallen for my own mad idea so completely? Goïmron pulled the book out of his shoulder bag. *How blind must I have been to think I might find Goldhand? To even believe he might still be alive? What kind of a trick was Vraccas playing on me when he sent the wooden chest my way?*

Family and friends in Sparklestone's High-Class Ornamental Jewellery and Gemstone Studio were back home waiting for him. The dwarf community of Malleniagard would be anxious for news of his safety.

Home. Goïmron weighed the book in his hands. *My home is in Malleniagard. That's where I'll go back to after this crazy adventure.* He placed the journal on one of the abandoned workbenches. *Let someone else find it. I want nothing more to do with it. Because of me, a Thirdling has met his death. And Belîngor nearly died, as well.*

In the distance a bugle sounded. The horn played a swift range of notes. Goïmron listened hard. *What's this? I thought we were alone down here underground.*

Hargorina came crashing noisily into the workshop. 'We've got to leave! Right now!'

She saw the book lying on the bench. 'Staying here? Or coming with us?'

'Whose horn is that?'

'One of ours. It's the call to action. Some Thirdlings need us. I can't imagine what they're doing here, but that's to figure out later.' The red-haired warrior walked backwards towards the doorway. 'You must decide.' Then she turned and ran out.

Telìnâs quickly entered the workshop and deposited one of the tiny paper figures he liked to make. This one was in the shape of a dwarf and he placed it in a niche on the wall. 'Well?'

Goïmron took a last look around the Hammerhome smithy – and then followed Hargorina.

Let me tell you what the buildings in the Black Abyss were like before the great earthquakes brought everything down. Down there, deep down, there are gigantic caves, bigger than anything any dwarf would ever have seen.

In one of these caves, ten miles high and twice as wide, there lived the cruellest of creatures. In the middle of this forbidding place, there was a gigantic building that was almost impossible to take in the sight of. Four square, fortified towers at the corners loomed straight up to a height of not one hundred, not five hundred, but one thousand paces!

On each of the four square towers, a further construction was placed, and its width and depth dimensions were twice the size of the lower edifice. On this second tower a third was built. And then a fourth on top. Can you even imagine what it looked like? The narrowest of the towers, the lowest one, carried the whole weight. Anybody with the slightest knowledge of construction would have to appreciate the masterly skill that had been employed here. And there was more.

These four strange edifices were interconnected by means of a number of free-hanging bridges, which gave the oddest appearance of a collection of webs between the towers.

Nothing other than pure stonework, unadorned, bald grey walls, of such a nature as to intimidate the beholder. Trolls and ogres, confronted with this building, would think themselves the size of tiny insects in comparison.

Excerpt from
The Adventures of Tungdil Goldhand,
as experienced in the Black Abyss
and written by himself.
First draft.

VIII

Girdlegard

Brown Mountains
Dsôn Khamateion
1023 P.Q. (7514th solar cycle in old reckoning), late spring

Klaey hurried past the great temple to Samusin and turned the corner into White Flowers Lane where it was quiet at this hour. *Tonight something tremendous will be happening!* In the course of the last few orbits he had managed to purloin several items of hooded clothing, so that, at least from a distance, and in the dark, he could more or less pass as one of the älfar. While the sun was still up, however, he would always stay in selected hiding places. *I shall make sure of that, you black-eyes.*

He had hoped that the älfar still kept human slaves for mundane tasks, meaning he might safely mingle with them, but Dsôn Khamateion had learned from past mistakes. Apart from the forty thousand inhabitants of the picturesquely sited city in its shaded valley, no other races or creatures were allowed. In this way, the dangers of insurrection or treason could be avoided. The stretcher-bearer party which had carried him to Brigantia and back had been specially chosen for the mission. Once their task was over, they had been killed.

Klaey walked slowly along the outer temple colonnade, keeping to the shadows.

To honour the god of wind and of retribution, the building had been constructed in triangular form, fashioned to resemble a block of storm-weathered marble. Coloured bone had been used to decorate the white façade, with the addition of white feathers and pieces of dark green and black glass. The dynamic arrangement gave the impression of a strong wind whirling around the temple.

Three älfar out walking took no notice of him, so deeply were they engaged in conversation with each other.

Excellent. Off you go, don't look at me. Formerly, his heart would have started racing at such an encounter, but now he could rely on knowing his way around the city and would be able to evade trouble. The danger of attack did not occur to the Brigantian. Not even in a dream. It would have meant his immediate death.

The ten-pace-high marble columns of the temple colonnade had elaborate carved reliefs showing triumphant älfar in combat. The decorations had been executed using the actual bones and teeth of vanquished foes. When first exploring the city, Klaey had not noticed the artworks, but now he had an eye for the cruel implications of the aesthetic habits of this dark race.

The city extended into a beautiful side valley, which mostly lay in the shade of mighty mountain peaks, whose names Klaey did not know. In the main valley, which ran from the far side of a wide basin and then gave on to a third valley, there were vestiges of the forests the citizens had cleared to build their town. The original buildings had been made of wood, but the more recent edifices were from blocks of different types of stone from the surrounding mountains.

The architectural style was bold and unlike anything adopted by elves or meldriths. The älfar preferred clear lines and inverted symmetrical shapes. Even in the case of a monumental building such as this temple, or the old valley fortress, the master masons had managed to change the impression of the massive walls to give a light and airy appearance. From his day-light hiding places, Klaey had listened in to the conversations of locals, picking up significant details, overhearing secrets and even witnessing forbidden actions.

In this way he had learned of the Secret Chamber meeting which was to take place in the Hall of Beautiful Bones in the temple of Samusin. Vascalôr had issued invitations to a cere-mony of sacrifice to the god, after which some important news was to be discussed, with the aim of thus invoking divine bless-ings on the Secret Chamber's decisions.

As soon as the three walkers had left the colonnade, Klaey climbed the rear wall of the temple and got up on to the roof, and then in through a small ornamental window.

At this giddy height, he made his way from one column cap-ital to the next. This meant he could avoid moving on the ground, where he might easily be spotted by one of the priests. He noted the smell of fire and spices, mixed with incense and a powerful flowery fragrance.

Klaey found a place to sit in the shadow on the top of one of the supporting columns. From here he could look down into the sacrifice hall. *Best possible view. The acoustic's good, too.* He kept his breathing controlled and shallow, for fear the fumes might hold intoxicants.

Now for the wait. He used it to think about what he should do following this meeting he had come to spy on. What he might learn would only be of any value if he managed to return to Brigantia and to his brother.

In the interim there had been plenty of opportunity for Klaey to learn the layout of the city. He knew the side streets and the gardens, but kept away from squares and public spaces where it would be difficult to hide. The älfar thought he had escaped and were convinced he was dead, so he was no longer being actively hunted. *Or maybe they just want me to think I'm safe . . .* Klaey studied the huge wall mosaic that was ten or twenty paces in length. Down below, priests were chanting praise hymns to Samusin. *And perhaps the älfar are only waiting for me to make a mistake. But I'm not going to do them that favour.*

The mosaic was formed with fragments of assorted bone types, some coloured and the rest left natural, some as large flakes, others worked as intricate filigree beads. Painted sections of bone gave the decoration a three-dimensional effect, so that Samusin himself seemed ready to step out of the wall to receive the älfar praise in person in their place of worship.

One by one, the members of the Secret Chamber arrived.

The ghostly figure of Vascalôr, wearing red, was the first, soon joined by the female älf of the particoloured face Klaey had observed on the battlements.

All in all, there were two dozen attendees, some in elaborate body armour, and some in glamorous robes as if for a significant social event.

Klaey made himself more comfortable. He had yet to work out a plan for escaping from Dsôn Khamateion. Going through the mountains would not do, as he would be spotted at the pass. He hoped that what he learned now would give him inspiration.

The service began with hymns in praise of Inàste and Samusin, followed by ritual denunciation of all other deities and cursing of any other forms of being. The priests then ceremoniously consigned a beautifully drawn chart of Girdlegard to the flames on the altar.

That's quite an agenda. Klaey was careful to make no move, although he had pins and needles in his right leg from his cramped position. Surely, even were all forty thousand älfar to take up arms, their army would never be powerful enough to conquer the whole of Girdlegard. *This policy will remain a theoretical threat.*

There followed a fervent chorused prayer to Inàste and Samusin, and with that the ceremony drew to a close. The priests left the sacrificial hall.

The Secret Chamber members sat down in a circle on comfortable cushions in the vestibule and were served with drinks and light refreshments by young novices. There was also a large dish with pieces of raw meat. No one touched these.

'I suggest we remain here to be closer to Samusin than we would be in the Hall of Beautiful Bones proper.' Vascalôr had waited until they were alone. He adjusted his embroidered dark red robe with its high black collar and stood to address the company. 'This will be a memorable night. For a number of reasons. I am looking forward to seeing how you react.'

He regarded the others with a satisfied smile. 'But first let me tell you the news I have received. Our spies reported that one hundred Thirdlings were on the march to the Grey Mountains. Going at speed, not sparing their horses, and without regard to the vagaries of the weather or any hindrances.'

'Are they following the band who seek Goldhand?' Ascatoîa looked doubtful. 'That would mean they were hurrying to offer support.'

Klaey watched her. With her striking hair, half black, half white, she was conspicuous. Over the recent period when he had concealed himself to observe the älfar, he had noticed several different colourations of eyes and skin and hair. Those with strange colouration were treated no differently from the others and no one was excluded, but they did seem to be given the less prestigious tasks as their responsibility. Ascatoîa was an exception. He had not yet found out the significance either of her title, zhussa, or of the distinctive jewellery she wore on her forehead, round her neck and round her wrists.

'That is also my own view.' Vascalôr took up a goblet filled with wine. 'Someone of very high status must be in the original search party, but this only became apparent later on. As tharks are being dispatched, I would guess it was a member of the royal family in the original party and that the ruler's consent had not been sought.'

'Do we want to capture that someone alive?' one of the female älfar suggested. She was wearing a blue silk garment worked with silver thread. It was low-cut and displayed her fair skin. 'It might be wise to have some leverage to use against the Thirdlings. Even if it is merely to force them to wait.'

'We should try,' said an älf whose full armour sported numerous inlaid ornaments made of the bones of his vanquished opponents. 'But not at too great a risk. Fighting one hundred tharks would not be easy, and combat in the mountains would mean an extra complication. If a favourable opportunity occurs, then let's grab and capture the scum. Otherwise, just kill them as normal with all the rest. It is not of ultimate importance to our plans.'

The assembled company murmured their agreement.

'I have furthermore received communication from our ships. The first small ones have got through the marine fortifications in the Red Mountains, disguised as merchant vessels. The groundlings had no idea who they were letting in,' Vascalôr told them. A ripple of malicious laughter indicated general approval. 'The initial preparations are underway.'

What preparations are these? Klaey found these vague hints intolerable to listen to. The south-west was a long way from Brigantia, but he got the uncomfortable feeling that sooner or later his own homeland would be affected. He was aware of the stories about how, thousands of cycles previously, älfar in the Outer Lands had set to sea on gigantic vessels, equipped with everything they would need for extended voyages across the uncharted oceans. They had taken stores of water, provisions and livestock with them.

'Arrival time is set for autumn.' Vascalôr addressed Ascatoîa. 'What have you heard from Undarimar? Are they with us?'

'They are. On my last secret mission on Arima, I was able to bribe Queen Aloka with gold, some construction plans and the prospect of having her own empire. So she has agreed to much of what we asked.' The striking-looking älf thanked the members of the Secret Chamber with a modest gesture for the applause they had given her contribution. 'As soon as our fleet sails through the groundlings' ruined eastern fortress into the inland sea, Undarimar will attack the adjoining states, to create a diversion.'

Aloka! That miserable little water rat! Klaey knew his brother had been in talks with the marine nation to try to form a pact. The centre of Undarimar was Arima, the largest of the islands in the inland sea, but Queen Aloka laid claim to the whole of the sea together with an encircling ten-mile-wide coastal strip. This attitude brought her many enemies and the nation was in a permanent state of hostilities on land and at sea. Cities and towns that refused to pay tribute, and any ships afloat that had not rendered the requisite sail-money, were attacked, plundered and destroyed.

Aloka had in her possession the swiftest vessels anywhere. And she had the formula for floating fire. Due to the use of specially treated timber, her ships could navigate their way through burning flames while ordinary craft caught fire and sank at once. It was thought that Aloka was making use of ancient älfar shipbuilding techniques. *Now I know where she got them from.*

'And what about Kràg Tahuum? Have Krognoz and his monsters been brought into the alliance?' One of the female älfar, sporting spectacularly long fingernails sharpened to resemble knife blades, addressed the zhussa. '*You* seemed very confident about this in your last report, Ascatoîa.'

'I'm afraid I am still waiting to hear from the orc fortress,' she answered, somewhat put out. 'I'm sure we'll have word soon.'

'They won't join us,' Vascalôr predicted. 'They feel safe in Kràg Tahuum. I know those green-skins and their limited powers of reasoning. They're content to terrorise their immediate environs without considering the bigger picture.'

'But Krognoz is a very clever orc. Tion gave him the gift of a quick mind,' Ascatoîa contradicted him. 'There must be another circumstance delaying his response. I think we should smuggle a spy into their fortress.'

'But if the spy were caught then we'd never get Krognoz to join the alliance. I'm against it.' Vascalôr surveyed the circle of faces. 'What do you all say? Is anyone in favour?'

Only two put up their hands. 'Then we continue to wait for their answer.' He reached for a dish of sweetmeats and helped himself. 'Before we move to the most important item this evening, I should like to hear from our noble friend Horâlor concerning the hunt for the missing mortal.' The threatening tone was unmistakeable. 'Have you found Klaey Berengart's dead body? You promised you would.'

Fear struck Klaey at this. *Curses! I thought they'd forgotten about me.* His name, pronounced by the spectral älf, seemed to make its way in the air round the whole hall and up to where Klaey was hiding at the top of the column, ready to shriek out his whereabouts.

Horâlor was nervously taking a drink before answering. For the evening's event he had chosen a flame-red robe with white sleeves and embroidered with black symbols. His long brown hair was kept back by a bejewelled helmet. 'We noted several thefts of garments, Honoured Members of the Secret Chamber. Berengart is undoubtedly using them to disguise himself. As one of us.'

'As I've heard nothing from the guards at the gate, I presume the mortal is still in Dsôn?' Vascalôr raised one eyebrow. 'Explain this, if you will. How is it that they cannot locate this human? His offensive barbarian smell should make him easy to find.'

'We thought at first we would find him in the sewers. The stench would cover his own. But there was nothing there,' Horâlor admitted. 'Every now and again the patrols sound the alarm, but by the time we get there, he has gone.'

'Pathetic. And that's our wonderful city guards at work, is it?' Ascatoîa's face showed dozens of black anger lines and one eye went dark as a starless night sky. 'Berengart could have killed dozens of us in the meantime.'

'He has his reasons for not doing that.' Vascalôr placed a hand on her arm to calm her. He gave Horâlor a reproachful look. 'He is spying. Trying to find out our secrets.' His expression grew merciless. 'Should this human get out of Dsôn and spread his new-found knowledge about us throughout Girdlegard, it will be immensely damaging. It is bad enough that we are forced to allow Stémna in.'

'I shall locate him.' Horâlor bowed an apology to the assembled members of the Secret Chamber. 'By the end of the—'

'No. You will be replaced. You have failed. You have not protected us.' Vascalôr looked round the circle. 'Who is for his immediate dismissal on the grounds of incompetence, lack of initiative and lack of prompt action?' All of those present, save the accused himself, raised their hands. 'Resolved in the name of the Secret Chamber. From the morrow you will be relieved of your post and a competent officer will take charge.'

This meant that Klaey's spying could not safely continue. *I have to find a way out.* He would not be able to leave via the city gates, and climbing through the mountains was out of the question. The älfar had soldiers everywhere.

'If we are currently on the topic of efficiency, what have you achieved in the case of the stolen relics from the sacred memorial?' Horâlor asked tartly. 'Perhaps you would be good enough to tell the Secret Chamber how successful you have been in this matter.' His smile was full of malice. He relished launching this accusation of failure at his opponent. 'What did the Brigantian tell you about this scandalous crime, Vascalôr? Let us forget for a moment that it was *your* custody that Berengart escaped from. Or maybe I should put your own competency to the vote?' He made a pretence of being sympathetic. 'We seem to have a similar weakness, you and I. And weakness is not what Dsôn Khamateion needs right now. There are others better qualified to lead than us. Don't you agree?'

The mood of the meeting became tense. Even up in the roof, Klaey was acutely aware of the change in the atmosphere. He could not feel his leg anymore. It had gone to sleep. He concentrated on not losing his balance. He did not want to plunge into the midst of these älfar. *They would be so thrilled if I did.*

'The name of the thief,' replied Vascalôr slowly, after taking another bite of the sweetmeat, 'is Mòndarcai.'

A ripple of outrage went through the Samusin temple. Two älfar sprang to their feet, while others froze in angry disbelief. Fury lines appeared on all the faces. The name seemed to evoke genuine hatred.

It's like with Vascalôr, when I told him the name. Under Klaey's right hand, a piece of the coloured plaster decorating the capital of the column became dislodged. He managed to catch it before it fell. But two small fragments escaped, falling and disintegrating on the floor.

Oh, Samusin! Please! In terror, Klaey held his breath. *Cadengis, protect me.* But the älfar were too busy being furious to notice. *Four or five heartbeats earlier and that would have been the end of me.*

'Quieten down, everyone,' Vascalôr suggested calmly, pouring himself more wine. 'I feared you might react like that and this is why I sought to spare you the news.'

'How long have we been searching for Mòndarcai? Our spies are at work throughout Girdlegard to find him. No trace. And then he just breaks in and robs us of our most treasured items?' The älf with the sharpened fingernails expressed her deep displeasure.

'He did not break in randomly. He had planned it meticulously,' Vascalôr corrected her assumption. 'Putting two and two together, according to what the barbarian told me, Mòndarcai came to Brigantia disguised as a meldrith, and sold the chart to some cut-throat out for profit. Berengart's troops then set off with it. Mòndarcai followed them and attempted to make it look as if the whole enterprise had been the work of the Brigantians. Had I not saved the barbarian's life, we should have known nothing of this.'

'But now he's roaming at liberty through our city!' Horâlor objected. 'Because you let him escape! Let's not forget that. We should ask the Ganyeios to judge your failure before the council pronounces a verdict on mine.' But no one took his side. 'So be it! I shall submit to the Ganyeios' decision! He shall hear my case.'

'What can the Originals want with the relics?' This enquiry came from the female dressed in the blue silk robe decorated with silver thread. She drained her goblet of wine. 'Or rather, *is* there anything they can use them for?'

Klaey paid special attention. *The Originals* once again. Up to now he had thought the murderer was a simple criminal, but this description implied membership of an order or a sect, perhaps. *A cult.* Something the Dsôn Khamateion loathed.

'There are no such beings as the Originals,' contradicted Horâlor. 'Not as we are being encouraged to think of them, at any rate. And so they can't do anything with the armour and the spear. No more than we can.'

The spectral figure of Vascalôr remained calm. 'I have sent out two scouts to follow hot on Mòndarcai's heels. Wherever he goes, we shall find him. And his brood of so-called Originals.'

So there are two distinct factions of älfar. Klaey glanced down at the treacherous bits of broken plaster on the floor. *By Cadengis' mother! What else is afoot without Girdlegard being aware of it?*

'Enough! I don't wish to hear any more bad news. And let's lighten the mood, please,' said Ascatoîa. 'You have promised the Secret Chamber something amazing, Vascalôr. Time to tell us about it, otherwise a fight will be breaking out here.' Her suggestion met with immediate approval. 'I expect that's what you needed the raw meat for?'

Vascalôr clapped his hands. The two novices opened the great door at the entrance and then stood aside, bowing. 'As you well know, in the course of hundreds of cycles, numerous magic beings have come here who were thought in Girdlegard to have died out. They will assist us with our undertaking.' Reaching into the dish, he lifted up a bloody piece of meat. 'Many unicorns, from which I have bred a new night-mare generation, died in the experiment to transform them. Which was unfortunate.' He tossed the meat over to the threshold.

The meat flew through the air, releasing a trail of bloody drops on the marble floor before landing with a slurping smack on the stone.

Klaey adjusted his position in order to get a better view. *What is this ghostly black-eyes up to?*

The sound of hooves was heard, together with an audible snorting noise.

The älfar craned their necks to see, some getting to their feet. Black horse nostrils appeared, followed by the muzzle and the head, in which blood-red eyes glowed. Then a slim neck. On the horse's brow, Klaey discerned the mark where a horn had been cut. Älfar blood had been drizzled on to the stump to effect the creature's transformation.

'Oh! What a beautiful night-mare,' whispered Ascatoîa, spellbound.

'It is extremely . . . slender,' added a stunned Horâlor. 'Is it still young?'

Carefully, the lethally elegant black creature stepped into the temple, snorting. It went towards the offering of fresh meat. As it stretched its neck forward to grab the enticing food, its long sharp incisors became visible.

Vascalôr whistled and threw a second hunk of meat extremely high into the air. With a neigh, the night-mare took off, and in mid-leap, it unfolded a pair of mighty wings which brought it swiftly up to where the meat was. Grasping the prize between its teeth, the animal executed an arc, landing gracefully back down on the temple floor.

That creature very nearly caught sight of me up here! Klaey wished fervently to be the size of a mouse. *Or an insect. Better still.* Something too small to be seen.

'I call my creation a flight-mare,' Vascalôr explained with pride, casting another piece of meat the animal's way. 'Created from a particular type of unicorn we found about ten cycles ago. It took some time for us to succeed in capturing one alive to experiment on.'

'All praise to Inàste! Just look at that!' Ascatoîa was beside herself with delight. 'It is . . . absolutely beautiful!'

'It certainly is that. It goes by the name of Phlavaros. It will be the basis for a whole army of flight-mares that can take us anywhere we want to go in Girdlegard, much quicker than we could get there with any cavalry regiment.' Vascalôr bestowed on the demoted guard commander a look of contempt. 'Combined with the weapons we have on our ships, even the dragons will be in awe of us.'

The Secret Chamber älfar congratulated Vascalôr heartily. Horâlor slipped out of the room. It seemed the evening had brought him one defeat after another. He had lost his post, his task and his reputation.

The flight-mare stood waiting in the temple. Stamping its fore-hoof on the marble in such a way as to cause sparks to fly, it eyed the dish of remaining meat eagerly.

Airborne cavalry. Klaey saw something other than the prospect of future military superiority or conquering the skies. He saw the possibility of escape. *That's how I can get out of Dsôn.* That's if the beast didn't have him for dinner first.

Girdlegard

Grey Mountains
Kingdom of the Fifthling dwarves
1023 P.Q. (7514th solar cycle in old reckoning), late spring

Bringing up the rear of the group running through the tunnels, Goïmron was fighting for breath. He was no longer in charge of operations and had taken on a heavier luggage burden in order to relieve Chòldunja. Hargorina was now the commander and led them through the corridors and halls according to Barbandor's directions. Brûgar was always muttering about having no time to light himself a war pipe.

The distant bugle summons was now constant. However, Goïmron felt the call to the attack was now sounding further away, as if they were being teased and led a dance as they advanced to assist.

In his new role as kitbag-bearer, he felt fine, apart from the weight of the equipment he was carrying. *We've been going round in circles for ages.* He recognised the detour they had made because of his insistence that they go to the Stone Gateway. Hammerhome was situated near the entrance, in the south. *It would have taken us less than an orbit to get there.*

Hargorina took a side turning, calling back to the others, 'Mind the cracks and obstacles underfoot. It doesn't bode well.'

'I'd say that *war bugle call* doesn't bode well either,' Goïmron muttered.

Apart from his axe, his darts and a sling, he carried no weapon. He wasn't bad with a sword blade. Like most Fourth-lings, he showed more talent with crossbow and slings than with a battleaxe or a war club. He now wished he had been more ambitious about winning the shooting competitions the dwarf community liked to hold, back in Malleniagard. His father had been a champion.

Sònuk appeared at his side. 'All right?'

'Don't tell me you can smell my fear?' Goïmron looked at him imploringly. 'And even if you can, then please don't let on.'

'It's not precisely fear. But I can sense that you are uneasy. In your position I should feel the same, I know.' Sònuk raised his spear with its broad, jagged blade. 'I'll watch out for you. We have ended our mission, but I shall continue to protect you.'

'Many thanks.' Goïmron was genuinely grateful.

'We are nearly there. I can hear the noise of fighting. Brûgar, to me! Get ready,' ordered Hargorina. 'Long'uns! Stay back. You as well, Goïmron. I can't guarantee your safety. We'll meet up again after the battle. We'll drink to the deaths of our enemies!' As she ran, she jettisoned her kitbag and her Thirdling soldiers followed suit. Lamps and weapons in their hands, they entered a hall that a faint light was coming from. 'For-ward! For Lorimbur!'

The clash of steel and the crash of shields sounded out to the others in the tunnel. They could hear a shout, a grim peal of laughter, a command and a many-throated confirming response.

Sònuk took up a position in front of the women and the Fourthling, to protect them. 'Let me and the elf go first. We are used to fighting and to the sight of open wounds.'

Telìnâs agreed, his expression determined. 'No one will get past us to hurt you.'

The elf sounds as if he were two hundred cycles of age, not twenty. It was hard for Goïmron to look past their defenders to see what was happening in the hall that had once served the Fifthlings as a stable, as was clear from the wooden stalls and iron wall-mounted rings for tethering horses. 'Let me have a look.'

A unit of Thirdlings was standing in a closed tortoise formation in the centre of the room, holding their shields over their heads. Arrows arriving out of the dark bounced off or shattered.

At a command from the protective wall, one shield opened to make a gap and a cloud of crossbow bolts shot out. Immediately the gap was covered once more. These Thirdlings were implementing a well-rehearsed manoeuvre. Several armoured dwarf soldiers lay dead or injured on the ground, having been hit by arrows, or slashed with swords. There was blood coursing along the floor and seeping into the cracks. The enemy had done away with at least a dozen, without apparently sustaining any losses.

Who . . .? The glimpse Goïmron managed to catch of their shadowy opponents made his blood run cold. *Älfar!*

One of the enemy archers leaped up on to a high rocky outcrop, took a shimmering bow from its holder behind his back, and in a swift, fluid movement, laid a black arrow in place and fired.

The missile went straight through one of the shields, creating a momentary gap in the shield wall. The air was full of the swish of arrows. The super-length älfar arrows rained down mercilessly on the opening in the Thirdlings' defences. Cries of pain indicated the number injured or dying. The upturned dish of shields began to topple.

In the nick of time, Hargorina darted forward with her soldiers, making enough noise to prove a distraction, and letting the defensive shield formation gather once more.

Up on the high outcrop, the älf took another deadly arrow out of the quiver at his belt.

'Wretched black-eyes!' yelled Telìnâs, grabbing an abandoned crossbow and taking aim. 'Get you gone to your false gods!' He fired.

Coming from below, the bolt hit the älf under the unprotected chin, just as he had been in the process of pulling back his bowstring. He was thrown aside by the impact.

'They can't hold out much longer,' said Sònuk. 'There are at least twenty black-eyes against them. They have strong steel bows. The dwarves have no chance. They'll be shot down like gamebirds in a clearing.'

Chòldunja pointed something out to Rodana. 'Look! What's going on up there?'

Goïmron could make out some drill holes on the ceiling, similar to those they had observed at different points on their journey through the Grey Mountains. At the next bugle call from inside the shield formation, cracks appeared and widened, making deep crevices between the drill holes.

Immediately a huge block of stone, the diameter of a wagon wheel, came loose from the ceiling and crashed down, taking two älfar by surprise and crushing them.

The shock caused the ground underfoot to shake terrifyingly.

It's all going to collapse! Goïmron instinctively ran out past Telìnâs and Sònuk.

'Hargorina! Get out of here! You must get out! All of you. The cave . . .'

Whole slabs of stone fell crashing to the floor, raising great clouds of dust. With the first impact, his vision was impaired by the smoke-like debris. The pressure wave knocked him off his feet but he was caught before he hit the ground.

'You have been courageous enough. But now it is time to leave,' said Sònuk, lifting him to his feet. 'I will take you. Don't try to resist. You can be proud again later.' The walls, floor and ceiling continued to shake. The Grey Mountains were trying to rid themselves of the intruders by burying them alive. Goïmron heard the rocks cracking and bursting, the noise mixing with the sounds of the Thirdlings' war shouts. He did not want to be carried away from the fighting like a coward. But he was not able to loosen the grip the srgālàh had on him.

'Where are Hargorina and the others?' He had finally managed to get the dirt out of his eyes. His lantern showed the clefts and fissures in the tunnel walls. They would not be able to withstand the damage for long.

'They're close behind us. I can smell fresh air. If we follow this corridor, we can get . . .' But Sònuk halted abruptly and quickly raised his spear.

There was a clang as the jagged blade met steel.

An älf in black armour confronted them, leaping out of a side tunnel. 'You shall die along with the groundlings, you misbegotten freak,' he threatened, kicking the srgālàh in the belly. 'None shall escape us!'

Sònuk released his hold on Goïmron and parried the swift attack from the älf's two swords.

But where is Hargorina? Whichever way he looked, there was no sign of the others, but a thick wave of dust was rolling towards him. There had been a new collapse in the tunnel to their rear. *They are sure to find themselves a different way out.* Goïmron fought down his fear and put the lantern aside. He quickly prepared his sling and shot at the älf, who was getting the better of Sònuk.

The steel ball from the sling hit the enemy with a crack on the back of his neck, just above the black armour.

The älf jerked round, cursing, hurling the shorter of his two swords at the dwarf.

Goïmron dodged the flying blade and it crashed into his lantern, extinguishing its light except for a residual glow from the wick.

As a Child of the Smith, Goïmron could see well in the half darkness and was able to keep firing his slingshot at his opponent, aiming at his knees. The älf cursed, staggered and began to limp.

Sònuk took advantage of this weakness to stab his blade into the chest of his foe. The sharpened steel spear penetrated the black armour plates, then went through skin and bone and heart. The älf collapsed with a groan, his long sword clattering to the floor.

Goïmron blew gently on the glowing wick to bring the lantern flame to life again. 'Where is Hargorina?'

Sònuk sniffed the air behind them. 'She's not here any longer. She'll have gone another way.' As he walked past, he placed a hand on Goïmron's shoulder. 'Thank you for what you did. That black-eyes would have finished me off.'

'But of course.' They hurried along the tunnel side by side. Bits of stone and crumbled rock were still raining down. The dust was making it difficult to breathe.

Goïmron espied new drill holes and test shafts made by greedy hands in search of treasure. *The Grey Mountains will not forgive them. They want revenge.*

At last they found themselves approaching a huge broken door through which rays of sunlight shone.

'Quickly!' Sònuk urged. 'I can hear more cracks forming. They're going into the depths and right up to the heights.'

Goïmron had never run so fast in his entire life. Behind them, the roof of the tunnel fell in with an enormous series of crashes. Staggering, he and Sònuk emerged from the destruction of the tunnel, accompanied by rolling clouds of dust and debris.

Hardly had they reached the outside world when they lost their footing on the shaking ground, and both slithered down the slope on a landslide of pebbles, finally ending up in a meadow fifty paces below, with scattered blocks from the collapsing tunnels all around them.

His mouth was full of dust. He spat out the dirt and levered himself upright. *Where are the others?* His back hurt, and his arms were grazed and throbbed painfully. He turned his blue gaze back up to where they had left the mountain. His breath failed him as he took in the scene with horror.

The last of the mighty peaks had collapsed in on itself, sending up a fountain of debris and dirt. A volcanic magma eruption was in full swing on the left, sending ash and glowing rocks hundreds of paces into the air. Where ancient rock formations had disappeared there were now gaps like bloodied wounds.

The Grey Mountains . . . are disappearing! Goïmron staggered back. The holes that had been drilled and the shafts that had been dug had hollowed out the underlying rocks and weakened the whole structure of Vraccas' mighty work. With tears in his eyes, Goïmron watched the continuing devastation. The billowing clouds of ash increased in size. *The long'uns are to blame for this. With their greed they have murdered the mountains!*

A black arrow whirred through the air, striking Sònuk in the shoulder. Making a noise like a combined scream and a bark, he grabbed the shaft and snapped it off. 'Those confounded blackeyes. Why didn't the mountain bury them all?'

Goïmron caught sight of a handful of dust-covered Thirdlings moving higher up on the slope. Their armour and shields were dented and scraped. The dwarves were in a reduced wall formation, trying to fend off an älfar attack. 'There! It's Hargorina! We've got to help her.'

He bounded up, leaping from boulder to boulder, to get to the dwarves fighting for their lives. If he could cause a momentary distraction by firing slingshots at the attackers and thus save his companions, all would not have been in vain.

But twenty paces further on and with two black arrows forcing him to seek cover, Goïmron had to admit defeat. *I can't save them.* As soon as he dared peek round the rock he was hiding behind, another arrow flew his way. He had no idea where the archer was shooting from.

Again they heard the bugle call to battle, urging the Thirdlings to fight on.

By now there were fewer than two dozen still on their feet, aiming their crossbow fire at the wraith-like älfar flitting in and out. *It's as if they were shadows!*

To his right, Goïmron glimpsed Rodana and Chòldunja sheltering behind a rock. Telìnâs was in close combat with an älf, trying to protect the two women. The young elf was revealing himself to be a skilled fighter. *It's obvious he's fought against them in the past.*

'Now I've got you, wretched groundling,' came a voice at his ear. Goïmron was grabbed by the collar and dragged off his feet so that he landed face down in the long grass. 'Did you think my arrows were missing you? No. I wanted you to stay here so I could come and get my hands on you.' He felt the weight of a soft-booted foot on the nape of his neck. 'You must be the Fourthling trying to find Goldhand. Your scrawny size betrays you.'

Goïmron could not wriggle out from under the pressure on his neck and spine. 'May you be prey for the hungry demons!' he cursed, gasping.

'I certainly shan't.' The älf laughed down at him. 'You can't see it, groundling, but your mountain maggot friends are falling.

One by one. You'll be the last one to die. I've killed Fourthlings aplenty in the past. They have their uses. I can do a design or two for myself, using your preserved heart's blood as ink.'

Goïmron's despair was overwhelming. He lay caught like some worm wriggling under the enemy's foot, destined for an unseemly and undignified death. And then to serve as material for the dark aesthetics of a cruel race.

'Say – what made you believe it?'

'What?' asked Goïmron.

'That Goldhand might still be living. He would have to be more than one thousand cyc–' His opponent was abruptly silenced, following loud crashes and clangs.

The pressure on his neck had gone and he felt a warm liquid splash down on him. *Blood! It's the älf's blood!* He rolled quickly on to his back and looked round.

But there was no one to be seen.

His torturer had fallen face down on the ground. A brutal cut had sliced him open through his armour from nape to buttocks, his spine divided lengthwise.

'Sònuk?'

There came no reply from the srgàlàh.

Telìnâs was still occupied. Rodana and Chòldunja had attempted to intervene, but because of the speed at which the älf moved, they had not been able to score a hit. But they had both suffered blows and kicks.

The Thirdling battle horn sounded again.

I must help them! Goïmron sprang to his feet. The sight of the sliced-open corpse made him retch but he mastered his nausea and hurried to the place where elf and älf were fighting. As he made his way there, he loaded his sling with metal.

Another älf suddenly loomed up on his left-hand side, with a shining steel bow in his grip aimed straight at red-haired Hargorina as she stood boldly in front of her troops, as if she

MARKUS HEITZ | 261

were invulnerable, though all she had to protect her was her shield.

Without pausing to think, Goïmron loosed his missile.

The metal ball hit the älf's armour. Black eyes turned to focus on the dwarf – and then the dark figure toppled slowly forward, crashing on to the grass. His bow and his black arrow landed harmlessly beside him.

What is . . . By Vraccas . . .? This time it was clear that a blade had opened the flesh up with a horizontal slash, slicing the älf practically in two. He was held together solely by his armour.

'Look out, gemstone carver!' Brûgar yelled, pointing upwards. 'There's another one.'

Goïmron reloaded his sling and aimed it but the archer had already released the shot. The black arrow flew straight at a blonde dwarf in Hargorina's troop.

Seeing this, Hargorina sprang into the path of the missile, holding out her shield to intercept the arrow, but the protection was insufficient. She was struck through her armour and arm, and the arrow buried itself in her side. There was no defence against an archer's shot from such a distance. The dwarf commander fell, badly injured, her arm and shield now pinned to her body.

'For Lorimbur!' yelled Brûgar, stepping in and whirling his war flail. 'For Hargorina!'

'No!' she called. 'Protect Gata! Get her away from here!'

Before Goïmron had recovered from the shock, he saw the dark archer collapse at his feet. A battleaxe with a mighty blade was stuck in his back. *Another one!* He lifted his arm with the sling, ready to fire. *We'll have them all soon! There can't be many more!*

An älfar command sounded and three remaining enemy figures sprang from all sides at the Thirdlings, who were desperately fighting to protect Gata.

Goïmron's sling seemed to him a pathetic weapon. *But it's better than doing nothing.* Yelling furiously, he stepped forward, sending out shot after shot. He hit his targets often but the power behind the metal balls was nothing in comparison to the force of a mechanised sling device. He tried to aim for the unprotected faces. Of the Thirdling band, only Brûgar, Gata and some of the soldiers from the Black Mountains were still standing. *Vraccas . . . the älfar are wiping us out.* Goïmron fired his last shot and took out his axe. *It is all my fault. If I hadn't talked Regnor into sanctioning the mission, no dwarf life would have been lost here. No Child of the Smith deserves such a senseless death.* In total despair, he flung himself at an älf, convinced, however, that it would be the last act of his life. 'For Hargorina!'

A vague shape raced past, shoving him aside, and a double axe whirred through the air to strike the älf in the belly. Felled, the älf toppled backwards.

What Goïmron saw was an ancient dwarf with a flowing silver beard, and polished armour shining dazzlingly bright in the sunlight. In his hands, he bore a long-shafted axe with which he was setting out to belabour the remaining adversaries. A golden mark glinted on his hand. *Goldhand!*

'Attack!' shouted Brûgar enthusiastically, whirling his flail. 'Death to the black-eyes!'

One confused älf tried to defend themself against the Thirdlings, but the other stepped back, taking his bow from his shoulder and aiming at the ancient dwarf, sending out a swift volley of arrows.

Goldhand did not step aside, but, on the contrary, stood fast and sliced at the black arrows with his axe as they flew towards him. He caught two or three in mid-air – until finally an arrow tip struck home. But instead of falling to his knees, he continued to march towards the älf.

Goïmron hurled his own axe at the enemy, who sidestepped without interrupting his volley of shots. As a last resort, Goïmron grabbed his set of darts. *You've got to make this the best throw you've ever done. Pretend you're in the tavern aiming for a high score at the dartboard.*

The dart flew to its target: the right eye. The wounded älf screamed and cowered in agony. At this, Brûgar used the opportunity to lunge forward with his war flail, whacking the skull with such force that the bone shattered. 'One to me!' he yelled, raising his bloodied weapon in delight. 'He was the last one! By Lorimbur, we've done it! We've beaten the black-eyes!'

'Celebration will have to wait.' Gata was kneeling at the side of her injured commander.

Goïmron raced over to Goldhand, who was teetering, with arrow wounds, four of them, in arm, shoulder and chest. *Vraccas! No!* 'Wait! Let me help you!'

'I think they've got me,' the old dwarf groaned, gasping for breath. 'Why did you bring them here? What are you doing in my mountains?'

'Girdlegard is in dire need of you. The Children of the Smith need a leader . . .' Goïmron's voice failed him. His words seemed senseless, even though he had found what he had been searching for. Not only was the greatest hero an ancient dwarf – the black arrows would shortly put paid to his life. *What have I done?*

Goldhand cast a glance at the disturbed mountains. 'I can no longer go back. You have prevented my completing the task Vraccas gave me.' He looked down at the arrow shafts sticking out of his armour, and the blood coursing down over the metal plates. 'Take me to King Hargorin. I must speak to him.'

The other dwarves stared in astonishment. Hargorina gave a concerned reply:

'My ancestor King Hargorin is long since dead. Our clan no longer supplies the ruler in our land.'

'What? Then . . .' Goldhand's wrinkled countenance showed his confusion at this news. Goïmron had needed to hold him up to let him speak. 'I must . . .'

'My father will give you an audience,' Gata interjected. 'I am Regnorgata Mortalblow of the clan of the Orc Slayers. I am heir to the Thirdling throne. The best of our healers will be summoned to attend you both.'

'I take you at your word. Let's get to the Black Mountains,' said Goldhand, fighting for breath. 'As quickly as . . . if Death-bringer is not . . . No! No!' He gestured wildly, struggling to stay on his feet. 'Everything – it is all in danger now!'

'Stay calm, or you'll make your injuries even worse.' Goïmron passed the old man a flask of water and helped him drink, but he seemed to choke, and the liquid ran down through his silver beard and washed the blood off his polished armour. *I didn't imagine it would be like this.*

Telìnâs, Sònuk, Rodana and Chòldunja came towards him. They had not been wounded. The young apprentice inspected the injuries.

Gata turned to Goïmron. 'I see guilt in your eyes, but none of this is your fault. The whole adventure is down to my decision. I let you think my father had asked me to accompany you. It is I who should bear all the responsibility for what has happened.' She kissed the ailing Hargorina on the brow. 'Your loyalty shall not cost you your life. I swear it, my teacher.' She ordered the sparse remainder of the troop to carry the wounded away. 'Now we must hurry.' Rodana and Chòldunja saw to bandaging the cuts. The rest of the band were then to carry off the patients.

Goldhand grabbed Goïmron's arm with more strength than would have been expected. 'Tell me, my boy. Who rules the Red Mountains?'

'King Gandalgir Irongrip of the . . .'

'Curses! We'll have to go there, too. Swift as the wind. Swifter!' Goldhand shut his eyes and a groan escaped his lips. 'I need to sleep. To rest . . . Wake me when we get to the Black Mountains.' His grasp lessened and his arm fell back.

Goïmron could smell the blood of the dead and the injured. His instincts had been correct all along and he had found Tung-dil Goldhand. Those who had laughed at him would now be forced to believe what he said.

But for him there was no joy nor any confidence that the future of Girdlegard was going to be safer.

On the contrary.

I know why the parsoi khi were admitted into Girdle-gard. They hunt down the creatures and the humans transformed by magic spells from the Land of Wonders. No one likes to talk about it, but this is the greatest threat confronting our homeland. Because we cannot recognise the danger.

We should offer the parsoi khi extra coins to entice them to come here in their droves. And hunt down what we cannot see.

'Concerning the Monsters in Our Midst',
an article in the *Malleniagard Advertiser*

Has anyone asked what the parsoi khi actually do with the humans and creatures and plants they hunt? Or to what purpose they hunt them down?

Or what they gain from it?

That is what we should focus on investigating. I do not know anyone who could, if necessary, hunt down the parsoi khi in their turn.

Reader's letter in reply to the article
'Concerning the Monsters in Our Midst'
in the *Malleniagard Advertiser*

IX

Girdlegard

United Great Kingdom of Gauragon
Province of Grasslands
1023 P.Q. (7514th solar cycle in old reckoning), late spring

'How are they both doing?' Goïmron looked up expectantly at Chòldunja from his place by the fire. She had just changed the dressings of the two badly injured members of his party. 'Any better?'

He put down the skeletal flame-flyer beak he had been examining by the light of the campfire. So far, he had not been able to discover how it had stayed intact and stable. If asked about what he was doing, he always replied that he was just admiring his trophy. He was keen to find the answer to the riddle all by himself.

Hargorina and Tungdil Goldhand were both being transported in Rodana's puppet theatre caravan and the group was taking the quickest route through Gauragon to get them to the Black Mountains. On the way, they had collected Belîngor in Platinshine. He had, for the most part, recovered, but still had to avoid strenuous activity so that his recently stitched injury was not put under undue strain. Dwarves from the surrounding settlements had managed to rebuild the fortified township the dragon Ûra had destroyed and Barbandor had stayed behind with them. The group made camp when the horses needed to rest, sometimes staying overnight in dwarf villages.

As Chòldunja shook her head, the long brown and black plait of thick hair fell forward from her shoulder. 'They aren't any better and they aren't any worse.' With a shudder, she chucked the soiled bandages into the fire, where the flames crackled up round them.

'What we really need is some magic assistance.' Brûgar surveyed the circle, a campfire pipe in his right hand. 'I appreciate it's a bit odd to hear a dwarf say this, but I think we should really get them both seen by a maga as soon as possible.'

'You mean – go to Rhuta?' Gata looked doubtful. 'But they refused us entry last time, remember?' As the blonde heiress to the throne stretched her hands out to the flames for warmth, the vraccassium and gold bangles shone on her arms. Since her true identity had been revealed, she no longer felt the need to conceal her status.

'But things were different then. Now we have proof to give Vanéra, so she can't turn us away. We've got Goldhand himself!' Goïmron thought the suggestion a good one, but he was no longer the leader of the group. Perhaps he never really had been the one making decisions. 'Highness, I think it's our best hope, if we are going to keep your mentor's life-forge alight.'

'We've nothing to lose by it.' Rodana looked up from writing in her notebook by lantern light. The company had settled this evening on a small hill in what must once have been a mighty Ido fortress. They had shelter here from the icy wind. 'We won't let the maga send us away again.'

'Strong words for a puppet mistress. Are you going to put the fear of death in Vanéra with your marionettes, to make her help us?' asked Brûgar with a grin. He picked up the skeleton beak and tested the sharpness of its tip.

'I'll see how it goes.' Rodana leafed through her notes. Goïmron tried to avoid watching her too closely. His fascination with her had only increased during their journey. He was attracted to her slender figure, blonde hair and dark skin. 'There's material here for ten new dramas. A whole variety of main characters . . .' She turned the notebook round so the others could see. 'Look, I've been sketching you. You'll live for ever in my stories.'

'That's a lovely idea.' Sònuk returned with a pile of kindling and logs he had found in the ruins. 'Girdlegard's folk will learn how much my race has done for their benefit.'

'Don't kid yourself they'll ever show you any gratitude.' Brûgar tossed the skeletal flame-flyer beak over to Goïmron, then went over to help the srgàlàh stack the firewood. 'Where's our young elf got to? Still green behind the pointy ears, that one.'

'Keeping watch, apparently, and doing fancy origami with leaves. I told Telìnâs I will smell and hear anyone coming close, but he insisted.' Sònuk tested the air. 'We are alone. Nobody far and wide.'

'We can certainly depend on your nose.' Goïmron had not forgotten how the srgàlàh had warned them about the älfar and told them about Goldhand's presence. He stowed his flame-flyer trophy away since he was not making any progress with his investigation. 'Highness, we . . .'

Gata frowned, bringing a slight bloom to the fluff on her cheeks. 'I don't like to be addressed like that. Call me Gata. I say let's make for Rhuta. It is my fault Rodana and Goldhand are in this position. I agree with the suggestion.'

'You don't regret having brought your people along on my mission?' Goïmron heard the uncertainty in his own voice. 'I mean, I've doubts enough myself, given the lack of success so far.'

'Very diplomatic,' said Brûgar, taking out his dagger and shaving the sparse hair growth on the back of his head.

'We are returning with the greatest hero our tribe has ever known, just as you promised,' Gata replied. 'That is—'

'An ancient dwarf, a thousand cycles old. He did not bring us back his magic Keenfire sword and he's in no fit state to lead us into a glorious future,' Brûgar muttered into his dark blue beard, while puffing smoke from his pipe as usual.

'*Regnor is going to be furious. He'll be incandescent.*' Belîngor signed his silent comment, glancing at the heiress to his tribe's royal throne. '*Your decision has cost more than a hundred Thirdling lives.*'

'It wasn't my decision; it was my father's, when he apparently decided to pursue me. I wonder if you would judge the matter differently if it had been him who had set out with Goïmron on this quest?' Gata snapped, fingering the silver brooch on her collar. 'Does it matter whether it's me or him giving the orders?'

Belîngor returned his gaze to the fire. His hands gestured: '*Forgive me. That was thoughtless of me.*' His reproach remained unspoken. They would, after all, never have left, had the heiress to the throne not told a lie.

Goïmron still felt guilty, even though Gata had accepted responsibility. *All my fault.* Hargorina was struggling to overcome a severe case of blood poisoning after being struck with an älfar arrow, Tungdil Goldhand lay in a kind of coma, and a hundred Children of the Smith had lost their lives. *My brothers. It's absolutely vital that we save these two. Otherwise everything will have been in vain. Everything.*

Rodana's eyes kept closing. 'I think I'll have a little nap,' she said sleepily, going off to lie down. 'Wake me when it's my turn to keep watch.'

'A puppeteer as our night-watch sentry? I don't think so.' Brûgar blew the bits of hair off the blade of his knife. He looked at Belîngor and put his pipe away. 'Come on, you. Let's do the rounds and check whether our young pointy-ears hears us coming. If he doesn't, he's in for a shock.'

The two Thirdlings set off, accompanied by Sònuk.

'I'm going to see how Hargorina is.' Gata nodded to them and went into the caravan.

Goïmron, unobserved, was able to steal a glance at Rodana. She was so unlike other human women, so slender. For a dwarf, of course, far too slender and delicate. He was drawn to her. *I'm sure Gandelin would have wanted me to look after her.*

'Quiet at last at the fireside,' Chòldunja murmured, covering her mistress's shoulders with a sheepskin for warmth. As she bent over, the pendant swung forward, although now the medallion was encased in a little leather bag. It did still, however, emit a faint glimmer. A dirty, dark red glow. *Surely not!*

A corona of evil surrounded the diamond, as the Fourthling was able to see through the leather. The aura of red light hovered round the gemstone like a promise, a statement that this was, as yet, only the start of things. He could not read the engraving on the wood and bone talisman but the stone itself was unmistakeable.

Chòldunja tossed a log into the flames and turned to him. 'You can always hear the dwarves stomping around. Enough to make everything else take flight.' She noticed his shocked expression. 'What is it? Is there a ghost behind me?'

'Why are you wearing a moor diamond round your neck?' he asked her roughly. Goïmron had his right hand placed on the handle of his dagger.

Chòldunja's laugh sounded false. 'Me? Why, by all the gods, would you say that?'

'Because I can see it. It is shining.'

The young apprentice laid her hand on her breast, covering the leather bag. 'How can you see it?' she whispered, horrified. 'What do you mean?'

'But it's only me that can see it.' Chòldunja screwed up her eyes. 'Unless . . .'

'What?'

'Of course. You're a Fourthling. You know all about jewels, don't you? Please don't let on. Don't tell anyone!'

'So not even Rodana knows?'

'No, and she mustn't.' Chòldunja moved closer. 'So, for you, the moor diamond shines *through* the leather pouch?'

He nodded cautiously, keeping hold of his knife.

'Does it happen a lot?'

'Me seeing moor diamonds?' His grip tightened.

'No. I mean . . . that gemstones speak to you?'

'I . . . would say I have an innate talent for recognising certain characteristics of gemstones.' He did not let himself become distracted. 'Why are you wearing this diamond? You do understand its power?' Goïmron was reluctant to jump to the one rational conclusion, seeing how much he owed the young woman. She was nursing Hargorina and Goldhand and keeping them alive. But this, too, made sense. 'Are you . . . a . . .?'

'My mother was one. I rejected the old beliefs,' she said, interrupting him. 'That's why I'm with Rodana. I wanted my life to be different. I wanted to entertain people, especially children. To make people laugh. That's all I ever wanted.' Chòldunja lowered her head and her long particoloured plait dangled on her back. 'Please, keep this to yourself. Otherwise I don't know what I can do.' She took his free hand. 'I swear to you: I have got nothing to do with the old ways. That's why they keep hounding me. They can't abide the thought there are dissenters alive with access to the same knowledge as themselves.'

Goïmron saw the fear in her features. He felt pity for her and knew she was speaking the truth. *Can I really read it in her eyes or is it that I want to believe her?* 'You have to swear that you have kept away and will keep away from the things you are accused of.'

'It is not an empty allegation about our kind – it *is* so. Our people are vicious and they deserve the cruel reputation they have.' Chòldunja sighed and gave him a grateful smile. 'I swear it from the bottom of my heart. On my life. And I'll owe you a great deal for not revealing my secret.'

He hesitated somewhat before nodding. He hoped he was not making a serious error. Slowly he released his tight grip on his dagger. 'So, tell me. What makes the stone glow?'

'It's to do with the phases of the moon. The diamond's strongest at full moon.'

'But what is the link with me?'

'I am certain that you are a Fourthling with an aptitude for gemstone magic. Not that you were aware of the gift. The talent is latent in you.' She tapped herself on the spot where the amulet hung under her robe. 'Otherwise you would never have been able to see the moor diamond. Not through the leather pouch.'

Goïmron was surprised to hear this. *The magic of gemstones? Me?* In the dwarf community in Malleniagard there had always been sagas told and myths recounted about this legendary mystical power ascribed to his tribe. But their creator, Vraccas, had no love for magic, and most dwarf folk were deeply sceptical about it. For hundreds of cycles now, there had never been any evidence of gemstone magic. It was all a question of tall stories and ancient tales.

The apparent advantage inherent in gemstone magic was supposed to reside in its ability to function independently of spells or magic fields. Its power source was in the jewel itself. According to what type of stone it was, different effects could be conjured up. That's what people said.

Goïmron made up his mind. 'You must be mistaken.'

'No. I am sure. Let's do an experiment.' Chòldunja saw that her mistress was still asleep. The puppeteer's eyelids fluttered as she dreamt. 'Close your eyes, count to five and then open them again.' He did as she told him. 'Can you see the moor diamond now?'

Goïmron immediately caught sight of a glimmer in the grass next to a weathered gravestone three paces away. 'Over there,' he said. 'Below that inscription.' He was astonished. *So it's true!* 'What can you tell me about this gift of mine?'

'Gemstone magic is well known among my people.' Chòldunja got up and wandered over to the monument. 'I could teach you what effect each stone has. Then you would be able to produce more magic than any maga.'

Goïmron gave a quiet laugh. 'Vanéra can do any amount of magic.'

'Wicked tongues say she is only able to utilise the magic that is bound up in her artefacts. And that she doesn't even know any spells. Or incantations.' Chòldunja picked up her pendant and hung it back round her neck. 'But Vanéra would still be able to see me for what I am. I don't want her revealing my secret. I haven't finished my training with Mistress Rodana yet, so I can't leave her. I'll come up with some excuse not to go along with you all to Rhuta.'

'And you'll teach me what you know about jewel magic?'

'We can start tomorrow. But as soon as we reach the maga's realm, you'll have to meet with me outside whenever you can.' Chòldunja came back to join him at the fireside. 'I shall keep your secret, Goïmron. Your talent will make others envious. You'll have enemies. It will be dangerous.' She looked at him boldly. 'I wonder how quickly you'll learn.'

Goïmron still could not believe it. 'Me too.' His thoughts were all over the place. His mind was struggling to deal with what had been happening.

Part of his head was telling him to be wary of trusting Chòldunja. Her people were on the same level as the black-eyes. They were feared. Nobody in the four southern coastal kingdoms of the inland sea ever dared enter the swampy regions where the ragana followed their wicked cult.

I shall wait and see what she can teach me. Goïmron had something he wanted to ask but he saw a white figure stepping out of the shadows of the ruins. 'A ghost!' he exclaimed in fright.

Rodana woke with a start. Chòldunja turned to face the shadowy figure calmly approaching the circle of firelight.

'Forgive the intrusion.' It was a light-haired woman in her forties, all in white from her boots to her mantle and striking wide-brimmed hat, which had two long feathers, glowing like orange flames, at either side of the crown. 'I'm on my way to Cliffton. But I heard the celebrated puppet mistress was en route with a group of companions. I absolutely had to come and see for myself. I've made a special trip.'

The dragon's messenger! Goïmron would much have preferred a visit from a ghost. Anything rather than meeting Stémna. Her turning up here was a sign of nothing good.

Rodana got to her feet, rubbing the sleep from her light-green eyes. 'Sit, Stémna. What can we do for the Voice of Ûra?'

'Oh, I'll be off again before you know it. I just had to see if the rumours were actually true. It's the talk of all the ports and palaces and townships.' Stémna stopped and looked at the caravan. 'So, is he in there?'

'Hargorina?' Goïmron pretended not to understand. 'She was hurt in an attack . . .'

'You know who I mean.' The dragon's envoy made her way over to the wagon, pushing the Fourthling and then Rodana and, finally, Chòldunja out of her way. 'Don't be so modest about your precious cargo.'

'Hargorina needs rest.' Goïmron tried again, looking around. *How did she get past the Thirdlings, Telinâs and Sònuk?* He was afraid the others might already have been fed to the white dragon and that now he and his companions were being played with before Ûra's flames burned them to ashes.

Stémna opened the caravan door, stepped inside, and halted by Goldhand's bed. She carefully lifted the sheet and looked at the fresh bandages on the four separate injuries he had sustained. 'An old dwarf. His life-forge is failing.' She looked around. 'No Keenfire. No hint of the hero. There's nothing here to worry my mistress in the slightest.'

'We found Goldhand and want to take him back to the Black Mountains so he can die among his own kind,' Goïmron lied. 'The legend should come to rest by its source.'

'How strange. Half the world has been telling me a hero has returned. That there will be a new age in Girdlegard. That all the dragons will cease to be.' Stémna jumped down from the wagon. 'They must all have misunderstood. But I'd love to hear your version.' She shot a challenging look at Rodana. 'I'm certain you can do a wonderful narration of events. You're so good at that kind of thing.'

Rodana sketched a bow.

She began: 'This is what occurred.' A nicely measured mix of truth and falsehood slipped past her dark lips. The tale was told in such masterly fashion, using her skill with words and her enchanting voice, that Goïmron could only gape in astonishment. 'Hardly had we made camp here and you arrive,' she finished.

'So the älfar attacked you?' Stémna started to move away from the firelight. 'They seem to be worried about the news. *That* is concerning. Don't you think so?' The brightness of her white clothing faded slowly into the darkness. 'I shall report to my mistress. You will very soon learn at first hand whether or not she is satisfied.' Stémna gradually disappeared into the shadows.

'To Tion with her!' Rodana sank down on to a stool by the campfire. 'I could not have kept that up for a single heartbeat longer.'

'What's happened to our very attentive guards on watch? How did she get past them?' Chòldunja poked the fire to bring it back to life. 'How much light do they need to notice one woman stinking of dragon and all dressed in white?'

'Will you get me the bottle with the strong mead?' Rodana asked her student. 'I need some.'

'At once, mistress.' Chòldunja hurried off.

Goïmron had not missed the looks Stémna and the puppeteer had exchanged. 'You know her, don't you?'

Rodana buried her face in her hands, her shoulders shaking with sobs. 'I only hope I have not brought death on us all.'

'Why would you think that?' Goïmron came closer and placed his hand on her shoulder. He could feel the warmth of her skin through her clothing and was aware of her delicate figure. 'Come, we're still alive and there was no dragon fire. You told the story well.'

Rodana was forced to laugh in spite of her misery. She took her dark-tipped fingers from her face. 'I didn't doubt my storytelling ability.' She wiped away the tears. 'I . . . wanted to go with you to find Goldhand, in order to get out of Girdlegard. To escape from her.'

'The dragon's envoy?'

They heard the tramp of feet as the dwarves approached, talking with each other. 'I'll explain another time.' She took a deep breath. 'Not a word about Stémna's visit if Gata and the others haven't noticed anything.'

'But . . .'

'She reduced Platinshine to ashes. How do you think the Thirdlings would react?' She begged him to understand. 'They would pursue Stémna and that would be the death of them. It is not time for revenge on the dragon. That orbit will come, Goïmron, but not yet.'

'I've found it, mistress!' Chòldunja called out, stepping down from the wagon, holding the bottle. 'Half full still.'

At that moment the Thirdlings and Sònuk reached the fire.

'Hey, is that the strong mead?' Brûgar said. 'How come you've only just thought about serving it up now? We've all been needing to celebrate the fact we're still alive.'

Chòldunja glanced questioningly at Rodana, who warned her with a gesture to say nothing about her real reason for requesting the mead.

'Let's drink to a full and speedy recovery for Hargorina and Goldhand,' suggested Goïmron, thinking quickly. 'We'll call up the healing spirits with a toast.'

'Good idea.' Gata came over with the others to sit by the fire. The flask passed first to her. 'A toast to the heroic friends we have lost on this mission. May their life-forges burn for all eternity.' She drank from the bottle and passed it round.

'And let's drink to all the dragons disappearing overnight.' Sònuk's long muzzle sniffed the air. 'An excellent omen.'

Brûgar took a drink. 'You and your jokes, by Vraccas!' The Thirdlings laughed. 'There will come a dawn when I'll play a joke on you. The sort only the Children of the Smith can come up with.' He passed the mead on.

Goïmron looked at Rodana and Chòldunja before taking a sip from the bottle.

Girdlegard

United Great Kingdom of Gauragon
Province of Grasslands
Near the border of the enchanted realm of Rhuta
1023 P.Q. (7514th solar cycle in old reckoning), late spring

Chòldunja sat up on the driving seat of the coach, taking the well-made road to the north-east. 'We have talked about gemstones, and I realise you already know a great deal, without having actively studied it. Their various characteristics. The effects they can have. But what do you know about the classic art of magic? You've had no reason so far to think about it.'

Mile by mile they were getting closer to the border between Gauragon and Rhuta. If the weather held, they could reach it by evening.

'I don't know much at all.' Goïmron was sitting next to her, eagerly soaking up everything the young woman could tell him about the magic of jewels. Some of it was new, but he had already unconsciously acquired a little knowledge during his training as a gem cutter. *More than Gandelin and all the other apprentices put together.* What he had seen as tricks of the light, he now recognised as his own natural gift for perceiving the energy and magic vibrations of the precious stones on his workbench. 'I heard that many of the records kept by the ancient magae and magi were lost.'

Chòldunja nodded. 'There are hardly any copies of the magic spells or anything about handling magic properly. And if any books are found, they turn out to be in some arcane language that nobody nowadays can understand.' She grinned cheekily. 'That's why Fourthlings like you have a distinct advantage. You can use the power of the stones.'

'There hasn't been a magus with that gift for hundreds of cycles.' Goïmron racked his brains. 'No ... that is ... I don't think ... there's ever been one.'

'Just imagine what you'll be able to do.' Chòldunja gave him a friendly nudge. 'You'd be the only one who wouldn't have to go out to seek the Wonder Zone when the magic fields change.'

'Apart from Vraccas, of course,' he corrected her. 'Or the älfar with their inborn abilities.'

Long ago there had been fields of magic in Girdlegard stretching over wide areas, feeding the various enchanted realms. These had shrunk considerably over time and were often hotly disputed, or else the magic community kept the locality of the sources a closely guarded secret. Nowadays even the borne no longer existed.

Instead, at the beginning of each new solar cycle, somewhere in Girdlegard a so-called Wonder Zone would emerge.

Anyone versed in, or imbued with, magic could go there and replenish their store of magic energy by entering the source area. This energy would last for exactly one cycle, staying strong no matter how much it was used, and elapsing promptly at the end of the cycle.

It was said that one could take soil, plants or animals from the Wonder Zone to bring the energy to someone else, but this theory had never been proved.

'I heard that magic can affect the environment.' Goïmron gave himself a shake. There were records about devastated cities with ghosts and demons and living dead. But there was also talk of there being miracles and healings.

'Yes. Magic can change creatures and alter nature itself,' Chòldunja told him. 'Sometimes for the better, sometimes for the worse. At one time, the Wonder Zone was in a swamp in my region. The changes that happened then remained even after the end of that cycle. The mutated individuals, animals or objects are highly prized. We had to cope with the strangest creatures for a very long time.'

'I take it you kept quiet about having the magic source in the swamp?'

Chòldunja laughed. 'But of course! We didn't want anyone knowing about it. That cycle all the magi and magae were left without any magic energy. It made them vulnerable. They could be preyed on by anyone wanting revenge or harbouring resentment.'

So Vanéra is wise to rely on her artefacts. They had spells incorporated within them. That was why Rhuta had not suffered. *They never went through a period of weakness.*

Sometimes it took an age for the new power-source zone to be located. It could be found by chance or sometimes with the help of specially trained hunting animals.

This had, in the past, led to whole empires arising, if the new source was found by the same people on their land. With a huge store of magic, and together with the dragons they controlled, emperors and empresses were able to tyrannise the whole of Girdlegard. But when the next new zone could not be located, those rulers would succumb, either to the fire of the dragons or to the fury of their own rebellious subjects.

There haven't been any magic emperors for a long time. Goïmron grinned at the thought that he might have the capability to be the next to found such an empire. *A dynasty, perhaps. With Rodana . . . and without recourse to any Wonder Zone.*

'Well, then. I've got something for you.' Chòldunja took a white onyx out of her shoulder bag. 'Let's disregard the magic of formulae and spells. That's not right for you. You don't need that sort of thing. Nor the magic gestures or the calling up of spirits.' She handed him the teardrop-shaped gem. 'What can you see in it?'

'Where did you get it?'

'A gift. An admirer somewhere. He wanted to get me a diamond heart but brought me this instead.'

'Then he must have been from Malleniagard. I recognise Master Sparklestone's technique here. This is the handiwork of Guntrabil. He was from the workshop next door. Gandelin was super keen to get this white onyx.' Goïmron noticed Chòldunja go pale. 'What's the matter?'

'I'm so sorry . . . I didn't want to upset you by mentioning the friend who was murdered.'

'That's all right. You couldn't have known.' He addressed himself to the onyx, focusing hard, in order to push dark thoughts away.

He was aware of a bright misty glow from the interior of the gem. This hinted at its stored energy. Whether enough for single use or multiple applications, Goïmron could not say. 'Its nature is good,' he said quietly, turning the gemstone over.

'What might a healer do with this?'

'Rub or crumble it and anoint the eyelids of a sufferer.' Goïmron recalled its properties. 'You can put the powder on an infected wound. Taken internally, it helps with a weak heart or dizziness.'

'So what kind of magic do you think you could do with it?'

'Healing.'

'What about black onyx?'

'The opposite effect.'

Chòldunja grinned. 'You've got the theory off pat. A genuine son of Goïmdil, your tribe's father.'

Goïmron weighed the stone in his hand. Recognising a stone's qualities had never been difficult for him, and under Chòldunja's instruction he was making steady progress. One question remained: 'How do I call up the healing magic?'

'Well, that's something only Fourthlings will be privy to. I'd try, in your place, concentrating really hard. Gather the power you can see in the stone and transmit it into the body you want to heal.' She looked back over her shoulder to where the two badly injured patients lay in the wagon behind them. 'But I wouldn't start with them. Experiment with a small cut on a finger or a scratch on an arm before you use it on someone that's already near death.'

Goïmron looked at the horses' backs to see if he could find any small injury. His mind was busy. Could the magic of different gemstones be combined if you applied them one on top of another to increase the energy?

How about using an amethyst, which had the power of driving away snakes and poisonous worms? Now, could that perhaps make enough magic to deal with the breed of dragons in Girdlegard?

And if so, how much energy would you need? Goïmron was very taken with the thought of one day proving to be more than the weakling, the quarter-Fourthling, his friends back in Mallenia-gard had always made fun of. *I could be useful for once. Not just a not very talented gem cutter.*

Moreover, he needed the proof that the legend was true: despite not loving magic, Vraccas had compensated the Fourthlings for their small stature by giving them magic gifts. Goïmron would be able to perform wonders by using jewels. The strongest effects would surely be achieved with precious stones found in the mountains, and those from his own homeland, of course, would be the most effective.

But the Brown Mountains are part of Brigantia and of Dsôn Khamateion. He sighed at the thought. Practically impossible to get to where the best jewels could be mined. *But isn't there a particularly valuable diamond?* He seemed to remember something like that from his training. *What was its name?*

'Are you thinking how to use the magic or are you falling asleep?' Chòldunja's voice roused him.

'I . . . was thinking.' He hadn't the faintest idea how to employ the power of the onyx. 'Maybe I should put the stone – or keep it in my hand and place my hand there . . .' He pointed to the withers of one of the horses where it had been scratched by some thorns. 'Shall I have a go?'

'Can you scramble over?'

Goïmron did not want to appear weak. 'Of course.' He stood up and jumped rather clumsily on to the startled horse, which neighed loudly. 'Shh. I'm going to help you.' He placed the stone carefully on the scratch and concentrated on trying to release the energy of the onyx.

When nothing happened, he touched the graze again, enclosing the gemstone inside his hand this time. Once more, no effect.

'It's not working,' said Goïmron crossly. He was disappointed. 'So maybe I'm not a jewel magus after all. Merely a gem recogniser?'

'Don't talk so loud, for the sake of all the gods,' Chòldunja hissed. 'What did I tell you? Nobody must find out.'

'What must nobody find out?' Rodana appeared from the interior of the wagon and came over to occupy the empty seat on the driver's bench. 'And what are you doing on Ilante's back?'

Quick, an excuse! Goïmron patted the horse's neck. 'The reins had got twisted. I've sorted it out.'

'While we're moving? You might have fallen.'

'Never. I'm good at climbing. We all are, us Fourthlings. Born in the mountains, aren't we?' He slipped and grabbed hold of the horse's mane. 'Occasionally I'd like to ride a bit on Ilante, if that's all right. Bit out of practice.' He quickly stowed the onyx. *Vraccas, don't let me fall off!* It occurred to him that the proper stone to help horse and rider would be a turquoise. *And I don't have one.*

On the horizon they now saw a flagpole where the Rhuta banner was fluttering in the afternoon breeze. The design was a white background with one blue and one yellow wand and a stylised sun above them.

'Chòldunja, would you see to our patients, please. There's something I have to discuss with Goïmron.' The apprentice obediently handed over the reins and entered the wagon. 'Can you come over here and sit beside me? I think you've done enough practising now.'

'Right away.' Making quite a song and dance about it, he managed to clamber his way back to the driver's seat. It was not just the exertion that was making his heart race. 'What's on your mind?'

'Remember the night that Stémna turned up and decided she wouldn't do anything to Goldhand because in her opinion he was dying?'

'Of course.' How could he have forgotten?

'There was a reason she asked me to tell her what had happened. Even if I did change a few things.' Rodana had lowered her hypnotic voice so that no one could overhear. 'I can't enter Rhuta. One of you must drive the wagon and take Goldhand and Hargorina to the maga.'

'What?' Goïmron was unhappy about this. He would have loved to have the slender blonde woman by his side, although he realised he was unwise to think these selfish thoughts.

'I . . . already confessed that I can't go to the Grey Mountains with you to verify the facts of your adventure. Even if there would be wonderful material for some stories.' Rodana took a deep breath. 'The truth is, I was hoping to be able to leave Girdlegard. For ever.'

'I know. Because of your story about the death of Ûra. Stémna threatened to kill you.'

Rodana shook her head. 'It's worse than that. I am her spy. I am to report to her about everything I hear on my travels. Anyone turning against Ûra will feel the flames, teeth and claws of the dragon.' She laid her hand on Goïmron's, her fingertips even darker than normal. 'If I accompany you to Rhuta and you start scheming against Ûra, I'll be forced to tell Stémna.'

'And what if you don't?'

'Then whole villages and towns will go up in smoke. I can't have that on my conscience.' Rodana gulped. 'But if Chòldunja and I wait at the border for you to bring me my wagon back, then I can't possibly have learned anything I'd have to report.'

Goïmron attempted to work out her meaning. 'But . . . are you always going to spy for the dragon? All your life?'

'Yes. Otherwise she will take her revenge on all the villages I've been to, and where I grew up.' Tears were glistening under her eyelids and starting to roll down her cheeks. 'There's nothing for it. It can't be changed. Unless either I leave – or I die.'

'That . . . is downright cruel.' He experienced a whole gamut of feelings: attraction, sympathy, anger at Stémna and at Ûra. 'We've got to do something about this!'

Rodana's dark lips smiled weakly at him. 'I don't want to criticise your people, but *this* Tungdil Goldhand won't be able to change anything. He can't protect anyone against the dangers that beset us in Girdlegard.'

Goïmron bit his lip so as not to reveal the secret. In his pocket, he closed his fist over the white onyx. *But I shall be able to do something. And soon.* 'Let's wait and see.'

'Stémna let Goldhand live because she saw how far gone he was. Ûra would have burned him to ashes if he'd represented any kind of threat to her reign.' Gratefully, Rodana pressed, and then released, his hand. 'Tell the others that Chòldunja and I aren't permitted to enter Rhuta. Say it's . . . because I once wrote a play about the maga and she hadn't liked it. That's the best way.' She handed him the reins and got up. 'I'll just pack a few things. Chòldunja and I will wait at the border for the wagon. Good luck!' She disappeared into the van.

The vehicle had reached the flagpole where the well-known sign bade visitors welcome, reminding them about registration and the necessary fee to be paid. Here too there was the same kind of golden shelf and the huge mirror within its jewelled surround as last time. There was also an iron chest.

Goïmron brought the horses to a standstill and was about to get down, when in the mirror screen he suddenly saw the reflection of a young man with a pointed dark beard in the shape of a quill and long blond hair artistically framing his face. 'Welcome, Children of the Smith! The good maga has heard of your approach and asks you to be her honoured guests. Please continue on this road until you reach the next town. You are expected there and your every need will be catered to.'

'Oh, that is most kind of the maga. Please convey our sincere thanks. We have in our entourage two badly injured companions,' Goïmron responded, surprised at the friendly reception. 'They are in urgent need of magic attention if they are to survive their injuries.'

'My mistress is aware of this. You will receive the help you need.' The young man in the mirror bowed and waved them courteously in. 'Make haste. Everything has been prepared.'

'Off you go,' Rodana called. She and her aprendisa had got down from the caravan out of the door at the back of the vehicle. With their luggage on their backs, they stood at the side of the road under the blossom of a broad-leaf tree. 'We'll do what we arranged.'

Goïmron flicked the reins. 'I'll be back soon,' he called out to the two women. To one of them because his heart insisted on it, and to the other because she was helping him with his gemstone magic. Both of these things must remain his secrets.

They waved. The wagon moved away.

Gata rode up beside him. 'Whatever's happening? Why aren't they coming with us?'

'Tell you later.' Goïmron clicked his tongue and the horses picked up speed.

We need to discuss Firewall. They have fifteen thousand inhabitants and are behaving in ways the United Great Kingdom of Gauragon can no longer tolerate.

Originally founded by my forefathers as a simple fire observation post to warn of danger caused by lava from the volcanoes, the place grew rapidly, and was fortified using special fireproof stones in the defence walls as protection against potential lava streams. This makes Firewall strategically extremely important.

Their surrounding farmland produces abundant crops because of the volcanic ash and rich soil.

Then there is the basalt and volcanic glass so useful in tool-making and for forging weapons and other equipment. This has brought Firewall considerable wealth.

Moreover, it is the way into the Grey Mountains. Because of the secure passage it offers, avoiding the fire eaters, most adventurers start from there. But on their return, any items they may have found must be shown to Firewall officials, who impose a tax.

It has come to my attention that explorers selling their discoveries in Girdlegard without a licence from the Firewall authorities are being subjected to great difficulties. Imagine: so-called Inspectors of Finds are being sent out to roam the countryside and ensure this presumptuous regulation is observed!

And all this in a settlement that has never yet been recognised with civic status. Their coffers must be overflowing with coins, but they are not passing on the requisite amount to Gauragon.

But even more concerning is the fact that älfar have settled within their walls.

Rumour has it that they are artists utilising the lava fields. I am unwilling, however, to believe that they pose no danger.

Excerpt from a speech given on the occasion
of the third jubilee of King Gajek,
ruler of the United Great Kingdom of Gauragon

X

Girdlegard

Red Mountains
Kingdom of the Firstling dwarves
Wavechallenge, western harbour
1023 P.Q. (7514th solar cycle in old reckoning), early summer

Underwater in the mobile *Elria Bonnet*, Xanomir was surrounded by a silver river of shimmering fish shooting past him into the entrance tunnel through the Red Mountains. Occasionally there was a bump when one of the sphyrae collided with the diving bell. *They are wonderful to look at. But dangerous.*

The *Elria Bonnet* protected the dwarf from these huge fish, each the size of a human, swimming in a dense shoal into the canal lock. They had become quite a plague. Had he not had his safety covering of metal, Xanomir was aware the predator fish would have descended on him eagerly and torn him to pieces.

Harbour master Bendabil voiced the theory that the sphyrae were heading through to their spawning grounds in Girdlegard.

But Xanomir was dubious. If they had not appeared near Wavechallenge for many cycles following an urge such as that, why should they be doing it now? *Predators such as these would fear and flee from few dangers.* He observed their elongated heads and sharp teeth. *And one of those dangers? Some other predator that's larger still.*

At the harbour master's request, he had installed fixtures for metal steering nets and folding planks to enable the fish to be directed out of the main canal into a side branch where they could be caught. Their numbers were far too high for the health of the inland sea.

If only the älfar could be dealt with as easily. Xanomir had fastened mechanically worked grippers to the outside of the submersible to facilitate underwater work without any need for the operator to leave the bell. He had no wish to become fish food. The iron claws could cope with all kinds of heavy manoeuvres, but for delicate repair tasks he would have to leave the safety of the diving bell and use his hands. That is, as long as there weren't any sphyrae in evidence. *Wherever the black-eyes have got to, I hope they'll have starved to death by now.*

The guards had searched everywhere but found no trace of the älfar spies that had reached the Girdlegard frontier. They had dragged the canal and found one älfar corpse. It seemed that one had a broken neck from a failed attempt to climb. The predator fish showed no interest in dead flesh. They had not touched the carcass.

Let's hope the others have met a similar fate. Xanomir anchored the hook for the next metal net in the side wall and hammered in several iron retaining clips. Two of the sphyrae tried to bite the diving bell's gripper claws before shooting off to look for more suitable food.

Xanomir became aware of a darker figure among the fish, near the tunnel spikes that could be lowered when the passage of some ship needed blocking. *So what kind of a thing are you?* Using the levers to steer, he moved the bell forward. The air was getting stale. He would have to refresh his supply soon. *Are you the hunter the sphyrae fish are afraid of?* He bent forward to get a better look through the window.

At that very moment something crashed against the porthole. The thick glass cracked and salt water sprayed through.

Xanomir jolted back and looked around. *That was never a sphyrae!*

Several dark bodies were swirling round the *Elria Bonnet*. The dancing shoal of fish made it impossible for him to see what was happening.

They suddenly came closer. Xanomir could make out shapes in silver armour over transparent bluish skin – humanoid beings with gills at the neck, and long, flipper-like feet. They were wielding three sharp-headed splitting hammers. As they smashed against the glass window, water streamed in, affecting his vision.

What in Elria's name did I just see? Xanomir took one more deep breath and waited until the interior filled up with water. Once the bubbles had ceased he could see better.

One of the creatures swam in front of the bell, hammer at the ready in webbed fingers. The narrow, streamlined head stared at him out of large round eyes with rainbow-coloured pupils. The individual was waiting for him to come out of his safe shelter to finish off with his implement whatever the ravenous sphyrae had not claimed.

The other attackers disappeared among the fish.

Nesodes! Xanomir weighed up his chances. The assailant did not need air to breathe and with those flippers could certainly swim ten times as fast. And the sphyrae would not attack a nesode. *I don't stand a chance.*

A surprise was needed. Swiftly he grabbed the mechanism for the grippers and made them snatch at the opponent. The nesode dodged out of the way and used his hammer to try to destroy the metal claw.

Now! Xanomir pushed up from the floor and shot through the broken inspection window, arms outstretched above his head.

But before he reached the surface, several sphyrae collided with him and swept him into the midst of their shoal. He was bitten often, their sharp teeth burying themselves painfully into his skin. All he was wearing was the loincloth.

Don't open your mouth to scream. You need that air! Xanomir tried to swim upwards, using strong arm movements, but the huge fish shooting past pushed him down again by swishing their whip-like tails.

On peering through the shoal of fish, Xanomir could see one of the nesodes, hammer in hand, destroying the levers for operating the underwater spikes used to block the channel. Now the spikes would no longer function; they would no longer be capable of piercing through the bottom of enemy vessels. *What is happening?*

Xanomir grasped the dorsal fin of one of the sphyrae and let himself be carried along until his breath ran out. The shoal grew less densely packed as the fish reached the deeper water of the main channel. In places there was a strong undertow dangerously dragging everything down to the bottom.

Up to the top before it's too late. Bleeding from a number of small bites, Xanomir reached the surface and swam strongly to the far end of the narrow maintenance platform that led to the outside. Exhausted, he pulled himself up on to the path and crawled along. Water dripped from his hair and grey beard.

Harbour master Bendabil will hate me. It's always me bringing the bad news. Xanomir clambered over the overhang on to the path that widened here into a road. He got to his feet, groaning with the effort, and stumbled along to the guard post.

His friend Buvendil, watching out for him by the crane for raising the diving bell, saw him first. 'By Vraccas, how did you ever get out of the bell? And why?' He looked very concerned. 'The sphyrae have given you a hard time.' He ran over to the faltering dwarf. 'Whatever happened?'

'Underwater creatures,' Xanomir gasped, grateful for his friend's supporting arm. 'They've broken the blocking spikes. I've no idea what else they've done. Or how long they've been there.' He pointed to the sphyrae swimming past. 'Could be nesodes, I think. They wore armour and they were using the fish to hide. That's why we didn't notice them. This is their work.'

'Nesodes? I thought they'd gone for ever. Curses on them!' Buvendil alerted the harbour guard. 'How many of them?'

'I counted three.'

'Hm. Why would they want to put the blocking spikes out of action? They can just swim through to Girdlegard without us noticing.'

Xanomir opened his mouth to answer but his words were drowned out by the alarm signal from the north side of the fortress. Other warning alarms followed as the watchtower reported unfamiliar sails on the horizon. For the first time in more than three hundred cycles, something was happening that Xanomir would never have imagined possible: Wave-challenge was preparing for an attack.

'Our channel defences are down. We must warn harbour master Bendabil about what I've seen.' He limped off, leaning on Buvendil. The stinging on his flesh indicated the sphyrae bites were becoming inflamed from the fishes' poison. 'We can't rely on our defensive blocking mechanism in the channel.'

'Wavechallenge's walls are strong enough and our catapults have a range of a thousand paces,' Buvendil replied. 'We only need the spikes in the unlikely event of—'

A loud hiss accompanied long tongues of fire bursting from the fortified tower. Clouds of smoke rose to the sky. Soldiers enveloped in flames fell through the windows and toppled from the platform into the waters of the harbour or crashed down on to the walls.

In spite of the pain, Xanomir took off at a run.

Girdlegard

Brown Mountains
Dsôn Khamateion
1023 P.Q. (7514th solar cycle in old reckoning), early summer

Klaey approached the slender flight-mare in its generously sized stall, and proffered a hunk of raw meat on a long skewer. Best fillet steak. 'Good boy. Do you like me a bit better today?' He spoke in a low croaky voice to make the stallion think he was an älf. He was also wearing älfar clothing and had intentionally lost weight. His face was in shadow because of his hood, so the family brand on his forehead was hidden. 'I need you, if I'm going to escape from the black-eyes. Without your help, I'm stuck fast.' He moved the meat closer. 'How about a little outing? Up through the air?'

The flight-mare snapped, showing long, sharp teeth that could easily bite through a forearm. The flight-mare took the offering greedily. Meat juices and blood dripped from its mouth as it chewed. The Brigantian felt the stallion was mustering him, wondering how tasty he might prove.

'Friends now?' Klaey bravely stretched out a hand, ready to stroke the soft black nose. 'Will you let me near?'

The muscles in the animal's neck clenched. Recognising the danger, Klaey swiftly withdrew his fingers. The vicious teeth closed on empty air and the flight-mare gave an angry snort.

'Wretched beast.' Klaey put the skewer back in the bucket of raw meat. 'I thought you were getting used to me.'

He had been sleeping in the stables for thirty orbits now, hiding in the straw from the grooms in charge of the horses and the conventional night-mares. Vascalôr insisted on no one else but himself being near this specimen.

The spectral älf had no idea that he was, in fact, not the only one the beast was getting accustomed to.

Klaey was fortunate in that no one had thought of searching the stables compound of the valley-head fortress. From his hiding place, he had overheard the servants talking about the hunt for him and placing their bets. The odds were not great.

'All right, Deathwing. Ah, you *do* recognise the name I've given you. It's better, isn't it, than the one the black-eyes thought up.' Klaey hooked his thumbs in his belt. 'I'll let you try that one more time, the biting, tomorrow, and then I'll come up with a different idea.'

The flight-mare made a shrill noise as if laughing at the man. Raising its head and pricking up its ears, it directed its glowing red gaze to the doorway.

'Someone coming?' Klaey quickly dropped down behind a heap of straw in one of the other stalls. 'Don't you dare tell on me, Deathwing. We're friends, aren't we? Don't forget.'

'Thank you for allowing me to see the flight-mare. I really appreciate it.' It sounded like Ascatoîa's voice, Klaey thought.

'How could I deny you? I wonder if Phlavaros will let you get close. He is proving difficult to tame,' said Vascalôr. 'Perhaps he'll be calmer with you.'

Klaey peeked out from between the stalks of hay, just as the two were passing the open doorway to the stall. Both were in dark leather and high boots, ready to go for a ride, as long as the winged night-mare was prepared to carry one of them. His dark clothing made Vascalôr look more like a ghost than ever. Depending on the light, his eyes changed from black to red.

'Oh, doesn't he look marvellous!' Ascatoîa exclaimed. Her appearance was every bit as striking as her companion's. It seemed she never took off the rings, bracelets and necklace made of bone, pearls and precious stones. 'The first in a proud line of flight-mares.'

'We've managed to produce four young females. But they are too weak at present to start breeding. Their physical make-up is not as strong as that of the unicorns. And the transmutation takes a lot out of them.' Vascalôr picked the skewer out of the bucket and banged it on the side of the pail. He was wearing his pale hair tied back and fixed with long silver needles. 'Here, Phlavaros. Here's a treat for you.'

'What sort of meat are you giving him?'

'Beef. It's the only thing he'll eat.'

'You've chosen a lovely name for him.' Ascatoîa clicked her tongue. 'Come here, my beauty. Let me stroke you.'

Its real name is Deathwing. Klaey raised his head and saw her move near the stall. The upper part of the door was opened and the flight-mare eyed the piece of steak. *I hope it bites her.* If only he had a new lucky talisman to kiss to make his wish come true.

But the stallion remained at the back of the stall, snorting through flared nostrils and looking at both of them in turn. It seemed wary of the älfar.

'How long before we have an army of flight-mares?' Ascatoîa drew back. 'You've heard the reports from Girdlegard.'

'I estimate it will take five cycles. At least. In normal circumstances that would not matter. But I hear what you're saying.' Vascalôr put down the skewer with the hunk of raw meat. 'It is true that all the groundlings from the settlements are heading for Rhuta to see their returned hero for themselves.'

'And that is only because Horâlor failed. First, he rode out in my place with our troop on the instruction of the Ganyeios, and even then, he didn't do what he was supposed to. He deserved to die at the hands of the mountain maggots,' Ascatoîa spoke resentfully, pushing a strand of her dark hair back under the black velvet turban.

'Forgive me. As Speaker of the Secret Chamber, I had to allow the Ganyeios to entrust Horâlor, after his demotion, with a task beyond his capabilities. The intention was to give him back some dignity.' Vascalôr gave a cold laugh. 'At least we're rid of him.'

'I should have had that task. I'd have brought you the groundlings.' Ascatoîa tossed the free end of her head wrap over her shoulder to fall on her riding jacket. 'They will expect Goldhand to bring the tribes back to their old strength. That could put paid to our plans.'

'It is already affecting them.'

'What do you mean?'

'Word of the old hero's return is going round like wildfire. I have been informed that some of the human kingdoms are sending delegations to the realm of the maga to witness the miracle of the ancient dwarf's return and to negotiate with Goldhand.' Vascalôr sounded annoyed. 'These cowards.'

'What do you think is behind it?'

'If this half-dead groundling remains alive and starts to get the tribes to unite again, I'm sure they'll get the humans to do their dirty work. Just like before.' Vascalôr turned his red eyes on his companion. 'The elves and the meldriths, too. First they'll incite all the mountain maggots to attack Brigantia and Dsôn, then they'll get the forges in the Red Mountains making new weaponry that's easier to move about, so they can use it against Ûra.'

'I'm surprised the dragon hasn't intervened. There's lots happening in Girdlegard that can't be what she wants.'

'Perhaps the scaly one hasn't realised the seriousness of the situation. Or thinks a few bolts of flame at the right moment will sort things out.' Deep in thought, Vascalôr studied his flight-mare. 'But *we* cannot stand idly by. Events are taking an unpredictable turn. If the groundlings put an army together by summer, with all the others, and then march on Brigantia, we'll be in trouble. Our plans to wield supreme power in Girdlegard will certainly be in jeopardy. Our relief fleet would not arrive in time.'

'Right. At our next session in the Samusin temple, I'll suggest to the Ganyeios that we bring about a meeting with the dragon's envoy. Stémna must know that Ûra's reign is endangered.'

'No. I can't rely on that. The dragon's messenger has taken a look at the decrepit Goldhand and has decided he wasn't a threat.' Vascalôr leaned against the stall with its wood and metal construction. 'In my view, the dragon won't mind a few changes taking place in Girdlegard. Perhaps the Brigantians have crossed the line and she wants to be rid of them?'

'So Ûra would let the mountain maggots do the dirty work. And then she'd turn round and wipe them out . . .' Ascatoîa rubbed the spot on her chin where light and dark skin met. 'I've got an idea: let's attack the delegations the humans are sending to Rhuta. As a warning to all not to disturb the status quo.'

'Not a bad ruse. You are the best zhussa of all! We'll ensure no one knows who's responsible for the attacks. We don't want suspicion to fall on us at this stage. The blame will be put on Brigantia.' Vascalôr looked pleased. 'Who would have thought that a trip to admire the flight-mare would give rise to such a valuable and productive exchange of views? I'll speak to the Ganyeios this very orbit. We don't need to summon the Secret Chamber for that.'

Zhussa. Klaey wrinkled his brow. That älfar name again. *A pet name? A title?* Was there a connection to the elaborate jewellery she wore?

Ascatoîa nodded gracefully. 'The pleasure is all mine. Oh, yes, why don't we kill Goldhand? He's in Rhuta, lying helpless and defenceless. Ought to be easy.'

'What? And incur the maga's wrath? No. Everybody would know we were behind it. Brigantians wouldn't be able to get into the magic realm without being detected and then secretly murder him.' Vascalôr detached himself from the wall, wiping the dust from his dark leather clothing. 'Let's start with a few delegations. That'll be sufficient to make them think twice about going off to meet with Girdlegard's great new hope. Anyone trying to get there will die. That's the ominous message. The Ganyeios is sure to agree to our plans.'

'Yes.' Ascatoîa hesitated. 'Why not kill the king of Gauragon? With a forged greeting from the Omuthan and his cut-throats?'

'We don't want to go over the top. Otherwise that's too much terror all at once and it'll turn to rebellion and it'll be even worse in the Brown Mountains.' Vascalôr tried once more to coax the flight-mare over, but the stallion ignored him and spread out its wings in a bored fashion. 'In case the stream of delegations keeps going despite our attacks, I'll mount Phlavaros and fly round from palace to palace, killing the human rulers. Vacant thrones and empty seats in council chambers will send Girdlegard hurtling into chaos. And we'll be the ones to profit. But not until our ships have arrived. We need that extra leverage.'

'You are right. A lot could happen by autumn.' Ascatoîa stood watching the flight-mare before turning to leave. 'Shall I see you this evening for painting in the Silent Tears Square? They've caught a huge troll and his blood will be ideal for doing a sunset scene on canvas.'

'I'll try to get there.' Vascalôr pointed at the winged stallion. 'He and I are going to work a bit more on our relationship.

It will be hard work. And I've got to go and see the Ganyeios, too.'

'May Inàste bless your endeavours.' Ascatoîa left the stables area, calling out, 'Don't let him eat you.'

By Cadengis! Klaey could not stay here in Dsôn even one more orbit. What he had overheard here affected the safety of his homeland, his siblings and, most importantly, his eldest brother. It was one thing being, for whatever reason, unpopular in Girdlegard, but quite another to be falsely accused of numerous attacks and murders.

You black-eyes are the most hateful creatures ever. Klaey watched the älf attempting to win the stallion round with soft talk and flattery and offerings of meat. *Rotten to the core.*

He resolved to try his luck with the winged stallion as soon as Vascalôr was out of the way. And if his life were to be forfeit, at least he would have tried to warn Brigantia. Klaey ducked down and waited, eyes closed, for the älf to finish his lesson and finally leave the stables.

'You're snoring,' someone whispered in his ear, speaking in the common vernacular. Klaey shot up – only to see his face reflected in the black orbs of Vascalôr's eyes. 'I nearly took you for an älf, what with the hood over your face. But your crude facial features betray you.' He laughed out loud. 'By Inàste! The whole city is out looking for you and you have nothing better to do than sleep in my stables.'

'Being hunted down is a tiring business.' Klaey was aware of the blade at his throat. It brought back a terrible flash of his mortal fear in the shrine to the älfar warrior. 'There was no one here when I lay down.'

'I don't believe you, Croaker.' Vascalôr stood up, keeping the tip of his sword on the Brigantian's throat. 'You were going to steal Phlavaros and try to escape. What an insane idea. Courageous, though.'

Klaey made no attempt to be quicker than the älf. He would not be able to reach his concealed dagger in time. *I need a different approach.* 'You may be right.'

Vascalôr gestured to him to get up. 'Just try it.'

'How do you mean?'

'I'll give you the chance to mount Phlavaros. Let's see how well that goes. If you fail, at least my night-mare will have himself a nice feast. Up you get, Croaker. Or, if you prefer, I can kill you right now. You choose.'

Klaey got to his feet uncertainly and made his way carefully over to the stall where the winged night-mare was stabled. All the time, he felt the sword at the nape of his neck. 'I would prefer the name Whisperer. You know, Croaker sounds a bit—'

'Get in.'

He heaved himself up over the lower door, landing in the straw. He raised his arms to show the stallion that his hands were empty. 'Right you are, Deathwing. I haven't got any meat for you this time,' he murmured, approaching the animal cautiously. 'Good boy. I'm not going to hurt you.'

'Look, Phlavaros. He has come to fly off with you,' Vascalôr said, leaning on the lower half of the stall door. 'You can have him as a special treat for dinner!'

Klaey reached for the dagger at his belt. 'I shall kill this beast if you don't let me out of the stables, black-eyes.' He took a sideways step so that he could keep his eye on both of them at the same time. 'I know how much it means to you.'

Vascalôr realised his mistake. 'Don't you dare touch him!'

'I'm good at throwing. And this flight-mare would be impossible to miss. If I get him in the eye, he'd be no good to you anymore. You'd have to come up with another idea for your military flying corps.'

The black älfar eyes widened. 'How do you know about . . .?' Then he realised. 'By Inàste and Samusin! You were listening in when Ascatoîa and I were talking. You understand our language!'

Klaey was annoyed with himself for having let this slip. Now Vascalôr had been alerted, he would do anything to stop him escaping. *But if I vex him further, perhaps he will make another mistake.* 'I know about your fleet that's due to head past the dwarf fortifications this autumn. And that your spies are already ensconced in all the coastal regions preparing for your invasion.'

'By Inàste!' Vascalôr vaulted over the half door, sword drawn, to stand in front of the stallion. 'So you've spied on us and worked out our plans and you reckon you'll get away?' He started to call an alarm.

Klaey hurled his knife, aiming at the älf's chest.

The weapon flew through the air and landed in Vascalôr's hand. He had grasped its handle. 'A weak throw, human scum. But wait! I'll throw it back. And you can try again—'

Suddenly the flight-mare leaped forward, burying its long incisors in the älf's neck and tearing a great hunk of flesh out. Blood spewed everywhere, drenching the sides of the stall. Before Vascalôr's body could fall to the floor, the stallion had struck again, this time grabbing at the head, yanking it off the shoulders. Then the creature sank to its knees and covered the corpse protectively with its wings, all the while chomping at the meat, its red eyes aglow.

Klaey stood rooted to the spot.

Bite by bite, the body of the älf disappeared down the stallion's gullet. Leather clothing was torn off and discarded; the bones were ground to fragments by the mighty jaws. Only the broken skull remained, for the flight-mare to suck out the brains.

It's now or never. Klaey darted forward, picking up a bloodied piece of leather from the straw. He jumped on to the animal's back and quickly bound its red glowing eyes with the improvised blindfold.

Whinnying shrilly, the flight-mare shot up, moving its wings and trying to rid itself of both rider and blindfold. Wind from the wings sent dust and straw into the air.

'Stop! Quiet now! Keep still!' Klaey clung fast to the warm slender neck, using all his strength. 'I'll direct you, do you hear? I'll tell you which way to go. Get me out of this place and over the mountains. Then I'll set you free.' He did not think the flight-mare would understand him, but his voice had a calming effect. 'Calm down now. Good boy, nice and steady.' Gradually Deathwing quietened down and Klaey stroked its head and neck. 'Just follow my touch.'

As a skilled rider, he tried to communicate first by thigh pressure. After initial difficulties, the stallion understood what was wanted and which way to move.

'Very good. My clever boy.' Klaey directed his mount towards the doorway and managed to undo the catch without getting off, then he rode slowly past the array of bridles and reins, taking what he needed from the tack-room shelves. He decided against taking the specially made saddle. It would take too long to put it on the stallion. 'And now we're off. Either we'll both get out of Dsôn alive, or you'll be rid of me once and for all and free to eat as many älfar as you want.'

He rode the flight-mare out of the stables into the courtyard.

Half a dozen älfar were busying themselves with grooming the horses and practising with the night-mares. At first they took no notice.

'Right. Now up with you, Deathwing! Up! Fly up and away!' Klaey croaked into the animal's ear and tapped against the creature's wing. 'Up!'

The stallion neighed and, spreading its impressive wings, it galloped along and took off. It shot into the air, clearing the court-yard wall, to the astonished shouts of the grooms and the soldiers. Whinnying, it moved its wings steadily for a steep climb.

Holding tight to the black mane, arms round the creature's neck, Klaey clung on. 'Samusin, my thanks,' he exclaimed, in a mixture of euphoria and terror. 'Goodbye for ever, Dsôn! Curses on you, damned black-eyed filth!' He spat down at the city beneath them. 'I'm going to put paid to your evil plans!'

Alarm bells were sounding and a crossbow bolt skimmed past his head.

He realised that this was only the beginning of his escape. And that there were four other flight-mares that could pursue them.

Girdlegard

Vanélia, capital of the magic realm of Rhuta
1023 P.Q. (7514th solar cycle in old reckoning), early summer

Goïmron looked in on Tungdil Goldhand as he did every orbit in the mornings, before then checking on Hargorina, where he found Gata by her bedside. The blonde dwarf had swapped her heavy armour for an ankle-length dark brown dress that flattered her figure; she still had the small silver brooch with its elaborate symbols.

Goïmron nodded at her, coming quietly to stand beside her. He had taken a bath and shaved his beard, leaving only the side whiskers. He was wearing a tunic, breeches and town shoes. He felt much more comfortable without the hard leather armoured jacket. 'How is your mistress doing?'

Gata looked worried. 'I don't know.'

Both patients lay on soft beds in their own bright rooms. The maga's servants changed their bandages every day.

'I'd have to say the same about Goldhand. Any human would have been killed by those four arrows. But a dwarf of his lineage and his battle experience seems able to withstand the effects of the älfar poison. So far, that is . . .' Seeing the cold compresses recently applied to Hargorina's limbs to bring down her fever, Goïmron thought the treatment ridiculously pedestrian, given they were now in the hands of a magician. Vanéra was not one for incantations and healing spells. 'Did the maga say what else she plans to do?'

'She's still hunting for a special artefact in her Chamber of Wonders. There's one that can heal the worst injuries, she said. A dark red carnelian knife with a white porcelain handle. But she doesn't know where it's got to. Not *exactly* where.' Gata heaved a sigh. 'It must have been good in the old times, when real magicians just had to snap their fingers to get things done. But nowadays a maga can't do more than–'

'. . . than search through a roomful of artefacts to find something to use.' Goïmron was dissatisfied and impatient. Vanéra did not seem to have grasped the seriousness of the situation and she appeared totally out of her depth in the quest for the right treatment. *I can't stand by and watch any longer.* 'Do you maybe know where I can find this Chamber of Wonders?'

'I seem to remember the servants saying it was in the middle of the building.' Gata looked at him incredulously. 'You're not going to try to locate the artefact yourself?'

'I am a Fourthling. If anyone can find a carnelian in the middle of a pile of stuff, it's probably going to be me. Without any magic.' Goïmron was delighted with his idea. 'And anyway, how big can a "chamber" be?'

'But you must ask Vanéra first. She is not likely to leave her valuables unguarded. Who knows what magic beings–'

'Or artefacts.'

'Or, indeed, artefacts, are charged with guarding her things?' Gata looked at him imploringly. 'Would you try? We can't lose Goldhand or Hargorina – not either of them. In my eyes, she is the greater heroine. If she were to die . . .'

'But of course. I'll go and find the carnelian knife.' Goïmron was already half out of the room. 'I'll have found it by this evening.'

His legs carried him swiftly through the extensive corridors and arcades. Left and right were statues, busts and paintings all created by the maga. She had a high opinion of her own artistic talent. Not only was she two hundred years old, it was said, having kept the appearance of a forty-year-old, but she considered herself to be the most powerful maga there had ever been.

Goïmron remembered how disdainfully Chòldunja had spoken of Vanéra, who was, in the young woman's opinion, merely able to make use of objects and spells that cleverer heads had invented and written about in former times. She was apparently very skilled in handling such items, but, in truth, any famula or famulus would learn these arts in their first cycle of training. You just had to be careful with some of the magically charged artefacts, or with specific spells written on paper or parchment.

Goïmron was more generous in his judgement. *As long as she's prepared to help us, it doesn't really matter.* He expected to find Vanéra in the Chamber of Wonders. *She'll be looking for the carnelian.*

A flight of stairs led down to a small room deep underground. On the walls there were trompe l'oeil paintings to give the impression of being in the open air, or looking out of palace windows on to a splendid vista of Rhuta. Goïmron had expected a servant or a famulus to stop him and ask his business, but he went through an archway decorated with magic symbols quite unchallenged. He found himself in a hall.

Opposite him he saw a double portal of polished light-grey liguster wood with gold fittings. The right-hand door stood invitingly open.

Goïmron was not going to pass up this opportunity.

He stepped carefully over the threshold and into the brightly lit room. 'Esteemed Maga Vanéra,' he called out. 'It's me.

Goïmron Chiselcut. I've come to help you look for your healing artefact. We Fourthlings have a bit of a talent for finding jewels and semi-precious stones.'

As he uttered these words, he looked around—and needed a few heartbeats to recover from his surprise.

The word *chamber* did not come close. Even the largest and most elaborate ceremonial dwarf hall in Malleniagard was nothing compared to what he saw on looking down from the balustrade.

His blue eyes took in the sight, thirty paces below him, of total confusion: overflowing shelves and cupboards, crates and boxes, obscure structures and abstract creations. The rectangular hall, forty by a hundred paces, was full to bursting with piles and heaps of densely massed objects. He espied items of jewellery, pieces of armour, rolls of parchment, weighty tomes, tapestries, lamps, pottery horses: everything remotely possible and a lot of impossible things, too.

But this was not all.

Some of the cupboards and shelves had collapsed under the accumulated collections, spilling their contents on to the floor. In places the mounds were piled knee-high. It would be like wading through a field of mud to start looking for anything here.

Generous light was afforded by lamps and chandeliers hanging from the ceiling, casting no shadows.

'By Vraccas!' Goïmron murmured. No wonder Vanéra had not been able to lay her hands on the carnelian knife. There was obviously no one in charge of sorting this archive. *This is going to be tough.* 'Esteemed Maga? Where are you?'

To his right was a broad spiral staircase leading down. As he went down the steps, he felt as if he might drown in the sea of junk. *This is worse than Solto's back room.*

He was missing his lessons with Chòldunja; she and Rodana would be waiting for him back at the border. He had had no opportunity to pay them a visit because he did not feel able to leave Goldhand's side, given the ancient dwarf's parlous state of health.

And he was missing Rodana.

If I can only lay my hands on this artefact, I can take the caravan back to the two of them and explain what I have seen. Who, apart from himself and the famuli, would ever have been able to cast an eye in this Chamber of Wonders? A chamber that turned out to be a vast hall?

Reaching floor level, Goïmron stood in the middle of a veritable forest of piles of random items. It made him feel extraordinarily small. Here and there, he noticed suspended metal ladders movable to wherever they were needed. The terrifying thought of balancing on a ladder forty paces up in the air made him break out in a sweat.

'Esteemed Maga Vanéra! Where can I find you?'

There was no answer, so, as Chòldunja had taught him, he closed his eyes and focused his mind on the carnelian. His people had a special gift for seeking out particular stones. This talent should put him at an advantage here.

Gata had told him that the artefact in question was dark red. This meant it was a masculine carnelian. The majority were flesh-coloured, but they could vary from deep red to nearly white with red specks. The bright or pale yellow ones, on the other hand, were female and even more powerful for healing purposes, according to Chòldunja.

Goïmron knew carnelians were popular for signet rings. In expert hands, a carnelian could function as a magic stone for enchantments such as emitting an astral body. It also offered protection against accidents and could neutralise poisons. In addition, it worked for ousting demons and dispelling melancholy or fear.

That's exactly what Goldhand and Hargorina both need. After a while, Goïmron began to notice gentle vibrations that could be coming from a carnelian. *Won't Goldhand be surprised when he gets up from his sickbed and sees what's changed in Girdlegard while he's been away? And the changes still happening now.*

Orbit for orbit, the Children of the Smith were streaming in, eager to see their hero and hear what he had to say. The first delegations sent by humans, elves and meldriths were on their way. The reappearance of the legendary dwarf had brought a new sensation to the inhabitants of Girdlegard: the feeling of hope.

There's an artefact at the back there! He opened his eyes and set off. 'Esteemed Maga! Where are you?' He was bothered by his conscience in invading her privacy in this way. But there was no going back. 'I think I know where the carnelian is that you're looking for.' His voice did not carry far because of the insulating effect of the piles of collected items.

There was no answer. He moved past the strangest of random objects – there were precious items of goldsmith's decorative work, set with coral, pearl and mountain crystal, enormous ocean clams, goblets of delicate metal, ostrich eggs in a gold setting, and carvings done with the bones of trolls or giants. He saw mysterious mathematical and scientific equipment with pointers, pendulums and springs. And then surgical instruments, distorting mirrors and a huge kaleidoscopic tunnel four paces long he would be able to walk through if he bent double.

Why does Vanéra keep all of this? Goïmron had reached the far end of the hall and was concentrating again with his eyes closed. To his immense relief, he was able to locate the carnelian ten paces above his head on an extremely deep shelf that went back five paces. *At least I shan't have to climb right up to the ceiling.*

With the help of the movable ladders, he quickly got to the right level. A glass lamp floated over to Goïmron of its own accord. On reaching the front of the shelf, he realised what was needed. *Curses. I'm going to have to crawl right in.*

Sighing deeply, he carved himself a path in through the piles of stuff: books, toys, bits of armour, small boxes that turned out to be surprisingly heavy, dolls the size of humans, a few stuffed animals – examples of species long extinct in Girdlegard. *What if all these hunting trophies were to come alive?* With a shudder, Goïmron worked his way forward on hands and knees. The lantern glided along at his side.

He set off once more past a mound of clocks, unfathomable automatic machines, models of the heavens, strange glasses, and fruit stones with intricately carved patterns. If indeed all these items were magical artefacts and not just junk, then Vanéra had surely accumulated the biggest collection there had ever been.

Occasionally the oak planks of the shelf creaked under Goïmron's weight as he tried to make himself thin enough to get through a forest of obstacles.

He could not begin to imagine what power these objects might possess. It would be amazing if the maga were able to use most of them. His respect for her grew.

It must be back there. He was just about to move a small chest from his path when, out of the corner of his eye, he noticed the glow.

To his right, there was a dragon carved from bone. It was holding a shining light-blue stone the size of an egg, and protecting it fiercely. *But that's . . . a sea sapphire!* Goïmron had heard about these legendary gemstones from the Brown Mountains. They used at one time to be set into crowns for rulers and magicians. Every couple of thousand cycles, a specimen would be found down one of the mines. That's if people knew where to look. *I want to find out more about them.* Without pausing to think, he stowed the precious item in his pocket so he could ask Vanéra later.

MARKUS HEITZ | 315

Then he pushed the final obstruction out of his way and there, suddenly, was the carnelian knife with its white porcelain handle. *There you are!* Its tip was buried in an overturned drinx the size of a bear dog. A very skilled taxidermist must have prepared this mini version of the fabled being following descriptions from books. Drinxes were similar to a mix of a brightly coloured ape and a black blood-collar bear. But these creatures had never lived in Girdlegard. They were the kind of fabled monsters you scared children with.

Goïmron reached out for the artefact, grasping the handle and pulling. *We'll soon have you doing your good works.*

Hardly had the tip of the knife been freed from the animal's body when there was a faint crackling sound, closely followed by a bright shimmer that flitted along the cobbled-together stuffed body of the drinx.

The dead glass eyes of the fabled beast shone brightly. The hairy body gave a spasm and the creature doubled in size. Bones and muscles woke to new life and, with an eerie, penetrating scream, the drinx bared its vicious fangs. Furious, it turned its turquoise eyes on the dwarf.

Vraccas, protect me! Grasping the priceless knife between his teeth, Goïmron crawled backwards, making painfully slow progress because of the confused mess of objects and artefacts. He shoved stuff aside, pushing things off the shelf entirely and hearing them land with a crash below. *Keep that beast away from me!*

The drinx thrashed around wildly, rearing up and thereby breaking the wooden shelf above it – and it went in for the attack.

I was in the abyss for a long time.

In the ravine known as Phondrasôn, which is what the älfar call it.

Two hundred and fifty cycles in darkness.

A darkness due less to lack of light than to a feeling.

There were three phases to my life in darkness.

And none of them good.

Excerpt from
The Adventures of Tungdil Goldhand,
as experienced in the Black Abyss
and written by himself.
First draft.

XI

Girdlegard

United Great Kingdom of Gauragon
Province of Fruitlands
1023 P.Q. (7514th solar cycle in old reckoning), early summer

'Have you seen how high the rye is growing, Your Princely Highness?' Altorn pointed to the crops surrounding them on all sides, the fields interrupted only by orchards and a clump of trees with cattle grazing in their shade. This dark-haired man of mature years was the captain of the guard and in charge of security for the heir to the Gautaya empire's throne. 'And the cereals are looking good! The province of Fruitlands will be bringing in a splendid harvest.'

'They are lucky.' Prince Ocdius, in his mid-twenties and with a wild mane of curly hair, could not get enough of the sight of these fertile acres. He was on horseback, as was his accompanying retinue of thirty. Two wagons trundled along with their luggage. Because of the rising temperatures, he had eschewed the idea of doing the journey in armour. 'Tell me – is it correct that one of the previous realms in my land used to be known as the Granary of Girdlegard?'

'Indeed so, Your Princely Highness.' Altorn sat upright in the saddle and took out his viewing glass to observe the fields more closely. It was purely a reflex. He had no concerns about the area. Gauragon was one of the safest realms, as long as you avoided the orc fortress of Kràg Tahuum or the frontier with Brigantia. 'It used to be called Tabaîn. They had wide plains, wider than our vista here, all full of cereal crops. Enough for their own land, and the rest available at bargain prices to merchant traders.'

Ocdius sighed. 'And we have now . . .?'

'A barren land with a giant volcano. We are beset by Ûra, harassed by orcs from the Salt Sea, and plundered by Undarimar's pirates,' Altorn reeled off soberly. 'And it has rendered Your Highness's father, let us say, despondent.'

'A harmless word for the desperate anger he feels about the unholy mess he is faced with, old friend.' Ocdius was imagining how it might be to reign in a land like Gauragon. Apart from the few danger spots, it must be child's play.

In Gautaya, by contrast, there was little potential for farming because of the recent volcanic activity in the plain at the foot of the Grey Mountains, together with the spread of the dry and inhospitable salt flats. True, there was income from selling salt and high-quality granite, but without imported grain supplies, they would not be able to survive. This made the empire reliant on others, a dependency deeply resented by the proud people of Gautaya. At least there was an abundance of fish at their disposal, thanks to their long coastline.

Ocdius symbolised hope of future prosperity, a sign to the younger generation not to desert their land wholesale in search of riches in other realms. Emigrants boarded ships and headed west through the sea gate, never to return.

'You appreciate the importance of your mission, Your Princely Highness.' Altorn put down his viewing glass. As expected, he had not seen anything of concern. The ten torkel vultures circling on the horizon might be waiting to descend on the carcass of some cow breathing its last under an orchard tree. 'If it fails, your parents and all their subjects will soon be having to seek a new home outside Gautaya.'

Ocdius laughed quietly. 'I've heard that life is good in Fortgard.'

'No life for a prince on whose land the town was illegally erected. You would soon succumb to ... an accident.' Altorn looked at his charge intently. 'Should it prove true that Tungdil Goldhand still lives and may unite the dwarf tribes, they could be our salvation. Except not against Ûra, I'm afraid. The groundling folk, too, are powerless against the white demon of the air.'

'But they are strong enough against the salt sea orcs. I know.' Ocdius had grown up with the northern danger and had slain several of the beasts. However, humans could not survive for long in the salt flats and travelling deep into the territory was impossible. The burning air stripped mucous membranes and corroded lungs. The orcs were well aware of this and had taken over the region in the north all the way up to the slopes of the volcano; their physical constitution was adapted to the hostile environment there.

Gauragon and Undarimar had rejected Gautaya's requests for assistance. Ocdius could appreciate why the marine kingdom was not willing to help, as their ship-based forces could achieve little on land. And there was a long-standing dispute with Undarimar about a certain coastal region. Neither Ocdius nor his father could accept the validity of this claim.

Gauragon had offered only feeble excuses, although it would have been in their own interest to assist in combatting the salt sea orcs and in ejecting them before they took a fancy to some of the neighbouring provinces. Orcs were immune to suihhi, the plague that King Gajek usually deployed against his enemies.

Relishing the warm air, Ocdius closed his eyes. 'Isn't it great for once not to have to worry about being ambushed by beasts and monsters?'

'But if we had the dwarves to protect us against the orcs, Your Princely Highness, then we could feel safe.'

'That's true. Do you really think we can persuade Goldhand to bring his united dwarf tribes to our aid?' Ocdius hardly dared to hope that the ancient hero would agree.

'If we were the only petitioners, I think we could. But half of Girdlegard sees his return as a sign from Vraccas.' Altorn was under no illusion. 'We will be in competition with them for his help.'

'We have the advantage of our proximity to the Grey Mountains, the homeland of the Fifthlings. I'm sure he will look kindly on our request.' Ocdius opened his eyes and looked at the road running straight ahead through the fields all the way to the horizon. 'Orcs are arch-enemies of the groundlings.'

'But the dwarves have not yet met the salt sea orcs in a fullscale battle, only in skirmishes in the Fire province. The orc scouts were beaten back, I understand.' Altorn turned back to watch their convoy. The troops in their full armour looked tired, and the horses, hanging their heads, were making slow progress. 'We should stop for a while. The sun has grown very hot. We're all roasting.'

Ocdius indicated the small clump of trees. 'It looks nice and green over there. I expect there'll be a stream. Shade and some cool water. A very welcome idea.'

A sudden gust of wind went through the cornfields, so that ears and stalks bent and waved in the wind. A dancing eddy of dry earth rose up near the soldiers; the top of the column of swirling dust, dirt and straw seemed to be high above their heads, reaching up to the midday sun.

'It's a Samusin twister,' said Ocdius happily. 'I haven't seen one of those since I was a child in the salt plain.'

Altorn looked up dubiously towards the burning daystar. 'The sun is at its highest point. This could have a different meaning.'

The prince looked at him in surprise. 'What do you mean?'

'The ancient legends of Tabaîn told of a demon that likes to frequent the ripe corn fields, especially when the sun is high. Then it grabs something living as its prey in order to drench the crops with blood to ensure a strong harvest.' He took his shield out of its holder by the side of the saddle. 'Pay attention to the whole area,' he called out over his shoulder to the soldiers. 'Two of you go on ahead to reconnoitre.'

The tired soldiers were slow to implement the abrupt order. The ride had been a long one and their shields were heavy.

'So you believe in the fairy tale?'

'It's a *legend*, Your Highness. Legends often have a basis in some truth.' Altorn took up his viewing glass again, then stood up in the stirrups and scanned the area below the circling vultures.

The expertly ground lenses brought the dead bodies closer as they lay at the side of the road and in the apple orchard. Humans and dwarves had had limbs hacked off with sharp blades. Heads and arms and great hunks of flesh were missing. The corpses were strangely pale in colour. Here and there the birds had picked at the injuries. Spears and lances were planted in the ground, with pennants fluttering from them as if in warning not to approach.

'What, by . . .?' Altorn quickly reported what he had seen. 'The flags belong to different kingdoms. I recognise the colours of Khalteran, Palusien and . . . that must be Ribasturian, Highness.'

Ocdius swore and looked for his own spyglass.

'Did they kill each other, do you think?'

'Unlikely.'

'You're sticking with the corn demon story?'

'Could have been orcs. Gangs of orcs from Kràg Tahuum have sometimes been sighted here, trying to set up an outpost. Maybe they ran into some of the delegations.'

'But I can't see a single dead orc.'

'They could have carried off their dead and wounded.' Altorn moved his spyglass round to the little wood and the whirlwind column disintegrated, depositing its load of straw and soil dust. 'They could have been hanging out there in the wood, hiding, ready to rush out for a quick attack and then back in to await their next victims.'

'Hardly. There are no signs. No hint of monsters like that. The undergrowth is quite dense and looks undisturbed.' Thinking of his exhausted troops, Ocdius ordered them over to the shelter of the trees. 'We'll examine the situation when we've rested. At any rate, we shouldn't . . .'

He was interrupted by the sound of terrified screams and a rustling noise.

Altorn and Ocdius turned swiftly round in alarm, putting their viewing aids down.

Two riderless horses stood on the path, blood dripping from the saddles. With a quiet rustle, the trampled stalks of corn righted themselves, concealing how the missing riders had been dragged off through the fields.

'Report to me!' commanded Altorn, protecting the prince with his shield. 'What happened?'

'We don't know, Captain. They were . . . torn away by an invisible hand,' replied a guard, chalk-white with terror. 'Carried into the field . . . and then they disappeared!'

Ocdius could clearly see where the life-juice of the missing guards had been absorbed up into the ears of ripe corn. A hitherto unknown fear spread rapidly among the company from Gautaya. 'Altorn, from this orbit on, I believe in legends,' he whispered. 'We need to get out of these fields. Everyone over to the trees,' he ordered. 'Ride as fast as you can!' He pressed his spurs sharply into his horse's flanks and was off. 'Follow me!'

A few moments later, Altorn and the vanguard had encircled him for his protection and together they thundered along the road to then take the pathway leading to the grove. Judging from the hoofmarks in the sand, it seemed that others had recently attempted to find safety there.

Riding diagonally ahead of the prince, Altorn turned to look over his shoulder at his troops. Horror filled his spirit when he saw how few were left. They had lost at least five, and the baggage wagons had been abandoned. *Palandiell, I beseech you, come to our aid!*

Abruptly the captain was seized by the shield and dragged from his horse.

Altorn was hurled through the air, landing on his back in the middle of the field of rye. For several heartbeats he had neither breath nor vision. All he could see were stars. *But the prince!*

'Ocdius!' He groaned instead of shouting out the name. He rolled to the side, coughing, and staggered to his feet. 'Your Princely Highness!' He found himself in waist-high crops that rustled and moved in the breeze.

Altorn was alone except for the riderless horses running around. The guards had vanished, along with Ocdius. 'By all the gods!' He pulled his sword out of its scabbard and waved his shield. 'Come and try it, Corn Demon! I'll hack you to pieces for what you've done!'

A new gust of wind went through the rye field, creating a wave that seemed to acknowledge the challenge. Altorn felt his heart gripped with icy fear despite the hot sun burning above. His hands began to shake.

'Altorn! Here to me!' Ocdius was calling from the clump of trees. 'Come on! You can make it!'

He is safe! Gathering his courage, he charged through the field, holding his shield and brandishing his sword, ready to do battle. Any foe in his path would be pierced and knocked to the ground.

The corn demon, however, appeared to be replete and content.

Altorn plunged through the undergrowth unopposed, slashing his way through creepers and bushes. 'Your Princely Highness!' Ocdius was down on his knees and staring blankly into space.

Behind the young man there rose a mighty black-barked oak and in its branches hung the two guards who had gone on ahead. Small twigs had fastened round their throats, strangling them, so that their faces were bright red. Kicking and struggling were to no avail.

A lurco oak! Altorn felt another wave of fear. 'Come to me, my prince. You are too close to the Gobbling Tree. If it stretches out its catcher branch, it'll have you.'

Ocdius did not move. But he turned his gaze to Altorn. 'Tell my parents that I love them.'

'Come away from there!' Altorn moved slowly forward. 'Quick! While the tree is still busy!'

The magical lurco began to stuff a struggling victim into a cavity in its trunk. Bones, splintered by the immense pressure, pierced the man's flesh and blood sprayed out. The oak creaked as it ingested the body of the dying soldier.

'We have a pact, the prince and myself. *He* surrenders his life *for yours*.' A woman's icy voice issued quietly from the shadow of the trees. 'Such a noble gesture. Ocdius would have made a fine emperor.'

Startled, Altorn turned to where the words had been spoken, and saw a female älf step out from behind a blood beech tree. She wore no armour. One eye was whitened over, the other black as ink. At neck and wrist and on her brow she wore elaborate jewellery. She had on a long black dress and over it a light-coloured mantle. Her countenance was half-light, half-dark. 'Whatever in the name of all the good powers is an älf doing in these parts?'

'I am heralding the onset of a new era.' As she pointed at the young man, her rings and bracelets shone in the light. 'I proposed to Ocdius that we spare you so that you can return to Gautaya to make the announcement. And to warn his parents. Let us play with cards open on the table.'

Having completed its consumption of one victim, the lurco oak began stuffing in the next, to the accompaniment of the same hideous noises.

Altorn had never seen one of these Gobbling Trees before. Created by magic in the Land of Wonders, their seeds had spread throughout Girdlegard. Most had by now been destroyed but occasionally an old specimen might be found. *Why now?* 'What does that mean?'

'We set a trap for you. Not just for you. For all the delegations intent on paying their respects to Goldhand,' the striking-looking female älf calmly explained. 'There's only the one road west to Rhuta. Neat, isn't it?'

'But the corn demon . . .'

'An old legend, a little sleight of hand, a pinch of fright and a good turn of speed. Enough to make you believe the legend and to bring you *directly*' – she tapped her foot – 'here to the lurco oak.' She watched, impervious, as the tree finished its meal. 'Such an interesting species, created by magic and nature. We'll be growing more of them. Useful for executions, once we have established our power base.'

A catcher branch shot out to grab Ocdius, encircling his upper body. The prince made no effort to resist.

'No!' Altorn sprang forward, wanting to slash at the tree with his sword to save this young prince whom he had known from the cradle.

But before he could reach the tree, the anonymous älf woman stood in his path and delivered a sharp blow to his chin, knocking him off his feet so he landed on his back. Altorn could have sworn her bracelets and bangles had lit up when she punched him. 'Listen to my words. No delegation on this road will ever reach Rhuta. Nobody should dare to form an alliance with the groundlings. *We* shall rule in Girdlegard. The era of the älfar is nigh.'

Gasping for breath, Altorn pushed himself up on his elbows. His ribs were painful, probably cracked or broken. 'Spare the prince's life. Let me die instead of Ocdius.'

'No. The pact we agreed stipulates that your life be spared and that you should try to warn his parents.' The älf bowed ironically towards the prince in farewell before the branches jammed themselves through his unresisting body, shattering his bones, to make him fit within their grasp. 'If you are quick enough, you may be able to save them.'

'Save them? From what?'

'From our assassins. Every palace in Girdlegard will receive a visit. Our murderers are already underway.' She gave an icy smile, which was made more uncanny because of the particoloured face. 'Hurry, Captain Altorn! At the double! You might save the emperor of Gautaya. And you can tell him his son gave his life for you.' She retreated slowly. 'Imagine what would happen if you were to fail. What would your own life be worth to you then?'

His eyes streaming with tears, Altorn was forced to watch Ocdius being thrust through the opening in the black bark of the tree. He had to listen to the awful sounds as the oak crunched up his precious young charge. There was nothing left of the heir to the imperial throne, no trace of the symbol of hope for a brighter future.

Uttering a strident cry of despair, Altorn wiped the tears off his cheeks and ran out from the trees to find his horse and swing himself, in great pain, into the saddle.

'Fly!' Against all normal practice, Altorn threw away his shield and belaboured the exhausted horse's flanks with the flat side of his sword. 'Fly! Get me to Gautaya. As quick as ever you can!'

Riding precipitously, Captain Altorn headed for home to avert a further catastrophe. That is, if he escaped the clutches of the älf woman.

Girdlegard

Vanélia, capital of the magic realm of Rhuta
1023 P.Q. (7514th solar cycle in old reckoning), early summer

The furious drinx, now double its original size, leaped forward into the shelf and grabbed at Goïmron.

You'll not get me! He dodged its claws and, with all his strength, thrust back to get away from the fabled creature, now magically awakened. There were objects clattering and clinking on all sides as more of the shelf's contents flew out and down to the floor of the Chamber of Wonders.

Goïmron noticed, too late, that he had reached the end of the shelf. He was tumbling down a full ten paces, but he still held the vital carnelian knife in his teeth. Above him he could see the ape-bear face of the drinx roaring at him and about to follow him head first. It was obviously adept at climbing.

Vraccas! Let me live! Or get the knife to heal me after it's gone through my skull! He closed his eyes and waited for the impact. *Better still, Vraccas, let me fly!*

SO BE IT. He heard the authoritative voice in his head.

His fall ended abruptly.

What . . .? Looking round, he saw he was floating close above some of the random objects that he had previously dislodged.

Then he slumped down a little further and landed with a bump on some scattered artefacts. *Thanks, Vraccas!*

He got hurriedly to his feet, stowed the carnelian knife and ran along the crowded gangway hoping to shake off his pursuer, or at least to get to the door before the drinx did.

But the mythical creature's screeches were uncomfortably near at hand.

I'm not going to get away like this. Goïmron stopped short and drew his dagger, but he soon put it down and chose the sea sapphire instead. *How stupid of me. Was it the stone speaking to me just now? Did it read my thoughts?* The egg-sized gemstone gave off a bluish glow in his hand, as if it were really happy.

By now the drinx was three times as big as the dwarf and had grasped hold of a silver chandelier. Swinging it like a club, it hopped along on two legs and one hand and got ready to strike.

Goïmron concentrated on the sapphire. *Make it fall asleep!*

SO BE IT. There was a flash in the middle of the stone. A thick ray of light shot out, zigzagging towards the drinx, hitting it in the chest. With a dull thud, all the fur and flesh and bones inside exploded and it was torn to pieces. The hand with the silver lamp sailed past Goïmron's ear and clanged on to the floor of the corridor.

The force of the detonation had thrown the dwarf on to his back and propelled even more artefacts out of cupboards and off shelves. A heap of clothing and textiles smelling strongly of lavender floated down over his head.

Goïmron was stunned and confused. He could still hear the noise of the explosion in his head. *Didn't I ask for a sleep spell?*

SORRY. BIT OUT OF PRACTICE.

'What in Samusin's name is happening here?' Vanéra's infuriated voice echoed from the walls. 'Adelia! I told you not to come in here without permission! And I told you not to go trying out any of the artefacts inside the chamber.'

'Excuse me, Esteemed Maga,' came the prompt answer from the famula, 'but that wasn't me! I was starting to secretly do a bit of cataloguing in the archive, hoping to please you. I'm sorry. But I swear on my soul I never touched anything.'

Under his pile of robes and other material, Goïmron thought it wise to keep quiet. *Maybe they won't notice me.* The last thing he needed was trouble. He did not want to have to explain what he'd been up to. *And I certainly do not want to give up the sea sapphire.* The gemstone had definitely spoken to him. He was keen to discuss this with Chòldunja.

'Nonsense, Adelia! Who else could it have been?'

'Maybe one of the artefacts went off all by itself, Esteemed Maga.'

'It's good of you to think of helping with the archive, famula. But don't change the subject. What did you touch?'

'Nothing, I promise. On my life. It came from over there. Shelf number eighty-three. Let's have a look. You'll see . . .'

'If you're trying to cover up for something you did, you'll be out on your ear and looking for a new position.'

'I'd never do that, mistress.'

The women's footsteps were getting nearer.

The carnelian knife! Goïmron pulled it out of his shoulder bag and threw it at the drinx cadaver, where the women would be sure to see it. Then, his task fulfilled, he could just wait for an opportunity to sneak out of the Chamber of Wonders unseen.

Through a gap in the heap of piled-up textiles, he observed Vanéra and Adelia, still far off, squeezing through between the shelves. They noticed the carcass of the mythical being.

'We had a *drinx*?' The tall, brown-haired maga, in her dramatic gown of lilac and gold, looked at the mutilated corpse and then saw the surrounding mess. 'Oh, yes, I remember reading about it.'

'There! It's the carnelian knife!' Adelia stomped through the blood and guts in her grey robe and carefully picked up the dagger by its porcelain handle. 'It was stuck in the drinx. It must have brought him back to life.'

'Looks that way, yes.' Vanéra did not touch the dripping knife. 'It's disgusting. Take it upstairs and clean it up. Then take it to the dwarf's sickroom so I can treat him. Goldhand and the Thirdling woman, too.'

'Very good, Esteemed Maga,' Adelia said with a relieved smile on her face. 'So you believe me now, that it wasn't my doing?'

'Yes, I do, famula. Forgive me for suspecting you.' Vanéra looked around. Her gaze took in the total confusion that reigned, caused by the landslide of artefacts from the top shelves, and the subsequent detonation of the drinx. 'Sometimes these magically charged items do the weirdest things.' She gestured to the way out and Adelia hurried off.

In his hiding place, Goïmron held his breath as Vanéra wandered round studying the shelves, her hands behind her back. He reckoned she was about forty cycles of age. The pearl decorations made her appear older. *She certainly knows it can't have been a random event!*

'Adelia!' she suddenly called out in a loud voice.

'Yes, Esteemed Maga?' A faint response came from the distance.

'Send Mostro down here. Tell him to collect the drinx's remains and get it all cleared up. The blood and the carcass will soon be stinking to high heaven.'

'Of course, mistress.'

Vanéra looked up again to the place, ten paces up, where Goïmron had tumbled off the shelf. 'There used to be something up there,' she murmured, massaging her temples. Her engraved gold and pearl ring started to glow as if helping her remember. 'Something very valuable.'

Oh no. Goïmron cowered down under his mountain of fabrics. *Please don't remember. Forget about the sea sapphire.*

Vanéra suddenly turned and strode off.

Goïmron waited a few more heartbeats before daring to fight his way out of the pile of heaped-up clothes. He moved quietly towards the stairs. There was no way he wanted to get locked inside the Chamber of Wonders. Or to get found there. Nobody must ever suspect he was behind all of this. In spite of everything, he was glad he had made this sidestep into the hall. *I will have saved Goldhand and Hargorina.*

Because the maga was proceeding only slowly, stopping every so often to rummage through the contents of a cupboard, Goïmron managed to reach the steps before she did and to get out through the polished liguster-wood double doors without being seen.

Arrived in the outer foyer, he closed his eyes in relief and took deep breaths. *Thank you, Vraccas!*

'What do you think you're doing here?' Mostro's voice was half surprised, half chastising.

Goïmron quickly opened his eyes to see the famulus in front of him in his leather apron, carrying a bucket of water, a floor cloth and a sponge, and with several towels draped over his shoulder. Normally Mostro, like his mistress the maga, was fastidious about his appearance, with his abundant dark blond hair artistically arranged round his head in waves. Wearing a maid's apron rather ruined the effect. 'Oh, I heard there's been some kind of accident?'

'A terrible mess, yes. But nothing to concern one of the Esteemed Maga's guests.' Mostro pointed to the stairs that led to the main building. 'Go back upstairs, if you would, Master Chiselcut. Make yourself comfortable and soon you will be able to witness the maga healing the two injured patients.'

'Oh, so has the carnelian knife been found?'

Mostro's dark brows shot up in surprise. Even the hair of his elegant, pointed beard seemed flustered. 'How do you know about the artefact?'

'It was Gata. She mentioned it. Said it had got lost.' Goïmron hurried past, heading for the staircase. He was keen to avoid meeting Vanéra and having to answer questions. 'Great that it's turned up. And you're right, Famulus Mostro. I *have* to see the healing with my own eyes!'

Sweating with the exertion, he reached his rooms and collapsed on to the bed. *Vraccas! That was close!* He took out the sea sapphire and stared at it in fascination.

The mystical blue glow was throbbing less intensely now, but the tremendous energy in the stone was still obvious to the dwarf. The miniature dragon fashioned in bone held the jewel wrapped protectively in its wings, forming a small handle.

Did you really speak to me or did I imagine it? Goïmron rubbed the smooth surfaces of the polished gemstone, which had been prepared and engraved by a master craftsman. He noticed, however, certain faults on the facets needing immediate attention.

The stone remained silent.

There was a knock at the door and Brûgar burst into the room. Goïmron quickly hid the precious souvenir under his sheets. 'What is it?'

'They've found the carnelian knife!' The bald dwarf was ecstatic. His pipe wobbled excitedly in the corner of his mouth. 'Hurry up! You've got to come and see this! I've put celebration tobacco in my pipe already.'

In Goïmron's opinion, the smell of leather and grass was a bit strong for a feast day. 'I'm coming.'

Brûgar puffed smoke into the room like a beekeeper approaching his hives. 'Right, off we go!'

'I need to finish praying to Vraccas.'

'Understood. But you can save your words. They won't be needed. It's the maga, not the Divine Smith, who'll be saving our hero's life.' Brûgar was already half out of the door. 'Hurry up. Or you'll miss King Regnor and his entourage arriving at our artefact polisher's court. He won't be impressed if you keep him waiting.'

'Me?'

'You've got some explaining to do, gem cutter.'

'Me?' Not the wittiest of rejoinders, but the smoke was making him cough.

'Of course I mean you. Explain how you managed to persuade our heiress to the throne to tell lies for you. *That* won't be easy,' he chortled with dwarfish schadenfreude. 'You're lucky the healing artefact has turned up.' Brûgar made off down the hall, having closed Goïmron's door.

Goïmron was in no mood to appreciate the joke.

Girdlegard

Cliffton, capital of the kingdom of Palusien
1023 P.Q. (7514th solar cycle in old reckoning), early summer

Stémna was waiting on the drawbridge a good five paces away from the main gate to Cliffton. Intensely irritated, she surveyed the formation of guards pointing their weapons at her, faces hidden behind visors.

Behind the phalanx of soldiers stood Chancellor Yltho in his dark, embroidered robe of office and matching cap. He had got up on a crate to speak to her over the guards' helmeted heads. He had been speaking now for quite some time.

Stémna, lost in deep thought, was no longer listening.

Ever since becoming the Voice of the dragon Ûra, Stémna had known a handful of incidents where she had been denied access, or where the tribute for the Mistress of Girdlegard had been withheld. Sometimes it was impossible to understand the reason, or sometimes there would have been the silliest of excuses made. But each case had resulted in the same consequence: total annihilation by means of dragon fire.

But Chancellor Yltho had offered a new, understandable but extremely disturbing excuse for Cliffton's non-compliance: the capital city, and therefore the whole realm of Palusien, was unwilling to pay a single coin in tribute because of a reason of greater significance than any she had previously ever heard. A power struggle of enormous proportions was apparently the cause. That is, if the man was speaking the truth.

Stémna finally managed to quell her astonishment. She collected her thoughts. She raised her right hand, and the chancellor stopped talking. 'You expect me to believe that an älfar assassin has forced his way into the royal apartments and murdered King Kamred and his sons in their beds?'

'"... expect me to believe", indeed!' Yltho exclaimed in indignation, the chain of office jumping up and down on his chest. 'Have you been listening to a word I've said? Not only do we have a widowed queen in full mourning in charge of our kingdom, but we lost at least a third of our soldiers and palace staff before we were able to kill the murderous älf. Do you insist on witnesses? How many would you like? I can show you the assassin's body.'

'So the älf must obviously have wanted to be seen at his doings. Otherwise you, chancellor, would also be dead.' To Stémna, the whole situation seemed odd in the extreme. The ruler of Dsôn Khamateion would normally be content to remain at home, forging plans that he never actually carried out. That was one thing she had learned in the course of her visits. The Ganyeios might occasionally enter a pact with the Omuthan, with a view to taking over Brigantia at some future point, but for älfar to assassinate all the male members of Palusien's royal family made no sense at all. The territory lay right at the far end of Girdlegard.

A message to Ûra? To show her that Dsôn Khamateion can launch a deadly attack at any time? And anywhere at all? Stémna adjusted her white hat and felt the warmth of the setting sun on her skin. The daystar was painting delightful colours on the glittering waves as they crashed on to the beach below Cliffton's walls. 'I shall report to my mistress. You will be aware of the normal consequence of a refusal to pay tribute. But I'm sure she will take the circumstances into consideration.'

'The circumstances?' yelled Yltho, quite beside himself, his beardless countenance bright red. 'The kingdom of Palusien has contributed riches over riches for decades and decades to your beast. We have paid her for protection. But what sort of protection did we get?'

'My mistress protects you from other dragons that—'

'It was you, Stémna, who always promised us protection! Protection against any change. And in my view, that includes preventing the black-eyes swanning up and murdering us whenever they fancy.' The chancellor prepared to outstare her, remaining fearless and firm. 'Or has Ûra maybe lost her influence with the other beasts? It seems the älfar no longer recognise her authority. And if *that* should be the case, we'd do better to scrape our gold coins together to pay the black-eyes, and not you.'

'I would definitely advise against that course of action.'

'Then tell me what I should say to our poor widowed queen.'

Yltho spread out his arms. 'How should I break it to her that the protection offered by the greatest dragon is worth nothing? Or perhaps the dragon itself is long dead and the money goes straight into your pocket?' Exasperated, he pulled off his cap. 'Get out of here, dragon messenger! Don't come back until you can prove to me and the poor queen that a dragon's word can be trusted. That protection is worth paying for. Then you'll get your damned money. And only then.' He gestured disdainfully with his headgear and placed it back on his head. 'For now, you get nothing. Unless it's a steel arrow between the eyes. Or a golden one, if you like, if you're going to insist on a tribute.'

'I will pass on your words to my mistress. She may not be pleased.'

'So what? Is she going to come and eat me? And the queen? Burn our land?' Yltho was scathing in his mockery. 'Then she will learn that her simple, easy life is a thing of the past.' He signalled to the watch. The guards marched backwards, keeping their pikestaffs raised.

Stémna was lost for words.

Threats only worked if there was no greater suffering and no greater peril than that issuing from Ûra herself. The chancellor had been explicit about what he saw as a more serious danger for Girdlegard.

'Go and talk to the monster you call your mistress. Come back when you've got something good to report. Otherwise there'll soon be no tribute paid by any of the kingdoms. There might even be talk of rebellion. Revolt against Ûra.' Yltho jumped down from his crate and dropped from sight behind the guards. 'You will have heard the latest: the dwarves are gathering round their newly returned hero. Who knows what they may be planning in their new optimism? They can forge any amount of weaponry capable of piercing a dragon's scales.'

The heavy entrance gate to Cliffton rumbled shut.

I would have known. Stémna wheeled round and left. *My spy would already have told me.* As she crossed the long bridge over the gap separating Cliffton's black basalt promontory from the rest of the landmass, she heard the mocking shouts and abuse raining down from the battlements.

Swinging herself up on to her waiting horse, she rode away on the high coastal road along the clifftops, with its breathtaking view of the sea and the many sailing vessels, some of which were heading towards the capital city's port. Others, in the opposite direction, were bound for Litusien or Ribasturian, hoping to make it before nightfall.

Stémna brought her mount to a halt on a slight rise that afforded a wonderful vantage point. She needed to reflect on what had happened and to order her thoughts before calling Ûra to give her report.

Lovers sat here on stone benches or on blankets on the ground. Others had gathered to watch the sunset from the roofed arcade leading up to the monument. People of all ages had brought along food to share with friends. An artist had put up her easel and was capturing the moment on paper with rapid strokes, using silver pens, lead pencils and charcoal sticks: Cliffton, the sea, the sailing ships, the whole scene evoked in shades of grey.

The envoy's approach was hardly noticed. Nobody reacted to the appearance of the Voice of the dragon. Dismounting with a grim expression, Stémna tethered her horse to a convenient tree. *Only a few orbits ago they would have grovelled at my feet in the dust, terrified of Ûra's might.*

Cliffton lay on the end of the tongue of basalt rock running from the Cloudfire volcano in the interior all the way to the sea. The fire mountain had been formed just nine hundred cycles previously, devastating most of the forests and thus badly affecting the whole of the queendom. The stream of basalt had cut through the wide low-lying belt of swampland bordering the coast. These marshes made it impossible for neighbouring realms to build harbours, and they caused recurrent fever plagues costing many lives. On the other hand, there was an abundance of flammable gas which could be used in various ways – as long as the ragana people issued the relevant permits for gas extraction from what they considered their territory. Nobody wanted war with the moor witches, said to be capable of extreme cruelty and thought to practise cannibalism and black magic.

And yet they pay Ûra's tribute without complaint. Stémna sat on a bench near the edge of the cliff and stared out across the sea that had been formed less than a thousand cycles before. *But how long will they continue to do that?* On her journey she had heard rumours of attacks on palaces and on the delegations heading to Rhuta, but she had dismissed the talk as local washerwomen's gossip. *Are the black-eyes getting ideas? Or do they know something that I've missed?*

'Here you are. A picture for the dragon's messenger.' This friendly offer came from an elegant figure holding out a drawing in a gloved hand. It was a portrait done in lead and silver pencil with highlights in a reddish-colour paint that had not yet dried completely. 'As a souvenir of this orbit.'

Stémna accepted the gift, careful not to get red paint on her own white leather gloves. 'My thanks.' She could not take her eyes off the picture. The technique and skill were extraordinary. 'It is excellent!'

'Thank you for your praise. I'm afraid it is only a very amateur attempt,' the gentle voice went on. 'You should have seen what my father could conjure up on paper and canvas. Or on parchment sometimes. No matter what kind of skin was employed in its production.'

After a further glance at the picture, Stémna lifted her gaze to the artist at her side. His slim features were obscured by the hood of a dark mantle. 'Did you say *skin*?' Next to the easel lay the woman painter, motionless now. Blood was pouring from her throat. All the courting couples had disappeared. There was nobody else on the clifftop except Stémna and the dark artist.

It was at this point that she realised who she had facing her. *An älf!*

Quick as a flash, he stabbed her with the rune-decorated tionium spear he had been concealing behind his body. The blade went in under her collarbone, emerging out her back through the shoulder blade.

She screamed in agony. Blood coursed down her clothing at the front and the back of her body. 'Curses on you!'

'I hope what I've heard about you is correct,' he interrupted coolly, holding her suspended like a fish on the spear. 'It's said: "wound her messenger and the beast will appear".' He raised his dark eyes and studied the cloudless evening sky. 'I hope I shan't have to wait long. I have a lot to do.' He twisted the spear in the wound, making Stémna groan with pain. 'I'm sure it would be better for you, as well.'

I have conducted extensive research and have collected all the documents I could find: witness statements, sentries' records, patrol reports. Taken together, they give a picture of how the beasts' incursion happened.

In general, it should be noted that, in the utter confusion that resulted from the time of the earthquakes and accompanying catastrophes, beasts arrived via the unmanned north and south passes before these entrances could be closed off, and then spread out all over Girdlegard. In the present-day Brigantia, this influx has never abated.

There were two major orc realms that were destroyed in the course of time by alliances made between humans and elves. There remained the salt sea orcs and the beasts in Kràg Tahuum, although it should be remembered that they had not built the fortress themselves.

The majority of the monsters lived in inhospitable regions, originally in the vicinity of the volcanoes. This was because humans would not venture there for fear of the dragons.

I can state that the orcs are planning to revive their old kingdom of Toboribor in the south-east of Girdlegard, in territory that is now low-lying land. Apart from the orcs, there are forest trolls in the south-west *part of Ribasturian and cliff ogres in the west of the empire of Gautaya that are feared.*

Excerpt from
The History of Girdlegard Following the Great Quake
(vol III, p. 3213),
as compiled by Master Ukentro Smallquill of Enaiko

XII

Girdlegard

Brown Mountains
Brigantia
1023 P.Q. (7514th solar cycle in old reckoning), early summer

Klaey had finished relating his Dsôn Khamateion adventures. He took an oat biscuit from the plate and dunked it once, twice, three times in his almond rose water before nibbling at it with a private grin of pleasure. He would allow time for the hubbub of conversation to die down.

Life had been amazing for him ever since his return on Deathwing, with all the news and information he had gathered about the älfar realm. Far from being the ne'er-do-well youngest brother, he was now seen as the most valued of the Berengart siblings. His hoarse voice made him attractive to women, giving him a certain air of mystery. He relished his new status.

The zabitays were discussing what he had told them and Orweyn was studying the plans and sketches that had been made from his tales.

Things have changed for me. Klaey enjoyed the rest of his biscuit and looked over at Deathwing. The black flight-mare stood at the rear of the conference chamber, blindfolded and tethered on a long chain. In this way, the stallion remained dependent on him and would not attack anyone, which it otherwise would have done at the first opportunity. Its ears twitched and from time to time it pawed the ground with a front hoof, causing sparks to fly. Or it would spread out its wings from boredom, the draught disturbing the maps on the table and making the candle flames flutter.

'Good boy, Deathwing,' Klaey called out. 'We'll go up for a spin in a moment or so. Then you can get your exercise.'

The flight-mare snorted with satisfaction.

While travelling from Dsôn Khamateion to Brigantia, Klaey had managed to win the stallion's trust. It had been a capital idea to bind the creature's eyes. Deathwing answered exclusively to his master's directions. It was as if they had always been together. Fortunately they had avoided the other four flight-mares. *I wouldn't have come off well in air combat.*

He took his new lucky talisman out from under his custom-made garments. He had got the tailor to cut the dark brown embroidered fabric according to the älfar fashion he had observed in Dsôn. He wore a rapier at his side. The amulet was a blue poppy flower with petals of lapis lazuli slivers – an ornament like one his mother had worn. A memory and a charm. *May you serve me well.* He kissed the blue flower and replaced the pendant under his robe.

Orweyn got up from his chair. The conversations in the room died down, and then were silenced completely at the ruler's signal. 'You have heard what my young brother, Klaey, has brought us from his mission as a hostage.' He pointed at the flight-mare. 'And there you see it.'

'He ran off with it when he escaped. The black-eyes will come and get their flying horse back. People will die because of it,' objected one of the zabitaya angrily. 'Let's send it back to them. As a gesture of goodwill.'

'No,' Klaey exclaimed, his voice croaky. 'I am definitely not going to be giving up Deathwing. The black-eyes can make themselves another one. *We* certainly don't know how to. If we breed from him, perhaps we can get ourselves a flying cavalry unit? It would be irresponsible to pass up this opportunity.'

Orweyn nodded in agreement. 'The animal stays here and remains under Klaey's supervision. He is the expert.' Lifting a bundle of reports recently arrived from the south-west of the empire, he went on, 'We could really use just such an air cavalry section. In Rhuta, the dwarves are marshalling round their one-time hero. The Fourthling frontier posts round our borders are hotbeds of excitement. They are busy forging weapons, siege equipment, sling machines and catapults by night and by day.' He slammed the papers down on the table. In his orderly costume, with a ribbon in his hair and his perfumed neckerchief, he had the air of an accountant annoyed about ink blots on his tidy balance sheet. 'They are pinning their hopes on Goldhand's help to conquer the Brown Mountains. That's not all. They want all the wretched groundling tribes and the combined armies from the human kingdoms to help them, too!'

It's looking serious. Klaey fastened back his black hair tighter in its plait and helped himself to another biscuit. Since the founding of Brigantia and its gradual expansion, there had been frequent skirmishes, with the resultant surrender of certain tracts of land, when the Fourthlings and Gauragon had claimed back some of their original territory. But the borders had remained stable for over two hundred cycles. *Stable, that is, until Goldhand turned up.*

'It's getting dangerous for us,' said a zabitay, unrolling a large map, 'if we allow it to go ahead. Apparently Goldhand has more or less recovered from the injuries the älfar inflicted.' He pointed on the chart to five enemy fortresses along the frontier which had proved impregnable. 'We can wait until the groundlings and their allies are at our border.'

'Or alternatively?' Orweyn drank some wine out of a golden goblet, long ago crafted by a dwarf goldsmith, its ornamental runes now hammered flat and the Berengart crest superimposed.

'Or we attack them first.' The zabitay looked round expectantly. 'We can take them by surprise.'

'A raid on the dwarf fortresses would be madness.' Klaey drank his aromatic rose water. 'I know what you want me to do. But on our own, Deathwing and I have little chance, from the air, of vanquishing them completely.'

There was a polite ripple of laughter.

'What if we ignore the forts completely and swing in past? We can cut through at the weakest points on the border as we've done so often in the past, and then we attack the units marching towards us, but we'll do it further in – miles before they reckon on seeing us?' Orweyn suggested. 'Before they've had the chance to assemble a combined army, they'll be vulnerable. The forts don't have large enough garrisons to attack us. They are purely for defence.'

'A bold plan, Omuthan,' said the zabitaya enthusiastically. 'It might work.'

'It will. If we know exactly where the various individual units are to be found, we can pick them off one by one.' Orweyn looked at Klaey. 'We have our own flying reconnaissance team. It will be easy. You locate them and tell us where to attack.'

Klaey nodded. 'It will be a pleasure for Deathwing and myself to be the eyes and ears of Brigantia.' He thought the council had come up with a reasonable plan. 'I expect they will start gathering their troops together before winter hits. If they wait till spring, they know we'll have had enough time to secure the Brown Mountains against attack.'

'The human kingdoms will be wanting to act as quickly as possible in revenge for the black-eyes' murders. That means they will have to go into the Brown Mountains,' Orweyn surmised. 'I've been sent several reports saying delegations on the way to Rhuta have been attacked by assassins. The plans my brother overheard in his time as a hostage have material-ised as bloody actions. There are several thrones which have lost their occupants.'

Klaey would never have thought that Dsôn would put its plans into action so soon or that it would declare its responsibil-ity for the murderous attacks. Either the assassins had made mistakes or the älfar were keen to create an atmosphere of sheer terror.

At least Brigantia won't be blamed. That's something. But either way, they have to go through our empire to annihilate the black-eyes. He stretched his hand out for the next biscuit. *I really missed these pastries!* He would soon have regained his original weight. He'd have to get the tailor to let out a few seams.

Orweyn turned to him directly. 'What do you think, brother?'

'Me? I think these biscuits are amazing.'

The assembled commanding officers all laughed again.

'I shall pass your compliments on to your sister. But I meant, what is your view of the present situation?'

Klaey had actually been giving this some thought. 'In my opinion, the älfar are keen to provoke Girdlegard into attack-ing Brigantia first, with the aim of conquering us before they march through the mountains on their way to Dsôn Khamateion.' He swirled the almond rose water in his silver cup. 'They think the groundlings and their allies will have been weakened through their battle with us and they'll be able to deal with them more easily and then move on to vanquish the whole of Girdlegard with the help of the sea kingdom of Undarimar.' Klaey took another mouthful of his drink to rinse the biscuit crumbs from his teeth. 'The black-eyes are exploiting us in a perfidious fashion in order to take hold of Girdlegard. And it will be us paying the price.'

Orweyn sat down and examined the map once more. 'Good. Two things. Firstly . . .'

The doors to the conference chamber suddenly opened.

A guard escorted two female älfar and a male älf in ceremonial robes into the room. None were carrying weapons, as far as it could be seen. White, blood-red and silver symbols decorated the flowing dark fabrics of their attire.

Klaey recognised the one with the most jewellery about her person.

Ascatoîa! He saw the flight-mare's nostrils quiver. Deathwing's head turned towards the new arrival, sniffing the air for her scent. The flight-mare's mouth dripped gobbets of saliva and its ears were pricked and alert. Klaey placed his hand on the hilt of his rapier. *They shall never have Deathwing back.*

Although the älfar looked peaceful enough, all the others in the room made ready to draw their own weapons. More guards entered the chamber carrying loaded crossbows and short bows with arrows placed ready to fire.

At a signal from Orweyn, Ascatoîa stopped and bowed to him. As usual, she wore heavy goldware at wrists, neck and brow. 'Greetings, Omuthan. As ambassador, I bring the best of wishes from Dsôn Khamateion. My name is Ascatoîa.'

'Bringing greetings won't be the only reason for your visit, I suspect?' Orweyn looked at Klaey. 'But since you are here, let me thank you for looking after my young brother so well while he was your hostage. He did lose a bit of weight, but he has put on muscle and learned a new language, I understand.' Then he pointed at the flight-mare. 'And many thanks for the generous gift you let him ride home on. Or should we say, fly home? What is the term?'

'*Travel.*' Ascatoîa's smile was cold. 'We call it *travelling.*'

'Right.' Orweyn waved his hand in a semicircular motion over the map on the table. 'As you see, ambassador, we were discussing a few things that concern your own empire. It was as if you had overheard our talk, back in Dsôn Khamateion.'

'Almost, honourable Omuthan. Almost.' Ascatoîa cast a curious glance at the map. 'I expect Brigantia is well informed about Dsôn's plans for the future?'

'Indeed, we have guessed what our own role is to be.'

'Do tell. What role would that be, in your view?'

Orweyn turned to Klaey. 'Would you clarify, please? You know the älfar.'

'Our role is to be a buffer zone, where the groundlings and their allies are to exhaust themselves in combat, before, in a weakened state, they march on Dsôn Khamateion. You then defeat them. And subsequently go on to snap up an overthrown Brigantia and a subjugated Girdlegard. With the assistance of Undarimar,' Klaey explained calmly. In the älfar tongue he added, 'Don't assume I have forgotten anything at all. I recall the discussions you held with Vascalôr. On the battlements. In the stables. Or the ones with the Secret Chamber in the Samusin temple.'

'You are talented. Not bad for human scum,' she responded disdainfully, before continuing in Girdlegard's common vernacular. 'I am more than happy to contradict, Omuthan. Dsôn Khamateion offers yourself and Brigantia something quite different. Namely, a pact.'

'Ah, so you mean something on these lines: that we form the front line? I am well aware that you regard humans as slaves or as donors for your artworks, providing a source of blood, bone and skin.'

Ascatoîa smiled and this time her particoloured features appeared amused. 'How nice that you understand. We do, to be serious, have the same enemy.'

'An enemy you have provoked with your murders.'

'We attempted to kill Goldhand in the Grey Mountains before he could become a danger. A danger to ourselves and, even more so, to you. You owe us a favour, really.' Ascatoîa watched the flight-mare dolefully.

'Absolutely not. Goldhand is still alive. All you have achieved is having the groundlings and half of Girdlegard in uproar and revolt.'

'You must mean the attacks on the delegations and the royal courts? The Ganyeios decided to send them a warning. From Dsôn Khamateion.' The oddly coloured eyes and the two skin tones on her face made the ambassadress appear more sinister than her silent companions.

Orweyn regarded her steadily. 'Out with it! How do you envisage this pact?'

The index finger of her left hand touched the map. 'We move some of our best troops, here, into Brigantia. You deploy them wherever you see fit, Omuthan. To support you when the Fourthlings invade, demanding you relinquish their land.'

'And in return?'

'Nothing. We keep the foe, in the same way, off our own backs. It's strategically sensible to combine our forces until our two realms are both safe.' Ascatoîa nodded to her colleagues, who stepped forward to hand over some papers. 'Here are the treaties. They give you the authority to command our troops.'

Klaey did not believe a word she had been saying.

'Paper is always patient.'

'These are treaties to be guaranteed by hostages. We will send you one hundred of our most respected älfar citizens. Their loss would affect us greatly.' Ascatoîa was obviously making an effort to keep her temper and retain her dignity while delivering what seemed, to her, to be a form of capitulation. A darkened fury line extending from forehead to chin betrayed her true feelings. The lights in the hall dimmed and the Omuthan's guards shouted out a warning. 'This is not my decision,' she said. 'It comes directly from the Ganyeios.

Personally, I should prefer to carry out the course of action your thief there' – she pointed at Klaey – 'described. It would give me great pleasure.'

Orweyn said nothing. He accepted the treaty documents and skimmed through them before handing them round. He took some wine. 'The wording is as you explained. I am surprised.'

'So am I.' Ascatoîa had her emotions under control again and the anger lines disappeared from her countenance. The lamps in the room regained their previous luminous power. 'What may I report to Dsôn? Will Brigantia enter into the alliance?'

'We shall discuss this and come to a decision by this evening. You are my guests until then.' Orweyn indicated the door. 'You shall be given whatever you wish.'

'That I doubt.' The ambassadress turned and went to the flight-mare, accompanied by her colleagues. 'What I wish would be to be back in Dsôn.'

All of a sudden, stretching the chain to its utmost extent, Deathwing surged forward to bite Ascatoîa's female colleague in the shoulder. Its long incisors sliced through fabric, skin and bone. A loud crunching noise came at the same time as the agonised scream.

Tossing its head wildly, the flight-mare smashed its victim hard against the wall, where she slumped down on the floor, semi-conscious. A fierce kick from a flashing rear hoof felled the other, fatally shattering the älf's skull.

Ascatoîa's hand shot up in a strange movement, making the ornaments on her forearm start to glow.

'You won't touch me!' she said in her own älfar language.

Klaey supposed the jewelled bracelets must contain some spell protecting her against the stallion's attack. *Are these the powers she once spoke of? Does the word zhussa mean the same as maga?*

Before the guards could react, Deathwing snapped up the älf's body and sprang over to where the other victim lay. The stallion spread its wings over the two corpses and began to devour its kill with speed and relish.

By Samusin and Cadengis' mother! I've taught him to enjoy black-eye flesh. Watching in fascination, Klaey took another biscuit and slowly nibbled away at it.

Anger lines covering her face, Ascatoîa had remained motionless, observing the stallion at its frenzied feeding. She gradually lowered her arm and relaxed her fingers. 'You can keep this beast. It no longer has any value for Dsôn.' She followed one of the guards out of the room.

There was total silence in the chamber.

The zabitays watched the flight-mare. It had already finished off the first älf, discarding only the thickest of the bones. Now its teeth were pulling soft flesh away from the belly of the female.

'We've established, I think, that no black-eyes will ever dare steal Deathwing from me,' Klaey observed drily, chewing his biscuit.

Raucous laughter greeted this comment. The stallion refused to be distracted by the noise.

'You leave as soon as your flying horse has eaten his fill,' Orweyn told Klaey, quietly, so that no one else could hear. Klaey was surprised. 'But the troops aren't even on the march yet,' he whispered. 'Or do you want me to head for the five forts?'

'No. Go and find Ûra. Should be easy on your flight-mare. Begin looking near the biggest volcanoes.'

'Have you lost your mind, big brother?' He nearly choked on his biscuit and his hoarse voice was even scratchier than usual. 'What is the point of attacking her? She is a hundred times stronger! There's no way I can mount a super-size catapult on the back of my Deathwing!'

'You need to think big, little brother. You were born in the Land of Wonders, so you've a gift for picking up any tongue you hear spoken.' Orweyn placed a hand on his shoulder. 'That will work for the dragon language, too. She must talk sometimes, mustn't she?'

This is utter madness! Klaey took some hasty slurps from his flowered water. *Negotiate! With Ûra! Words failed him. What if it's not what we call language that she employs?*

'Got it? Good! We shan't need her envoy to mediate. We can talk directly to the mightiest of any of the beings in Girdlegard. You can warn Ûra in person about the älfar plans you heard in Dsôn.' Orweyn looked pleased with himself. 'And we can offer the dragon one hundred älfar hostages. And tell her where the Dsôn troops are stationed. And we can give her all the secrets about the älfar realm and their defences. You can tell her all of those things.' He put his large, ungainly hand on the nape of Klaey's neck and shook him as if he were a little apple tree. 'How could Ûra possibly resist that offer? She will be sure to want to rid herself of the älfar threat. All the black-eyes could give her would be trouble and uncertainty. You must find the right choice of words to persuade her to attack Dsôn.'

'And what do we demand in return for our kind offer?' Klaey finally forced out the question.

'Nothing. It's enough if Ûra likes us.' Orweyn pointed at Deathwing's bloodied muzzle as it pulled out and ate its victim's liver. 'That'll do for now, until we've built up our own flying cavalry unit, thanks to your terrifying creature. And once we've got that, we can soon wipe out the dragons. All of them.' He let his brother go and turned to the assembled commanders. *Fly to find Ûra. Conduct negotiations with her.* Klaey felt he might have been safer if he'd never left Dsôn Khamateion.

Girdlegard

Vanélia, capital of the magic realm of Rhuta
1023 P.Q. (7514th solar cycle in old reckoning), early summer

It was with an uncomfortable feeling that Goïmron went, at the bidding of a dwarf from King Regnor's retinue, up to the top floor of the maga's palace to the tract where Vanéra had given the Thirdling king rooms.

He had very recently spoken with Telìnâs and Sònuk. They were waiting to see how things developed, ready to join in the next stage of the adventure if Goïmron asked them to. The elf was making his little figures and other miniature items from shiny paper; Goïmron had been handed a tiny paper axe that he had said thank you for, nicely, and stowed carefully in his pouch. *We can always use allies. Whatever happens.*

Two warriors in full armour were guarding the door. Gata was there as well, in her normal iron-plate armour. She greeted him, 'Ah. There you are.'

'Indeed.' He tried to gauge from her expression what might be awaiting him. 'I assume your father is *very* displeased?'

'I should think so.' The blonde dwarf embraced him at once, her armour pressing painfully into his chest. 'But, you know, it was the best decision I ever made.'

Goïmron smiled and embraced her, despite the uncomfortable metal plates between them. He preferred what he was wearing now: shirt, jerkin and knee breeches. He had eschewed the cone-shaped hat Gandelin had always laughed at. 'You have set something amazing in motion. This could never have happened for our people otherwise. A new sense of harmony, like in former times. The good old days.' He released her and looked her steadily in the eyes. 'That's exactly what I'm going to tell the king.'

'Courageous. For a Fourthling.'

'That sounds like a criticism.'

Gata opened her eyes wide. 'Oh, I didn't mean it like that. You are . . . the bravest Fourthling I know. And probably one of the bravest dwarves ever. Full stop.'

Goïmron laughed. 'Let's go in before you mess up your next attempt at a compliment.'

She grinned at him sideways and set off. He followed her and the guards let them pass. 'I'd better warn you. My father and I don't get on especially well.'

'Because you choose to think for yourself, I expect?'

She grinned. 'That's not the only thing. Our opinions differ on the Thirdlings' future. This has become . . . apparent in recent cycles. I have often contradicted him, sometimes in front of his advisors. I often earned myself extra hours of duty in the eastern fortress as a punishment. This did not improve our relationship.' She sighed. 'I wouldn't say it's actually contempt on my side, but near enough. Basically, I think I ought to be in charge of the tribe.'

Goïmron exhaled sharply. 'But I wasn't purely an excuse for you to disobey his orders and do something on your own?'

'No, never! You really convinced me of the importance of your mission,' Gata insisted. 'That won't impress my father at all. But at least we bring him good tidings.'

'So Hargorina is better?'

'Nearly back to full health. As soon as Vanéra used the special artefact, you could see her improving every orbit. The healing magic was really effective. Even if Hargorina disapproved of being treated with invisible powers.' Gata looked at Goïmron expectantly. 'And Goldhand?'

'The poison the älfar put on their arrows is really dangerous. Their toxins have settled in the old dwarf's bones and they are still proving resistant. Even to the healing powers of the enchanted carnelian knife.' He had been trying to find better forms of treatment or some alternative therapy that could help restore the venerable dwarf hero to full health, instead of his current kind of twilight-zone existence. He wished he could get some advice from Chòldunja. He wanted to show her the sea sapphire and ask her opinion about its powers. But at present, there was no opportunity for him to leave Rhuta. He was expected to remain in the vicinity of the sick patient, given that he had been the one to go in search of Goldhand in the first place. *I so want to see Rodana. If only I could be near her.*

'So more time is needed,' said Gata.

'Or maybe a stronger artefact. I don't suppose Vanéra will ever be able to lay her hands on anything at all, the mess she keeps in that storeroom.' Goïmron spoke a little incautiously and laughed to himself. 'It's a miracle anyone can even see to find the stairs in that place.'

'One moment.' Gata stopped and took his arm. The brooch on her collar flashed. 'How do you know what the Chamber of Wonders looks like?'

'What? Oh no, by Vraccas! No, I . . . heard the famulus talking with the other assistant,' he stammered. 'How could I have seen it for myself?' The forced laugh did not sound convincing.

Gata's stare intensified. 'Goïmron Chiselcut, what are you keeping from me? Secrets? After all we've been through together?' She walked on, dragging him along by the arm as if he were a naughty child. 'I know I told you to look for the carnelian knife. Did you actually go into the storeroom?'

DON'T TELL HER! This was the sapphire, speaking inside his head. I AM YOUR SECRET. IF YOU SHARE ME, YOU WILL REGRET IT.

Goïmron gave a start. He removed her grip on his arm. 'Of course not.'

The doors of the next room swung open.

Goïmron was not going to be granted time to marshal his thoughts. Regnor Mortalblow was standing on the threshold, wearing a light leather tunic under chainmail with reinforced sections at elbows, chest and back. *I'm glad he isn't carrying a weapon, at least.*

'There they are, the two guilty parties. Get in here so I can give you both a piece of my mind.' Regnor looked scornfully at Goïmron's clean-shaven cheeks, such a contrast with his own full blue beard reaching down to his belt buckle. 'Lorimbur! Help us. I can't even grab you by the beard.' He turned on his heel and they followed him in.

The chamber was high-ceilinged with arched windows. Goïmron and Gata were now on their own in the king's presence.

'Father, it was totally my own idea,' Gata blurted out. 'It was not Goïmron's fault.'

'That is what I assumed to be the case.' He sat down, leaving the two of them standing before him. His beringed fingers gripped the arms of the chair, as if he were about to spring up out of it. 'With your mad, headstrong ideas, you have sacrificed the lives of nearly a hundred of my soldiers. And you risked Hargorina's life, too!'

'The mission we were on has brought us back the greatest hero Girdlegard has ever known. And, remember, he is a Thirdling, too,' Gata flung fearlessly back at him. 'And look at what his return has achieved. The tribes are united once more and they all long to re-establish their old harmonious cooperation.'

'We were never a part of that community. Even if King Hargorin Deathbringer claimed the contrary,' said Regnor, interrupting. 'Reconciliation. Togetherness. The other four tribes never truly wanted that, in their heart of hearts.'

'And is that the reason you wouldn't support Goïmron in his quest? Because you're afraid unity might mean the Thirdlings would be expected to join with the others, just like Death-bringer originally intended?' Gata asked sharply. 'In times like these, there is no place for one tribe insisting on going it alone. Girdlegard—'

'Girdlegard can manage. We have found our own way and we are guarding the entrance, just like King Gandalgir Irongrip is doing in the Red Mountains.' Stroking his bushy blue beard, Regnor fixed his eyes on Goïmron. 'It's the *Fourthlings* who have failed in this regard. It was our kingdom's fall that triggered the whole chain of catastrophic events.'

'And we want to contribute to putting things right.' Goïmron had no idea whether a response was appropriate, but he had held his tongue for quite long enough. There was no master of ceremonies standing by to upbraid him. 'You have not spoken to any of the four other tribes since arriving here, King Regnor. The others are elated at Goldhand's reappearance. In him they see—'

'I am well aware what *they* see. But what *I* see is this: war, suffering, death. Everything I have always wanted to protect Lorimbur's descendants from,' Regnor interrupted harshly. 'There are dragons, Brigantians, älfar and orcs all needing to be fought.'

'And we should have done that a long time ago,' said Gata, walking slowly up to her father. 'In recent cycles we have been no more than doorkeepers for Gauragon and King Gajek, and we've taken the easy way out. And we call ourselves Girdle-gard's defenders.'

'We *are* its defenders!'

'No, we aren't. We stand by and watch what's happening but we don't intervene. We do nothing.' Lowering her voice, she spoke insistently, 'Father, I set off with Goïmron to find the legendary hero so the tribes could once again become what, in the past, they were, always upholding their traditional standards. Surely we are more than simple officials minding the doors and managing access at the behest of some human ruler?'

'Oh, yes, in the Red Mountains they have been doing very well for themselves on it, what with the tolls, duties and taxes they earn from all the ships going in and out. Do you think King Irongrip is doing anything else, I want to know?' Regnor put his right hand up to his brow, so that the tattoos on one side of his face were in shadow. The meeting was obviously tiring him.

'Nothing! *That's* just what I mean. The Secondlings and Fifthlings – and even the Fourthlings – have put up forts at the vulnerable locations to stop beasts coming across through the lava fields and the caved-in mountains. And us? What have we done? We've waved travellers through and occasionally peppered the odd handful of monsters with some slingshot.' Gata was next to his chair now and she went down on one knee before her father so she could look him straight in the eye. Goïmron was aware of the effort it was costing her. 'The hundred soldiers we lost in the Grey Mountains gave their lives to bring Tungdil Goldhand back. Even the älfar fear his influence. Don't let their sacrifice have been in vain. I beg you!'

'You want me to send yet more of our people into battles we cannot win?' Regnor snorted, his beard quivering with anger. He turned to the Fourthling again. 'And the old one. How is it going? Can he even speak to us? Is he able to tell us his plans?'

'He is still being treated by the Esteemed Maga Vanéra. But his health is improving. He will get better. Soon.' Goïmron knew he was not being totally honest. 'What Gata says is absolutely right.' Gathering all his courage, he said, 'The delegations and the communications from various kingdoms make it clear that Girdlegard demands revenge for the murderous attacks the älfar have inflicted. Humans, elves and meldriths are forming an alliance to march on the Brown Mountains. We can destroy both Brigantia and Dsôn Khamateion.'

Regnor let out a peal of furious laughter. 'You've got a Fourthling there, scrawny as a little long'un, and you're talking about waging war! Wars, indeed! Sieges! Fighting the most deadly enemies imaginable.'

'I know that—'

'You! Know! Nothing!' Regnor shouted at him, the words falling like a slap in the face. 'You used to sit in your safe little goldsmith's workshop – and you're not even a very good goldsmith, at that – in the even safer little town of Malleniagard. I hear that you like to sing in the dwarf choir. And that makes you a Fourthling warrior? Gem-carving and some tra la la?' Incensed, the king leaped up and rushed past his daughter. 'Don't you dare tell me about waging war just because you once carved an axe on a piece of agate! They should have walled you up in the Grey Mountains as I commanded them to. But there weren't enough of my tharks left alive to carry out my orders!'

The king reared up in front of Goïmron: muscular, broad-shouldered, with his warrior's beard and his victory tattoos. The Fourthling moved his right foot backwards a step.

DON'T WALK AWAY. LET HIM SHOUT. LET HIM RAGE. REMEMBER, YOU HAVE MORE POWER THAN HE DOES. The sapphire was whispering inside his mind. THE ORBIT WILL COME WHEN YOU WILL SHOW THEM ALL WHAT YOU ARE CAPABLE OF.

'Father, it will need effort and it will cost lives,' Gata interjected, 'but it will mean we can once again be the dwarves who can look themselves in the mirror with pride and say: we have swept evil out of Girdlegard and we shall never allow it back in.'

'Is that so?' growled Regnor, turning his bearded face to his daughter. 'Right. Let's assume this assorted heap of combatants and the maga manage to destroy the Brigantians and even the älfar.' He pointed to the window. 'And the dragons? Ûra? Will she just watch? Or will she join in on the side of the enemy? And how much extra tribute will she be demanding after that?' The king stomped back to his seat. The wood groaned as he flung himself back on his chair. 'How will we ever be free of the pestilential flying creature?' Resentfully, he regarded the empty goblet on the table at his side. 'By Lorimbur, I could do with a black beer! Some mead! This sickly pink wine is only fit for pointy-ears.'

'I'm sure the Esteemed Maga will think of something.' Goïmron closed his hand round the sapphire in his pocket. The gem, set within the shape of a dragon, gave him confidence. 'I shall speak to the dragon's envoy and find out Ûra's intentions.' Regnor and Gata both stared at him in amazement, as if he had suddenly turned into an elf playing the harp. 'Well, that's the easiest way to find out, isn't it?' Goïmron recalled Rodana saying she had been forced to be the dragon's spy. *She can summon Ûra in the blink of an eye.* 'Someone has to talk to her. We need to prevent her feeling her status as Girdlegard's supreme ruler is endangered, or else she'll step in to help the Brigantians and the älfar.' Saying these words made him assertive. 'It would mean an apparent surrender, King Regnor. Nothing changes for us really. Except that we'll free Girdlegard of threats.'

'A wise idea,' Gata agreed.

Regnor sipped the wine and made a face. 'What if Stémna doesn't go along with it? What if Ûra forbids us to march on the Brigantians and the älfar?'

Goïmron smiled and held his sapphire tight, running his thumb over its facets. 'I think she will agree. It would make her whole realm more peaceful. More peace means more prosperity. More prosperity means more gold and thus more tribute for her. She can't really object.'

Regnor did not look keen. 'If you insist, Fourthling. Try your luck and get her envoy to listen to you. But if Ûra is against the idea, there's no way the Thirdlings will wage a hopeless campaign, risking huge loss of life. We have already paid a high price for bringing back the dwarf hero.'

Famulus Mostro hurried in, despite the guards' attempts to stop him. His appearance was immaculate: long robe and flowing locks. 'Come quick! Goldhand has woken up and wants to speak with you.'

'Good.' Regnor stood up and shook his beard.

'No, King Regnor. It's not you he wants. Apologies.' The famulus pointed to the Fourthling. 'He only wants Master Chiselcut. Nobody else.'

Goïmron felt uneasy. 'Let's not keep him waiting!'

His heart beating fast, he followed the famulus, passing the hopeful faces of the dwarves and the delegates from the various realms, who were guests in Rhuta. People smiled at him, clapping him on the shoulder encouragingly or murmuring words he was too nervous to listen to.

Goïmron finally made it to the chamber where the ancient dwarf lay on his sickbed. The white-haired patient's brown eyes were open now. He was looking out of the window, seeing the sunshine on the gentle hills, fields and woods.

When Goïmron stepped into the room, Vanéra stood up and stowed the carnelian knife she had been using to treat her patient. She was wearing a white apron over her lilac-coloured dress, and her long brown hair was tucked under an embroidered white headscarf.

'Don't make it too long, Master Chiselcut,' she said as she passed. 'He is very weak and his mind is still affected. I hope you will be able to make sense of what he says. I'm afraid I couldn't.'

Goïmron found himself alone with the hero.

Tungdil Goldhand immediately turned his gaze on the Fourthling. 'You are the one who found my book,' he said in a croaking voice that carried the weight of a thousand cycles in it.

'Yes . . . that's me,' said Goïmron, surprised at the clarity of the other's speech. 'It was in a simple wooden chest floating in the Towan river.'

'Ah, so it was in a chest. I forgot where I'd put it.' Goldhand shook his head and rubbed his long silver beard. 'Must be getting old.' He gave a quiet laugh. 'Is that what they think?'

You old fox! Goïmron grinned. 'You've been play-acting to Vanéra!'

'Pretending I'm senile and exhausted. Yes. To get some peace and quiet.' He waved him over. 'Listen carefully, Goïmron Chiselcut. You will be my confidant. I can trust you, I know, from what I've been hearing as I lay here, pretending to be asleep. No one else would have taken it upon himself, on finding my journal, to set off to find me.'

Goïmron nodded proudly. 'Well . . . it seems you have a plan?'

'I do, indeed. I can't let you know all the details yet.' Goldhand touched Goïmron's arm. 'Not till various things have happened as I want them to. Then you'll be the first to know. It's a matter of nothing less than the future of Girdlegard.'

Goïmron's excitement turned to curiosity and blossoming enthusiasm. 'I am ready.'

'I am not pretending, however, about the noxious effect of the poison on my bones. In my younger years, my body would easily have shaken off the älfar toxins. Oh, the things I have been through! And survived.' Goldhand winked. 'I don't need to tell you, do I? You've read my diary. It's all in the book.'

'Indeed, I have.' *More than once, at that.* It occurred to him that in all the confusion the book had been left back in Hammerhome. *Hope he doesn't ask to see it!*

'The poison in my bones will seep through to my bloodstream from time to time and pollute it. When that happens, my mind will become muddled until the malign force ebbs away. When that occurs, however long the phase may last, it is essential that you pretend there is nothing wrong.'

'Understood.' Goïmron felt it was a great honour to be taken into his confidence in this way.

'I won't speak to anyone apart from yourself. You will be my voice. That is to say, in official meetings as well. I shall whisper my responses to you,' Goldhand explained. 'This means that in the dark phases, when I am hors de combat, the difference won't be noticeable. You will just pretend I've murmured an answer to you.'

'Of course. I see.' Goïmron was slightly hesitant. '. . . But what am I supposed to say then?'

'You'll think of something. You're a clever young lad.' Goldhand put his hand under his pillow and took out a sheaf of folded notes. 'Here. I've put these together for you in secret. Make sure they get to the Red Mountains. I've written the recipients' names on them. It's absolutely vital they get them.'

Goïmron was starting to feel overwhelmed. 'Good . . . I'll see to it.'

'It's essential everyone gets to hear that I have returned. Even in the farthest flung corner of Girdlegard.'

'That's already the case.'

'No, not sufficiently. Make sure that the message gets taken to the slopes of the mountains that collapsed. Publish it on posters, spread the news.' Goldhand coughed. 'There's more depending on this than you can ever imagine.'

'How shall I . . .?' Goïmron's heart sank. *It's too much.* 'That's . . .'

Goldhand patted his cheek to reassure him. 'Tell the dwarves it's what I want. We'll summon everyone to a grand assembly soon. With all the delegations and envoys and national representatives who have come to Rhuta.' Slowly the old dwarf's eyelids were starting to droop. 'It's vital that Regnor attend. Sort that for me.'

'I shall.' Stowing away the letters destined for the Red Mountains, Goïmron got to his feet. He felt this new responsibility weighing him down. Not knowing what he was actually doing or what was going to happen now made the trust Goldhand had placed in him hard to bear. He made his way quietly towards the door.

'Goïmron.'

'Yes?'

'Where is my book?'

'I left it in the Grey Mountains,' he admitted. 'In Hammerhome, because I thought it should be put back where it came from. I never guessed the miracle would really happen and we would actually find you.'

'But it was me that found you. The book will be safe in Hammerhome. Who knows, maybe it'll find its own way out again?' Goldhand smiled, his eyes closed now. 'I want you to be a proud Fourthling and conduct yourself in the spirit of your tribe. Do not change one bit and don't let anyone put you down. Anyone at all.' He sighed. 'I know what it means not to be taken seriously and to be laughed at. Because I was different. But that proved to be my greatest strength. Never forget that.'

'I won't.' Goïmron left the sickroom as quietly as he could. Once outside the door, he paused and took several deep breaths. *He said I should be just what I am.* His fingers found the sapphire in his pocket. *My greatest strength. And nobody must ever know about it.*

Girdlegard

Cliffton, capital of the kingdom of Palusien
1023 P.Q. (7514th solar cycle in old reckoning), early summer

Racked with pain, Stémna looked from the spear in her shoulder to the part of the älf's face that was visible under his dark hood. Apart from the murdered artist's corpse, they were alone on the plateau high above the glittering sea. Despite the magnificent sunset and the warm breeze, there was nothing romantic about the scene. There was nothing here but cruelty and violence.

'Have the älfar all lost their minds?' she said with a groan. She could not move because the spear was pinning her to the bench. 'First you murder the delegations and the members of the royal houses and now you attack the dragon's envoy?' Stémna tried unsuccessfully to breathe her way through the pain. Her blood streamed down over her white robe from the shoulder wound. The runes on the spear started to glow green as if the weapon were being charged with energy. 'This means the end of Dsôn Khamateion!'

'I have absolutely nothing to do with those newcomer älfar that have inveigled their way in,' he responded disdainfully. 'They have their plans and me, I have my own ideas.'

Stémna looked up. The burning pain in her shoulder was getting worse. 'Of course you are a lone wolf. Does Dsôn think it will get away with everything if all the blame falls on *you*?'

'You mean what I'm doing with you?' The älf twisted the spear in her shoulder, making her gasp. He looked down at her mockingly. 'You have not understood, have you? I'm attacking you in order to attract the beast. I am summoning her.'

Stémna swallowed her scream of pain, to deny her opponent satisfaction.

'Do you really think you could survive a battle with Ûra? Just with a spear?'

'It's more than a spear.' The älf surveyed the skyline and the sea. Black strands of hair slipped out from under his dark hood. 'This is an ancient runic spear. An artefact with indescribable power, filled with the strength from thousands of inflicted deaths. It was made by the Unslayables.' He threw off his cloak. 'Like this armour, too.'

Black tionium plates became visible: they were directly sewn and hooked into his flesh. One of the plates had a finger-sized hole in it. Underneath, the skin over the stab mark had gone dark. Where the incorporated plating stopped, he wore tailored, reinforced dark red leather on his sinewy, muscular body.

Stémna was surprised to see this torturous application of tionium. 'Who are you?'

'Someone who remembers.' The älf twisted the spear again in her shoulder. 'Someone who never forgives.' His black eyes bored into hers, then he raised his free arm, revealing a black metal gauntlet reaching up to the elbow. 'Someone who can bring back those memories, so that incredible injustices will never be forgotten in Girdlegard.'

'You are talking in riddles.' Stémna had never seen an älf such as this before. Her tasks as the dragon's messenger had often taken her to Dsôn Khamateion, to demand the tribute the city state reluctantly paid in order to be spared punishment from Ûra's fire. She had often seen their artistic wonders with her own eyes. But this attitude, this cruel application of metal armour sewn directly into skin – this she had never come across, so strange. *Extraordinary.*

'What will the Voice of the beast do when I have killed her mistress?' The älf looked first at her and then swept the horizon with his gaze. 'You will have to remain silent for ever. If you are recognised, you must always be afraid you will be punished for the cruelties of recent cycles.'

'I am only the messenger. If I didn't carry out this office, Ûra would find another envoy.'

'That's the classic excuse.' The älf kept his eyes trained on the view to the north-east, his long black hair waving in the breeze. 'Ah, here she comes. Just as I expected. She's aiming to attack me out of the setting sun.'

'Tell me your name.'

'Do you want to do the formal introductions?' the älf responded in amusement. 'I think we'll skip the pleasantries and get straight to the point.' As he yanked the spear out of her shoulder, Stémna collapsed on the seat and tried to close the wound with her hand.

'Take a good look. This is going to be a spectacle like no other Girdlegard has ever witnessed.'

Tearing the white sleeve from her garment, Stémna stuffed the fabric against the deep cut to slow the blood loss. Without a healer's intervention, she would not live long. 'Alone against a dragon? You are completely mad! The emperor of fools!'

Ûra's shape became visible and her screech of fury could be heard over the sea in Cliffton, and clearly all the way up to the viewing platform where they both were. Stémna admired the mighty dragon, the pearly shimmer of her scales and wings. Each wing was thirty times the length of a haywain. Ûra's teeth were the size of short swords – they could bite through any armour and would certainly make short work of the älf's metal skin-plating.

The älf moved over to the edge of the sheer drop, taking long, elegant strides. 'Who says I am alone?' He jumped gracefully over the edge of the precipice and Stémna lost sight of him.

One blink of an eye later, he was on the back of a blue-scaled dragon soaring up into the air, brandishing his tionium spear.

By Samusin! Of course! Stémna knew the creature that carried the älf, who was riding it as if he had been doing so since earliest childhood. *He has made a pact with Ardin!* The strange pair swept upwards before her very eyes and immediately started to attack Ûra. *The old habits no longer hold!* Eager to see the outcome of the dragon combat about to unfold, she stood up from her place on the bench, ignoring the pain and the streams of blood coursing down, as well as the feeling of light-headedness. Ûra was attempting to grab hold of the extended neck of the smaller dragon, but the slighter male specimen had the advantage when it came to manoeuvrability and he was able to dodge her snapping jaws by ducking down under her and flying past her body.

Ardin certainly felt Ûra's sharp claws scraping along the scales on his back, tearing off strips that tumbled into the sea, but to compensate, the älf lofted his rune spear high.

The blade, which had easily sliced through Stémna's bones, cut into the light plates and the soft places of the white dragon's underbelly. A fountain of boiling hot blood rained down on to the water, causing yellow clouds of acidic steam to rise.

Ardin took a tail swipe on his left wing, which sent him off balance. Ûra followed through with her attack with a hate-filled roar and plummeted down after the treacherous blue dragon who had dared to try and usurp her position on Girdlegard's throne.

Stémna heard the alarms sounding out in Cliffton. Chancellor Yltho's recent decision to refuse further tribute payments must have seemed in his eyes to be justified. *No point in heading over there to look for a healer.*

The dark blue dragon swooped in a deep arc across the surface of the sea – a curve that Ûra could not follow, given her size. Ardin was behind her, snapping at her tail. The white dragon screeched angrily and whirled around, folding her wings sharply so that she reared up vertically to face Ardin, ready to destroy her rival with a blast of flames from her nostrils.

What's happened to that älf? Stémna could not see him. *Did he fall in the sea?*

A long tongue of flame sizzled along Ardin's spine, making his scales steam. In places the carapace was transformed into white puffs of dust, and glistening pieces of scale dislodged, floating up into the air.

Just as the smoke-draped, blue-scaled dragon roared and skimmed underneath Ûra to avoid her fiery breath, she whirled round and grasped hold of his blistering neck. Teeth as long as an arm penetrated his flesh.

Ardin has made a serious error. His new ally is useless. The mistress is not easy to defeat. Otherwise . . . Her train of thought was interrupted when she spotted the black figure crouching on the white dragon's back. *No! That cursed älf has somehow got on to Ûra!* She followed events in horror, seeing the rune spear bury itself in the central spot of flesh located exactly between the two wings.

With a shriek, Ûra released her blue-scaled opponent. Ardin plunged to the sea to bathe his blistering burns. The älf clung to the shaft of his spear and his gauntleted other hand grabbed fast at the horny scales of the white dragon as she slowed and tried random manoeuvres with her impaired wings, trying to rid herself of the hated älf invader. At the last, she folded her two great wings and took a headlong dive down into the water.

There was an enormous splash, with spray going as high as any house. Great tidal waves rushed towards the port of Cliffton and the coast.

Where is she? Fighting weakness, Stémna staggered to the edge of the precipice to look down.

But neither Ardin nor Ûra had surfaced.

No! That can't be true! The white dragon's messenger collapsed on to a boulder.

Cries of jubilation came up from the nearby city, the sound borne by the wind. The bells went on ringing and the humans who had gathered by the harbour were celebrating the two dragons' well-deserved deaths. This one orbit had seen the back of two terrible tormentors.

But then a white shape shot up from the depths and surged out of the waves. Ûra circled up into the air, screeching horribly and sending out a triumphant flash of fire before gliding over to where Stémna was standing. Water dripped from the dragon's body like a cascade of diamonds.

'Mistress!' Stémna fell to her knees and bowed her head. 'Forgive me for letting you down. The älf came out of nowhere.'

Ûra's glide lost any remnant of gracefulness, her wings faltering badly. She was unable to regain her balance, no matter what she tried.

No! This cannot happen! Never! Stémna could see the älf crouched on the dragon's broad skull, his spear rammed sideways through Ûra's eye, releasing a stream of hot blood. *This cannot be her end!* Stémna struggled to her feet.

'This must not be how she ends!' She uttered the words unbelievingly. The älf jumped off Ûra as the dragon started to fall and he pulled his spear out of her eye. At that very moment, Ardin, until then thought done for, surged up out of the sea, causing a giant fountain. He fielded the älf, catching him as he descended. Ardin's shimmering scales showed many burn marks, and cobalt-blue blood welled out of the place where Ûra had bitten him in the neck. But in spite of the injuries, Ardin had survived. From this moment on, he was the mightiest dragon in the whole of Girdlegard.

Stémna was overwhelmed by faintness and sank to the ground. Her limbs no longer obeyed her. From her prone position, she saw how Ûra was faltering towards the township of Cliffton.

When the white dragon took her final plunge down inside the city walls, many houses and part of the fortifications were flattened by the impact. The collapse of the guard towers strewed debris widely through the streets. The capital city was swallowed up in a cloud of dust and, one by one, the joyful bells fell silent.

The last rays of the setting sun showed the approach of six large vessels sailing under the ensign of Undarimar and making straight for the harbour of the city that now lay in ruins. It looked as if they were selflessly rushing to Cliffton's aid.

The älfar will be taking Girdlegard over, Stémna realised. *Who could hold them back now, with Ardin and this powerful black-eyes on their side?* Her gaze followed a dancing piece of paper being carried out to sea. *Oh, it's my portrait. It will be lost. It will die like me.*

Mountains are masters of silence and know how to keep secrets.

Joanbil Wulfganger, dwarf poet prince

XIII

Girdlegard

Vanélia, capital of the magic realm of Rhuta
1023 P.Q. (7514th solar cycle in old reckoning), late summer

'Let's get this urgent meeting going.' Goïmron addressed the assembled company. He was no longer so uncomfortable having all eyes on him and had taken his place at Goldhand's side. The ancient hero gave the impression of being asleep with his eyes open, or of being mentally absent. But at the crucial moment, his gaze cleared, and he whispered to Goïmron, who then relayed his words to the assembly.

The dwarf tribes had all sent representatives, as had the human kingdoms, elves and meldriths. Several maps of Girdlegard, both large and small scale, were spread out on the conference room table. Those unable or unwilling to risk travelling through Girdlegard during the present dangerous circumstances had either sent messages of support for the alliance or had indicated their refusal to join the campaign.

More and more troops were gathering in Gauragon along the northern border of the magic realm. They were in large encampments, preparing for a united attack against Brigantia as soon as the army had reached a suitable size. The alliance was taking shape.

'The reason this meeting has been called is a very positive one: we have received confirmation from several sources that Ûra is dead.' Goïmron flourished Palusien's communication. '"The white dragon crashed down on the capital, in her death throes, and, in doing so, has devasted vast swathes of the city of Cliffton. Our thoughts should be with its citizens."' His blue eyes skimmed quickly over the lines as he read the report. '"She was killed by the dark blue dragon, Ardin, and by an älf riding on Ardin's back." There follow various conflicting accounts concerning the älf's actual appearance. Reports agree that the dragon was killed with the älf's spear.'

'Was that all it took?' Telìnâs interrupted. The young elf had been folding a fresh green maple leaf into the shape of a little wolf, which he placed on the table in front of him as if it were guarding his goblet.

Telìnâs was with the Tî Silândur delegation, appointed for his outstanding contribution to the current mission. An emblem on his reinforced leather jerkin marked him out as a candidate for the elite fîndaii regiment. He had nearly achieved his ambition. Goïmron was delighted for him.

'Well, yes, one spear. And one dragon,' King Regnor added, causing stifled laughter in the room. The king was furious. 'So you find that amusing, do you?'

'It does sound rather funny. But given all the difficulties the situation gives rise to . . .' Vanéra responded, in an effort to restore order.

'A tamed dragon. We can't provide one of those. That changes everything.' Regnor held a tankard the famulus had brought him from the Chamber of Wonders. By magic it constantly refilled itself with beer. Even if the beer was not entirely to his taste, he thought it a great improvement on the pink wine the others were drinking. 'If we were just going to be marching on Brigantia, all right, I'd be in. We've got enough soldiers for that.

We can defeat them. But as long as there's the threat of Ardin hovering overhead with his dragon fire, we've no real chance, have we?' He looked round at the concerned faces, his hand on his dark blue bushy beard. 'Unless one of you has a useful magic spell up your sleeve that can make us immune to his flames?'

'Thirdlings demanding magic? I don't believe it.' The Gaur-agon delegate, Betania, sister-in-law to King Gajek, placed the tips of her fingers together in a steeple shape. The most striking thing about her was the strong perfume she wore. It had sent Sònuk scuttling for the exit. Otherwise she was attired simply, like the majority of those present. This was no time for attention-seeking or for trying to stand out with extravagant clothing and elaborate jewellery. 'What about the legendary courage of the dwarves? Aren't you supposed to be up to any challenge?'

'There's a difference between courage and insanity,' Brûgar muttered into his blue pointy beard. His pipe was filled with his special conference tobacco, but it kept going out because in his great excitement he would sometimes forget to draw on it.

'We'll need specialised weapons if we're to shoot Ardin down out of the skies.' Telìnâs expressed what everyone else was thinking. In his hands a second folded leaf was taking the shape of a catapult. 'From what I hear, the dwarves have bullet-hurlers that could do it.'

Bendoïn Feinunz of the clan of Arrow Seekers, high com-mander of the fortresses at the Brigantia border, now got to his feet. In his full armour, this Fourthling could almost have passed for a Thirdling. His determined gaze bore witness to his strong will. 'That is correct. Our heavy-duty catapults are powerful enough to pierce a dragon's scales, as long as the beast comes in range. We have also been experimenting with differ-ent kinds of projectile. But Ardin and his fellow dragons will be clever enough to steer clear.'

'Is there any chance we could put the catapults on some kind of mobile siege engine?' Telìnâs wanted to know. 'That way we could keep the winged monsters off our backs while we're busy fighting the Brigantians and the älfar.'

But Bendoïn shook his head, regretfully. 'The steel springs of the heavy-duty catapults use a counterweight mechanism. The weights are raised by chains operated from our tall defence towers. It would not be possible to rewind the heavy springs manually.'

'I see. And how often can the catapults be used on one winding before the tension lapses?' Betania asked.

'About half a dozen times with the heaviest ammunition, or more often if we are using smaller projectiles. But those ones would not be powerful enough to penetrate the dragon's scales.' Bendoïn had taken her meaning. 'Sure, for a while, we could manage without rewinding the springs. But then after a few shots, the machines' use on the battlefield would be severely restricted. They'd just be in the way. And they'd also be an obvious target the dragon would aim for.' The commander indicated a wall chart. 'It would mean the loss of protection against Brigantia for the defensive fortresses in the south-west. While we are fighting, here, you see, at the front, Ardin and his älf-rider can simply incinerate the fortifications.'

'We have to tackle Ardin first, of course,' advised Betania, a little arrogantly.

'Definitely. Nothing easier than shooting down a dragon in full flight as it zigzags and swoops.' This was Regnor's sarcastic response. 'Like hitting a swallow with a bow and arrow.'

We are making absolutely no progress here. Goïmron had been watching Goldhand. The old dwarf had not wanted to wear his shining armour this time, and this morning he appeared semi-comatose. It was the effects of the poison working in his bones. So it was up to the Fourthling himself, he now realised, to present his own opinions as if they were those of the hero. 'Wait. He is saying something.' Goïmron bent down to the old dwarf's mouth. 'We could wind multiple steel springs to full tension in advance, using the tower chain mechanisms, and then move them to the battlefront in carts. Keep them in reserve. That's what Tungdil Goldhand suggests.'

'Good idea! Could have been one of mine!' Bendoïn bowed in acknowledgement towards Goldhand and then resumed his seat. 'Such a shame we no longer have the famous fire-blade axe.'

'Indeed. Tungdil Goldhand also regrets the absence of Keenfire. The weapon was lost somewhere in the Grey Range when the mountains moved and the peaks collapsed. It was lost, together, of course, with Goldhand's son, the King of the Fifthlings,' Goïmron lamented. 'But the catapult plan is a good one.'

'The dragon could easily home in on our transports when we bring up the steel springs,' Regnor objected, rubbing his long beard, a habit that seemed to calm him. 'Ardin might not be very bright himself, but his rider certainly is. Clever and daring. As we've seen from how he defeated Ûra.' Regnor drank more beer and the tankard refilled itself, gurgling. 'We are totally lost without magic on our side. It is all far too dangerous.'

'So you just give up and return to your kingdoms? Is that the idea?' Bendoïn exhaled angrily, his moustache wafting in the draught. 'Absolutely not! Never! This is the best opportunity we've ever had to march on Brigantia.'

'Only a fool seeks to hide a bad idea behind pretty words.' Regnor was adamant.

'And if I tell you, Thirdling king, that my famulus is currently working on perfecting some powerful new spells?' Vanéra flashed a supercilious glance at him. For her role as conference hostess, she was dressed in a dramatic costume of lilac and gold and she wore strings of glowing pearls round her neck. 'I am aware of the rumours questioning my competence. It is said that

I am merely an artefact-enchantress. I take no offence.' She spoke calmly. 'All the more reason for me to expect greater things from the successors I am training. Mostro is a case in point.'

'How do you mean? Do you have a collection of old spell books, Esteemed Maga?' asked Telìnâs hopefully, placing his origami catapult in front of him on the table.

'Not personally, I don't. But the city of Enaiko has a rich arch-ive of treasures saved from various corners of Girdlegard. Saved, I must add, thanks to the efforts of the dwarves.' Vanéra looked at Goïmron. 'And thanks in particular to tireless collectors such as yourself, Master Chiselcut.'

Goïmron bowed, flattered by the compliment from the tall brunette maga. 'What kind of magic is your famulus capable of producing?'

'You will be pleased. Your own tribe is predestined for this branch of magic, so you can help him.' Vanéra paused dramati-cally. 'The magic I mean is that . . . of gemstones.'

By Vraccas. 'He can certainly rely on my support,' Goïmron finally blurted out, trying to conceal his nervousness.

'Mostro can also use a number of magic spells which he learned while studying in Enaiko. What he lacks, however, are the special jewels to accompany them.' Vanéra took a list out of her pocket and gave it to Bendoïn. 'I am sure the Fourthlings will have examples in their treasure hoards to put at Famulus Mostro's disposal.'

'So . . . he has learned the magic . . . but . . . only in theory? Have I got it right?' Regnor trowelled on the honeyed sweet-ness. He emptied his tankard again and watched it refill.

'Yes,' Vanéra admitted. The rest of her response was drowned out by the dwarf king's raucous laughter, and the lively exchange of confused exclamations among the conference attendees.

Goïmron did not know whether to be disappointed or relieved to learn that Mostro was not going to prove a rival. As long as everyone was concentrating on the famulus, he would be able to continue exploring his skills and refining his own knowledge. His magic differed notably from that of the young famulus who had so nearly caught him red-handed in the Chamber of Wonders.

'May we have quiet, please,' he said. 'Let us be glad that we now have at our disposal the very magic that King Regnor is calling for.'

'This list,' said Bendoïn, speaking slowly, and holding it up so the others could all see, 'contains names of some stones that are no longer available. And if they do still exist, they will be *there*.' He pointed to the map. To the Brown Mountains. 'And they'll be buried deep in the rocks.'

'It gets better and better, doesn't it?' Regnor raised his tankard in a toast. 'Then maybe we should send an advance party of Fourthlings off at the speed of the wind to dive into the mines and the shafts to search out the stones for our little second-generation wizard. Without the gems, he is utterly useless at present.' He turned to Vanéra. 'Or have I misunderstood?'

'You have understood correctly, King Regnor.' The maga remained dignified but her tone was no longer friendly.

'We do, of course, have garnets, malachites and rubies, which we can let the famulus have. But compared to the ones he is requesting here, they would be of inferior quality,' Bendoïn conceded.

'Then the magic will be less efficacious. But the spells will still work,' Goïmron interjected – then added swiftly, going red, 'That is, I would presume this to be the case. You will know that we Fourthlings know quite a bit about this subject. Personally, of course, I have no idea about magic.'

Bendoïn indicated one of the gemstones on the list. 'This one is a particularly powerful sea sapphire. I've heard of it. The old stories say that with this jewel, someone with a predisposition for magic can make absolutely any imaginable spell work, no matter how complicated or dangerous it might be.'

'I think there was a legend about it,' said one of the Fourthlings in the advisory group. 'But I don't remember the details. Wasn't it called the Troublemaker Stone?'

THAT IS A SLANDEROUS LIE, Goïmron heard inside his head. YOU SHOULDN'T BELIEVE EVERYTHING THE OLD LEGENDS SAY. SOMETIMES THEY ARE PUT ABOUT FROM PURE MALICE WITHOUT A SHRED OF EVIDENCE.

'I've got a suggestion.' Regnor's cheeks were glowing red from the beer. He twisted a blue beard lock round his finger. 'Let's send the Fourthlings to the mountains. If they can bring back the Troublemaker Stone, and *only* if they can, then I'll gladly contribute my troops to your army.'

'So you remain adamant about the Thirdlings not joining the alliance?' Betania exhaled heavily. 'This will be difficult to explain to the Gauragon fighters who are expected to risk their lives.'

'It will certainly be detrimental to morale,' Bendoïn added. 'All the Children of the Smith should—'

'Come now! You've got your catapults and a famulus and a handful of jewels and some magic.' Regnor pointed at the ancient figure of Goldhand. '*And*, of course, Girdlegard's greatest hero. What could possibly go wrong? You know what? You don't really need my people at all. I almost feel sorry for Brigantia and Dsôn Khamateion, in the face of all this superior force.'

'Spare us your mockery,' Vanéra retorted angrily. 'Put that tankard down. I'm going to take back my gift. It did not even begin to make you more amenable, as I had hoped.'

'You can't demand the return of a present.'

'You can if the recipient behaves extremely badly. And you are behaving so crudely. It is really an insult. For a monarch to conduct himself like that . . .'

'I won't give it back.'

'Be warned: the gift can change its nature.'

'Even if it serves up vinegar instead of beer, I don't care! It still won't be any worse than that piss-poor pink stuff of yours.' Regnor got to his feet. 'But I will do you – all of you – a favour and leave your assembly right now.' With the tankard in his hand, he made slowly for the door. 'On the morrow I shall leave, taking all my people with me. I have heard nothing here to make me change my mind.'

'How can you say that?' Gata stared at her father in horror. 'You are trashing the Thirdlings' reputation by your stance. Lorimbur would never have wanted that! Come back here, so –' She bit her tongue on the next words, because he had not even turned round to face her.

A worried silence fell on the company. People were outraged by the incident, and embarrassed at having witnessed this shameful dispute.

As Regnor left the chamber, a dwarf messenger arrived, face and leather armour caked in dust from the journey. His badges identified him as belonging to Bendoïn's fortress defenders.

'I bring news from the Brigantia border,' he gasped out.

'What has happened?' Seeing the Fourthling's anxious expression, Goïmron was sure it would not be good news.

'The Brigantians have marshalled an army. They are attacking in waves in various places along the wall. And they're ignoring all the shots from our catapults.' Bendoïn gave the breathless messenger some water which he hastily gulped down. 'The invaders are surging in through Gauragon, bent on conquest.'

'Orweyn has pre-empted our plans,' Betania called out, distressed by the report. 'His spies will have known for ages that we are marshalling a large force.'

'The *älfar* have known it for some time,' Bendoïn corrected her. 'Esteemed Maga Vanéra, we will set off immediately to locate the stones your famulus requires. He should get ready to leave with us. At once!'

'Then we must send our army out at full speed, to stop the Omuthan,' advised Telìnâs. 'I think he might well make a pact with the salt sea orcs. The monsters could attack Girdlegard from the north at the same time!'

Looking at the exhausted messenger, Goïmron realised there was yet more to report. 'What else? Speak freely.'

'The blue dragon is said to have been seen in the vicinity of the orc strongholds,' the Fourthling stammered. 'And we hear there's a new banner flying over Kràg Tahuum that no one in Girdlegard has ever seen before.'

'So the älfar have made a pact with that scum, Prince Krognoz. This is getting very tricky.' Bendoïn turned to the maga. 'I beg you, gather together anything in your collection that could be useful in battle, and get it loaded up. And then–'

'That's no good. There's too much of a muddle in the Chamber of Wonders,' Goïmron said, interrupting. 'Or rather, I meant to say . . . so I've heard . . . Forgive me, Esteemed Maga.'

Vanéra gave him a puzzled glance. 'You are correct, Master Chiselcut. I have not yet managed to archive my predecessors' valuable collections properly. Let me have a quick look and I'll follow on as soon as I find anything. In the meantime, I'll certainly send my famulus along with your army and you can do your best to locate the stones we need?' She stood up and, with a perfunctory bow, hurried out of the conference chamber.

It's not going to get any better. Time to close the meeting. Goïmron bent down again to Goldhand and pretended to be listening to him. 'Resolved, then! We set off and put a stop to this evil. Let all the troops make their way north as fast as possible. Vraccas is on our side!'

'Vraccas is with us!' all the dwarves responded – all, that is, apart from the Thirdling delegation and Gata.

The humans, elves and meldriths banged on the table in thunderous agreement, encouraging everyone to be of good heart. But somehow, to Goïmron's ears, there was a slight hesitancy there. Some reluctance. *A fearfulness.*

The assembly broke up; there were many dispositions to be made in preparation for the march.

I only hope I've done the right thing. He slowly placed his hand on Goldhand's shoulder. If only he could have heard some advice from his mentor, or received some instructions from him. *As it is, it's only my own orders that have been issued. And whatever happens in the next few orbits, it'll be my responsibility.* He had seldom felt less happy. There was not even any consolation to be derived from having that stone in his pocket.

Standing at the window of the rooms he had been assigned, a half-empty tankard in his hand, Regnor surveyed the parts of the town immediately surrounding the palace. With his free hand, he stroked his beard to try and calm himself.

The banners, flags and pennants of the various clans and tribes flew proudly in the warm air. Vanéra had arranged for the southern dwarves to be accommodated in the local hostelries at her own expense. Regnor could hear dwarf songs on the breeze. The sound of their tambourine, bagpipe, drum and bell accompaniments echoed round the narrow streets.

They are so stupid. He drank his beer in a foul humour. These were songs he knew well. *They're singing as if there were a victory to celebrate.*

To his mind, the forthcoming campaign against Brigantia was a hopeless endeavour. He recalled the words of his forebear Rognor Mortalblow, a previous Thirdling chancellor: he had held the view that, in the long run, the mountains would tolerate only the dwarf tribes, whether underground or on the slopes. The series of earthquakes, landslides and devastating volcanic eruptions were proof enough of that. The mountains would soon shake off the Brigantians and the älfar, too.

We must wait, that's all. We wait, rather than risk throwing away countless lives in an attempt to eradicate the scum. Deep in reflection, he continued to play with his beard. Ever since Goldhand had turned up, things were no longer going his way.

His greatest task as Rognor's successor was to enhance the memory and strengthen the reputation of the tribe's originator, Lorimbur. The one-time feud between the tribes had been over and done with for more than a thousand cycles. This smoothed the way for his ambitious plans to bring Lorimbur more to the fore. Hargorin Deathbringer had neglected the Thirdlings' roots, busying himself with alliances with the monarchs of the other kingdoms. *He nearly became exactly like one of them.* That was the reason the Mortalblows of the Orc Slayer clan had appropriated the sceptre of the Thirdling tribe. In a peaceful yet determined takeover.

Since then, the aim had always been to convert the other four tribes to the glorification of Lorimbur. To propagate his teachings slowly and surely over the course of hundreds of cycles, undermining and eventually displacing the worship of the hated Vraccas.

Initial successes had already been recorded.

Then along comes Tungdil Goldhand, back from the depths, and once again the name of the Divine Smith is being praised. Regnor swallowed the last mouthful of beer and watched the tankard fill up. *May they all go to blazes, consumed in the dragon fire, with Vraccas' name on their lips. I'm not sacrificing my own people.* And it was his own daughter who had been instrumental in bringing Goldhand back, thus ruining all his plans. Typical of her to contradict him and to be working in a way diametrically opposed to his ambitions. *Lorimbur, you know that I would never have sent troops along with that quarterling dwarf.* He turned round and plonked himself down on the chair. Foam from his drink slopped over the side of the tankard. *We protect the Black Mountains. Anyone who doesn't follow Lorimbur can fend for himself and take the consequences.*

Regnor was making an effort to feign indifference.

And yet it did not sit well with him, the thought of thousands of dwarves dying without his having lifted a finger. There might well be differences of opinion about Vraccas, but they did, after all, all belong to the same race.

On top of that, his daughter would be hurling recriminations at him, all the way back to the Black Mountains. And she would continue to do that once they were home. And she'd do it in public. *Perhaps she'll instigate open revolt among the people and find a following of like-minded individuals.* Indifference turned into concern. Concern on so many fronts. Concern about losing his own throne. *Curses! Why did they have to find that decrepit Goldhand dwarf?* Regnor put the tankard to his lips and took a long draught. *Couldn't they just have killed a few pig-faces and some black-eyes and then come home without succeeding in their mission?*

He tried to put the tankard down. But it did not work.

What the . . .?

Cool, fresh beer kept pouring into his mouth, a veritable river of beer; his raised arm was anchored fast, with the drink held at his lips.

Regnor was forced to swallow, or else drown. The drink flowed and flowed, unstoppably, slopping over the side of the tankard and getting up his nose, making him choke. He could not stop to breathe, and the beer kept coming. With the brewed juice foaming in front of his eyes, he could not see where he was going as he stumbled blindly for the door. Any attempt to call for help disappeared in a gurgle.

Regnor finally gave up the unequal struggle. The stream of liquid ran into his airways and flooded his lungs, robbing him of breath. He collapsed, semi-conscious, and the beer kept pouring down on him.

At long last the door opened.

Out of the corner of his eye, he caught sight of a pair of expensive-looking shoes. Women's shoes. Shoes decorated with pearls.

'Be warned: the gift can change its nature,' Vanéra whispered. 'You have only yourself to blame, King Regnor. Many an artefact develops a life of its own. I find it uncanny how they do that.'

She planned this all along! He could not answer, only splutter and choke. *She wanted to murder me!*

'They will find you eventually. You will have literally drunk yourself to death. Your daughter will assume the Thirdling crown. It's what she's been wanting for some time. Now she won't have to wait, hoping for you to have a fatal accident.' The pearly shoes turned away. 'Thanks to her affection for Goïmron and her well-developed sense of responsibility, she will lead Lorimbur's descendants against Brigantia. And she will do everything possible in order to be victorious. But not in honour of you.' The steps receded. 'Drink your fill, King Regnor. Empty the tankard, do. My treat. Every mouthful.'

As the chamber door closed, the King of the Thirdlings drowned. And the tide of beer ebbed away.

Girdlegard

Queendom of Undarimar
Island of Arima
1023 P.Q. (7514th solar cycle in old reckoning), late summer

'What a wonderful surprise!' Queen Aloka approached her guest with arms outstretched and a welcoming smile on her lips. The new arrival had turned up at the north fortress on Arima, the main island. 'A spectacular entrance, as I saw with my own eyes. No one has ever come to visit us riding on a dragon before. And nobody ever rode a dragon to kill another dragon, as far as I know! Welcome, welcome!'

The black-haired älf, his body concealed under a simple, pale blue robe, sketched a bow. 'My thanks.' In his right hand, he held a tionium rune spear engraved with the signs and symbols of his kind.

Since he had arrived unexpectedly and unannounced, her guest found the mid-fifty-year-old in a plain garment with maritime embroidery. She wore a gold chain incorporating tiny palandium shell-shaped beads round her neck. Her hair, bleached by sun and salt water, was piled high on her head.

'Had I guessed what power my allies have, I would have entered into the pact much sooner.' Aloka lowered her arms and indicated the laden table where bread, vegetables and grilled seafood awaited. 'Take a seat! You must tell me the whole story of your victory over Ûra. Now that she is dead, the crews on my ships have been unhindered as they ransack the ruined city of Cliffton. For this, again, my thanks.' She clapped her hands together enthusiastically. 'And you must tell me your name. I want to hear it from your own lips.'

'It was perhaps less epic a battle than rumour would have it. If you know where an opponent is most vulnerable, victory is not necessarily so difficult to achieve. No witchcraft involved.' The älf sat down, his upper body kept stiffly erect as if there were a suit of armour under his robe. 'I call myself Mòndarcai.'

Aloka took her seat opposite him and summoned the doulia servants over to bring the drinks and to serve the delicacies. 'A lovely-sounding name. And certainly worthy of a dragon killer.' She indicated the selection of food. 'I thought this might be the kind of thing an älf would like.'

'That is so. I see foodstuffs and can smell spices that my people enjoy most. How do you come to serve these foods?'

'I'm a great fan of exotic cuisine and I collect recipes from the foreigners as they arrive from overseas.' Aloka selected a pickled kiso-almond with a cheese filling. 'And we've had twenty of your people here helping us interpret the shipbuilding blueprints. Otherwise, I fear, my carpenters would be a bit, shall we say, at sea? Who understands the älfar language, after all?'

'Oh yes, of course.' Mòndarcai tried some of the vegetable dishes. 'Perhaps they will be coming to see me?'

'I'm sure they will be on their way. But it will take them a while to get here from the southern fortress. Not every älf has a tame dragon to ride on.' Aloka laughed with her mouth full, and her fingers played with her gold chain. 'I take it you came with the beast in order to support us in our sorties against the coastal realms?'

'Do you need support?'

'Well, yes. The Gautaya empire is weak. We can cope with them easily. And the larger cities on the coasts. But Litusien and Ribasturian are hard nuts to crack. If you could do a little over-flight with your dragon and knock out the defence works, that would be great. My commander can give me a list of the towns that are of the greatest strategic importance.' Aloka crossed her legs and arranged the fabric carefully over her thighs. 'How are things progressing with the plans in the Brown Mountains? Are you aiding the Brigantians in their attack, and their attempt to take Gauragon and the neighbouring empire?'

'No.'

'Oh.' Aloka's cheerful expression faded. She looked surprised. 'But I thought . . .'

'I do not belong to the scum from Dsôn Khamateion.' Mòndar-cai tasted the roast akra peppers and nodded appreciatively. 'And I prefer to pursue my own objectives.'

'You're not from Dsôn Khamateion? And you called them *scum*?' The queen hesitated, uncertain now. 'How is this? You *are* an älf, aren't you?'

'The salt sea orcs and I have formed an alliance. I promised they could have the whole empire, apart from a ten-mile-wide coastal strip. That is reserved for you. Along with anything you can conquer to the south.'

'The salt sea orcs. Well, well. And what about the orc fortresses?'

'Kràg Tahuum is with me in the alliance.'

'Which alliance . . .?' Then Aloka's countenance lightened. 'Ah, of course. An exiled älf crowns himself prince of the orcs in order to found his own empire. I presume you have fallen foul of Dsôn because . . .'

'It would take too long to explain all the background,' Mòndarcai answered, concentrating on making his selection from the plates of delicacies. 'For you, it suffices that you know I have come to have you join my alliance.'

To Aloka's ears, this was starting to sound rather like a threat. 'I am already committed to the alliance with Dsôn Khamateion.'

'You can change that. You should change that.' He selected some squid and chewed sceptically, before spitting the morsel out on to the ground. 'Too much siko pepper. Take care with the plisi seeds on the algae salad. They can have a detrimental effect on one's thinking.'

Aloka stared at her uninvited guest. Her response was a joyless laugh. It said more than any spoken refusal.

'You have seen my dragon. What will I do, if you *don't* join the alliance? Mm? Queen Aloka?' Mòndarcai banged the end of his spear on the ground with a metallic clang. 'Ask Ûra. She knows what I do.'

Aloka blanched and grasped her necklace as if it could give her assistance. 'What kind of älf are you?'

'An älf who hates Dsôn Khamateion. Who hates all those who live there. Who has nothing in common with the ones that slunk into Girdlegard one thousand cycles ago pretending to be elves in order to deceive the humans and the dwarves,' he said in a cold voice. 'I shall take away Dsôn's allies and I shall reduce their empire in the Brown Mountains to ashes.' The black tip of his rune spear poked the fifty-year-old in the chest near her solar plexus. 'And you, Queen Aloka, will belong to me. It will be worth your while: no duties to pay, no regulations to follow. I just need some of your ships when the time is right. I need those ships and I need you to reject your pact with Dsôn. You don't have to do anything else for now, apart from stopping the attacks on your neighbours. Send signals. Leave Litusien, Ribasturian, Gautaya and the other sea kingdoms in peace until I say otherwise.'

'But I can't . . . I can't do that!' Aloka was at a loss. She started to break out in a sweat. Her heart was beating so fast it felt as if it might catch fire from the fear. 'Dsôn will send assassins to punish me for my treachery if I do that.'

'Tell me, do you think I look so harmless, then?' The älf's voice was dangerously quiet. 'Do you think you will have long to live if you refuse my offer?'

With hands folded beseechingly, Aloka sank on her knees, although she could hardly breathe for terror. 'Please!' she begged.

'Do you swear loyal allegiance to me?'

'Can't we—'

'In order to convince you of my powers, I have sent my friend Ardin to set fire to five of your largest vessels. It was really so simple,' Mòndarcai broke in. 'If you do not change sides, Queen Aloka, I shall burn the rest of your fleet, along with the island fortresses, and then I shall look down from above to watch how the coastal kingdoms capture your family and execute them. You will be long dead when that happens.' The spear tip buried itself through the light-coloured fabric to touch her skin. 'There will be nothing left of Undarimar. Or of your line. I am more cruel than Dsôn, I assure you.'

'So graceful in appearance and yet so thoroughly evil!' Aloka collapsed down on to the tiled floor and let her hands fall. 'Then I must—'

And suddenly the door flew open.

Twenty älfar stormed in, armed and armoured. Without saying a word, some of them loosed their longbow arrows at Mòndarcai, while the others lunged towards him with drawn swords.

Elria be thanked! Aloka ducked down and rolled under the table to avoid the deadly missiles and whirling blades.

The black arrows struck Mòndarcai in the chest. But the armour under his blue robe repelled the shafts and even shattered the arrow tips.

The warriors from Dsôn moved in for close-combat fighting, blades swishing through the air at such speed that it was impossible for the queen to see who was winning. The opponents' movements were fluid and swift.

I must get away! Aloka was startled to see one of her allies fall dead to the ground. Another slammed, slaughtered, against the table; a severed arm flew through the air, followed by a head. The dark red, almost black, blood of the älfar spread wide over the carpets and trickled across the tiles.

Aloka managed to crawl through to the far end of the feast table, where she staggered to her feet and made a run for the door. Shouts could be heard in the distance as the palace guards reacted to the sounds of combat.

As if from nowhere, Mòndarcai loomed up in front of her, his robe slashed from sword thrusts and splashed with the blood of those he had killed. 'Where are you off to, queen?' The moistly shimmering rune-spear tip was at the side of her throat. 'I hope you're going to look for that treaty document?'

Aloka was conscious of the warmth and the smell of fresh blood cleaving to the tionium blade. 'Absolutely. That's just what I was going to do,' she stammered.

'Oh, and don't forget to recall your ships. Get the signal beacons lit,' he continued. 'Are we in agreement?'

Her gaze swept over the carnage Mòndarcai had created. The violence of the wounds he had inflicted spoke of the deep loathing he felt for her alliance partners.

'We are in agreement,' she muttered, pale as the sands of the southern beaches. 'You will protect me from the Dsôn assassins?'

'It is in your interest that Dsôn fall swiftly. Then you would no longer have to be afraid of them.' Mòndarcai lifted the spear tip away from her throat. 'It's only myself you need to fear, should you ever disregard our new alliance and act contrary to my orders.'

'Never!'

'Very good.' He indicated the exit and the guards running along the corridor, swords upraised. 'Go and look for that treaty, Queen Aloka. And tell your guards to withdraw. I never like to kill my allies.'

Aloka raised her hand and her armed soldiers hesitated and then stopped. 'I am unharmed. Don't be concerned. Summon the doulia to clear away the corpses.'

The captain took two paces forward and closed the door behind himself before bowing to her. 'My queen, something else has happened.' He pointed to the window. 'The advance fleet is here. And . . . it is hard to credit. More impressive than anything I've seen before in my life. The largest ships have eight masts with huge blood-red sails!'

'What advance fleet?' Mòndarcai cast a questioning glance Aloka's way.

'The advance party for the relief fleet that Dsôn promised us. So that we can quickly conquer all the kingdoms along the sea coast.' She looked at the armoured captain with a confused expression. 'They're not due here till the autumn.'

'It looks as if the plans have changed, or maybe there was an unexpectedly strong following wind. The älfar flags on the masts are unmistakeable, my queen,' he replied. 'Eight vessels.'

'Eight? That will be a lot of work for your dragon.' Aloka turned to the silent älf. Then she felt a hefty blow on her back, a thump that made her shell bead necklace bounce.

Mòndarcai had vanished without a sound.

An arrow tip from Dsôn stuck out through Aloka's breast. Even before registering the pain, she fell dead to the palace floor. The quick death spared her any agony. She landed on the ground next to the body of her guard captain, whose life-blood was still gushing out from the slash across his throat.

From the scaly back of his circling, dark blue dragon, Mòndarcai surveyed the group of eight mighty ships that Aloka had referred to as the advance fleet. From the safe vantage height, he could make out various details of the vessels' construction and noted the differences in size. There were two giant water vehicles at least one hundred and twenty paces long and fifty broad, each boasting eight masts. The blood-red fabric at the yardarms, a light silk, wafted in the breeze that had brought them close to Arima. The shape of the sails was distinctly different from those used in Girdlegard.

By Inàste! A whole floating city! The eight-masters were surrounded by six companion vessels in convoy. Mòndarcai could pick out not only night-mares and troops on the decks, but also barrels for provisions and water. The advance fleet was thus self-supporting and could remain at sea for extended periods without having to land to take on supplies. *Perfect for long voyages.*

The prow of each ship was decorated with an attractive face with a wide-open mouth holding a catapult inside it. On the decks, whether of the big ships or the smaller ones, there were movable slingshot devices on gun carriages with their leaf-springs, wire hawsers and piled-up boxes of ammunition or spears.

'I saw the guns too,' said Ardin, speaking inside the älf's head. 'They won't stop me. I'll fly over a couple of times and those little walnut shells of boats will soon be crackling with flames. Nothing can withstand the fiery breath of a dragon.'

Mòndarcai was rather more circumspect and cautious than his bold ally, who was gliding high above the fleet. 'The speed of their shots might be quite considerable.'

'You know they won't get to aim at me. What can they do against us when I go down in a nose-dive attack?' Ardin responded, heading into the wind and folding his wings back slightly to increase his speed. 'You choose the boat you want me to turn into a heap of ashes first!'

'Turn away! They know you are coming and they are prepared. Let's just observe for now.'

'Oh, go on! I deserve a bit of fun!' The dragon held its wings closer against its body. 'Hold tight. Or you'll be swirling down like a leaf in autumn.' Faster than a stone falling, Ardin shot head first straight at the first of the eight-masters.

Mòndarcai leaned back against the sparkling blue scales of the dragon, the wind catching at his torn robe. His dark hair fluttering wildly, he was forced to almost completely close his eyes against the wind.

The lookouts on the convoy ships had spotted the attacker. Whistles sounded out. Numerous large and small catapults were being manoeuvred into position as crewmen rushed to and fro. Straps and chains were being attached to the sides of the slingshot devices, although Mòndarcai could not guess their function. None of the crew's actions betrayed the slightest amount of fear. The artillerists were taking their places in the armoured pods behind the catapults and they moved their carriage barrels through ninety degrees to aim vertically upright.

They've been practising for dragon attacks! They are prepared! 'Abandon this attack! Pull out!' Mòndarcai yelled against the noise of the wind.

'Their steel and iron don't scare me. These are not dwarf weapons.' Ardin continued his dive. *'We'll soon be starting some nice little bonfires with all that wood and the enemy bones for kindling.'*

They were still some two hundred paces off from their target when the catapults on the decks of all the ships were brought to life.

By Inàste! Great showers of metal bolts the length of a man's arm came hissing at them from all sides. *At this range?* The hollow barrels of the catapults kept spitting out projectiles. The coiled metal springs were being rewound by means of the chains and were shooting automatically while the operators merely had to adjust the range and aim.

Then the first bolts struck home with a clatter. Mòndarcai ducked down as the first missiles burst apart and rolled off, narrowly missing the dragon's scales.

'What did I tell you?' crowed a triumphant Ardin. *'They've got nothing to get me wi—'* A howl of anguish escaped the scaled creature's open muzzle and a fountain of hot blood shot up, spraying past the älf; the dragon's boiling life-blood spread out behind them as a long blue ribbon in the air as they flew.

Curses! I knew that would happen! There was an open gash on Ardin's throat. *What was that?*

'Dragon bone! They're using bolts with tips made of dragon bone!' the scaled beast screamed inside the älf's head. The dragon spread his wings to draw up out of his headlong dive and swerve to the side. *'That's why they can pierce my scales!'* He flew to the right to escape the hail of missiles.

But the perfectly trained marksmen operating the turntable catapults had anticipated this manoeuvre and had swung their barrels round by using their foot-pedal mechanisms. Ardin was caught in the middle of a stream of steel and dragon bone.

We can't survive this! They had lost speed and altitude and now, as the blue dragon glided into range of the ships, they were presenting an easier target. Mòndarcai prepared to jump off.

At this point Ardin was struck again, his body pierced by a bolt. The dragon gave a great shudder and lost power. The swift glide across over the masts of the ships turned into an uncontrolled descent. The attempt to launch a final tongue of flame at his torturers resulted in only a puff of smoke and a miserable flame flickering out of the slash in his neck.

Immediately following this, Ardin received a glass pellet in the mouth, which broke open and shattered against his upper palate, releasing acid to pour down his gullet, burning him from the inside.

Mòndarcai leaped off and plunged to the waves from a height of fifty or sixty paces. *I have lost my best ally!*

Red-hot pain shot through his shoulder above the sewn-in tionium plates. One of the bolts had hit him and was stuck in his flesh. Groaning, he pulled out the bolt, even as he fell, and grabbed tight hold of his tionium spear. The spear's runes glowed green.

He plummeted into the water.

He became aware, as he sank down, that now Undarimar was once more an ally of Dsôn. A vital part of his grand plan was null and void.

A weighted net was thrown over Mòndarcai, covering and trying to entrap him. He split the fibres of the net using his spear to avoid being caught fast. He looked around. *Where is Ardin?*

Hardly ten paces distant, the dragon's corpse was sinking down to the bottom of the sea, with his life-blood boiling into the water around his dead body. The acid had destroyed a large part of his head.

That is the second of the two scaled creatures on my conscience. Mòndarcai caught hold of a rope dangling down from one of the ships. He let himself be pulled along. Otherwise the heavy tionium would have dragged him to the depths, to end up alongside Ardin. *They'll be calling me the dragon killer.*

He carefully climbed up the rope, hand over hand, until he was able to poke his head out into the foaming bow wave to take in a lungful of air.

Mòndarcai was going to need a different strategy to bring Girdlegard down. *A strategy nobody would have anticipated.*

I spent many cycles making a name for myself leading a company of mercenaries. Even when I accepted the office, I was aware of many intrigues and plots being hatched against me.

But the mercenaries needed me.

Still.

So I began to expand my power and the magic skills I needed for my own plans.

Excerpt from
The Adventures of Tungdil Goldhand,
as experienced in the Black Abyss
and written by himself.
First draft.

XIV

Girdlegard

Red Mountains
Kingdom of the Firstling dwarves
Seahold, eastern harbour
1023 P.Q. (7514th solar cycle in old reckoning), late summer

Xanomir watched, dejected, through his viewing glass as the blood-red sails vanished at the horizon. *We could not stop the advance fleet!*

Eight ships with silk sails, two of them larger than any other vessel he had ever seen, had come through the tunnel, shooting at anything and everything that had not taken cover. The arsenal at the disposal of the Outer Lands älfar could match anything Seahold had to offer, apart from the dwarves' great heavy-duty war wolves. The acid-shooters were a perfidious piece of weaponry emitting a substance that ate through metal and stone.

Under normal circumstances, the defenders on the fortress would have had their catapults and sling devices trained towards the sea. The giant ships and the accompanying convoy would have presented an easy target at this distance and could have been quickly sunk.

But the preceding strong earth shocks and the gas alarm that followed had forced the dwarves to abandon their positions in the bastions and head for the open air as quickly as possible. Often the open fissures in the ground could fling up lethal vapours and horrendous gusts of hot steam that would attack lung linings and fatally poison the blood when breathed in.

Hundreds of the defending forces stood in the open air on the town squares behind the protective walls of the port. Whitish-yellow clouds had surged out of the tunnel, enveloping the whole eight-vessel convoy.

Xanomir was one of the first to celebrate what was assumed to be the inevitable death of all those otherwise unstoppable älfar. There followed the bitter realisation that this was not gas but harmless steam. The attackers were soaked and, although discoloured by exposure to this vapour, unharmed and still all on their feet.

In the hail of fire from the eight ships, which all showed a vague resemblance to Undarimar's fleet, it had been impossible for the town's forces to approach and man their own catapults and long-distance weaponry. With their underwater ramming spurs, the convoy of ships had been able either to rupture the chains fastened across the canal, or else drag the fixtures out of the walls.

We were taken completely by surprise and have been overwhelmed. Xanomir trained his spyglass on the exit of the tunnel leading through the Red Mountains. Nine similarly deadly ship convoys were to follow, according to reconnaissance reports. *We can't let the same thing happen again.* 'The others will be turning up any moment now,' he said to Buvendil. *Except next time, there'll be more of them.*

In the course of the last quarter-cycle, the three älfar saboteurs and the nesodes working with them had managed in secret to inflict considerable damage on the Seahold defences, with the result that the dwarves' deterrent installations either did not function at all or else did so only at a fraction of normal efficacy.

Nine more convoys of eight-masted ships were heading for Seahold. Xanomir reckoned they each carried a fighting force of around thirty thousand. This meant that three hundred thousand älfar would get into Girdlegard at one fell swoop.

The western fortress of Wavechallenge had had no chance of withstanding the hail of heavy stones, acid and flaming projectiles. The defending soldiers had been forced to seek shelter in the interior of the mountains.

'Next time the gas alarm goes off, everyone's to remain at their post,' ordered Xanomir's commanding officer. 'Put your protective masks on and let's hope the saturated cloth will keep working long enough. One way or another, we will all give our lives for Girdlegard's sake.'

The soldiers on the open ground cheered and prepared to return to Seahold.

'What is the point of us dying in a cloud of sulphur?' Buvendil shook his blond head. 'There's no way I'm going to stand still in the smoke. If I manage to stay alive today, tomorrow I can hunt down one of those black-eye ships with your submersible craft. And sink it. They won't be expecting that.'

'Keep quiet,' muttered Xanomir. 'It isn't ready yet.'

'We would need at least ten of them. Otherwise it would take far too long to deal with their eighty ships.' His friend took half a step backwards, his eyes huge. 'By the beard of the Eternal Smith! Here comes the next contingent! We'll never be quick enough to get the fortress catapults trained on them.'

The bowsprits of two of the escort vessels were already poking out of the tunnel into the sunshine. Behind them came the mighty eight-masts carrying the blood-red sails.

'These black-eyes are certainly in a hurry.' Xanomir had to

quell his admiration for the enemy's efficiency. What their carpenters and construction teams had produced was infinitely more than the total shipbuilding capacity of the whole of Girdlegard. *Who can stop them?*

A loud roar issued from out of the depths of the earth, signalling an impending earth tremor. It was followed by the gas alarm, warning of deadly fumes.

'Everybody, run! Man the catapults!' the commander ordered. 'We must sink the two escorts and the eight-master in their wake. So they don't get through the—'

Xanomir heard the faint rumble of firing from the ships. At first, the missiles were visible only as tiny points, growing in size as they headed in, with plumes of smoke streaming after them.

'Take cover!' he shouted, hurling himself behind the harbour walls.

About thirty paces away from him, stones the size of a giant's head started to crash in through the arrow slits of the nearest empty defence tower, followed by the flump of flaming leather bags landing in the breach, spilling their liquid fire. The defenders' arrow catapults were burning to a crisp.

Xanomir peeked over the top of the wall to look at the huge, suspended crushing-stone devices in the roof of the cavernous tunnel. They did not move even though the two escort ships were directly underneath them. *Have the älfar got on to the overhead maintenance walkways and destroyed the machinery?* If so, that would be their last hope lost.

'To your posts!' came the command. 'To work! Let's send these abominable black-eyes to their deaths!'

'No,' countered Buvendil. 'Stay under cover. You will die a senseless death!' Pointing with his axe, he indicated the destruction in the blazing defence tower. 'That's what will happen to us. Let's wait here and grab—'

'Wait!' A dwarf covered in reddish stone dirt came running out of the side entrance of the northern gate in the cliff face, a stream of dust behind him as he whirled his arms. 'Get away! Stay back!'

Xanomir could not see who it was, but one thing struck him at once – *we don't wear armour like that anymore!*

'Speak!' the officer demanded, addressing the messenger, who was having a coughing fit. 'What has happened?'

'It isn't–' he said, gasping, then placing his signal horn to his lips. The sounds were pathetically weak, but the correct sequence of notes to command the troops to retreat. 'It's not . . . gas you can see.' Xanomir noticed the dwarf's hand. *Two crossed hammers on an iron ring. The heraldic device of Hegomil Coalglow!*

'Stop! Who are you?'

The underground rumble developed into loud crashing and bursting sounds. The rock arch above the entrance to the tunnel showed a definite vertical gash travelling swiftly upwards. Fragments of stone were falling on to the decks of the ships and into the water. The wave of destruction continued back into the tunnel, as Xanomir could see through his viewing tube. *The tunnel! It's collapsing!* He felt no tremor, nor was he aware of the ground shaking beneath his feet. His spyglass lens showed him a mark, up from which a second fissure was travelling.

'It is intentional,' he whispered, lowering the glass.

'It was our king's plan!'

Suddenly, huge blocks of stone crashed down out of the roof and the upper side walls of the passage, sending up fountains from the water of the canal. Others struck the planks, firing devices and masts of the ships. Cross-beams shattered and sails were torn to pieces.

'Not *your* king's,' the dirt-covered dwarf amended happily, wiping his bearded face in utter relief. 'Another's.' Alongside the two shocked and surprised Firstlings, he watched with satisfaction as the tunnel collapsed and the mass of rock over it slipped sharply down.

High waves surged out of the underground waterway and crashed against the harbour walls. The dull thuds of breaking stone mingled with the sounds of splintering wood and the muffled älfar screams wafting over from the distance. Dust clouds billowing out of the tunnel obscured the rest from view.

'By the beard of Vraccas!' Xanomir turned to the new arrival, with many different emotions swirling through his head: delight, disbelief, astonishment, and incredible relief. 'What did we just see there?'

'The end of the älfar fleet. The end of the sea passage through into Girdlegard,' came the dwarf's relieved response. 'The first attempt went wrong. We had miscalculated. That trick with the gas alarm saved your lives.'

'Who planned this? Who is we?' the commander wanted to know, raising his spiked metal morning-star flail. 'And who in the name of all the shameful titles of Tion do you think you are, to know all of this?'

'I am called Hegobal Coalglow. I am the son of Hegomil Coalglow, and one, together with yourselves, of the many saviours of our homeland.' He sketched a bow. 'We did not expect the fleet until the autumn and we had to rush through with everything. But it has worked . . .'

Xanomir found he understood very little. He put his hand in his pocket and pulled out the amulet he had found in the mouth of the giant fish. 'Did this belong to your father?'

'But yes! Where did you get this? And how do you know . . .?'

'Your signet ring. I noticed it and put two and two together.'

Hegobal took it gratefully and displayed his own ring to prove his relationship. 'It belonged to him. Where did you find it?'

'In the sea,' was Xanomir's simple response.

'Then it made a long journey.' Hegobal sat down and Buvendil passed him his bottle of water. 'My father died quite some time ago. He fell. It was during the preparatory works for this destructive miracle that you have just witnessed.' He took a quick draught from the flask. 'Thank you. And now you must excuse me. I must . . .'

'No way! You are under arrest, Hegobal Coalglow!' the commander thundered. 'Until we know the meaning of what has happened here, you're not going anywhere.'

'But I have to speak to King Gandalgir Irongrip.' Hegobal calmly finished his sentence with a smile. 'He is expecting me.' Pointing with the flask, he indicated the cloud of dust emerging from what was left of the blocked sea passage through the mountain. 'Do not concern yourselves. There'll be nothing else coming through.'

In the meantime, word had got about in the harbour town of Seahold that none of the älfar vessels had escaped. Seventy-two ships had been crushed and buried by the tremendous fall of rock. The Red Mountains had destroyed them and all their living charges were drowned. The first hesitant cheers went up.

It's over! By Vraccas! It is over! Xanomir exchanged relieved glances with Buvendil and then they both joined in the general jubilation.

Girdlegard

United Great Kingdom of Gauragon
Province of Mountainhigh
1023 P.Q. (7514th solar cycle in old reckoning), early autumn

Standing on the top of a halted rail coach for a better view, Goïmron surveyed the vast expanse of the camp by the light of the night constellations. There were countless illuminated tents and small campfires glowing round the last station where they had stopped.

So few, and yet it's still more than Girdlegard could ever have hoped to assemble.

The makeshift gathering of troops consisting of dwarves, humans, elves and meldriths would have to cover the remaining miles to the planned confrontation with the army from Brigantia either on foot, on horseback, or in battle carts. Goïmron could hear the sound of singing and flute-playing coming from groups round the campfires.

The commanders of the various contingents had met together on several occasions under the leadership of Tungdil Goldhand to discuss strategy and decide on the best site for the coming battle. Their plans frequently had to be adapted because the Omuthan's forces had, in recent orbits, been advancing rapidly. Brigantia's army was living off the land, rather than transporting its own food supplies. This being late summer, these tactics were proving sensible.

At the same time, the Girdlegard army was conserving energy by using Gauragon's express-rail network. Their heavy-duty catapults could never have been moved long distances as quickly without this mode of transport. This way they had not had to take the machines apart. They were ready for use.

The orbit after the morrow, then. Goïmron sat down. For the most part, he had had to be responsible for Goldhand's decisions, since the ancient dwarf was currently badly affected by the älfar poison in his bones. The hardships of travel had not improved the state of his health. *The butchery begins the orbit after next.* He let his gaze drift over the encampment. *What shall I do?*

During the journey, he and Chòldunja had met in secret to work with the gemstones other dwarves had managed to bring along from where they lived. As a Fourthling, he had been given charge of assessing their quality. He had thought it right to keep a few back in case his gift for magic were needed in combat.

'Ah, a dwarf resting out under the stars and not hiding away in the back of a truck somewhere because it would be more like his own comfortable, dark cave.' Rodana pulled herself up through the hatch in the carriage roof. 'You have always been a bit different, haven't you?'

'Not just by being a Fourthling?' He watched the blonde puppet mistress come over to sit by him, carrying a flask of red wine. She was wearing a long shirt and leather hose and was still very graceful in appearance.

'Not only that. There's more to you.' She took a sip of wine. 'I've got an instinct. Believe me.'

Goïmron concealed his eager feelings. This delicate woman, who had captured his heart more than any other he had known, could hardly have been sitting any closer. 'How did the performance go this evening?' he asked.

'Very well. Even the most terrifying of hardened warriors will turn back into small children if you sit them down and tell them a story.' Rodana grinned, showing her dimples. 'You know, even the elves were clapping. Imagine that! They did it in a very refined manner, of course!'

Goïmron laughed. 'Well done, you! Which play did you do?' He pushed aside the thought of how it might feel to kiss those dark lips. As she had never indicated that she shared his feelings, he was left with the delightful, if painful, fantasy.

'I showed them the *Death of Ûra*. My version is a little different: I have her being killed by the citizens of Cliffton. I'm not letting the älfar have all the glory.' Rodana gave a sigh. 'But what a relief to know the beast is dead! I am no longer forced to spy and betray others to her. It was the right decision to come along to help entertain the troops. They need the distraction.'

'Apart from earning yourselves a few coins, you and Chòl-dunja are doing the community a service.'

'Since you mention her: I know she's looking for you.'

'Thanks.' Goïmron understood the message. They were to conduct an experiment that evening. Before the battle began. To give extra safety. 'I'll go to her in a moment.'

Rodana took another mouthful of wine while she surveyed the camp. 'It's like a military review of troops from all over Girdlegard. Archers from Tî Silândur, Malleniagard's heavy vehicles, phalanx-fighters from Gautaya and cavalry from Khalteran. And not to forget the dwarf troops. Even if I must say the Thirdlings look more dangerous than all the rest put together,' she said, twinkling. 'But your lot are the shiniest.'

'They'll put us at the front to dazzle the Brigantians,' Goïmron said with a soft laugh, enjoying having her near. But she was a human and would prefer her own kind. *What would she do with a quarterling dwarf jeweller?*

'Have you heard about the winged night-mare the scouts reported?' asked Rodana, passing him the bottle.

Goïmron declined the offer of wine. 'Terrifying, if the story is true.'

'If it's true?'

'Well, how can they have created a winged night-mare? Unicorns certainly can't fly.'

'There are some with wings, I understand. Beyond the Brown Mountains. Maybe they've caught some and adapted them.' Rodana's good humour disappeared. She brushed a tendril of hair back behind her ear, emphasising her high cheekbones. 'What if they have hundreds of them?'

'If they did, they'd have invaded long ago.' Goïmron pretended to be more confident than he actually was. 'They'll shoot the strange bird-horse out of the sky with their metal bolts if it gets close.'

'Will . . . will you be in the fighting the orbit after next?'

He liked to think he could hear a touch of fear in her voice. *Concern? For me?* 'I intend to go to war, yes. So far I don't know which unit to join, but . . .' Confusion made him hesitate to finish the sentence. All of a sudden the hope he had suppressed flamed up. His fantasy of the two of them being a loving couple might come true. 'You'll be in the infirmary, Chòldunja said?'

Rodana nodded. 'I can defend myself, but I would never be able to fight my way out of a battle alive. I'll stitch up the wounded instead.' She placed a hand on Goïmron's back. 'I pray to Samusin and Palandiell you won't be among them. The gods keep me from ever having to place a shroud over your face.'

'Nothing will happen to me. I think I'll be with the artillery.' Her dark fingertips gave him a warmth that went deep and filled him with energy. *Such a good feeling.*

'The enemy catapults have the same range as our own. On a battlefield, no one is safe, Goïmron.' She raised the wine to her lips. 'Oh, I'm sorry. Perhaps I shouldn't have said that?'

'It is the truth. And I am fully aware of it.' All the same, he would have preferred not to have been reminded of it. *Or of a shroud.* 'We have Famulus Mostro and a whole wagonload of artefacts with us. Victory is certain, whether the älfar have one, ten or a hundred flying night-mares.'

'It's said there was someone astride the beast.'

'Is that substantiated?'

'It's as certain as anything the reconnaissance party can say. Dsôn and Brigantia must have formed an alliance.' Rodana swirled the rest of the wine around in the bottle. 'And another thing: magic from artefacts and precious stones. What do you think about that?'

'Me? I'm just a dwarf,' Goïmron lied, knowing his voice was pitched too high and might betray him without her having to ask any more questions.

'You are a Fourthling. Your people are the best jewellers in Girdlegard. Are there no records in your archives?'

'Yes . . . I'm sure there used to be. But Brigantia will have them now, or the occupying forces will perhaps have destroyed them.' Goïmron felt he was on thin ice here. 'I have heard that the troops have received fifty magical artefacts from the famulus. The soldiers have been trained in their use.'

'That is so. But I'm not sure whether the things Vanéra gave us from the Chamber of Wonders will really be able to help us win the battle.'

'What do you mean?'

'That cage with the stuffed orange bird. Apparently it comes to life as soon as you open the cage door and attacks whoever tries to touch it.' With the bottle in her hand, she described the arc of someone throwing an object. 'Shall we lob the cage over to the enemy? How dangerous can a small bird be for a warrior?' She laughed. 'It's funny, rather than dangerous.'

'Let's wait and see what the bird is capable of.' Goïmron was relieved that he had turned the talk away from gemstones. He recalled the episode in the Chamber of Wonders. If the bird could suddenly increase in size the way the drinx had, then its effect would be devastating. *It could peck away at the enemy's heads.* 'Let's hope he gets his objects back again afterwards.'

'Who? The famulus?'

He nodded. 'We don't want the soldiers keeping the bird for a souvenir.'

'Vanéra would turn them all into pigs if there was a single artefact missing . . . that's if she's actually got a pig-transformation artefact up her sleeve.'

Goïmron got to his feet, despite being reluctant to leave Rodana. 'I'd better go and find Chòldunja. Are you staying here?'

'Yes. The view is amazing. And I like listening to the soldiers' songs.' Rodana closed her green eyes and swayed gently in time to the music. She pulled an orange-coloured feather out of her pocket and blew it up into the air. The breeze took it away.

She is simply wonderful. It took quite an effort for Goïmron not to kiss her. The lightest of innocent kisses on the cheek. To show her, before he went into battle, that he cared for her. To show her how much he cared. The urge was strong, and his heart was beating wildly. *But it's not appropriate.*

'Goïmron. Are you still there?'

'I . . .' He cleared his throat. 'Yes, I'm still here.'

'Promise to come back safe out of the fighting? It would be such a shame . . .'

'I'll take care!' He was about to launch into a declaration.

'Gata would never get over it.'

This mention of the Thirdling queen had the effect of a bucket of ice water over his head. Gata was bearing the tragic death of her father with a dignified equanimity, but had decided to postpone the normal period of mourning, sending his body back to the Black Mountains. He would be laid to rest in the family crypt without any pomp and circumstance. This was not the time, she had said firmly.

'Oh, I thought . . .'

'She has just lost her father and has to bear the heavy weight of the crown and leading her people into war. She bears the responsibility for the decision her father would never have made,' Rodana explained, her eyes still closed. 'That is an enormous challenge for such a young dwarf. I admire her. Don't you?'

'Of course.'

'I think Gata would like to think you admire her.' Slowly she opened her eyes and looked at the dwarf with a mischievous grin. 'She has taken you into her heart.'

Goïmron was at a loss for words. He went over to the hatchway. 'We shall have victory, Rodana. I'll see you in the morning.'

'Until tomorrow, Goïmron Chiselcut.'

Quite out of temper now, he made his way down and stomped through the camp to the puppeteer's caravan, where he had arranged to meet Chòldunja.

Frustrated at not having declared his feelings to Rodana, he was not looking forward to a lesson in gemstone magic.

He and the young apprentice had intended to try out various combinations of jewels in order to increase their magic power and to trigger several effects at once.

But the only effect he was interested in causing was the power of love.

I am so wretched. Goïmron tapped on the caravan door, noticing the pile of gifts and bouquets of flowers lying there. *So many admirers. Each one better looking and sturdier of build than the next. And then she tries to matchmake for Gata!*

Chòldunja opened the door. 'What sort of a face is that? Didn't your supper agree with you?' She adjusted the long blue woollen shawl she wore over her beige dress.

'I don't want to talk about it.' Goïmron walked in past her and dropped on to a chair. Listlessly he put his hand into his pocket and took out a polished ruby, a noble garnet and a diamond. He had not told the famulus he had these in his keeping. They were high-quality stones. Nobody at all, by contrast, knew about the sea sapphire in the dragon setting, not even Chòldunja. 'Behold, the experiment begins.' With bad grace, he placed the jewels one on top of each other and held them up to the lamp. 'Change the small flame in the lamp to a huge flare of ice . . . and make it taste like spun sugar.' He blinked once. 'There. You see? Nothing! End of experiment. Good night.' He got quickly to his feet.

But Chòldunja pushed him back down. 'What was that?'

'The experiment. It didn't work.'

'You can't call that an experiment. That was pathetic.' She looked at him quizzically. 'What is the matter with you?'

'I don't wish to discuss it. As I said.'

'Ah. Lovey-dovey stuff. A dwarf affair.'

'No.'

'A human, then?'

'No, dammit!'

'Oh, so it's Rodana, is it?' Chòldunja smiled sympathetically, knotting her brown and black hair in a bun at her nape. 'Did you think I hadn't noticed you beaming at her and always trying to be near her?'

Goïmron sighed heavily. 'That makes me feel even worse.' Hesitatingly, he looked up at the young aprendisa. 'Has she . . . has she said anything about me? I mean . . . anything positive?'

'She speaks of you only in the most respectful terms,' said Chòldunja, neatly evading his meaning.

'As I thought.' He rubbed his face disconsolately. *I feel like throwing myself on to the sharp beak of the flame flyer.* 'I'm off to bed. You'll have to excuse me. But we have the whole of the next orbit to repeat that trial.' He pushed himself up to standing. 'Sleep well.'

'You, too. Do you want me to give you something to help you sleep?'

'I've got beer. Strong noble black beer. It works well.'

'I meant a special herbal sleep concoction.'

'No, thank you.' He walked slowly over to the door.

Chòldunja patted his shoulder as he passed. 'I'm so sorry.' She picked up a topaz that had fallen out of his pocket and handed it to him. 'Keep all the jewels properly safe. If anyone sees, they'll want to know what you are up to.'

'I'd find some excuse.'

'But the famulus could get suspicious.' Chòldunja's tone was earnest. 'Don't show anyone your talent. *Not* yet. And not in the battle, either, no matter how great our losses may be,' she insisted, opening the door. 'The orbit will dawn when your power will be of greater value than now.'

Goïmron nodded and shuffled out and down the steps. He took care not to step on the bunches of flowers. *I want Rodana to enjoy them.*

Chòldunja had turned round, about to help herself to a slice of her special smoked ham, when there came another knock at the door.

'Did you forget something?' She opened the door. 'Or . . .' She stopped short for the length of a heartbeat when she saw who the unexpected visitor was. 'I'm sorry. My mistress is not here,' she said, starting to close the door. 'She'll be back tomorrow.'

'It's fine.' Mostro had put his foot in the door to prevent her from closing it. 'I had been hoping to find you here on your own.' His wavy, dark blond hair framed his face like a helmet. 'Rodana is sitting on the roof of her rail carriage with a nice bottle of wine, singing along with the meldriths. We shan't be disturbed.'

Chòldunja was not going to relinquish her hold on the door handle. 'Unless you have some great idea for a play script, Famulus, you and I have nothing to discuss.'

'I disagree.' In his hand Mostro held a thumb-length rune stick carved from sigurdacia wood. The tip of the tiny wand glowed red. 'I thought at first the groundling had some kind of magic gift. I suspected it after catching him coming out of the Chamber of Wonders.' He shoved the door open, forcing Chòldunja to take two steps backwards. 'But I see that *you're* the one.' The famulus was wearing a dark brown hooded cloak over his mint-green robe. A dagger and several artefacts hung ready at his belt.

'What is that thing?'

'A magic-indicator. I brought it along in case the Brigantians have a magus or similar with them. I was so surprised to find it giving me a strong reading here.' Mostro rubbed one of the runes at the end of the wand. 'This symbol helps me to identify the kind of magic being employed.'

'You are wrong. Your artefact must be faulty, Famulus.' Chòldunja stole a hand behind her back to find her knife.

'I don't think so.' Mostro showed her the greyish-blue shimmer. 'Do you see? *That* is *not* a good sign. Not outside of your swamps.'

Chòldunja put a hand under her robe on her hidden talisman, noting through the leather pouch the new charge of energy from the moor diamond. 'You are mistaken. Go now.'

The magic-indicator flared up. 'You are not going to try to attack me, ragana?' His laugh was nasty. She noticed the crumbs on his pointed beard and between his teeth. 'I am the army's only hope for magic assistance.'

'Get out!'

'Show me the amulet!'

'No! I'd rather—' Chòldunja bit her tongue. *Curses!* She had avoided Vanéra herself but it would be appalling to be unmasked by the Rhuta famulus in the middle of the military camp on the eve of battle.

'Rather ... *what*? You'd rather attack me?' Mostro came closer. He put the magic-finder away, instead pulling a flattened silver disc from his belt. It had magic symbols engraved in its surface. 'Go on. Try. The shield of Awizu will counter anything you have to offer.' He stretched out his free hand. 'The amulet! If it is a moor diamond, then . . .'

Quick as a flash, Chòldunja stabbed at his hand with her dagger.

The tip of the knife went straight through his outstretched palm. The famulus yelled out and snatched back his arm.

'It seems the shield of Awizu doesn't work against a ragana blade,' she said with malice in her tone. 'Get out of here. And not a word to anyone, or the next time I use my knife . . .'

Cursing, Mostro kicked her in the stomach, throwing her against a table. She fell down between the storage units for the marionettes but she kept hold of her weapon.

The famulus took out a second artefact from his belt with his bloodied hand. Only the grip was in view; it looked like it belonged to a switch or a strap. As he swung it, there was a whirring noise and the leather cut through the skin on her upper arm.

With a cry, Chòldunja dropped the knife and put her hands up to protect her face. The strange whip slashed down, tearing her dress and the flesh beneath it. Wedged as she was between the cupboards, the young woman could only crawl backwards, but there was no escaping the unseen leather strap.

'Give me the amulet,' Mostro demanded. 'I don't want to have to kill you, even if I'd be doing Girdlegard a tremendous favour, moor witch!'

When the famulus drew back his arm to strike her once more, Chòldunja clasped the talisman and murmured a ragana spell.

At this, the caravan lamps went out and the young woman had the protective cover of darkness. 'I've got you now!' She quickly got to her feet, gripped the dagger tight and hurled herself at Mostro. 'Tomorrow's battle will take place without you!'

But the blade met thin air.

Instead, Chòldunja received a blow to her chin as an elbow hit her in the face, sending her half senseless to the floor. The crack of her fractured jawbone resounded through her skull. Blood came pouring out of her mouth.

Then the light level was restored and Mostro was looming over her. 'It's not that easy to deal with me, you know. A good magus also knows how to fight with his fists. I'm always telling Adelia that.' He grasped the neckline of her blouse, tearing the fabric. 'Give it here!'

She could only offer a modicum of resistance. The magic whip struck at the hand she held up in defence. Two fingers were slashed open, exposing the white bone before the blood came spurting out.

Mostro broke the ribbon at her neck with a jerk and shook the contents out of the small leather pouch. 'A moor diamond,' he whispered in awe. 'And a powerful one, judging from the colour chart in my textbooks. How many children have you captured and eaten, ragana?' With a laugh, he pocketed the diamond and grabbed Chòldunja's hair, hauling her to her feet. He shook her by the shoulders. 'How many lives are inside you and in your diamond?' As he threw her brutally against the wall, her bodice ripped. She fell over again. 'So young and so corrupt. Mean and evil through and through.'

The entrance door swung open.

Rodana charged into the room, knife held high. 'What is happening?' Horrified, she looked at the bleeding half-naked body of her apprentice on the floor. 'You damned swine. You are no famulus. You filthy bastard!'

'No. You've got it wrong,' Mostro tried to explain. 'I didn't take her against her will, on the contrary—'

'I can see exactly what you've done,' Rodana yelled, rushing towards him with her knife. Her delicate figure did not make her any the less dangerous. 'Get yourself right out of my caravan! When I have seen to her needs, I will tell the generals what you have done.'

'But I—'

'Yes, you may indeed be important for the battle, but that is not going to protect you from the might of the law!'

Mostro raised his hand with the amulet and the moor diamond. 'Your apprentice is a ragana. Did you know?'

'So now you are going to tell filthy, slanderous lies as well?' She stepped towards him and slapped his face twice, sending him staggering back against the wooden wall. 'I'll see you in the commanders' tent. You coward! You swine!' She spat at him and dragged him to the door, kicking him out.

'You will regret this!' Mostro called, banging on the side of the caravan in his fury. 'You will burn at the stake, together with your ragana. She is a murderess and you are her accomplice!' He hurried away, clutching his bleeding hand.

'Mistress . . . I . . .' Chòldunja groaned, her broken jaw grinding horribly and causing her intense pain. The injury swelled up and made speech almost impossible.

'What did he do to you?' Rodana knelt at her side to examine the wounds. 'Are those the marks . . . of a lash? By Samusin! What a son of an orc whore.'

A loud hubbub was heard outside. People were shouting. The struggle itself and the loud exchange of words between the famulus and the puppeteer had been clearly audible.

'A ghost knotstrap.' Chòldunja pushed away Rodana's helping hand. 'Thank you. But you must get away! Leave me here. I shall make sure you are not implicated in all the allegations.'

'What are you talking about?' Rodana was totally confused.

'It's true. I *am* a ragana. Mostro is right.' She wiped the tears away. The loss of her amulet robbed her of any remnant of strength. The lashes, the pain, and the damaged jaw were taking it out of her. 'And I have deceived you. But you must not suffer . . .'

'Never. I don't believe you. He's put a spell on you, hasn't he? He wants to avoid blame for what he has done.' Rodana grasped hold of her hands and pulled her up. 'But we should get out of here until the fuss has died down. We'll discuss it with the council tomorrow.'

'No! No, I . . .' Slowly, awareness of her surroundings ebbed away and faintness placed a black cloth over her senses. It was like the curtain coming down at the end of the performance. 'Don't . . . you should . . .'

As her senses failed, she realised she was being lifted up and carried outside. Then Chòldunja was freed from pain by passing out completely.

Forcing his way through the crowds, Goïmron stormed over to Rodana's caravan. The uproar had startled him into action before he had managed a first drop of the strong beer. *Don't let anything have happened to Rodana!*

'Let me through!' he insisted. 'What has happened?'

Mostro was on the steps by the caravan's open door, his hand bandaged. Telìnâs was at his side, deep in discourse with a second fair-haired elf.

'It's a good thing you've come, Master Chiselcut,' the famulus said in greeting as soon as he noticed the dwarf. 'You are the chief expert concerning any kind of gemstone, aren't you?'

Some armed soldiers were searching the interior of the caravan and they were not holding back, it seemed. Valuable puppets and the special silhouette shapes, along with other theatre accessories, lay scattered on the floorboards, trampled on by heavy boots.

'What is going on? Has there been an attack? Was it älfar assassins?' Goïmron cried out, leaping up the steps. 'Be careful with her things! They are precious items!'

'An attack on the puppet mistress? Hardly.' Mostro's uninjured hand dangled the chain of the wood, bone and diamond amulet. 'No. It was Chòldunja who attacked me because I found out she is a ragana.' The necklace swung to and fro. 'That is, if this is a genuine moor diamond, Master Chiselcut?'

Goïmron felt his blood run hot and cold. *Oh, no. The secret is out!* 'Where are they both?'

'They have fled. It doesn't speak for their innocence, does it?' Mostro looked keenly at the Fourthling. 'What's your opinion, Master Chiselcut? Is this an authentic moor diamond?'

Goïmron went through the motions of giving the stone an extensive examination and then pretended to consider the result. 'Yes,' he admitted finally, because he knew that Mostro would not let any other verdict pass. *How did he find out?* 'Yes, it is a real moor diamond.'

'And they come from *where*?' Like a judge in court, the famulus kept digging.

'In the ragana swamplands.'

'Exclusively there?'

'Exclusively.'

'There we have it! As I said! Master Chiselcut has confirmed what the runes on my magic-indicator revealed.' Mostro turned to the crowd to show the thumb-sized piece of sigurdacia wood, its symbols glowing bright. 'These sorts of talisman are intimately connected with the wearer. It only works with that person. And it is charged with the energy of the unfortunate children that a ragana likes to entice, capture and consume!'

A wave of outrage went through the assembled throng.

'To travel the country with a puppet theatre! Perfidious! That way her little victims will come running to her.' Telìnâs was incensed at the thought. 'The evil witch could just take her pick!'

'But the two of them were in it together, of course,' said the older elf. His badge showed he belonged to the fîndaii regiment. 'Who knows what the cannibal witch gave her in exchange for her help?'

Goïmron was far too shocked to be able to think clearly. 'I don't . . . I can't think Rodana knew anything about it,' he stammered. 'She would . . . she would never have covered up anything like that. She loved, above all things, the sound of children's laughter. It was so much more important to her than the takings from the adult audiences.'

Telìnâs looked deadly serious and seemed suddenly to be older than his years. 'You are good to speak so highly of her. But the fact that she has run away with the moor witch makes her guilty. Why would she not stay and face up to the allegations?'

Mostro held up his bandaged hand in accusation. '*This* is her work. This is what the ragana did. The puppeteer attacked me as well.'

'No, I don't think so . . .' Goïmron was desperately trying to defend the reputation of the woman for love of whom his heart was beating so wildly.

'Famulus Mostro! We have found something!' One of the guards came out with a chopping board on which there was a small joint of ham. 'This meat is not from any animal. Not a calf. Not a pig.' In the other hand, he presented two pieces of jewellery. 'We found these under the witch's mattress. Beard clips, made of onyx. These aren't the sort of thing a witch would have. Maybe pilfered goods.'

Goïmron felt a blow in the pit of his stomach. He wanted to throw up. He knew these items very well. *They had belonged to Gandelin!*

That his friend's beard clips had been found in the caravan under Chòldunja's bed had the most terrible implications. Gandelin's death had thus perhaps not been the result of a random mugging in Malleniagard.

Just as I did, Gandelin will have seen her talisman and will have asked her about it, Goïmron guessed. *By Vraccas! And I've been listening to her and letting her teach me!* At the next intake of breath, he was heaping recriminations on himself for not having gone to Rodana straightaway with his revelations. *Chòldunja must have put a spell on me, that's it. That must have been it. I was bewitched!* His head started to spin.

'You're looking rather pale, Master Chiselcut. What is troubling you?' Mostro asked.

'It's that . . . ham,' he said, almost choking on the words, and having to clutch at the door frame for support. 'The very idea that it could have once been part of an innocent young child. I feel dreadful.'

'Bury it,' Telìnâs told the guard. 'As if it were a human and not something to be eaten.'

'And what about the loot?' the man asked, weighing the onyx clips in his hand.

'They belonged to my best friend,' said Goïmron, wanting to make sure the jewelled items did not go elsewhere. 'I recognise his handiwork. He was murdered in Malleniagard. When . . . that is, when . . .'

'. . . when the puppeteer and her student were performing in the city,' the famulus continued. 'Say, did any children disappear at that time?'

Goïmron had no idea. 'Can I have the clips? As a keepsake?'

'Certainly.' Mostro nodded to the guard to show he should hand them over to the dwarf. 'All of you go back to bed now,' he addressed the crowd. 'Sleep and rest. The battle will be soon. That's all that matters for now.' Then he issued instructions for the caravan to be boarded up and kept under guard. 'If Rodana comes back, bring her to me.'

'No one is to touch a hair on her head until the facts are established,' Goïmron insisted before he turned to leave. He ignored whatever Telìnâs was calling out to him. He could not stay there a moment longer.

I know how to find her. Sònuk can track anything with his nose. He will soon find which way she has gone.

While Goïmron was stumbling back to his accommodation in the Thirdling encampment, where he heard the dwarves singing, he was overwhelmed with doubts.

Doubts about whether or not he should follow the words Chòldunja had hammered into him – namely, that he should hide the fact that he had a magical gift with gemstones.

Perhaps that was all in her plan? Does she want to weaken the army?

Is that why I mustn't let on I'm a jewel magus? Does she intend us to lose against Brigantia? The darkest of thoughts went tumbling around in his mind. *And what if the moor witches had also made a pact with the black-eyes? Has Chòldunja been in the alliance from the very beginning? And that's why she was summoned from the swamps, in order to cause mayhem and confusion?* With every step, his despair grew. *I ought to have told Rodana!*

Downcast, he sank down on a bench next to a campfire, without noticing where he was. Someone pressed a mug into his hand. The fumes from the hot drink had a sharp, pungent smell. There was an accompanying sound of friendly words and loud laughter.

He drank the bitter liquid like an automaton. *I carry the responsibility for everything that has happened. How many children do I have on my conscience because I kept silent?* Goïmron gave himself a shake and then drained the cup. It was immediately refilled and he downed it again. *Was it a witch spell or was it my own complete failure? My stupidity?*

These depressing and worrying thoughts circled faster and faster in his mind until he saw the world spinning around him. Laughing, distorted faces floated round him and he heard his name being spoken again and again.

But Goïmron did not react.

It's all my fault. Swaying, he got to his feet and dropped the mug.

He staggered through the camp, falling several times when he tripped over tent lines or stumbled over cooking pots and piles of firewood, getting up each time and staggering off, until finally falling drunk to the floor and closing his eyes.

In his ear, he heard a calming tune, sung softly by a dwarf. But in his imagination, it was Rodana singing him to sleep. She was singing for him alone.

*What for others is the highest peak will, for a dwarf,
be merely a bend in the road.*

Dwarf proverb

XV

Girdlegard

United Great Kingdom of Gauragon
Province of Mountainhigh
1023 P.Q. (7514th solar cycle in old reckoning), early autumn

Klaey entered the tent where Orweyn was conducting the final evening strategy meeting with the zabitay generals. They were waiting for him to report on his findings from his latest ride in the clouds.

'Good news,' he rasped, as he approached the table, where there was a detailed, large-scale map spread out. Figures of various colours indicated the current positions of army units. 'We have reached Two Stream Hill before them. If we get our catapults set up there, we'll be able to wipe them out. Whether with magic or without.'

'Fantastic.' Orweyn beckoned him over. Surrounded by all the generals in full battle dress and armour, the fifty-year-old looked as if he had wandered into the wrong tent. What with his civilian attire and his thin hair topped by a black silk scarf, he had the air of a well-to-do merchant, not a commander-in-chief. 'Take a seat and tell us what you have seen.' A servant poured him a dish of tea. 'Are there any changes or any more support troops we hadn't known about?'

Klaey was surprised that nobody had voiced a reaction to his excellent news. Occupying the highest piece of ground for miles was going to be an enormous advantage in battle. *Has something else happened?* 'No, no further troop arrivals. But several contingents have moved off. All the ones from the coastal regions.'

'Very good! Just what we were hoping!' Orweyn slapped the table. 'Undarimar is keeping to the promise to attack the sea-bordering lands with their ships. They are being forced to withdraw soldiers to protect their own hinterland.'

'There was also an incident last night,' Klaey continued. He stood out from the others in the room by virtue of his tailored garment of dark brown embroidered fabric. *If you have the ability to fly high above the world, why should you need armour or fear any earthly foe?* 'The magus – but really, he's simply a famulus in training – was apparently attacked by the puppeteer's young assistant. I saw both the women escaping from the camp.'

'Has the famulus survived?'

'Yes.'

'Then nothing has changed for us.'

'Except that the girl assistant stands accused of being a ragana.' Klaey took a sip of the cold tea which had some corkut leaves floating in it; even just the fresh, sharp fragrance was stimulating. 'If the moor witch is after revenge, we could maybe get her to fight for us. How about that?'

Orweyn considered the suggestion and surveyed the troop dispersal display on the map. 'No. The ragana can never be trusted. They may have legendary powers, but they are as unpredictable as a pack of hungry wolves.' He raised his gaze to meet his youngest brother's eyes. 'Next time you see her, kill her. The fact she's roaming round in the north at all is a bad sign. There's no place for any ragana in the empire I shall be building.'

'As you wish.' Out of his shoulder bag, Klaey took the notes he had made on the way. 'Here we have the plan of their camp.' He passed it to his brother.

Orweyn studied it and adjusted the campaign map accordingly. 'A classic formation. That's how the Girdlegard army has always fought, for over a thousand cycles,' Orweyn said, laughing. 'That works in our favour.'

Klaey sipped his tea. He glanced over the large-scale map where Brigantia's army was now represented by small figurines. Because the Omuthan had ordered a swift sortie to take advantage of the gaps in the walls between the dwarf fortifications, their front-line forces were composed, in the first instance, of brigades of light and heavy cavalry, but few foot soldiers.

Without the infantry's unwieldy catapults, they only had relatively lightweight collapsible slingshot devices that used arrows, balls or bolts. But they did have mounted divisions that could manoeuvre at speed, in small units of archers, and they could make a series of feigned attacks. In this, they were superior to a classic army formation that was more or less static. Orweyn liked to refer to this as a flock-of-starlings tactic.

Klaey had seen the Brigantia deployment without understanding its significance. None of their own troops were placed on the hillock. *It doesn't make any sense.* 'Why would you leave the rock to the enemy? From that elevation, they'll be able to shoot us all out of the saddle.'

Orweyn ignored the hint. 'Then our riders will have to move very quickly.'

The commanders made no comment, seeming similarly at ease with the strategy. It was as if they thought it was the easiest thing in the world to storm up an incline while under bombardment.

'You'll be up there on your little flying horse, tipping incendiaries on their catapults and the archery units,' Orweyn told him. 'If you fly high enough, they can't reach you with their arrows.'

'How long for?'

'Constantly. Till your beast's wings get tired. You are an undeniable advantage for us, little brother.' Orweyn gave him a smile. 'And you represent a decisive factor in our victory. Without your part in this campaign, our cavalry would be hard put to get through.' He placed a stone behind the figures denoting his own troops. 'I'll have the incendiaries deposited at this point for you to collect.'

'That's very dangerous. The steel-spring catapults are long-range weapons. Deathwing might get hurt,' said Klaey, objecting in a half-hearted way. The resulting laughter from the generals maddened him. 'Keep quiet, all of you! He is a fantastic animal. Unique. There's not another like him in the whole of Girdlegard. And we've not bred from him yet. If we lose Deathwing, what happens to your dream of an airborne cavalry corps?'

'Well, then, look after him and keep him safe.' Orweyn put another stone down on the map, placing it beside a mark denoting a fire. It looked like a funerary pyre. 'This is where the älfar will be waiting,' he explained to everyone. 'One thousand black-eyes. They won't attack till I give the signal.' He drew a straight line uphill from the älfar position. 'It's their job to kill that famulus and anyone else carrying artefacts. But I shan't be sending them out until battle has actually commenced. In the resulting confusion of combat, they can easily advance on the flank, quickly and without being noticed.'

'Has their leader said anything about Ûra and the blue dragon? About the rumours going round that there was an älf involved?' Klaey enquired, stirring a spoonful of crystal honey into his tea. 'Or any mention of the incident at Arima's north fortress?'

'Nothing. I was told the Undarimar attacks on the coastal lands are continuing, with the aim of doing as much damage as possible. We've seen that it's effective. That's good enough for me.' Orweyn surveyed the campaign plan for the coming orbit with satisfaction. 'Very good.'

Very good? Klaey did not agree at all. 'I must draw your attention again to the point here, brother.' With his spoon, he tapped the place on the map where the high ground was shown. 'We get there before—'

'Leave that all to me,' Orweyn interrupted. 'And kindly do not cast doubt on the strategy I have decided on.'

'It's not a question of doubt, Omuthan. But I know—'

'If, brother, after the deaths of every single one of our siblings, you should ever ascend to Brigantia's throne – and may Samusin and Cadengis please prevent this – then you can command the army in whatever way you see fit.' Orweyn drew himself up to his full height and his blue eyes flashed cold, colder than midnight ice. 'Until then, you will follow the orders I give you.'

Klaey saw from the faces of the silent commanders that no one was on his side. *This cannot happen! They'll be riding to their deaths!* 'Please hear me out! I know I have never studied battlefield strategy as you undoubtedly have. But you know how difficult it will be to storm up a slope—'

'We have finished the discussion, youngest brother mine.' Orweyn put his hands behind his back and still looked like a merchant in his counting house, not a commander-in-chief with his generals. 'You know what I expect from you. Without you and your little flying horse, we shall have no swift victory.'

Because you're sending your heavy cavalry brigade uphill. Klaey presumed the real reasons for this destructive tactic were being kept from him. 'One more thing.' He plucked one white and one red grape from the fruit basket on the table and rolled them accurately across the map. They wobbled along, coming to a stop on the northern edge. 'The salt sea orcs. And the banner of the orc fortresses.'

Orweyn looked surprised. 'Another army?'

'No. Two yurts. Fifteen to twenty monsters in each one, that normally stay separate and are quite peaceful.' Klaey had not been able to work out the orcs' intentions. 'It seems they've got themselves good vantage points for watching the battle tomorrow.'

'No sign that they're on a scouting trip, reporting back to a stronger force ready to bring up the rear?'

'No, brother, no sign. They have brought along truckloads of meat to grill, pigeons, and barrels of atrocious beer and some comfortable chairs,' Klaey reported. 'They've come for an entertaining spectacle.'

'They want to see lots of dead people. Dead human foes. Well. We'll ride them into the ground once we've secured our victory,' suggested one of the zabitayas. 'The only good beast is a dead beast.' This was greeted with applause and laughter. 'We'll drown them in their own barrels of piss-poor beer. And stuff their muzzles with the pigeons!'

Orweyn stroked his shaven cheeks. 'No. Those pigeons will be for sending messages. I don't want any untoward surprises.' He looked round the room. 'Fifty men – to watch the orcs. If they look like joining in the battle, you annihilate them with fire arrows.'

The female commander who had spoken furrowed her brow. 'Why would they do that? There are far too few of them.'

'To steal the artefacts.' Klaey understood why his brother was concerned. 'Or to take hostages once the battle is over, to get ransom money. I think the orcs are certainly up for something of that nature.' He examined the campaign map again. In his opinion, the plan was suicidal. He could not understand why they would relinquish the heights of Two Stream Hill.

To be on the safe side, he kissed the lapis lazuli poppy on his lucky talisman.

'There we are, Master Goldhand.' Goïmron felt uneasy standing at the spearhead of the battle forces, looking down on the Brigantian enemy's heavy cavalry. The fact that Gata, Belîngor and Famulus Mostro were at his side was immaterial. Sònuk had insisted on going ahead with the reconnaissance party to ensure they were not ambushed.

If he were honest, Goïmron would have to admit to feeling troubled about being anywhere at all on a battlefield, even in the vicinity of the most legendary of dwarf heroes. Despite his advanced age, Goldhand looked majestic – almost a reincarnation of Vraccas, one might say, what with his long, flowing beard and his highly polished suit of armour; he had two long-handled battleaxes ready to hand at the side of his saddle.

Goïmron, by contrast, felt like a clownish figure. Gata had found him some darkened armour, but it had had to be adapted by the smiths for his slight frame. It felt as if he were constrained in a steel barrel. He could hardly move.

The sun had come up over the distant mountain chain. Grey clouds sped across the sky, but so far the fair weather was holding.

What wonderful things one might have been doing on a lovely orbit such as this one. Behind him, Goïmron heard orders being issued by the troop commanders. Clanking and rattling, the units assembled according to instructions. Elves, humans, meldriths and dwarves were being shown their positions. Archers, pikemen, and mounted divisions took up their posts, creating the complex machinery of destruction. *And instead we are heading for the deaths of the unlucky and the reckless.*

It had been a stroke of luck to gain the considerable advantage of the high ground before the enemy could get there. Two

Stream Hill was named for its one-time ring of rivers that used to meander at its foot. The island-like elevation had turned into a mound of shields and lances, topped by catapults and sling-shot machines ready to send out death and devastation.

There was enough wind blowing for the heavy manoeuv-rable kites to be flown. From their tails there hung bags of a lethal flammable pitch mixture that could be ignited by means of a second line. At present they were flying within their own archers' range, but the strings coiled on the kite capstans were long enough to let these airborne devices rise up high over the heads of the Brigantians and their allied armies. One thousand mounted älfar had been reported by the scouts. These would be capable of a twenty-fold fire power.

'Ho, this is going to be a splendid orbit for us!' said Brûgar as he sat on his horse in full armour, his war flail over his shoul-der. 'My battle tobacco is going merrily.' He blew a little cloud of smoke out of the corner of his mouth. 'That's a good omen.'

'We'll take these wretched gnomes apart,' Belîngor indicated in his sign language. *'At long last, a real fight and not just a silly scuffle with a few giant trolls.'*

Goïmron attempted to calculate the size of the opposing forces. He did not like the answer. 'There are so many of them. More than us. And most of them on horseback,' he said thought-fully, not wanting to sound afraid. 'And they are archers.'

'I know the tactics,' said Goldhand, speaking slowly.

'We all do,' replied Telìnâs, who had come riding up. His elfish bronze-coloured suit of armour was more playfully decor-ated than the sort a dwarf would wear for protection. 'Brigantia is employing a technique used in the past by the Ido before they switched to using heavy cavalry and battle wagons. They call it the flock-of-starlings method. We shall ignore their feigned attacks that will be intended to lure us out so they can then catch us in a pincer movement.' He looked up at the banners waving in the breeze. 'The wind will carry our missiles further than they will be expecting. It will be a nasty wake-up call for them.' He held a tiny folded-paper bird which he blew off from the flat of his open palm. A sudden gust seized the little figure and carried it away.

All at once, a division of five soldiers broke out from the enemy lines and started to ride slowly towards them up the lower slope, displaying a white flag and a Brigantian banner.

'They want to parley,' Goïmron assumed, trying to hide his relief as well as he could.

'The cowards.' Brûgar took the pipe out of his mouth and spat. 'They have realised that they're going to lose.' He took a few more deep puffs of his pipe.

'Let us talk with them.' Goldhand looked at Goïmron. 'Every one of our people's lives we can save will be worth it.'

'I don't think that's a good idea,' said Gata. On her left arm she wore a mourning band. Goïmron had noticed her occasionally smiling when she touched the black fabric. 'We are the superior force. Let them try and attack! Brigantia will be defeated. And we can help the Fourthlings regain their old homeland.'

The ancient dwarf turned to face the rising sun, then to the dark clouds on the other side. 'Let us listen to what they have to say. Perhaps Vraccas has given the Omuthan some degree of wisdom for once.' He pointed to Gata, Telìnâs and Brûgar. 'You three come with me.' He spurred his horse forward. 'Don't forget the white flag. There must be no misunderstanding here.'

'Don't move too fast, gem cutter,' Hargorina advised him. 'It might lead to a misunderstanding. It would be a shame to lose you as the first casualty.'

'And what about me?' Famulus Mostro wanted to know. 'Why am I not coming with you?'

'Because of your supremely all-important status,' responded Brûgar drily, sticking the pipe firmly between his teeth. 'And because you're even weaker than Goïmron.' The dwarves rode off, grinning. 'You've got to be well protected. Belîngor will look after you. And he won't annoy you with lots of talk the way I do.'

Very soon the two delegations met halfway.

'I am Orweyn Berengart, Omuthan of Brigantia.' He had taken off the lamellar helmet with its mask and iron rings at the lower edge, placing it on his saddlebow. He wore reinforced steel armour. On his forehead, the monarch showed the family brand enclosed in a tattooed surround with the addition of applied gemstones. Only the neckerchief seemed not quite in tune with his martial attire. A breath of perfumed water hung in the air. He did not incline his head with its sparse hair in greeting at all. 'Tungdil Goldhand. I regret very much that this is to be the way we both meet.'

Goïmron was impressed by the armoured Omuthan's demeanour. In his retinue, he had three bodyguards and also a younger man on a winged night-mare. With each step that the fiery-eyed stallion took, lightning flashes played round its fetlocks. And in each hoofprint there were scorch marks. *Wings! It's got wings! The creature really does exist!*

'You could have waited in the Brown Mountains to surrender the territory to me and the Fourthlings,' replied Goldhand. 'But you have decided to wage a war.'

'Not a war. Only the completion of the conquest which began some time ago. The whole of Gauragon should belong to me. It was always intended to be mine. The Brown Mountains and the surrounding area were only a compromise.' Orweyn indicated the two yurts where the colours of the salt sea orcs and of Kràg Tahuum fluttered in the strong breeze. 'My allies are over there. They can call up fresh contingents at any time. Should they even need them in a battle against yourselves, that is.'

'Is that so? You work with beasts.' Goldhand smiled faintly. 'We know that these pig-snouts will not actually do anything.

They are only looking forward to your deaths and our own. They have their beer and grills ready.'

'Don't be too sure, Goldhand. I planned it to look that way. To give you a false sense of security.' Orweyn laughed. 'No, you are too clever to fall for that inferior type of trick. Anyone who has reached your own great age will be well placed to recognise trickery or falsehoods.'

'Which brings me to your wish for negotiation.' Suddenly Goldhand sounded neither decrepit nor exhausted. He sat upright in the saddle, as full of energy as any young dwarf. 'What are the conditions for capitulation?'

'Lay down your arms—'

'Another of your little jokes? Omuthan, we are discussing the terms of *your* surrender. Or why else are you wanting to negotiate?'

'Yield now, Goldhand. Withdraw your troops and do not oppose my army when we take Gauragon.' Orweyn pointed to the thousand älfar waiting on the sidelines of his army. 'You know that Dsôn Khamateion is an ally of ours.' He raised his hand and the banner carrier waved the white flag.

At this, fires were lit on the right and on the left of the Brigantian army. Kindling and extensive piles of firewood in heaps ten paces wide were going up in flames.

'Undarimar has also entered into a pact with Dsôn,' said the Omuthan. 'If the battle begins, the coastal regions will be paying more dearly than they expect. As of this moment, they still have the option of turning round and going back to protect their homeland.'

'And I think the salt sea orcs and Kràg Tahuum will attack you as soon as you advance towards them. Their princes also lay claim to Gauragon.' Goldhand looked at the mighty fires burning down below on the plain. 'Are you making preparations for disposing of your many war dead?'

'The fires are for our victory feast. For grilling, we'll need to get the charcoal glowing red-hot. That's why we've started the fires now.' Orweyn indicated the winged night-mare that had just taken off. 'See sense, why don't you? What do you have to compete with that? Or my cavalry?'

'The hill . . .' Goldhand froze. His lips quivered and his speech issued as a confused babbling.

By Vraccas! Not now. 'He says that we have a living mountain,' Goïmron quickly interjected, leaning over towards Goldhand's ear to give the impression he was listening intently to the ancient dwarf's words. 'Brought to life by the Girdlegarders who want to be free of your oppressive regime. Just as do the Brown Mountains.'

Orweyn looked at him sceptically. 'And what are you? A dwarf-prompter?' His companions laughed quietly.

'One who has his confidence. One who understands him best of any and who expresses his will when his voice becomes weaker.' Goïmron had had practice at appearing assured, but he realised now that it was more difficult in the presence of the enemy than when among friends.

'Ah. The old mind failing a bit sometimes, is it?' Orweyn gave a sympathetic glance to Goldhand, who was now motionless. 'All the more appropriate, then, to surrender right away. I've no wish to kill a hero who is not capable of defending himself.'

Goïmron bent his head once more and pretended to listen. 'He will teach you, he says, what it means to challenge a Child of the Smith. He expects you to capitulate and all the inhabitants of the Brown Mountains to withdraw to the Outer Lands. The decision is up to you.'

Orweyn gave no reply. Instead, he looked over their heads up to the top of the hill, over which the sun was sending its blazing rays down to the Brigantian army, as if keen to melt them in their armour. 'Are you aware of the peculiarities of this region?' Goïmron noticed the wind drop suddenly. 'As soon as the daystar comes over the peak of the hill and warms the land, the prevailing wind ceases.' The pennant hung down and the white flag moved in a sudden flurry of air blowing uphill from the plain. 'And then it changes direction.' Orweyn turned his horse. 'You should have consulted the locals as to why they still call it Two Stream Hill even though the rivers are long gone. I did ask them, you see, and was planning to use this amusing little interview for the miracle to happen. You will see that the advantage you were so proud of will be your undoing.' The Omuthan and his escort raced away, laughing.

'What does that mean?' Goïmron looked round at the helpless expressions on the faces of the elf and the Thirdlings.

Suddenly, there was a whirring diagonally over their heads. The dirigible kites, that until a moment ago had been riding proudly on the wind, crashed to the ground and their flammable payloads exploded among their own ranks. Fire took hold in the lines standing ready and the whole battle configuration was now in disarray. Other flying devices tugged at their anchor lines and pulled free.

'So that is why Brigantia let us get to the hill.' Gata cursed loudly. 'Now the wind is against *us*.'

'And not only that!' Goïmron pointed to the lower ground.

Round the burning fires there were huge bales of strawlike material being unloaded from carts and fed to the flames. The harmless grey smoke from before was now turning a toxic green colour; clouds of it were drifting towards them on the wind.

The thick oily swathes rolling slowly up the incline surrounded and enveloped the Girdlegard troops who had marched up the hill.

Immediately they started to cough and choke. People, animals, elves, dwarves and meldriths were soon vomiting, down on their knees, trying to escape from the fumes without landing in the fire from the incendiaries that had been accidentally ignited. Where the toxic vapour touched the flames, it turned greenish yellow and burned more fiercely still.

'Plague weed,' Telìnâs exclaimed in horror. 'They're burning plague blooms and other poisonous herbs! The Brigantians must have stolen it all from a Gauragon land-guard depot on their way over.'

The constant wind produced great swathes of smoke, rising way up the hillside like fat green snakes, wrapping themselves around the fighting men, not only robbing them of any view of the enemy, but also affecting them physically. There was no time to use the artefacts or to get the famulus to produce an incantation. The Girdlegard troops were forced to abandon their formations and race down the hill willy-nilly to escape the deadly fumes and the unquenchable flames from the crashed fire kites.

Goïmron realised that the battle was lost before it had ever begun. The plague blooms were those used to make the serum for suihhi, the fatal disease that was used against invaders. *We are lost.* Grabbing the ancient hero by the shoulders, he shook him in desperation. 'Master Goldhand! We need a miracle now!' Over his shoulder, he saw ranks of Brigantian cavalry riders at full gallop, bows and arrows held ready in their hands. This was the opening move of the flock-of-starlings tactic. 'What shall we do?'

But the elderly dwarf seemed to be in a trance. Only his lips were moving feebly.

Vraccas! I beseech you! Bring him back to his senses! Goïmron put his ear by Goldhand's mouth to catch the mumbled words.

'What's he saying?' Gata came over.

'He ...' Goïmron blinked in surprise. *This cannot be. I must have misheard.*

'By all the gods! What did he say?'

'He said: play the melody of "The Lonely Dwarf". As loud as ever you can.'

Rodana watched Chòldunja as she slept. The two of them had found shelter in a remote, rocky part of the forest. They had found a moth-eaten blanket in an abandoned barn, and, using that and a small makeshift fire, they were coping with the cold of the night. Chòldunja's badly torn garments could not keep her warm. *Best rest.* The young assistant's swollen jaw proved to have been dislocated rather than fractured. And she had lost two teeth.

Rodana was not prepared to gloss over what had happened. She had fled the camp for her own safety, and not as any kind of admission of guilt. The fact that they had taken flight must not be seen as counting against either of them.

I've got to speak to Goïmron. He will ensure people listen to me. Rodana got up and went off, leaving the little clump of trees and making for the army encampment.

Chòldunja had confessed to being a ragana. But the long journey in Girdlegard and the puppet theatre tour had changed her way of seeing the world, she had insisted. She had come to feel affection for young children and could not abide the thought of their deaths.

The moor diamond was bound to Chòldunja herself, as the famulus had stated. This extremely rare stone belonged to her family, and the energy it held resulted from the deeds of her sister, who had previously owned the gem before becoming ill and dying. Chòldunja swore she had never added a magic charge derived from the life of a single child. The ham that was alleged to have been the flesh of a young child was in fact a piece of smoked watersnake: a traditional recipe from Chòldunja's birthplace. The delicacy was at one and the same time provisions and a reminder of home.

Rodana believed her. She knew the young girl well. *I have seen her with the boys and girls in the audience. Laughing and playing with them. She could never have hurt a child. But it will not be easy to convince people of her change of heart.* Rodana reached the road that led to the camp. She was not willing to be chased away on the strength of a misunderstanding and on the say-so of a wretched famulus intent on intrigue and mischief. *As a child murderess. As a ragana's accomplice.* Mostro would have trumpeted his accusations against Chòldunja far and wide by now. *And against myself, too.*

From a distance, Rodana could already see that, of the vast encampment of the evening before, nothing at all remained.

Except for her own caravan.

Parts of it had been burnt away. There was a big hole in the roof and the soot-covered windows and door had been boarded over. There was nothing left of her puppets, scenery and theatre equipment.

No! Rodana felt tears brimming. *All that work. My heart and soul. All gone.* She looked closer. There was a letter pinned to the door:

TO THE CHILD-EATER AND HER FRIEND

was written on the envelope. The red wax seal had been broken. It must have caught the eye of some curious soldier.

Wiping away her tears, Rodana read the message.

To Doría Rodana de Psalí and Chòldunja:
You have committed gruesome and terrible acts and are both guilty of many lies.
    Your flight is seen as proof of and admission of your guilt. Your lives shall no longer receive any protection and you have both forfeited the civic rights of Girdlegard.
    You are, from now on, considered to be outlaws.

Doria Rodana de Psali:

You will not be sought or hunted down, but if you are seen and recognised and captured and killed by someone because of your deeds, that person will not be punished.

Chòldunja:

There will be a reward for your capture. Go back to your swamps before we find you and burn you at the stake as you deserve.

Since there was no signature, Rodana could not see whether this communication had any official backing. Was it purely a threat and intended to intimidate? The seal was that of Rhuta, she saw.

Maybe these lines were penned by the famulus. She screwed the paper up in her hand and threw it in the dirt at her feet. She was not going to let the matter rest and she was not going to give up her life's work like that. Her name was celebrated. Even in the largest towns, she filled the theatres, and people were always keen to welcome her back with her puppet show performances and the stories she told.

Rodana would follow the army and, as soon as the battle was over, she would make sure, whoever was victorious, that the leaders got to learn of Mostro's shameful behaviour. Until after the battle, no one would find the time to listen to Chòldunja's story, and thus understand that she had never killed any children herself even though she did belong to the ragana.

Moor witches. When she was a child, Rodana had thrilled to the horror stories from the swamplands. This treacherous, boggy region, which also included sandbanks, wooded areas and meadowland, bordered the sea to the south. You could not establish a harbour or a town there if the moor witches would not let you. The ragana ate small children – any, that is, that were not of their own kind. They worshipped a demon who gave them black magic. This was what people had been saying for many hundreds of cycles.

Punitive expeditions against the ragana were doomed to fail, and in most cases, the troops were never heard of again. On one occasion, two soldiers had made it back, but they had lost their minds, been blinded with red-hot knives, and had obscure symbols cut into their skin in a demonstration of ragana power.

Rodana sat down on the steps of her ruined caravan. *It will take me a whole cycle to replace everything.* She could not bear to take a look inside. *But I shall come back. Nobody is going to drag my name in the mud. And certainly not that cursed famulus!*

'You really didn't know, did you?' It was a familiar female voice, but not one that was welcome. 'Perhaps I ought to have warned you.' Rodana turned and saw Stémna emerge from behind the vehicle and stand leaning against its side. The forty-year-old had exchanged her usual striking costume for more conventional attire. The circular-brimmed white hat with its two orange feathers was the only thing to link her with her previous manifestation. 'Then you would have been spared this sad episode.'

'Get yourself to the underworld where you belong, Stémna. I did not summon you. I've thrown your feather away,' Rodana said in reply. 'They hate you as much as they hate me. I have nothing to say to you. And I owe you nothing at all. Go find yourself another spy if you still need one.'

'These are turbulent times.' Stémna scratched at the sooty deposit on the wood. 'They will kill us on sight. That's what unites us, isn't it? Three persecuted women. Two of them innocent. But that little moor witch is capable of anything, I'd say.'

'Did you think I'd sympathise with you?' Rodana laughed. 'I would hand you in if I wasn't sure they'd hang me, too.' She looked at the empty campsite. 'Why are you here? Did you intend to join the army in order to make up for all your evil deeds?'

'I want revenge. For the death of my mistress.' Stémna crossed her arms.

'You say that as though the dragon had been the friendliest and most peaceful of Girdlegard's creatures.'

'She was betrayed. By an älf who has been in Undarimar, too. And now his banner is flying over the orc fortresses.' The older woman spoke clearly and thoughtfully. 'I hope to meet him on the field of battle. So that I can kill him.'

'I don't know which of you I should wish luck to.' Rodana was tired and did not want a stressful conversation. 'So it was an älf riding on Ardin who put an end to Ûra?'

'Yes. One in particular.' Stémna kept her pale orange eyes fixed on Rodana. 'This one possesses an antique rune spear which was made by the Unslayables. And he has black tionium plating incorporated into his flesh. The rest of him is protected by dark red leather armour.' She stood upright now. 'He left me to die, but I survived. And I went to the city of knowledge to find out about the spear and the tionium plates.'

'Why are you telling me all this?'

'Because you and I and the young witch are going to travel together.'

Rodana laughed incredulously and spat at Stémna's feet. 'I'd sooner—'

The woman who had been the Voice of Ûra raised her hand. 'Be careful what you wish for.' She removed her white hat. 'How about this: I promise to protect you and your apprentice during the entire journey.'

'Why would you do that?'

Stémna fiddled with the brim of her hat. 'I'll stay in the background and will protect you and her from out of the shadows, and you will both let me know what is going to happen. You will be my eyes and ears. If the älf does not turn up for the battle, we go in search of him. The three of us.'

'I'm having nothing to do with it. It's your revenge, not mine.'

'That's as may be. But without my protection, both of you will die.'

'You are a voice without a body, without that white fire-breathing air-demon you served. Why should anyone fear you now?'

Stémna stroked the orange plumes adorning her hat. 'I hope it will not be necessary to demonstrate.' She replaced her head covering. 'You will help me to track down and reveal a secret to the benefit of the whole of Girdlegard. The three slandered women will become three heroines – doesn't that sound enticing?'

'What secret would that be?'

'The secret that surrounds the älfar.' Stémna put her hands in her coat pockets. 'I talked to the älf who murdered my mistress. He said he was someone who never forgives. Someone who would bring back the memory of an appalling wrong and that it would never ever be forgotten in Girdlegard.' She took a deep breath. 'His appearance, the armour, and the way he hurled out the words when he spoke – I'd never heard any other älf talk like that. He is extraordinary. Unique. So I investigated.'

'An älf is always an älf.'

'No. He wears the armour of a legend. Another legend. First we had Goldhand and now we have him.' Stémna placed her right hand on the hilt of her slender sword. 'I found out that the name of the actual bearer of the tionium armour and the rune spear is Aiphatòn. He was the son of the Unslayables. He was defeated a thousand cycles ago.'

'So this älf is not Aiphatòn.'

'No. Certainly not. But why did this älf kill Ûra? Why is he waging his campaigns on his own? Why aren't there any other älfar with him?' Placing one foot on the caravan steps, Stémna went on, 'Why did Dsôn Khamateion never mention one of their people had made a pact with the dark blue dragon? Wouldn't they have wanted to vaunt this achievement and then lay claim to the land of Girdlegard?'

The answer occurred to Rodana quickly. 'Because he isn't really one of them.'

'That's what I think. But then, what *is* he?' Stémna smiled. 'Aren't you fascinated to find out? To solve the riddle, knowing that I will be ensuring your safety?'

Rodana knocked the scorched side of the wrecked puppet theatre van. 'The only thing I want to do is to clear our names from the slander proclaimed by that shameful youth. And then to get myself a new team of horses and get down to replacing all the puppets and equipment that have been destroyed. To tell my stories again. Give pleasure to children. And live in peace. That's what I want.'

'You have had adventures enough with your puppet theatre to provide many stories.' Stémna gestured to her to stand up. 'And as we go on our travels together, you will have much more material.'

Rodana waved the offer away. 'I am not going with you.'

'Just over to the battlefield. After that, you may find you will change your mind. As I said, I will keep you safe.'

'I don't want your protection.'

'But what if there are robbers? Or if someone tries to arrest you?'

Rodana cleared her throat and looked the older woman up and down. 'What can you do to protect me, on your own?'

Stémna placed a hand on her solar plexus. 'The mistress and I were united. She gave me some of her boiling blood to bind us. Not all of her previous Voices were able to survive the procedure.'

'And that gives you dragon powers?'

Stémna prised out one of the feather fronds and blew it into the air. 'Watch this.'

Rodana followed the flight of the tiny fibre with her gaze.

It floated up and down on the breeze as if it were relishing its freedom – until Stémna snapped her fingers and it exploded in a ball of bright red fire. A wall of hot air surged past the puppeteer, choking her and making her fall to the scorching ground.

'People always thought it was Ûra destroying the towns, and they were taken by surprise, because they never saw her coming. Like a white shadow in the night. Moving too fast for human eyes. That only served to feed the myths about her,' Stémna went on, unmoved. 'You now know what means I possess. The power that resides in these feathers. The power that I can bring to life. Have you any idea what else I might be capable of?'

'I take your meaning.' Rodana pushed herself up to standing. In front of her was the destroyer of settlements, villages and whole townships. The bringer of thousandfold death. Just by snapping her fingers. On the older woman's face, Rodana detected neither remorse nor pity. The only thing that counted for this murderess was the thought of avenging the death of a beast she had so loyally served. *I shall ensure justice is done in the name of your victims. And you will not see it coming.* 'You do not leave Chòldunja or myself any choice,' she said.

'We understand each other, I see, Doria Rodana de Psalí.' Stémna turned to go. 'Let us go and collect the little moor witch. And then we shall set off. The battle will have started by now. I absolutely do not want to miss this älf. I shall not give him a second chance to use his spear against me.'

There is one thing for which Vraccas will throw me out of the Eternal Forge, because it is unforgiveable. Because in my time in Phondrasôn, I was a dwarf hunter.

It made me feel invincible. My benighted spirit told me I was not one of them. Vraccas, have pity and show me your mercy! You know it was not from my own free will!

Excerpt from
The Adventures of Tungdil Goldhand,
as experienced in the Black Abyss
and written by himself.
First draft.

XVI

Girdlegard

United Great Kingdom of Gauragon
Province of Mountainhigh
1023 P.Q. (7514th solar cycle in old reckoning), early autumn

Klaey loaded up the blindfolded flight-mare with bucket-sized leather bags filled with flammable pitch, tethering them to the specially crafted freight saddle. The firepots would be ignited by means of a smouldering storm fuse. A swift knife slash to the rope and the deadly cargo would plummet directly on to the enemy troops.

A messenger came with a note. 'The new target instructions for you, zabatay.'

Klaey unrolled the paper. He was enjoying his new rank, the insignia of which he now wore instead of the banner officer cadet badge. Before the battle he had insisted on promotion to commander of airborne cavalry. He was not bothered by the fact that he was the only member of this new unit. *The catapults on the hill?* He pulled out his spyglass to observe the high ground, which was, for the most part, obscured by smoke from the plague-weed fires. 'Why? They can't do our people any more damage. We could still make good use of these steel-spring devices.'

The courier saluted with an indifferent air and hurried away.

Well, whatever my brother thinks, I suppose. Klaey tightened the chinstrap of his helmet, swung himself up into the saddle and urged Deathwing off at speed. The lightly built stallion struggled to manage the extra weight. More than two or three flights of this nature would not be possible without frequent rests.

'We'll be done soon,' Klaey murmured into the flight-mare's ear. 'Victory will soon be ours.'

Spreading its strong wings out wide, the flying stallion used the prevailing wind to gain height, thereafter responding to its rider's thigh pressure and spurs. The stallion trusted the man on his back and was now accustomed to flying blind. Klaey seldom had to use the reins.

At a safe altitude out of enemy arrow range, Klaey was able to survey the battle's progress, with Orweyn's trick now successfully implemented.

The Girdlegard forces had split into two large blocks to the right and the left of Two Stream Hill, with the high ground at their backs for protection. Lightning attacks from the Brigantian cavalry were causing them trouble, while the elves, humans, dwarves and meldriths were still attempting to get themselves organised. Arrows rained down constantly. The mounted troops had to withdraw after loosing five or six shots. They then regrouped and attacked elsewhere. Wherever an opportunity occurred, the armoured cavalry regiment would cut through, creating a swathe of death, before turning, as one, pulling out on the flank and retreating momentarily.

If the mounted troops of the enemy made a sortie, the Brigantian forces avoided lance thrusts and arrows by means of a series of zigzag manoeuvres and sudden changes of direction, causing confusion and never offering a static target.

The flock-of-starlings tactic works well. But Klaey could also see how the famulus and some of the others who had brought artefacts to the battleground were using their powers to tear holes in the Brigantian ranks. A magic device had released a cloud of glitter, terrifying the horses, making them rear up in panic and bolt straight into the middle of a deadly dwarf onslaught.

That famulus is our cavalry's main concern here. He was using spells to send up clouds of dry earth or, alternatively, to make the ground so muddy that the horses' hooves foundered. Their attacks were losing momentum, thus allowing the opposition enough time to fire or to regroup as a wall of shields. Surprisingly, the same was occurring on the other side of the high ground. It seemed the famulus was able to utilise his powers in two places at once. *Or might there be more than just one of them?*

The clouds of toxic smoke from the plague weeds were steadily shifting uphill and thus splitting the enemy ranks, seriously impeding their progress. *Not long now and it will all be over.* Through the fog, Klaey glimpsed the outlines of the enemy catapults. *Seems a shame to burn them.*

He was about to ignite his incendiaries, one after another, when he spotted the group of figures on the top of the hill, standing in the open space between clouds of swirling vapour but seemingly unaffected by the poisonous gases.

Are they scouts? The lenses of the spyglass showed him the group was composed of dwarves of varying stature, and one elf. And one extremely old dwarf in the middle of the group, wearing dazzlingly bright armour. *Goldhand! That is the delegation! They have held the position.*

Klaey took the spontaneous decision to disregard his brother's orders.

The death of the legendary hero would throw the dwarf forces into despair. They would be utterly destroyed, with morale at rock bottom. Swift victory for Brigantia would be assured.

By applying pressure to the flight-mare's flanks and adjusting his own weight in the saddle, he steered Deathwing directly at the small group on the hill, so far undetected by the cavalry.

Having ignited the storm fuse, Klaey took the first of the incendiaries and cut through its retaining line. *Good landings!*

The missile caught fire as it fell, releasing a plume of black smoke.

Becoming aware of the attack, the small group dispersed in agitation. The blazing container crashed to the ground, spilling liquid fire all over the grassy hill. It had struck neither elf nor dwarf.

'Curses!' Klaey checked his reserve ammunition. *Next time I'll send them all off at one go.*

Arrows and crossbow bolts came shooting his way, but he and the flight-mare were too high up to be in any danger from them.

Klaey sought out his target once more.

The dwarves and the elf were trying to hide behind some small boulders, but there was very little shelter available, given how the poisonous plague-weed fumes were drifting. The polished armour of the old dwarf made him conspicuous.

'Come on, Deathwing! Let's burn these mountain maggots. Then we'll land and see how they taste once they're roasted.'

The stallion dived steeply earthwards.

Klaey kept the spyglass to his eye in order to be able to target his victims more accurately, and then, with his free hand, he lit all the fire-bag fuses. Because of the unevenness of their swift descent, it was not Goldhand he now had in focus, but the slight figure of a different dwarf holding out a blue sapphire the size of a hen's egg in a dragon-shaped setting. The dwarf's eyes were shut and his lips were moving.

What is he up to? Klaey was struck with a sudden fear. *Is that an artefact? Is he the second magus? A groundling magus? How, by the mother of Cadengis . . . ?*

Opening his eyes, the dwarf stretched out his left hand, balled in a fist. The jewel glowed bright blue and sparks danced around its faceted surfaces.

A hefty blow struck both Deathwing and Klaey. One of the creature's wings had become dislocated. Instead of being in a graceful dive, they were now spiralling out of control, with the flight-mare screaming in agony.

He is, curses! He is a damned magus! Klaey's chest and face were smarting from the force of the blast sent their way. A second wave threw him out of the saddle.

As he fell, he managed to grab hold of the stirrup, while Deathwing, bellowing loudly, flexed his injured wing, which snapped back into the joint. The chaotic, uncontrolled descent resolved itself into an unsteady flight.

'Back, Deathwing!' Klaey commanded, trying to haul himself back up on to the stallion. The corrosive, stinking fumes from the firepots tied to the saddle choked him and robbed him of the ability to see.

But the flight-mare was lost without guidance from the reins and the accustomed pressure on its flanks. Whinnying furiously, it flew in wild, ever-descending circles, heading directly for the group of figures on the hill.

We're now in range of their weapons!

'Fly higher, Deathwing! Higher!'

Down on the slope, the dwarves and the elf fired again. And this time two metal bolts struck the flight-mare in neck and breast.

Though the shots were insufficient for a fatal injury, Deathwing reared up, mid-air, wings flapping crazily. The strings attaching the bags of burning pitch ruptured and the firepots plummeted down.

At long last and after a momentous effort, Klaey, bathed in sweat, pulled himself up on to the saddle. He looked around him. *Have I at least put paid to the groundlings?*

The shock went through him, cold as ice. Deathwing had overshot and was now heading for their own battle lines, where their cavalry troops were positioned. The incendiaries had hit the Brigantians, setting the tent shelter ablaze where his brother, his other siblings and all the generals were gathered.

Oh no! The elaborate swathes of decorative cloth were an inferno. Burning figures staggered out of the tent. Soldiers raced up by the dozen, carrying buckets of sand in a futile attempt to extinguish the rapacious flames. *Cadengis! I beseech you! Don't let Orweyn die!*

Deathwing uttered an ill-tempered shriek and flew round in a wide arc. The stallion no longer had the strength to use its wings properly and was plunging earthwards.

'No. Don't do that! You must turn around!' Klaey tugged the reins sharply.

But the flight-mare skimmed over the dangerous plague-weed smoke and came to land on the northern edge of the battlefield in the direct vicinity of the two orc yurts.

Before the sparks from its hooves had faded, Deathwing attempted to pull the steel arrows out with its teeth.

'Let me,' said Klaey, dismounting swiftly. 'Quietly now, do you hear?' He removed the metal bolts as carefully as possible. 'Then we must head off again at once!' He was forced to snatch back his hands to avoid the angry creature's snapping teeth.

'Ho! What sort of a feathered horsey have you got there? Did its dam mate with a hen?' This was a loud comment from some distance away, made to accompanying laughter.

'We'll look after it nicely,' was another mocking suggestion. 'We've been wondering what that thing was. Now we can see it up close. But you aren't a black-eyes. How come it lets you ride it?'

Klaey turned hopefully to the east, where, half an arrow shot away, the banners of Dsôn's allies were fluttering. They must have seen exactly what had happened and would know he was in need of help. *Right, here I am!* He waved in that direction. *Come and help!*

Then he remembered that the thousand älfar had orders not to move until they received the secret signal from his eldest brother.

And Orweyn had been in that burning tent.

That cursed dwarf magus!

Klaey turned to confront the orcs, who were ambling over at their leisure, but with weapons held at the ready. Three of them, judging by the whitened armour they wore, were salt sea orcs, and five bore shields with the insignia of Kràg Tahuum. *That magus has ruined everything.*

'Three cheers and a hearty hussa! We've shot down the ugly, flying little night-mare!'

Brûgar flourished his heavy crossbow. 'My combat tobacco helped me aim straight.' Smacking his lips round the mouthpiece of his pipe, he stroked his pointed blue beard.

'And it has set fire to its own ranks!' gloated Telìnâs.

'We'll get well-deserved praise for our actions,' Brûgar said, rewinding the crossbow mechanism. 'I don't think these horse-things are so bad. They can send a few more over our way. I've got plenty of tobacco to see me through.'

Sweating profusely, Goïmron quickly hid the sea sapphire. *It worked! I hit him!* His companions had not noticed the marvel. They thought they had achieved this resounding success with their crossbows. *That's fine by me.*

TWICE. THAT WAS VERY GOOD, the stone told him. YOU ARE CAPABLE OF WAY MORE THAN THAT. I SHALL HELP YOU.

'Hand me a bugle, someone,' Goïmron demanded.

Gata handed him her own horn. 'So you really want to carry out Goldhand's instructions?'

'I know, it does sound mad, this idea of playing a nursery tune in the middle of a battle.'

Goïmron recalled the last time he sang the melody, back in the Black Mountains. He applied his lips to the instrument and blew a lungful of air powerfully into the mouthpiece, letting the sounds ring out.

The strong wind tore the musical tones up and wafted them uselessly away. The tune of 'The Lonely Dwarf' hardly even reached the foot of the hill where the battle was raging.

'Nobody will have heard that. Not even Vraccas,' Brûgar commented baldly. He had his loaded crossbow in one hand and his tobacco pipe in the other. 'You have the lungs of a quarter-dwarfling.'

'And what's it supposed to achieve, anyway?' asked Gata. 'We've got to get back to help our people.'

'As loud as ever you can,' whispered Goldhand, his gaze absent at first, but beginning to sharpen. His clarity of mind was returning. 'As loud as you can, Goïmron.'

'Put your fingers in your ears, everyone!' With his right hand, he clutched the sea sapphire before putting the horn to his lips again. *The melody must sound out as loud as claps of thunder and must travel swifter than a swallow can fly.* Concentrating hard on the effect he was intent on producing, he sent the tune blaring out once more.

At the first note, the hillside shook beneath his feet. Brûgar was so surprised, he dropped his pipe. Gata, Telìnâs and even Goldhand were all startled and quickly shielded their ears from the noise.

Note by note, the sounds formed the well-known tune. The movement under their feet quietened to a gentle rocking. The noise of battle died down and even hand-to-hand fighting slowed and then ceased. Horses reared up, eyes wide in fear.

For as long as the melody was playing, there was no other sound to be heard on the hill. Everything happening elsewhere was done to the accompaniment of this song.

Tungdil Goldhand slowly raised a long-handled axe to the skies, any hint of frail old age and decrepitude having now vanished. His gaze was steadfast and unshakeable.

Goïmron had gooseflesh all over, and a strange, sublime emotion sent shivers down his spine.

Then came the final note.

For the length of a heartbeat all remained still, apart from the wafting of the breeze round the flagpoles and past the rocks up on Two Stream Hill.

Goïmron lowered the horn. *What did that achieve?*

Suddenly there was a rumbling noise rolling in from both sides of the hill. Dust rose up and dwarf armies stormed out of the flat valleys.

'What . . . by Lorimbur . . .?' Gata stared down at the plain as it filled with warrior hordes. Heraldic devices and tribal flags fluttered in the midday sun. The steel of countless shields and weapons dazzled their opponents, promising great things.

'Sitalia! I praise you!' Telìnâs sank down on one knee.

The very miracle we were so sorely needing. 'There must be hundreds of them,' Goïmron exclaimed. *Those are the traditional ancient symbols on the flags. Symbols that have not been used for a thousand cycles.*

'We are the Children of the Smith!' Goldhand called proudly to the army. 'We protect Girdlegard. Now more than ever before!'

Without hesitating, both fresh dwarf armies took the Brigantian forces from behind and attacked the relief troops on the flank. The fires were quickly extinguished and the evil vapours from the plague-weed smoke dispersed safely.

Up on the hill, the outlines of the two undamaged catapults and the other battle engines emerged from the smoke as it faded away. These weapons were ready and waiting to be activated against the Brigantians.

'How . . . how did you do that?' Goïmron stared at Goldhand. His own sapphire could never have summoned two armies like that.

'I'll tell you later, my boy. Now, off to those catapults. We have a battle to win.' The ancient dwarf raced past him. 'On your way, everyone! Standing around won't bring us victory!'

His jaw dropping open, Brûgar stared at Goldhand's departing back, until Gata picked up his pipe for him, grabbed him by the arm with a laugh and pulled him along.

Klaey had never had to confront eight orcs on his own before. He was not wearing armour, having selected a light helmet and an elegant embroidered uniform for the new airborne cavalry unit. His chances of emerging from this fight alive must be about one million to one. *If that.*

'Wait! Do wait,' he said, indicating he wanted to negotiate. 'I'm from Brigantia. We are . . . sort of . . . almost . . . allies.'

'Yes, we know. And we saw what you did. Couldn't have missed it, could we?' said the first salt sea orc. 'And we certainly are not almost-allies.' Their lamellar armour, the skin, the thick hair – apart from the eyes, everything was covered in a crumbly layer of crystals, serving simultaneously as protection and embellishment. Full of pride, the beasts showed their origins. 'What's gone wrong with your voice? You sound like a crow.'

'That thing with the firepots was going well. Until your scrawny chicken-horse got the wind up,' the second orc put in, its teeth white, sharp and threatening.

'Caught fire nicely, the Omuthan's tent, didn't it?' chimed in the third. Under the orcs' layer of salt, Klaey could not really make out what colour their skin was. It seemed to be a patchy mixture of green, brown and black. 'What a wonderful smell! Roast human is absolutely irresistible!'

'Yes, that did not . . . go quite to plan.' Klaey looked at the five beasts from Kràg Tahuum mostly hidden behind their long shields, but with throwing spears in their clumsy hands. It was obvious these orcs did not trust the others. *Maybe I can make use of that fact.*

Klaey planted a quick kiss on his lucky talisman. 'What do you say? If you protect me from the salt sea orcs, I'll reward you well.'

The three monsters in whitened armour laughed. 'They won't dare. Otherwise we'll tear down their little castle,' said the leader.

'As if *that* would work,' flung back one of the shield-bearing orcs. The orcs from the fortress were just as broadly built and their strength and wild nature were generally feared. 'We've always held our ground against any attacker, for hundreds of cycles.'

'That would be because you've never had *us* to deal with,' came the response.

Klaey managed to suppress a grin. *They're quarrelling among themselves. Excellent.* The greeting to his amulet had worked. He watched Deathwing lick its bleeding wounds. The creature's own saliva would close up the injured flesh and help the gashes to heal. *I hope it will be strong enough to take off again with me.* A few hundred paces would be enough to get them away from the monsters and closer to where the thousand älfar were waiting.

'Don't fall for his tricks,' said one of the fortress orcs. 'Let's do it *together*. Let's grab him and demand the ransom money from Brigantia. He must be valuable if they let him ride on this demon's spawn.'

The largest of the salt sea orcs nodded. 'What do we do with the flying night-mare?'

'A thousand gold coins for Kràg Tahuum if you protect me from the salt sea orcs,' said Klaey, pulling out his rapier reluctantly. 'And a further thousand if—'

'Let's grab the little human *and* the horsey first and *then* we can work out what to do,' proposed the smallest fortress orc. 'Let's leave each other in peace, shall we?'

'Agreed.' The three salt sea orcs stomped forward. 'We'll take the fellow. You lot get the flying thing.'

Curses on their sudden concord. 'Get back!' Another kiss on the lucky charm, then Klaey raised his blade, pointing the tip at the monsters as they approached. *I have never needed the assistance of providence more than now.* 'I'm warning you, I'm the best swordsman in Brigantia.'

'But obviously not the best horseman,' taunted one of the fortress orcs. 'They should have sent you off to the front instead of letting you sit on the saddle.'

The comment earned throaty laughter.

'Come on, then. Show us what you can do, Crow Voice.' The largest of the salt sea orcs towered over him with a broad sword and a dagger in its hands. The dagger was as long as Klaey's rapier. 'I'll trim your wings. Come on, attack me—'

Klaey executed a swift side swipe with his rapier, freeing the flight-mare's blindfold.

Neighing furiously, the stallion flared its nostrils and turned its rolling red eyeballs on the orcs. Its front hoof pawed the ground, striking up sparks round its fetlocks. There was a smell of burning grass. A loud, aggressive snorting sound followed and the dangerous incisors were bared.

The fortress orcs cowered behind their shields, their spears aimed at the stallion. 'Call him off or we'll do for him. We've run out of provisions and can really use some fresh meat. The grill is still hot.' This challenge issued from behind the shields.

Klaey was not going to comply. The orcs would be fiercer towards him than towards the stallion. 'Neither of us will give in.' His heart was racing.

Beads of sweat coated his brow. He could defeat one of the beasts perhaps, if he were fast enough. *But then I'd have to get out of here very quickly. On Deathwing.*

A tiny filament from an orange feather floated past on the wind, touching Klaey's cheek before wafting over to the salt sea orc.

'Ah, look, little human with a big mouth. Look how I can brush this feather away. That's just what I'm going to do with you.'

The filament danced in the air around the huge monster. The beast tried at first to blow it away. Then to wave it off. But the tiny plume whirled around, just out of reach of the creature's clumsy paws. There was raucous laughter from the other seven orcs. Until the feather hovered above the head of the middle salt sea orc – and detonated.

The blast from the lurid fireball tore the beast's skull apart and the other two white-armoured orcs, ablaze and smoking, were hurled several paces through the air. The pressure wave struck down two of the long-shield carriers and the rolling heatball singed the hair and the armour of all the others.

Klaey received the brunt of the stinking gust of wind but was untouched by the lethal flames and appalling heat. He lifted his arm to shield his face and grasped Deathwing's bridle so the stallion would not bolt off in panic. *The dwarf magus!*

Fearlessly the winged horse sprang forward, yanking itself out of Klaey's grip, and bit the nearest orc in the neck, tearing out a lump of flesh to swallow. The injured beast fell screaming on to the grass, desperately trying to stem the stream of its own dark green blood.

'We'll cut you and that cursed animal into little pieces!' The last two of the fortress orcs raised their shields and rushed towards Klaey, short spears at the ready.

So where is the magus? Klaey was delighted at the support given him by the enemy. *I'd rather be captured than end up in an orc's belly.*

To his astonishment, a woman of about forty attacked the beasts from the rear. She wore no armour and there was no insignia to be seen. With her long straight sword, she felled one of the orcs with a blow to the back of its unprotected neck, then she gave him a mighty kick at the back of the knees and then another to the spine. The monster lay groaning on the ground. The woman touched the brim of her round white hat. The crown of the hat had long orange feathers on each side.

It was her! Klaey dodged a spear thrust from the remaining orc but was struck by a blow with the long shield that sent him flying. From close up, he could see the many little spikes on the front of the shield. And the dried substance adhering to them. *Poison!* He had been supremely fortunate not to have been grazed by one of the barbs.

'I'm going to eat you up even before your heart has stopped beating,' roared the orc as it made another lunge at him. 'I'll stuff you inside the chicken-horse thingy and cook you on a low heat!'

The long shield blocked Klaey's view and he could not reach round its edges to use his rapier. The orc's short spear scraped his arm and along his ribs, leaving a long, painful slash. It would be senseless to try running away. His adversary only had to throw the spear. And there was another in reserve on the creature's back.

This close combat with the orc cost Klaey every bit of concentration, so that he lost sight of how the battle was going, and, more to the point, of where his flight-mare was. Only when he heard the stallion neighing loudly and the sound of wings beating did he turn his head. *Deathwing!*

Two other women had arrived, taking knives from the fallen orcs and hurrying over to help him. But in the saddle of his flight-mare sat the unknown female who had saved him from the beasts. She was dragging at the reins with one hand and forcing the stallion up into the air without regard to its injuries. In her free hand, she held a glowing feather threateningly against its neck.

'Oh no, you don't! Bring him back here!' Klaey yelled, incandescent with rage. Out of the corner of his eye, he saw the long tower shield coming at him but it was too late to dodge. The hard surface caught him on the head and, in spite of the light helmet he wore, the impact sent him stumbling stupefied on to the trampled grass.

'What a nuisance. The chicken-horse has gone.' The bottom edge of the shield was lifted and was aimed straight at his head. 'So it's just you I get to have for dinner.'

The dagger Rodana had retrieved from an orc corpse looked enormous in her hands. She could only use the blade as if it were a short sword. The smaller of the knives she left for Chòldunja.

Suddenly she heard the sound of the wings beating – and she saw Stémna on the strange night-mare. 'Hey! We had a pact! You promised to protect me!'

'I did protect you. But I can't take you along with me, I'm afraid,' she replied. 'We shan't be travelling together anymore so the agreement is terminated.' Stémna directed the furious stallion by means of the smouldering feather in her hand. 'There's only the one flying night-mare, as you see. Find another one and follow me if you can, and you'll be under my protection once more.'

'Damned treachery!' Rodana heard the beat of hooves behind her. 'You said there would be room for all of us!' She glanced quickly over to the battle.

The dwarf armies were cleverly forming an impenetrable wall of shields on the enemy flanks and were bombarding the Brigantian cavalry with steel balls from the dreaded spring-loaded slingshot engines. At the same time, the catapults up on the hill were sending out clouds of spears, bolts and small missiles at the enemy riders, who were forced to retreat and gallop off under this constant fire. Then the heavy Gauragon armoured divisions hit home, mowing down the lighter Brigantian cavalry troops as they fled in disarray.

The smoking remains of the Omuthan's blazing tent had a demoralising effect. The majority of the mounted troops turned to the north-east, abandoning the infantry to their fate, surrounded now by the lethal military vehicles from Malleniagard.

This afforded the Girdlegard forces the opportunity to take on some of the scattered enemy units.

And to tackle the orc yurts.

Two dozen heavy cavalry trotted up in a loose formation with half-lowered lances sporting the Gauragon colours on their pennants. The lance tips were directed defensively against the flight-mare and then were swept round to confront Rodana, Chòldunja, the Brigantian and the last of the orcs as soon as they glimpsed them.

'There! It's the child-eater!' cried one of the riders. 'We've found the ragana! An excellent chance to rid the world of this evil!'

Rodana quickly worked through their options. The young man with the conspicuous Brigantian uniform bore the badges of high office on shoulder and breast. *If we save him, we'll be saving ourselves.*

'Hold on! We'll be with you in a trice!' she called. 'Chòldunja, come on!'

Her student assistant picked up on her plan and struck at the orc's neck from behind; the beast was more than twice her size. She kept stabbing her knife into the gap between the face and the edge of the creature's armour. Blackish-green blood spurted from its neck as the orc lumbered around, groaning and wheeling its arms wildly, but the girl was too nimble for it and managed to avoid its claws. Finally it collapsed to the ground, falling on top of the shield, directly in front of the young Brigantian, who was struggling to get up on to hands and knees, unaware of the mortal danger he had been in.

Rodana was in awe of Chòldunja's bravery. *There was a touch of madness in that courage.*

'If the flight-mare were in good form, it could carry all three of us. *That* was what I said. But it has been badly injured.' Stémna brought the stallion under her control and flew it close, skimming over Rodana's head. 'I'll help you one more time. Then you'll both have to see how you cope by yourselves. I'm off to find the one who murdered my mistress.'

All of a sudden, there came a loud crashing sound.

A hot gust of air lifted the puppeteer, swirling her in the air like a leaf torn from a shrub. She landed on the grass several paces away, tumbling over and over.

'Use your advantage. I've given you a head start. It won't last long.' Stémna's voice came from somewhere overhead. 'I wish you both all the best.'

Rodana got to her feet and spat out some dirt. A huge explosion had torn a crater in the earth, wiping out most of the Gauragon mounted riders and their horses. Warriors lay dead on the ground, their armour either badly dented or in shreds.

The detonation and the flying night-mare had caught the victorious army's attention. The next mounted unit on the right flank of the battlefield was preparing to charge over towards them.

And they'll recognise us just like the others did and the famulus will make sure that we are executed in the heat of the battle bloodlust. Rodana skilfully caught three horses which had been wandering around riderless. She brought them over to where Chòldunja and the high-ranking Brigantian were standing. They needed to go somewhere safe, where they could work out their next steps. Somewhere outside of Girdlegard.

'No time for introductions. My assistant saved your life. You are in our debt,' Rodana said assertively. 'We want you to take us to Brigantia.' She handed him the reins. 'We'll explain on the way.' Chòldunja mounted her horse. 'Or else we all die right here, right now.'

The Brigantian put one foot in the stirrup and heaved himself up. 'Whatever,' he said in a croaky voice, turning his horse to the south-east. 'Keep close behind. And be prepared for a whole load of questions.' Then off he galloped.

Exchanging relieved glances with each other, Rodana and Chòldunja raced after him.

I am surprised that the dragons reacted to the volcanic eruptions. The heat and the energy that was released must have attracted them.

On comparing the reports and the source material, I found that a dozen of them flew in over the mountain ridges, creating havoc and terror. After fighting with each other for territory, nine remained – of them, three small ones were killed by humans and one was killed by orcs. The others were either too powerful or else they found themselves eyries out of reach of armies with any heavy weaponry. Humans agreed terms with the dragons because they lacked the means to combat the scaled monsters.

I assume that Ûra has been living in Girdlegard since the first of the earthquakes and that is why she considers herself the supreme ruler. But there is a slight discrepancy in the reports. And perhaps there is another dragon that has not yet been sighted.

Excerpt from
The History of Girdlegard Following the Great Quake
(vol III, p. 3229),
as compiled by Master Ukentro Smallquill of Enaiko

XVII

Girdlegard

United Great Kingdom of Gauragon
Province of Mountainhigh
1023 P.Q. (7514th solar cycle in old reckoning), early autumn

Goïmron's state of exhaustion was making him yawn and think of sleep even though the fighting was still in progress on the battlefield surrounding the hill. Neither the rumbling sounds from the catapults nor the constant rattling of the winding cap-stans for the steel-spring mechanisms could keep him awake. His heavy armour was pulling him down to the ground.

YOU WILL NOT CLOSE YOUR EYES. TAKE THE GLORY YOU DESERVE, the sea sapphire said in his mind. WITH MY HELP AND WITH YOUR SKILL, YOU HAVE MADE A GREAT CONTRIBUTION TO THE VICTORY. THE MUD THAT STOPPED THE BRIGANTIAN CAVALRY. THE DEFENCE AGAINST THE ARCHERS' ARROWS.

'But nobody must know about that,' Goïmron muttered sleepily. 'I'll leave the cheers and the applause to the famulus and the artefact carriers. Enough lives have been sacrificed.'

BUT YOU SAVED GOLDHAND. WITHOUT YOUR INTER-VENTION, HE WOULD BE A LITTLE PILE OF VERY OLD ASHES, the gemstone contradicted him. MOSTRO IS AN UPSTART. HE WANTS TO HAVE ALL THE CREDIT. HE

WANTS TO BE THE HERO OF THE HOUR. THE MAGA WILL SOON REGRET HAVING TAKEN HIM ON AS AN ASSISTANT. SHE SHOULD NEVER HAVE DONE IT.

'I don't care,' whispered Goïmron. He yawned and plonked himself down on the ground. His eyes were getting smaller and smaller as he tried, using his spyglass, to follow the action. The last of the Brigantians were running off.

The älfar divisions were pulling back in formation to stand protectively round Brigantia's injured ruler and the Omuthan's flags and banners. The älfar had not entered the fray once in all that time. *Who knows what was holding them back? Nobody understands the black-eyes.*

The magnifying lenses of Goïmron's sight-tube picked out two familiar figures.

All of a sudden he was fully alert. *Rodana! Chòldunja!*

They were galloping along at the side of one of the Brigantians, whose badges showed him to be a zabitay. He was heading towards his compatriots.

The women are running away voluntarily with the enemy! He moved his glass back along the direction they had ridden from. Near the ruins of the two orc yurts, he saw several beast corpses and many armoured dead from Gauragon. Humans, horses and the orcs had been torn to pieces. *What can have happened there?*

Goïmron got painfully to his feet and searched the area with his spyglass again. But the puppeteer and her apprentice were visible only as a cloud of dust on the horizon.

I've . . . I've lost her. Horrified, he lowered the glass. *No. Something must have occurred to make her seek shelter with Brigantia. She would never . . .*

'Hurrah for our army!' shouted Gata, setting off the catapult. 'A parting shot – and then let's get to our horses and give chase to the bastards who were trying to suffocate us, smoking us out like vermin.'

'Not so fast.' Tungdil Goldhand came over to Goïmron's side and laid an arm round his shoulder. 'What's wrong, my boy? You look as if you'd been standing in the middle of the battle-field all the time, laying about you with a heavy club.'

'It was hard work loading the catapults,' he lied. 'It's taken it out of me.'

YOU DID NOT DESERVE THAT. THE FAMULUS IS GOING TO CLAIM THE CREDIT FOR EVERYTHING YOU DID!

'We've all earned a rest before we set off in pursuit. They'll get to Brigantia before us anyway. There'll be a siege of the Brown Mountains, I expect. But it'll be over fast. There's nothing that can hold back dwarves intent on taking a fortress.' The white-bearded figure of Goldhand was watching him critically. 'Lad, you're as pale as anything and you're sweating like a well-stone in the sun. What you need is a draught of nice, cool beer. Cold beer, that's what'll refresh you.'

Goïmron did not feel the need but nodded out of politeness. 'I'll be fine. I think I just need a helmet full of sleep.' He rubbed his face. 'Do we have to keep up our charade? And where did those two dwarf armies come from?'

'Patience, my boy. I'll tell everyone when we're all together. Otherwise I'll wear my tongue out with talking.' He clapped the young dwarf on the shoulder encouragingly. 'But I still need you at my side. The poison in my bones still has a long way to go before it vanishes. I trust you, Goïmron, like no other. Almost like a brother. Like my son.'

'Right.' He gave a tired smile and pointed down at the flat side of the hill. 'Here they come.'

'Then I'll get my little speech ready.' Goldhand went off, displaying nothing of the recent impairments to his health.

Brûgar came over and handed Goïmron his flask. He had exchanged his war pipe for a larger version which was puffing out small clouds of blue smoke. 'You are the slowest munitions carrier I ever came across.'

'Well, gems are lighter, aren't they?'

'That's what I thought at first.' Brûgar gave him a penetrating look and drew on his pipe again. 'But then I started to observe you. And I saw you were watching the battlefield through your viewing glass all the time. And then you were muttering to yourself.'

'Yes . . . I was praying . . . That's it, praying to Vraccas.' He drank from the flask, noting the taste of the herbs in the tea.

'Praying for a miracle?'

'Asking for his help.'

'How strange. I would have sworn there'd actually been a few miracles. There definitely were some wonders happening.' Brûgar took back his flask.

'No. That will have been the artefacts. Or maybe the famulus.'

'Hmm.' He stroked his pointed blue-dyed beard. 'You know what? This pipe is my thinking-things-through pipe. My let's-combine-things pipe. This tobacco mix speeds up my thoughts and my intuition. Works really well.' He took another lungful and then blew the smoke out at the Fourthling. 'Why would you be lying to me, gem cutter?'

Goïmron indicated the procession of army commanders moving their way: humans, dwarves, elves and meldriths. The soldiers of every division in the combined armies were massed at the foot of the elevated ground, cheering their leaders. Mostro was at the front, waving graciously, then came Sònuk, enjoying the crowd's appreciation.

'I must go to Goldhand. He needs me.' He went off quickly. He was not ready to share his secret. *And I certainly don't want to tell Brûgar.*

He was acutely aware that Chòldunja knew everything about who he was. And that she was currently riding off to the Brigantians with Rodana.

'I'll work it out, you know!' Brûgar called after him, waving his thinking-things-through pipe. 'Exactly what happened and just why you're denying it.'

Goïmron hurried over to Tungdil Goldhand, who was standing on the leaf-spring catapult platform waiting for the commanders to arrive.

In silence they relished the sight of the united armies approaching up the hillside, and they thrilled at the jubilant cheers from thousands of throats. The banners of the victorious lands fluttered in the breeze, with the runes and standards of the dwarves prominent among the other flags. The past had come alive.

Once again, Goïmron felt emotional and had goosebumps of apprehension. He had to suppress his exhaustion. It would not look good if he were to break into a cavernous yawn while standing next to the hero in his moment of triumph.

Gradually the space round the catapults filled up with the massed throngs of warriors. Finally, the ancient dwarf raised his hand for quiet. Silence fell on the hilltop. The tension was almost unbearable as they awaited the first words of the victory speech.

Goldhand lowered his hand with a smile. He opened his mouth to address the crowd.

'What a magnificent orbit!' announced Mostro, overwhelmed by his own importance. 'The army of Girdlegard, Tungdil Goldhand, and I myself, Famulus Mostro, emissary of the Esteemed Maga Vanéra, have defeated the Brigantian troops!' He thrust both arms up in the air and twirled slowly around in his mint-green robe, ensuring that his fine head of wavy hair appeared to best advantage. 'Ûra – vanquished. Ardin – gone. New times are coming.' With one hand, he indicated Goldhand. 'And now let us listen to his words. The words of one who was believed dead. Who set in motion what we have made possible on this momentous orbit. And what will be done on many, many others!' He slowly lowered his arm and waited to receive the applause and cheers of the crowd.

Nobody moved. Not a single voice was raised. Goïmron exulted at Mostro's embarrassment.

Goldhand broke the silence and began once more to speak. 'More than eight hundred cycles ago, I made a plan. The plan continued to mature in secret until it could be put to the monarchs of the times, those kings and queens of the dwarf lands of yore. In secret. So that neither friend nor foe in Girdlegard could get wind of it.' Goldhand smiled benevolently. 'Today it is not only over Brigantia that we have triumphed. All the old passes into Girdlegard have collapsed and are now closed off. For ever. Even in Brigantia!'

This was greeted with astonished chatter and murmurings.

'The dwarves, whose army came to our aid, hid themselves in the mountains with their children for hundreds of cycles. Unbeknown to the other inhabitants, they made all the preparations for the passes to be blocked, and they made new openings. And then they waited for a signal from myself to put the plan into action.' Goldhand laid a stately hand on Goïmron's shoulder. 'This young Fourthling did something I could never have imagined possible – he found my book. And he found me. Before the completion of the works and my preparations. That is why I had to improvise.' He laughed. 'By Vraccas! And *how* I improvised! Together with all of you! And victory is ours!'

Loud shouts of joy resounded on the hill. Shields and armour were drummed on in jubilation.

'My friends! Our homeland is walled off and safe. Brigantia is cut off from the Outer Lands and from any source of further supplies for food, labour or materials,' Goldhand announced. 'Let us march to the north-east and start to lay siege to the Brown Mountains. Let us wipe out the conquerors so that peace may return.' He pointed to the giant spring-driven war machines. 'And we no longer have to fear the dragons.' He looked at the famulus. 'We have an ambitious young famulus among us. He will also be a great help. Am I right, Master Mostro?'

Mostro confirmed his willingness to help, with a determined voice, his chin high with pride. 'And let me add that—'

'. . . enough words have been said,' added Goldhand, cutting short Mostro's next boastful claims. There was stifled laughter from among the audience. 'Set up camp. Let us rest, eat and drink and see to our wounded before we head out on the morrow to deal with Brigantia. For the sake of Girdlegard!'

'For Girdlegard!' came the booming echo from the crowds on the hillside and down on the plain.

'I shall hold conference this evening in my tent with the leaders of the human realms, the elves and the meldriths – and I expect you, too, Sònuk. I shall tell you everything that has been happening in the mountains while we were fighting. The coastal lands can withdraw their troops from here in order to go and defend their territory against Undarimar. We shall come and help them as soon as we have established what the situation is in the Brown Mountains.' Goldhand stepped down from the catapult platform and suddenly needed to lean on Goïmron.

'I could not have gone on for a single heartbeat more,' he muttered to the younger dwarf.

'Is it the poison again?'

Goldhand nodded and was glad that the war engines hid him from sight as he gave in to his weakness. 'I do not know how long I shall still be here, alive. Even for a dwarf, my age is incredible. But I have achieved a great deal to make Girdlegard safe again.' He placed a hand on Goïmron's breast. 'You will carry on the task if I should die.'

'Me? But I'm a Fourthling and—'

'I see a lot of myself in you, Goïmron. We are more similar than you can know. Soon I shall explain more.' He leaned back against a catapult. 'We gave the dwarves in the mountains a strategically superior position. The beginning is achieved.' He nodded encouragingly. 'Now let us finish the work.'

'Master Goldhand!' Mostro hurried up with one of the armoured soldiers wearing the colours of Gauragon. 'You must hear this. *Everyone* has to hear this!'

Goïmron lifted his hands in protest. 'Not now. He must rest. The day has exhausted him.'

'It cannot wait!' Mostro insisted, beckoning to the soldier. 'Come on! Tell them!'

'It's about the puppet woman and the moor witch, Master Goldhand.' The soldier made a bow. 'We were about to grab the two of them and the orcs, but the ragana hurled a fireball at us, leaving several killed and many injured. Then they escaped with someone from Brigantia.'

'And who was the Brigantian?' the famulus asked smugly.

'It was that zabatay who brought us the flying night-mare. But I think . . . I think that in the end it was Stémna that got away on the winged creature,' the soldier continued his report. 'The woman with the white hat that was in the saddle looked like Stémna. I met her once.'

The news hit Goïmron hard, but he had to support the old dwarf, who was staggering now. He could not under any circumstances show his feelings. *It must have been different. It can't have been like the soldier is saying.*

'Do you understand the implications of this? Rodana, the moor witch, Stémna and the Brigantian! They have been working hand in glove! The puppeteer and the child-eater were really spying for our enemies,' Mostro hissed. 'We should have had them killed straightaway! We must set a reward for the capture of these treacherous women! The whole of Girdlegard must be told about their shameful deeds!'

DO NOT SAY A WORD, said the sapphire in Goïmron's mind. DO NOT SHOW WHAT YOU FEEL.

'Had Mostro been the only witness, I would have advised caution. But there is no reason to doubt your words,' Goldhand said to the warrior who had brought the news. 'How could we have been so mistaken in them?'

'Those women will have found out nearly all our secrets. They've been with us all along.' Mostro's scorn was bottomless. 'That's why neither of them wanted to go to Rhuta. They were afraid the Esteemed Maga would recognise their intentions. That Vanéra would see through their disguise.'

Goïmron saw Chòldunja's pink moor diamond dangling from round Mostro's neck. Removed from its original setting, it had been included with other amulets on the same chain. *What's he going to do with that? Doesn't he know its power and its real significance?*

Goldhand moved his hand to show agreement. 'We'll talk about this outrageous incident later.' He turned to the soldier from Gauragon. 'You will be with us and you can tell us exactly what you have seen.'

'And so now Brigantia has the services of a ragana at its disposal.' Mostro balled his fist in anger. 'But she won't win against me. I'll smash her to smithereens!'

'You do that, famulus. One of your artefacts can work that wonder for us.' Goldhand was leaning heavily on Goïmron. 'I need to lie down. Take me to a bed somewhere. Now.'

There's nothing I'd rather do. Goïmron took his mentor's arm to escort him from the scene, to get away from Mostro and the soldier. He was hardly able to think clearly. In his mind's eye, he saw Rodana's visage and he could not believe her to be a traitor. *Never. There must be a different explanation. An explanation so improbable, it must be true.*

Girdlegard

Brown Mountains
Brigantia
1023 P.Q. (7514th solar cycle in old reckoning), autumn

'We need two war-wolf devices on the east side,' Goldhand decided, checking the detailed plan of the fortifications, which, although originally built by dwarf hand, had in the course of many past cycles been added to by the Brigantians. There were obvious differences in the quality of the construction and in the amount of ornamentation involved. All in all, it was clear that the ramparts they needed to storm were higher and more extensive than previously thought. 'They must be constructed and in place by the end of autumn.'

The commanders of the various divisions nodded.

'We'll recruit more carpenters,' said Hargorina, standing at Gata's side, her chin resolute as ever. 'We can use the material from the villages that have been destroyed. There should be plenty of strong wooden beams available.'

Goïmron kept to the background during the afternoon conference, ready whenever called for to assist Goldhand. He understood a great deal more, nowadays, of the talk of war and tactics, but this was still anything but his natural environment. He did at least know that a war wolf was the name for the largest counterweight catapult that it was possible to build. A war-wolf trebuchet could send a five-hundredweight boulder more than three or four hundred paces, accurately hitting its target.

'We must convince the Brigantians that we are trying to break through on the east. Our mining engineers will move forward underground in the meantime. We are already nearly at the first wall. And deep enough not to be heard when the tunnels are being dug. And there should be no chance of the enemy's detecting the vibrations at that depth, either,' Goldhand explained. He looked over at Telìnâs. 'What do your scouts say?'

'They've noted no attempts to get round us to the rear of the siege troops. Nothing happening on the slopes. Not even a hundred miles away. Sònuk is indefatigable. Never stops. He'll make sure nothing escapes our notice,' said the young elf, who had been promoted to the elite fîndaii unit following the battle at Two Stream Hill. Everyone had welcomed his meteoric and well-deserved advancement. Gata had seen to his being called in to the most trusted circle of advisers from Tî Silândur. 'They won't dare attack.'

'Not yet, they won't. But that will change as soon as they get wind of our two war-wolf engines. Let's keep our eyes open. And don't forget to watch the sky.' Hargorina pointed to the outside western limit of the ramparts securing the entrance to the Brown Mountains. 'We've received word from our observers on the lookout tower that the Brigantians are setting up steel-spring catapults. Can they get us in their sights from there?'

'We won't be in range unless they have a following wind to help them. And even then, it's unlikely they could reach us. If they use small-calibre stones, the wind will deflect them, altering their course. And if they use heavy stuff, it won't go far enough to touch us,' said Gata, after a moment's thought. 'I rather think they'll be using them to defend their own walls. They'll use them to shoot at us if we come up with our storm ladders.'

'That is why we shan't be storming the walls, then.' Gold-hand nodded at Goïmron, who was trying to disguise a yawn. 'You can take a break if you like. We'll be some time.'

'Do you feel – ?'

'I am fine. There are enough people here who can call you if my voice goes.' And he bent his white head to study the model of the fortifications once more.

On his way out, Goïmron picked up his mantle. He was glad to leave the stuffy atmosphere of the pavilion. The conference tent had been pitched on elevated ground to afford the commanders good oversight of the terrain.

In the centre of the huge encampment, they had erected a tall wooden observation tower, offering a good view over the curtain walls right into the Brigantian fortress. The enemy had covered over their walkways and streets with canvas, but a considerable amount of intelligence about movements within the citadel could still be gathered. Only the most courageous of the Girdlegard troops ever served on the observation tower, the crow's nest.

Slinging his mantle over his shoulders, Goïmron surveyed the numerous tents and the rough wooden structures the army had put up to house their troops. Thousands of dwarves, humans, elves and meldriths were here, preparing to liberate the Brown Mountains. The sun was going down now, and in the east, the sky was darkening.

And somewhere within those walls is Rodana. Goïmron sighed and found himself a seat on an uncomfortable bench. He still refused to believe that he had been mistaken in his impression of her. *How could I have got it so wrong?*

'Do you want to be on your own?' Gata appeared at his side, wearing her father's wolfskin cloak over her armour. 'Or would you like some company?'

'Company is always good.' This was not strictly true, but he did not wish to be discourteous. 'Why did you leave the meeting?'

'My Thirdlings aren't involved in the digging works. We're waiting to be allowed to storm through the tunnels to attack. And Hargorina knows all there is to know about mounting a siege. Much more than I do.' Gata took the spyglass out from her belt and observed first the camp and then the mighty fortress. She still sported the mourning ribbon on her sleeve, though she did not regret the late monarch's passing. She was keeping up appearances. 'The Fourthlings were better at building walls than we thought.' Then she dug him in the ribs. 'Hey, that was supposed to be a compliment, you know?'

'Yes, but in this instance, I should prefer it if my tribe had made more of a mess of things.'

The Fourthlings' five protective ramparts that had once secured the border with Brigantia about two hundred miles from here had closed the encircling belt so that not all the retreating Brigantian cavalry units had been able to escape after their defeat. Only one division had managed to make a breach and get away, as had also the one thousand älfar and the badly injured Omuthan.

What Goïmron had seen on his travels through the abandoned territory he was never going to forget. Everywhere they went, they found burnt-out villages, their inhabitants seen only in the form of huge piles of skulls. Bodies hung by the dozen from makeshift gallows at crossroads, to intimidate pursuers. The wells had been poisoned. *Scorched earth. What madness.* Horrific.

'I know what you're thinking. Me too. I'd never seen anything like that devastation.'

Gata took a pipe out of her shoulder bag and lit it. The tobacco she used was milder than Brûgar's herbal mixes. 'Why didn't the Brigantians just retreat instead of laying waste to the land like that?'

'They have to do what they can to make our siege as difficult as possible. The Brigantians know the inhabitants of the liberated towns would have rushed to our side, so they fled. Well; the ones who survived the assault did.' Goïmron sighed. 'How long will the siege go on?'

'It's not really a siege. A proper siege might take decades, faced with fortifications like these. The long'uns would die of old age. We're preparing to attack. But I'm afraid we won't be launching it this side of winter. It will be cold in the north.' Gata puffed at her pipe and polished the badge on her collar with one hand. 'And then in the summer, we'll be fighting Undarimar and the black-eyes with their pretty little boats.'

Goïmron thought the Thirdling queen was over-optimistic. 'The reports . . . worry me. Such huge ships! And weapons that can take on dragons.'

'Preparations are underway to form a combined fleet. Undarimar has lost its five largest vessels, probably to the blue dragon. And we've got the famulus on our side. He's a bit full of himself, I admit, but seems effective.' Gata tapped the bowl of her pipe, sending up sparks. 'Presumably he can sink the ships from a distance and then we'll be able to salvage their weapons and produce copies of their anti-dragon devices. Hundreds of them.' Pleased with the plans, she sat back, blowing smoke rings. 'We'll put them up on all the mountain peaks. And Girdlegard won't ever have to fear the scaled monsters again.'

Goïmron did not share her rosy vision of the future, but he kept his counsel on the subject. 'So we stick with the blocked passes?'

'Yes. Certainly until we have eliminated the älfar.' She tamped down the tobacco in her pipe and sucked at the mouthpiece, drawing in the aromatic smoke and then puffing it out. 'What an effort Goldhand went to! All those hundreds of cycles digging away, calculating exactly where to make the passes collapse, and then creating new access points.' Gata's face showed her appreciation. 'Nobody – not even us – noticed what was happening during their excavation works. With Lorimbur's blessing and assistance, lives have been spared in my kingdom.'

'In my view, it was less a question of divine assistance and more a case of perfect planning,' Goïmron countered. 'Gold-hand would not endanger a single Child of the Smith.'

'Well, yes. But in the Black Mountains, he did not always make friends, did he, when he insisted on going it alone? Several miles of tunnels, mine shafts and underground halls were lost in the rock falls. Lost for ever. Together with our oldest and most highly celebrated fortress in the east. Let's hope the orcs didn't take it over.'

'It was not a solo effort,' he contradicted her. 'The plans had been discussed and agreed with all the monarchs of the time.'

'You're a bit thin-skinned today, aren't you? It's not my fault, whatever's got into you.'

Goïmron stared at his feet. 'I'm sorry. I'm tired and—'

'You're worried about your puppeteer, aren't you?' Gata laughed. 'Don't look so surprised. I'd have to be blind not to have noticed your reaction when Mostro came charging up with his allegations and demands for a higher price to be put on her head.'

'Yes, you're right. I *am* worried,' Goïmron admitted. 'Because I don't believe she's a Brigantian.'

'The evidence of the Gauragon soldiers doesn't allow any different interpretation, really, does it?' Gata put her hand on his shoulder. 'We'll find her when we take the mountains. And then we can ask her. Nobody will touch a hair of her head. Is that agreeable to you?'

Goïmron had not been expecting that. 'Good.'

His gaze fell on her silver brooch with its mysterious symbols. *I must ask her about that some time.*

'I shan't make any promises, however, about the ragana woman. I think we'll be on the receiving end of her powers soon enough.'

'No, we won't.' He thought with unmitigated anger of the presumed murderess of his best friend. His thoughts were darker each time she came into his mind.

'What do you mean?'

'I . . . I saw the moor diamond round Mostro's neck. He had taken it off her. Without it, she can't do any magic. She'll get weaker and weaker. She is bound to that gemstone.' Goïmron shrugged. 'At least, that's what I learned in my apprenticeship. The ragana were more a theoretical item until I met Chòldunja.'

'But . . .' Gata looked at him in surprise. 'Why did you never say anything before now?'

'I am no famulus. Perhaps Mostro knows more about moor witches than I do,' he said, skirting round the question. 'Or maybe Chòldunja has found herself some new gemstone from a Fourthling hoard. But without small children to cannibalise, she won't really be very dangerous.'

'But Brigantians produce offspring, too. Maybe they'd even go so far as to sacrifice a few of them to help the ragana regain her powers.' Gata rubbed her lower lip as she contemplated the thought. 'I'll have to ask our would-be magus. Oh, and he needs to tell us where the rest of the artefacts have got to. We're going to need them when we attempt to breach the fortress walls.'

'Don't let on about me, though!' Goïmron did not want any trouble with the famulus. And certainly did not want suspicion aroused that he might have any acquaintance with magic himself. Or people would start expecting him to attack the fortifications with the sea sapphire in his hand. *And I don't think I'd be up to it.*

'Don't fret. I'll choose my words carefully.' She leaned back, looking satisfied. 'One thing at a time. And then we have to decide who will be the new High King.'

'Well, it'll be Goldhand, of course.'

'An ancient dwarf, likely to pop off to the Eternal Smithy at any moment?' She made a face. 'No, that really wouldn't be a wise choice. And I'm sure he would not accept, anyway. For exactly the same reason.'

There was no way this conversation was not going to take an uncomfortable turn for Goïmron. 'He has never been High King. The greatest dwarf hero ought to grace that office once before he dies. It would be such an honour for the Thirdlings, don't you think?'

But Gata did not take him up on this. She busied herself eloquently and silently with her pipe.

'I must get back to the meeting.' Goïmron got up abruptly. 'I'll see you in the bar this evening, I expect.'

'I hope to find you there,' the blonde-haired dwarf replied softly in a genuinely friendly tone. 'You're one of the best singers I know.'

'See you this evening.' Goïmron set off.

It's mad. There it was: a dwarf queen was ready to give him her heart, but his own was ardently dedicated to a traitorous puppet mistress currently stuck somewhere behind the walls of a besieged fortress. *What shall I do if everybody is right in what they say about her?*

Eager to leave these unhappy ruminations behind, Goïmron raced back to the pavilion where the strategy meeting was being held. A disagreement had emerged as to the proper siting of the two extra war-wolf devices. He took off his mantle and, in order to forget his own problems for a while, forced himself to try and follow the military pros and cons of the argument.

He did not completely succeed. Rodana was still in the forefront of his mind.

In the middle of the debate, the tent guard announced the return of one of the elf reconnaissance party who had discovered a puzzling artefact near the fortress.

The elf was directly summoned to give his report.

A tall, slender figure in a green, hooded mantle entered, a rune staff made of tionium in his hand. The symbols on it were of älfar origin. The elf's other hand was hidden within the folds of his garment.

Before the returned scout could say a word, Telìnâs took a step backwards and drew his rapier. 'This is not one of our scouts!' he called out in alarm. 'It's an älf!'

Weapons were drawn and there were loud shouts calling for more guards to come.

It's not just any old älf. It's the blue dragon rider, thought Goïmron, feeling in his pocket for the sea sapphire to have it ready to protect Goldhand and the others if needed. *If Sònuk had still been in the camp, he'd have sniffed him out straightaway.*

The unknown newcomer parried two sword thrusts with his spear flashing dazzling green rays from its symbols. He leaped surefootedly on to the map table in the centre of the tent and swept back his hood, revealing dark hair and an attractively clean-shaven face, with a pair of clear eyes slowly darkening.

'Stop!' shouted the älf, going down on one knee to demonstrate his peaceful intent. He kept his right hand, gauntleted, on the black shaft of the spear. The runes on it were pulsating threateningly. 'Listen to me. We have the same enemy!'

MAKE NO MISTAKES HERE, the sapphire warned. NO ONE ELSE HERE CAN DO ANYTHING AGAINST THE POWER OF THAT SPEAR. THANKS TO ME, YOU WILL BE THE ONLY ONE TO LEAVE THIS TENT ALIVE.

'We can't take the word of a black-eyes.' Brûgar brandished his war flail, his thoughtfulness pipe hanging from the corner of his mouth. Belîngor and Hargorina were at his side.

The canvas tent flaps were lifted from the outside, revealing a phalanx of tower shields. The high ground the commanders were meeting on had been surrounded.

'By . . . Vraccas!' Goldhand, astonished, placed his hand on beard and breast. 'That is the rune spear of Aiphatòn!'

'And this' – the älf declaimed, throwing back his purloined elf cloak – 'is his armour.' Underneath the mantle, they could see the mix of blood-red leather armour and the engraved tionium plates sewn directly into his flesh.

'But it can't be!' said Goldhand, stretching out his hand helplessly. Goïmron rushed to support him. 'I knew him. I knew Aiphatòn well and deeply regretted what became of him.'

'I have come because I knew that I would find you here, Tungdil Goldhand. Because you know what power I possess.' The älf got slowly to his feet. 'My name is Mòndarcai. Just as Aiphatòn once hunted the älfar, in order to destroy them because of the evil he perceived in them, I, too, pursue Inàste's creatures.' He made the runes glow more intensively. 'I killed Ûra with this spear, doing Girdlegard the first favour. I destroyed most of the Undarimar fleet. I took the salt sea orcs and Kràg Tahuum under my banner in an alliance.' His finger stroked the black tionium plates on his skin. 'But first of all, I stole this armour from Dsôn Khamateion because the älfar there are not worthy of it. To continue what Aiphatòn once began with good intentions, before his mind became befogged in bad magic and before his tragic end.'

'This is true. I spoke often with him and . . . By Vraccas!' Goldhand exclaimed. 'Put up your weapons! Now! All of you!' Guards and commanders reluctantly obeyed. 'You cannot know it, but Mòndarcai can kill us all with this one single weapon. Hardly any of you would be able to prevent him.'

JUST AS I SAID, whispered the sapphire in Goïmron's head. NOBODY EXCEPT FOR YOU.

Mòndarcai bowed in front of Goldhand. 'And so my hope was not in vain.'

'What is it you want, apart from trampling all over the map and making speeches?' said Brûgar roughly. 'Curses! There I've got a black-eyes in my sights and I haven't got the right tobacco in my pipe for the occasion!'

'I already told you. We have the same enemy – the älfar.' Mòndarcai let his gaze rove across the gathering, halting when his eyes reached Telìnâs. 'I despise Dsôn Khamateion and want to burn it down to its very foundations.' He banged the end of his spear loudly on the table. 'And the same fate must meet the ships that go under their flag in the inland sea. I underestimated them. This will not happen again.'

'Are you asking for an alliance?' Telìnâs raised his fair eyebrows. 'An alliance – with you?'

'Not just with me. At a word from myself, thousands of orcs will march up to the fortress.' Mòndarcai looked at Goldhand and Goïmron. The dark eyes in the pale visage swallowed every last speck of light, like a bottomless abyss. 'You trusted Aiphatòn for a long time. I would ask you to have the same trust in myself, O greatest of all the dwarves in Girdlegard.' He sank down on one knee, bowed his head and proffered his beringed hand to symbolise the pact. 'My orcs are waiting to take the fortress. Before the winter comes.'

'To use it for their own ends,' objected Hargorina under her breath.

'No. They will be with me, marching on Dsôn to destroy the älfar. I swear this on my life. I swear it to you all, here and now.' Mòndarcai had kept his hand outstretched. 'Do we have an alliance, Tungdil Goldhand?'

Now, for the first time, Goïmron was terrified for Rodana. For her life. He recognised the iron determination in this älf to breach the fortifications with all speed and vanquish Brigantia. *He is powerful. Unbelievably powerful.* No one else could have slain the dragon with a spear or could have made the salt sea orcs join their arch-enemies from Kràg Tahuum.

Goïmron had been hoping to have time till the end of the cycle to consider how to proceed. To find a solution, find a way to save Rodana. Mòndarcai's sudden appearance had put paid to his ideas.

The atmosphere in the pavilion remained extremely tense.

The älf's graceful hand stayed outstretched over the table, his manicured nails shimmering in the light of the oil lamps. 'What do you say, Tungdil Goldhand?'

When the ancient dwarf gave no answer, Goïmron realised what was happening. *The poison again! He is paralysed.* Slowly, he bent his head to Goldhand's mouth. The silver white bristles tickled his ear. But no words came.

Goïmron's moment had arrived.

His vital moment.

A hundred thousand thoughts swirled round in his head. Decisions came and went in a flood of imaginings: the falling walls of the fortress, Dsôn in flames. The end of evil, the lives of countless humans, dwarves, elves and meldriths saved through the help of the orcs, the total collapse of Brigantia and, finally, the return of the Fourthlings to their realm.

But the picture that swam to the fore was Rodana's beloved face.

May Vraccas be with me! Goïmron cleared his throat.

The End of Volume One

To be continued soon . . .

DRAMATIS PERSONAE

DWARF TRIBES

Firstling Kingdom

Bendabil Pincergrip, harbour master

Buvendil Shellgrasp, of the clan of the Hot Smiths, tribe of the Firstlings, engineer and constructor

Hegobal Coalglow, warrior and stonemason

Xanomir Waveheart, of the clan of the Steel Makers, tribe of the Firstlings, engineer and constructor

Thirdling Kingdom

Belîngor Blade-eater, of the clan of the Steel Fists, tribe of the Thirdlings, warrior

Brûgar Sparkbreather, of the clan of the Fire Swallowers, tribe of the Thirdlings, warrior

Hargorina Deathbringer, of the clan of the Stone Crushers, tribe of the Thirdlings, female warrior

Larembar Goodshot, of the clan of the Far Seers, tribe of the Thirdlings, commander of the eastern fortress

Regnor Mortalblow, of the clan of the Orc Slayers, King of the Thirdlings

Regnorgata Mortalblow, of the clan of the Orc Slayers, tribe of the Thirdlings, daughter of the Thirdling king

Romogar Bloodstab, of the clan of the Leaf Bells, tribe of the Thirdlings, master of ceremonies

Fourthling Kingdom

Bendoïn Feinunz, of the clan of the Arrow Seekers, tribe of the Fourthlings, commander-in-chief of the fortresses on the border with Brigantia

Gandelin Goldenfinger, of the clan of the Stone Turners, tribe of the Fourthlings, gem specialist

Goïmron Chiselcut, of the clan of the Silver Beards, tribe of the Fourthlings, gem specialist

Fifthling Kingdom

Barbandor Steelgold, of the clan of the Royal Water Drinkers, tribe of the Fifthlings, warrior

Gesalyn Strikehammer, of the clan of the Gold Biters, tribe of the Fifthlings, senior resident

Giselgar Hardblow, of the clan of the Hammer Blows, tribe of the Fifthlings, warrior

Glamdulin Goldenspark, of the clan of the Blossom Finders, tribe of the Fifthlings, healer

HUMANS

Adelia, Vanéra's famula

Aloka, queen of Undarimar

Altorn, commander of the bodyguard for Ocdius

Ayasta, female warrior

Betania, envoy from Gauragon

Chòldunja, Doria Rodana's female apprentice

Doria Rodana de Psalí, female puppeteer

King Gajek, monarch of Gauragon
Klaey Berengart, Orweyn Berengart's youngest brother,
　　　banner officer cadet
Mostro, Vanéra's famulus
Orweyn Berengart, Omuthan of Brigantia
Prince Ocdius, heir to the throne of the empire of Gautaya
Solto, owner of a curiosities shop
Stémna, female messenger for Ûra
Vanéra, maga
Yltho, chancellor of Palusien

ÄLFAR

Ascatoîa, zhussa
Horâlor, commander of the city guard
Mòndarcai, warrior
Vascalôr, warrior

OTHERS

Ardin, second-largest dragon in Girdlegard
Krognoz, orc prince of Kràg Tahuum
Nebtad Sònuk, srgãlàh
Telìnâs, an elf
Ûra, largest dragon in Girdlegard

PLACES

Arima, main island of Undarimar
Ceuwonia, sea realm in the Outer Lands

Dsôn Khamateion, älfar empire in the Brown Mountains

Enaiko, city of knowledge in the south of Girdlegard

Fire, a province in the United Great Kingdom of Gauragon

Fruitlands, a province in the United Kingdom of Gauragon

Gautaya, empire in Gauragon

Grasslands, a province to the west of the Grey Mountains in the United Great Kingdom of Gauragon

Idoslane, former empire, subsumed into Gauragon

Kràg Tahuum, orc fortress in the centre of Girdlegard

Landbolt, a mountain, eleven thousand paces in height

Mountainhigh, a province in the United Great Kingdom of Gauragon

Platinshine, a fortified dwarf settlement at the foot of the Grey Mountains

Phondrasôn (älfar name), underground place of exile

Rhuta, magical realm, capital Vanélia

Seahold, the Kingdom of the Firstling dwarves' eastern harbour

Smallwater, humans' village near Platinshine

Tî Silândur, elf realm

Towan, river in the north of Girdlegard

Undarimar, sea empire in Girdlegard

Wavechallenge, the Kingdom of the Firstling dwarves' western harbour

Wrotland, in earlier times, a kingdom in the Outer Lands

RACES AND SPECIES

bastard-horse, mounts the orcs ride on

by Cadengis, a popular oath

Cadengi, a group of divinities widely worshipped in Brigantia

Cadengis, the most dangerous of the Cadengi gods

Cadengis' mother, the most dangerous of the Cadengi goddesses

doulia, immigrants from the Outer Lands who volunteer to serve as slaves

drinx, a mythical creature

fire eaters, beasts in the lava fields in the north of Girdlegard

flame flyers, flying snake-like creatures, related to dragons

Ido, member of the ruling family of Idoslane

lurco, plants that are transformed into flesh-eating creatures under the influence of the magic fields

meldriths, people of mixed elf and älfar parentage

nesodes, an underwater race of people

parsoi khi, humanoids who possess super-sensory power and like to take on the shape of creatures

Phlavaros, the älfar name of the first flight-mare

ragana, moor witches

salt sea orcs, beasts living in the salt deserts of the empire of Gautaya

sphyrae, arrow-slash fish

srgālàh, humanoid with the head of a dog

Unslayables, one-time rulers of the älfar

TITLES AND DESCRIPTORS

aprendisa, female apprentice

banner officer cadet, junior soldier in the supply corps

famula/famulus, human with a talent for magic, in training

fîndaii, elite regiment in the service of the Kisâri

Ganyeios, title of the ruler of Dsôn Khamateion

Kisâri, title of the empress of the elves

magus/maga, sorcerer/ sorceress

obgardist, low-ranking member of Malleniagard's city watch

Omuthan, title of the prince of Brigantia

tharks, special unit of Thirdlings forming the front battle
    line

zabitay (m) or **zabitaya (f)**, rank of general in Brigantia

zhussa, female älfar magician

zolonarius, customs official

MISCELLANEOUS TERMS

bergschaum pipe, a pipe made from a pumice-like stone

butter hail-stick, a crunchy biscuit of puff pastry

caravel, a type of ship

Elria Bonnet, the name of a diving bell

express tunnel, means of transport using carriages on rails.
    In former times, a comprehensive underground network
    connecting the whole of Girdlegard

galley, class of vessel propelled by oarsmen

Gundelgund and **Gindelgund**, **Gunibar** and **Ganibar**,
    names of heavy catapults

kedonit tobacco, very expensive and exclusive brand of
    tobacco

P.Q., post quake

quid, chewing tobacco

shark class, a particular type of galley

stone-strike game, a dwarf puzzle

suihhi, name of a deadly plague in Gauragon

war wolf, a catapult of extremely large dimensions